# The Congressman
# Who Loved Flaubert

*21 Stories and Novellas*

## WARD JUST

A MARINER BOOK

*Houghton Mifflin Company*

BOSTON    NEW YORK

FIRST MARINER BOOKS EDITION 1998

This book was originally published in 1990 in hardcover as
*Twenty-one: Selected Stories.*

Copyright © 1990 by Ward Just

For information about permission to reproduce selections from
this book, write to Permissions, Houghton Mifflin Company,
215 Park Avenue South, New York, New York 10003.

Library of Congress Cataloging-in-Publication Data is available.

DOH 10 9 8 7 6 5 4 3 2

Printed in the United States of America

ISBN 978-0-395-90137-3

The stories in this collection were originally published elsewhere: "Honor, Power,
Riches, Fame, and the Love of Women," *The Atlantic Monthly*; "I'm Worried About
You," *Gentlemen's Quarterly*; "Journalism," *The Virginia Quarterly Review*; "The
Congressman Who Loved Flaubert," *The Atlantic Monthly*; "Burns," *The Atlantic
Monthly*; "Noone," *The Atlantic Monthly*; "Prime Evening Time," *The New Re-
public*; "A Guide to the Architecture of Washington, D.C.," *The Atlantic Monthly*;
"D.", *Redbook*; "The Short War of Mr. and Mrs. Conner," *The Atlantic Monthly*;
"Journal of a Plague Year," *The Atlantic Monthly*; "Cease-fire," *The Boston Sunday
Globe*; "Dietz at War," *The Virginia Quarterly Review*; "About Boston," *The At-
lantic Monthly*; "Maintenance," *New England Review*; "A Guide to the Geography
of Vermont," *The North American Review*; "The North Shore, 1958," *TriQuar-
terly*; "The Costa Brava, 1959," *The Virginia Quarterly Review*; "A Woman of
Character," *The Atlantic Monthly*; "She's Not Dead, Belle," *Ploughshares*.

"Honor, Power, Riches, Fame, and the Love of Women," "Dietz at War,"
"Journal of a Plague Year," "A Man at the Top of His Trade," "D.," and "Cease-
fire" appeared in the collection *Honor, Power, Riches, Fame, and the Love of
Women* (E. P. Dutton). "The Congressman Who Loved Flaubert," "Burns,"
"Noone," and "Prime Evening Time" appeared in the collection *The Congressman
Who Loved Flaubert and Other Washington Stories* (Atlantic Monthly Press).

*To my mother*

# Contents

# Introduction

I ALWAYS wanted to write short stories, mostly because I liked to read them. Fitzgerald, Faulkner, Hemingway, O'Hara, and James. I first tried to write them during a stint in Spain in 1964 but it was not a success. I was on a leave of absence from the London bureau of *Newsweek*, six months or don't bother to come back. The trouble was, I didn't know anything worth knowing; or, accurately, I didn't know what I knew that was different from what everyone else knew. This meant that I was not finished with journalism, nor journalism with me; that would take another five years, and Vietnam.

I was forced to try again as a consequence of an editor's rejection of a novel, his judgment rendered so cold-bloodedly and with such a vindictive spirit, and delivered with such enthusiasm, that I knew that if I did not publish something right away I might never publish anything again, and would be forced to return to the newspaper business, a woman I loved but could not live with. That was in 1971, when I was thirty-six years old and not getting any younger.

I had written a novel and seen it published to scant applause; but the applause wasn't the point, and I liked the book. I believed then that to master the short form you first had to master the long. You had to hit before you could bunt, and the novel was a mighty round-tripper compared to the short story's suicide squeeze. I had a number of theories like that twenty years ago, not all of them cockeyed. In the middle 1970s I actually made a sort of living writing short fiction, thanks largely to the patience and patronage of Robert Manning, then the editor of *The Atlantic Monthly* and the Atlantic Monthly

Press, who never wavered from his unusual belief that a reporter's training did not disqualify a man from writing fiction. (A good editor is a kind of miracle and I have been fortunate in having Ben Bradlee and the late Larry Stern at the *Washington Post,* the incomparable Richard Todd and Frances Apt at Houghton Mifflin, and the indispensable Sarah Catchpole at home.)

The working life, the war, politics, love affairs, and marriage seem to be the waters on which my boats set sail, men and women glaring at their compasses and navigating home — or anyway a port of convenience, some consoling anchorage, someplace *else.* The twenty-one stories in this book are culled from thirty-three published here and there over the past nineteen years. Most of the Washington stories were written in Washington and in Maine and Vermont. Most of the war stories were written in Vermont and Martha's Vineyard. The two novellas and the stories about the Midwest were written in Martha's Vineyard and Boston. "Belle" was written in Paris, the only story to be written there or anywhere else outside the continental limits of the United States, although it is fair to say that the plots for nine stories and two novels came in one trance-like hour in the thin air of the *altiplano* of Peru. I have moved around a little, but am settled now.

I had not reread any of the stories since seeing them in magazine galleries, and many of them surprised me. Some of the ones I remembered as *won*-der-ful turned out to be less so, and are not included here. These twenty-one have some ragged edges, now and again a failure of nerve or of insight, the bungled bunt. But there are virtues, too, as in any life.

WARD JUST

*Paris*
October 1989

◆

# HONOR, POWER,

# RICHES, FAME, AND THE

# LOVE OF WOMEN

◆

MY FATHER, now dead, was mayor of Dement. He served as mayor for three terms, twelve years, then resigned to run for lieutenant governor. None of us wanted him to run; it seemed reckless and eccentric and therefore out of character. We could not understand why he wanted to be lieutenant governor; in Illinois at that time it was an office without visible function. We assumed he wanted to use it as a base or platform for something else, Congress perhaps, or the U.S. Senate, though my father had no love for the federal government or "the East." He was a Taft man and feared socialism.

He was soundly defeated despite a Republican landslide that year, but I know what hurt him most was that he lost Dement. He'd always won his mayoral races by wide margins, and when the returns came in that November Tuesday he was angry and depressed, rejected by his own townspeople. Dement then was much smaller and less turbulent than it is today. I remember its stillness and innocence, a triangle-shaped prairie city isolated from Chicago. It was an unpretentious place of Protestant churches and family farms and small businesses, by its own lights a haven. Its untroubled skin may have concealed a riotous interior, but I doubt it; Dement was unscandalous in all respects. However, it had an inferiority complex common to small towns. Its citizens knew each other too well, and while my father may have been an excellent mayor, that did not qualify him for state office. Better he should stay where he was. I suspect that those who voted against him believed they were doing him a favor, saving him from the heartbreak of the outside world. They were at

I

bottom a suspicious people who perceived Springfield as a glamorous rival and my father's candidacy as a rejection of them. *Aren't we good enough for you?* Dement was fierce to protect its secret self.

It had a reputation as a tough little town, a hard audience. Dement was not hospitable to outsiders, ever. Not long after the war there was a governor who celebrated the land, the cornfields in the fall, finding something hopeful in the mile-long rows of plucked cornstalks, barren and beautiful in Indian summer. He believed that the infinite square of dead fields implied the durability of the land. As the land waited for winter it prepared for spring, leaped ahead one season. It was a definition of confidence and optimism, the fields always fertile and well tended, beautiful and at peace. This governor, campaigning then, made a short speech about it in Dement. He addressed the audience in the gymnasium of the Dement Township High School, standing under the threads of a basketball net.

No one applauded after he spoke; it was as if the words were taken as a prayer or benediction. The crowd dispersed sullenly into the night and the high-minded governor reckoned that he had made an error, given them an unlucky speech that was not understood or appreciated. He had meant to encourage and inspire. This was the heartland, after all, and much depended on its stability, its adherence to fixed principles. He wanted them to *persevere*. The governor's friends, sympathetic always, thought that the speech read very well. They told him that the message was necessarily difficult and elusive, and that he was a man ahead of his time. Ideas endured, men did not.

"You can use it as an introduction to your memoirs," one of them said.

But the governor never spoke of it again in the campaign and in Dement people referred to it as that *damn* speech and shook their heads, bewildered and angry. Then they forgot about it and it was never used as an introduction to a book or to anything else. It is remembered only by me; it exists only in my memory, an episode of singular passion.

◆

I was my father's driver in his campaign for lieutenant governor, and for twenty years I have associated autumn with the special stiff atmosphere of small Illinois towns. Dixon, Alton, Kankakee, Centralia, Mattoon, Waukegan, Bloomington. I see myself still, hunched over the steering wheel of the blue Buick, driving at breakneck speeds

down narrow two-lane highways, the highways bisecting fields of
corn, soybeans, oats, alfalfa, tame hay. Burma Shave verses on red
signs. My father is in the rear seat, revising his speech; his cigar
smoke fills the air. Up one rise, down another, up and down, and
abruptly a familiar settlement. He says, "Slow down." I remember all
of them, the American Legion post in Alton, the Elks Club in Centralia, the old Karcher Hotel in Waukegan. He spoke in a half shout
from notes, his themes as familiar to me as the cigar smoke in the car;
standing in the shadows in the rear of the hall, I dozed and counted
the house.

In Cook County we always appeared with my father's running
mate, the Republican candidate for governor. "In a heavy rain," my
father used to say, "you need an umbrella." The candidate for governor, better known and better financed and organized, was my father's umbrella in the hostile and unfamiliar suburbs of Chicago. He
was a willing umbrella until mid-October, when it became clear that
he was running well and would win and my father was running
poorly and would lose. Then we were on our own, and the final
weeks of the campaign were desperate and unbearably lonely. The
campaign manager returned to his law practice in De Kalb, and the
two advance men drifted off to other, more promising campaigns.
Even my mother seemed to lose her enthusiasm, and my father's
telephone calls home became less frequent. The campaign became an
erratic odyssey with no inner logic, like a love affair doomed and out
of control. In the car, my father and I barely spoke; as he sensed
defeat he withdrew, growing colder and angrier and more passionate
with each new bit of depressing evidence.

Yet he did not break stride; he threw his full energies into his manic
courtship, rising at dawn and never retiring before midnight. Reaching out to audiences, he could not stop talking. He spoke of the
enormous odds he faced; he said his advisers were discouraging. But
odds could be beaten and advisers were often wrong. In any case, he
would not quit; he was not a quitter, they had to understand that.
But his cadences, insistent and irregular, irritated his listeners; he
seemed to be daring them to reject him. He constructed his speeches,
sentence by heavy sentence, during the long drives between towns.
He'd mutter bits and pieces of the harangue and then, under his
breath — "shit" or "you whore," pronounced *hoor*. The last week
we worked the Republican counties downstate, speaking before any
crowd that would listen. Applause, any applause, no matter how
perfunctory, would buoy his spirits. We would return to the car and

he would speak briefly with animation — *Good crowd, I got to them
that time, we'll make hay here* . . . Then he would wind down, physically sink into the Buick's cushions, and presently I would hear his
pen scratching across the yellow pad. Fresh proposals for the next
speech.

And me? All of it was newly minted. I was twenty, just graduated
from college, fascinated by the process. I absorbed it like a sponge,
becoming a connoisseur of effects. I listened, and when I could not
listen I watched, and when I could not watch I closed my eyes and
imagined it, hearing and seeing in my mind only. I observed his
maneuvers in small Illinois towns, a gruff word to the men, a shy
smile to the ladies, then an earnest lecture from the podium. Acknowledging the cheers at the beginning of each speech, he would
clasp his hands above his head like a prizefighter. I watched the others
watching him and I knew instantly the moment he lost them. I noticed
the moment they grew restless and I was vexed that he did not know
it. I knew it, it was perfectly obvious, why didn't he? I watched the
smiles of the audience dissolve, their mouths grow tight with disapproval. Too serious. I believe my old man was too serious, because in
every other way his views were theirs. It wasn't politics that divided
him and the audience, it was passion. He wanted it so much.

The Sunday afternoon before the election he spoke at an I.O.O.F.
picnic in Bloomington. We were to spend the night, then drive to
Dement the next day for the final appearance of the campaign. En
route that morning I decided to break silence and tell him what I
thought. I tried to tell him why I thought he wasn't connecting. I
suggested that he tread a little lighter. Open with a joke, I said. In the
Midwest, people came to political rallies to be entertained. Entertain
them a little . . .

He listened in silence. Then he said, "You drive. It'll be over in a
day and then you can go home to your friends. I appreciate your
driving. It must be very *boring* for you, these little towns that you
don't like. What did you call them the other day? Tank towns.
There's only one more day, and then you'll be home. You can do
what you want, then." I could hear him breathing hard, believing
that he had put me down in a decisive way. Except we both knew
that he spoke the truth. I was bored, I hated the small towns. And I
did want to go home, if only to prepare to leave for somewhere else.

Autumn was almost over; the trees were bare and the fields stripped,
desiccated in a hot spell. It was warm in Bloomington. Children

skylarked on bikes and a softball game was in progress on the worn diamond. It might have been mid-August except for the look of the trees and the haze in the sky, and the smell of burning leaves. I remember standing at the rear of the picnic grounds, leaning against a tree, listening to my father. He was attacking Communists in government and drawing applause for it. The applause seemed to encourage him, because he continued on that theme for thirty minutes, describing himself as the Number One Target of the Communists. Of course, by then he'd lost the audience.

A girl in a print dress came over to me, carrying two bottles of Hamm's beer. She offered me one and I took it and thanked her and we stood there a moment, saying nothing. I could not place her; she had been one of a blur of introductions when we'd arrived. She asked me if I was having a good time in Bloomington and I nodded politely. Then she smiled and gestured toward the stage and my father, talking.

"That's your dad, isn't it?"

I nodded; it was suddenly embarrassing and tiresome to me. I was tired, sick of the campaign, sick of the small towns and afternoon picnics, sick of small talk, sick of being a chauffeur, sick of watching my father try and fail. He had completely lost the audience now and was talking into a din of conversation. The truth was, I believed I had no more to learn from this campaign.

"Well, that's *my* dad," she said. "The other one."

"The president?"

"None other," she said. "The president of the I.O.O.F. — the eee-oof." He was seated to the left of my father on the stage. He seemed to be the only one who was truly listening. She was smiling broadly now and leaning toward me, as if sharing a secret. "He is in his second term as president of the . . . Odd Fellows." She drained her beer and we listened to my father; his speech was winding down and his voice was blurred. She said, "My father hates Communists. Always has."

"Always?"

"Since he was an itty-bitty baby," she said.

"Well." I could think of nothing else to say.

"He thinks they are running Springfield. Governor Stevenson brought them in and hid them in the various departments. They are like time bombs, set to explode at intervals. They are there now, and when the Kremlin gives the signal they'll take it over. My father has specific evidence relating to the infiltration of the Department of

Motor Vehicles. He believes the Reds are interfering with auto registrations." She spoke as if reading from a prepared text. "He believes that unless your father is elected lieutenant governor, Springfield will be the first to go." She nodded gravely and moved off to a table nearby. This was apparently a table of friends, for she fetched two more bottles of beer from the ice chest and returned. My father had warned me not to speak to strangers. He believed the Democrats would do anything to compromise him, and he also feared the press, specifically reporters from the *Chicago Sun-Times* and the *St. Louis Post-Dispatch*. He'd said to me, "They'd like nothing better than to print some stupid remark you might make, so mind your *p*'s and *q*'s and don't say anything to anyone you aren't sure of. Check with me first."

She said, "How about yours?"

"He believes they are in the schools," I said.

"Underground?"

"Yes," I said. "They are underground men."

"Any particular department?"

"History mainly," I lied. "He has made a study of the . . . texts." I was improvising now, having fun. "He believes that the first step is a falsification of history. He believes they are altering the documents." I looked at her. "He intends to put a stop to it, after he is elected."

She nodded uh-huh.

"I do not know what steps two and three are."

"Well," she said. "It's obvious they would be concealed."

"No doubt," I said.

She said, "The Communists. Is that why he is running for lieutenant governor?"

I looked at her and shrugged; it was all hopeless. And it was no longer funny. This day in November, unseasonably warm; I was in shirt sleeves and perspiring, but she looked cool and fresh. I surveyed the picnic grounds, the tables laden with food and drink; the two men on the platform, the one talking, the other listening. No one else was listening; my father was talking to an audience of one. The softball game continued, hits, errors, base runners sliding in clouds of dust. Dust rose over the diamond. Behind the third-base line was a mound of leaves, a mound five feet high; I wanted to go roll in it. Nearby there was laughter and I could hear a phrase or two of my father's. *An uphill fight,* he was saying. Then: *We must be vigilant.* I could not imagine what I was doing there on a picnic grounds in Bloomington, Illinois, and told her that.

"We are here because they are," she said, gesturing toward the platform. "Isn't that clear enough?"

"No," I said.

"That's because you haven't thought about it."

"I was kidding about the history," I said. "It's just a vague thing with him, the Communists. He's a good guy, really. He'd be all right as lieutenant governor." I paused. Why was I saying this? "The Communists are just a momentary thing. He's worked like hell, he's tired." She was looking at me with wide blue eyes. "He wants it so damn badly." Then: "He knew it would be a popular thing with this crowd, so he's talking about the Communists. It could as easily be about farm price supports or . . . anything else." I shrugged. "Himself. The odds against." I suddenly felt very sorry for my father, and angry at myself.

She touched my arm and smiled sadly. "I wish I could say the same," she said in a low voice. "He really believes it. Poor old bastard."

Suddenly we were on a different plane altogether. I was surprised at the word; it was not a word girls used then about their fathers. But she said it with affection; there was no rancor in her voice. I knew we were in agreement and I was happy she was there. I was happy we were together, drinking beer and talking.

"Hell," I said. "If it isn't Communism it's something else. It doesn't matter anyhow."

"It matters," she said. "That's the sad part." Then: "You looked so sad when I walked over here —"

"This has not been my best day. Or his, either."

"You are not enjoying yourself?"

"No."

"And you haven't told me why he is running."

I could feel the first effects of the beer, and of her. But I remembered the warning. Anything could happen in this campaign. Enemies were everywhere. "You're not a reporter, are you?" She looked at me hard, hurt, not knowing whether I was serious or not. I quickly added, "A Democrat? A conscious dedicated agent of the conspiracy?" She smiled and moved her head, her hair brushing my shoulder. All my defenses went at once and I wanted very badly to tell this girl about the past two months, all of it, every rally and chicken dinner and Main Street walkaround. And my own careful observations, effects crowding my memory.

I said, "Whoever you are, I don't know why he is running for office. None of us knows, and I'm not certain that he knows; all he knows for sure is that he *wants* it. But it doesn't make any difference, because he's going to lose. Then he will go back to his insurance agency in Dement and I will go with him, until the first of the year. Lewis and Sons Insurance. Fire, theft, casualty. We have known he would lose for three weeks, but we never speak of it; he speaks of odds against, and of prevailing in the face of pessimism. It gives him confidence, God knows why. We both know he will lose but we don't say it. We have traveled from one end of this lousy state to the other, driving two, three hundred miles a day. I drive and daydream; he sits in the back seat, revising his speeches. We try to make at least two speeches a day, but lately it has been three speeches. Never the same speech, understand that: fresh crowd, fresh speech. Since the campaign manager left and the advance men joined other campaigns, it's been very difficult. He has to make the arrangements himself, he has to plead with people like your father. He is popular with the Legion and with the I.O.O.F., so he can usually get a hearing. I have seen a hundred Legion posts in this state and I can recite the Pledge of Allegiance backward in my sleep. I have met every Legion official in the state of Illinois and I want nothing more now than for a new war to break out. Except that this would be a war by invitation only to men over the age of forty. Restricted to members of the American Legion. Every morning before the assault they could recite the Pledge of Allegiance among themselves, tell some war stories to get in the mood, and then pick up their bayonets and charge the . . . Department of Motor Vehicles. This place, whoever you are, is *insane*. The Legionnaires, they're a genuine National Guard, they're making Illinois safe for —"

"History," she said.

"Yes, exactly that. So that is what I have been doing for more than two months, and tomorrow, when this is over, I will return to the office. I will write casualty insurance. Then, at Christmastime, I will take my savings and leave, God knows where . . ." I paused; her friends at the table were looking at me strangely. She caught my hand and held it, squeezing. She was grinning, her eyes bright.

"Sandra," she said.

"Tom Lewis," I said.

"Come on."

"Where?"

She was still holding my hand. "Home," she said. "Geez, you really got wound up. That was terrific."

"I can't —"

"He can find his way to the hotel. My father will look after him, they'll have a lot to talk about. It's all right, you don't have to worry."

As we walked away from the picnic grounds I could hear scattered applause. She moved close against me, waving casually to the group at the table. Then she began to run. We both ran away from the picnic grounds, our feet slapping the cement sidewalks. Bloomington reminded me of Dement, identical frame houses, porches facing similar streets, blinds drawn within. It was very quiet in the streets. Each house was shaded by a tree, an elm or a hickory. It was as if a single architect had designed both towns; perhaps he was a circuit-riding architect like a judge or a physician. I knew without being told which houses belonged to professional people and which belonged to merchants or shopkeepers.

Dusk was coming on and we ran faster and faster beneath the bare branches of the huge trees, cutting across lawns and through alleys, still holding hands. Leaves were piled on front lawns and in the gutters and the scent of burning was in the air. We ran for three blocks and then we walked, out of breath and laughing. Her face was damp and we were both perspiring; my shirt was stuck to my back. I still carried my bottle of Hamm's and handed it to her. She took a long swallow, draining it, and tossed the bottle into the gutter, where it fell soundlessly among the leaves. My thumb was wet from the lip of the bottle. We walked for a while, talking, and then we ran on. She tripped once and fell, skinning her knee; there was a little blood and dirt where she had fallen and tears jumped to her eyes. She daubed at it with a handkerchief and said it was nothing, it would leave no mark, and didn't hurt much. We began to run again. The town passed by me in a blur, the streets undulating. Now the houses were close together and bushes obscured their façades; brittle ivy, pale green and flecked with brown, hung in dry patches from the brick and the clapboard. Vacant lots were thick with vegetation, overgrown with high weeds and scrub oak. Tree branches touched over the narrow deserted streets, natural trellises spanning the concrete. From somewhere nearby I heard faint laughter and familiar voices. I could not identify them and I touched her arm and we both halted, skidding to a stop, listening; it was the radio, metallic voices drifting through open windows in the evening stillness. I looked at my watch. It was Jack Benny, had to be; Benny and Rochester and a studio audience. The voices were more distinct now as other radios were switched on; I sensed movement behind the windows. I heard two words, *Mistah Benny* . . . Darkness was gathering quickly now; it seemed to me that we had run for hours down these streets. The trees were black against the lawns and there were few lights inside the houses. In the heart of Bloomington, in darkest Illinois, there was only the radio. I laughed, gazing skyward; what were the first words heard in this heart of darkness? *Mistah Benny* . . .

She tugged at my arm, impatient to be off. We picked up the pace and were running again, the picnic grounds far behind now. We drifted easily down the sidewalks and across lawns. Then we were moving up the stairs of a front porch, taking the steps two at a time. The screen door banged and we were inside. The house was cool and ablaze with light. Every light in the house was on. We stood in the middle of the parlor, panting; I bent at the waist, trying to catch my breath. The light hurt our eyes, and she methodically moved around the parlor switching off the lamps. Presently we were in darkness again. She laughed for no reason and left me a moment, disappearing through the swinging door into the kitchen. I heard the icebox open and close and the water run and her humming, and then she was back.

"No beer," she said. She took my hand and we mounted the stairs. They were narrow and uncarpeted and we bumped the walls as we climbed. I put the palm of my hand on the small of her back and felt her heat. She laughed softly. Her room was at the top of the stairs, the door closed. We burst through it and I led her straight to her bed. We fell on it together and embraced for a long moment. It was very still; the only sound was the rustle of our clothing. We did not kiss right away; it was enough lying together on the bed, our bodies touching everywhere. Then we kissed, delicately, lips barely touching. I kissed her chin and her eyes and then we lay apart for a moment. Her eyes were closed, her long lashes touching her cheeks, her mouth upturned at the edges and slightly parted. I felt her breathing, her breasts rising; I timed my own breathing to be in tune with her. I wanted no part of us in disharmony. She ran her hand slowly down my cheek, caressing very lightly; I did the same. Her hair, light brown and thick and soft as down, was in curly disarray. I smoothed it and took two strands and arranged them around her ears. Her eyes popped open then and I found myself in her pupils; her eyes were like mirrors, my face convex, my grave expression distorted. I moved closer to her and we kissed again, this time longer and deeper. She smelled wonderful. Her hands went around my back and squeezed and kept squeezing. I drew her as close to me as I was able, wildly happy at that moment. She was not slight but she felt slight, small-boned and slender, my arms around her, our legs twined like vines. We lay together in the big soft bed, arms around each other. Time suspended itself. I could not stop touching her.

After a while she pushed me away and we lay six inches apart and talked. I talked about everything in my life; it seemed to me there was nothing I might say that she would not understand. We made jokes about the conspiracy: Was it true that Tom Dewey took his orders from Moscow? We joked and then we talked seriously, and then we kissed some more. I would tell her everything that mattered to me, every fact and emotion; then I would listen as she explained her life to me. We were hearing our own harmonies, mounting the scale as if it were a staircase, each story improving the one before. We prepared the ground for disclosures, things we had never discussed with anyone. I told her repeatedly that I could not believe this was happening, I did not believe in chance encounters. Was it true that she was an undercover agent for the *Post-Dispatch*, anxious to pry compromising information from the son of the candidate?

I listened to her breathing. We saw each other dimly in the blackness of the room; occasionally I would squeeze my eyelids shut to see her in my mind only; then I would open up and find there was no difference. I imagined her to perfection, every detail. She described her life: her mother was dead, there was just she and her father. Ever since the death of her mother she felt . . . at loose ends. Literally, she did not feel whole; she felt her emotions were leaking away through her nerve ends. One day she would awaken and find herself parched, dry as dust. What was there for her in Bloomington? She would succeed at something, make no mistake; she did not intend to stay in this house. But she felt her life was muffled, smothered in cotton batting; all escape routes were blocked; she was wrapped in mufflers. She could not escape from the place or reconcile herself to it, either one. Bloomington: it was supposed to be the center of the continent, one could gaze east or west with equal ease; but she did not find it so. She said that the walls of Bloomington were higher and thicker than the walls of any prison. The truth was, she was afraid to leave. She said she noticed me right away at the picnic and knew from the look on my face that I felt as she did; she had an instinct for looks, it was an instinct she'd always had. I was living under the same conditions, wasn't I? In that way we were brothers, except being a man it would be easier for me; it would always be easier. And I had some money and she did not. Up close, her mouth almost touching mine, she whispered that we were both on bivouac. She chuckled dryly; we were on night watch surrounded by enemies. We laughed together, improving on that image. We discussed the weapons we'd need and the tactics we'd use to exfiltrate the prairie. Passion, she said finally; that was all there was. It was evidence of life. She looked at me fiercely in the dark, her fingers on my chest. Not sex, she said; passion. There was a difference. Then she smiled and added, Though not always.

I took her hand and kissed it; I was bound to her. It seemed to me that she knew everything, her understanding was limitless. I told her she'd cast a spell. We were so close in spirit now that there was no difference between us at all. She rolled over on top of me, burying her face in my neck; she was murmuring something, I did not hear what it was. Light as feathers she slipped out of her dress, her skin shining in the faint light from the street. Her hair fell to her shoulders in loops and her eyes were open and glittering. I moved slowly, as slowly as time itself. *One*, she said. And again, *One*.

I heard a noise in the street and presently the front door slammed and we both sat upright. We could hear conversation and then, quickly, the clink of ice cubes in glasses. I looked at her: What do we do now? She smiled ruefully, hugging herself, her arms covering her breasts. Then she put her arms down and just sat for a moment, looking at me with a smile. She whispered, *It's a farce. Everything collapses into farce.* She sighed and climbed over me and stepped on tiptoe to the door and listened, one leg bent, her arms at her sides. I watched her from the bed, every movement. Then she motioned me over and we sat on the floor together and listened.

It was her father and mine, both mid-drunk, sitting in the parlor, their voices just louder than they needed to be. It was evident that they thought the house was empty. She lay in my arms on the floor and we listened to them.

Her father was telling mine that he was a great American. There weren't many left; Truman had ruined it. The Communists were everywhere now, they were like termites eating away at the foundations of the house. The house could collapse at any time and Eisenhower was too dumb to do anything about it. "Never trust a general," he said. But thank God the polls had Eisenhower winning and with any luck in two days they'd be rid of the haberdasher forever. He and Hiss and Harry Dexter White and the whole rotten barrel. General Vaughan, the five-percenters. Bad as Eisenhower was, at least he wasn't Stevenson. They all knew about Stevenson; he had grown up in Bloomington and owned a piece of the local rag, the newspaper. As governor he had reduced Illinois, Land of Lincoln, to a Poland or a Czechoslovakia. Illinois was no different from any of the satellite Russian states. When Stevenson used the state police to break up the gambling, he had served notice and signaled his intent: it was to establish a KGB in Springfield, a secret police. J. Edgar Hoover knew all about it but was powerless to act. Stevenson had tried to dismantle the National Guard but was prevented by the many scandals. The cigarette stamp tax scandal, the horsemeat scandal, and the others. There were too many scandals to count. Ha-ha, he said. I heard a good one the other day. Man goes into a meat market to buy hamburger and the butcher asks him if he wants it win, place, or show.

I heard my father grunt and sigh, and then a fresh tinkle of ice cubes. The voice droned on. I knew my father had disconnected from the conversation and was thinking private thoughts.

Her father said, You know he's a fairy.

My father said nothing. I tried to picture him in the chair, stiff and morose and exhausted and pulling on a highball, and listening to the president of the I.O.O.F. beat up Adlai Stevenson. My father had always described the governor as a bad politician, often feckless and weird in his choice of friends and associates, but not a bad man.

That is what they say, her father said. And not only that (his voice lowered to a confidential level), but he has a woman in the mansion. There's a woman who's in residence around the clock to service him.

Her face was buried in my chest, her shoulders were shaking with laughter. Her hands beat a little tattoo on my back. She whispered to me that much of this material was new to her. Her father had hinted at private scandal but had never spelled it out. Too *risqué*. She giggled.

Well, her father said at last, here's to victory on Tuesday.

I heard the clink of glasses and my father clear his throat. I was waiting for him to argue, though I guessed he would not. He hated references to private lives, and I never heard him gossip. He was a practical man and hated confrontation. He would know there was no convincing argument he could make. I was amused at the lunacy of it, Stevenson a secret voluptuary, saturnalias in the mansion at Springfield.

My father said, "I'm still wondering where my son is."

"He and my daughter went off together. They were talking during the speech. They're all right, don't worry about them. She's probably showing him around the town, there's quite a good deal of local history here in Bloomington. She'll take good care of him, you shouldn't worry."

"I'm not worried," my father said. There was a strange timbre to his voice, a rattle that I had never heard before. "But we've got to leave early; there's a rally in Dement at noon and I've got a speech at night. The Elks."

"Fine people."

"Yes, I've been an Elk for — twenty years."

"Give it to them hard, Giles. Tell them about the screwballs in Springfield. I can tell you, when you get there, you have only to call on me if you need any help in Bloomington. I can give you support. I can do *things*. I'll do anything I can for you, anything at all to help clean up the mess —" Her father abruptly stopped talking. There was an awkward silence, punctuated by sounds I could not identify. I leaned forward, my ear against the doorjamb. I heard *unh-unh-unh*, as if a pillow were being punched. There were no other sounds, just those. It was my father, and I understood in a frozen second that he was crying. I could not move, I was paralyzed; my hands fell away from her.

"Well," her father began. It was an awful moment.

"Shit," my father said. He blew his nose. A thick silence seemed to spread through the house, the air suddenly compressed and made heavy. I imagined the other man turning away in embarrassment. "There isn't much for a lieutenant governor to do," my father said slowly. He was not prepared to acknowledge that he had been weeping. He spoke in a broken undertone, to himself alone. "There isn't much to the job, it's a largely ceremonial thing. Ribbon cuttings. Banquets." Then, in his familiar voice: "Guess we'd better get back to the hotel, get some sleep. Heavy day tomorrow."

"I guess we better," the other said stiffly. I could have killed him, his tone was so condescending.

"I want to be there by noon, not a minute later." The other one was silent. "Goddamnit, if you'd pay attention, stop dreaming, keep your eyes on the road. The other day, outside Alton, that semi ——" I realized then that he was talking to me. He believed I was in the room with him. "You've got to concentrate. Good driving is just' concentration, no more and no less. Understand where you are, where you're going. Know the rules of the road and obey them." Her father coughed and I could hear him rise. "Christ, to have to depend on *you*." Then he was silent, and I could feel — *feel* — the atmosphere change.

He said, "I believe now that I should have stayed in the agency. My three boys are there. It's a good agency, none better in Dement. The other two understand about business. The one with me here now, it was important for him to see the state. His mother felt it would be helpful to him to see all the state. Her people came from around Centralia. He's been my driver on the . . . campaign. It's a responsible post, because everywhere I go I've got to be on time. Punctual. But he's restless. He's very much like his uncle, my brother. Two peas in a pod, they should both be in Chicago. They're *sophisticated*." He spat the word out, an obscenity to him.

"I can take you back to the hotel."

"You know," my father said, "Stevenson isn't the worst of the lot by any means." He spoke very softly; it was difficult for me to hear. It was just a statement; I could tell that he would not pursue it.

"Well, I suppose he's not as bad as Williams. Compared to Williams, he's all right." The other was making a concession; I relaxed. I had had a feeling there would be a fight between them, and I would have to go down and break it up.

"Williams is in the pocket of Reuther," my father said. "Reuther owns him. That Reuther's a cold one."

"A menace to America. Soapy Williams is a screwball, always was, always will be." Her father went on to describe social and political subversion in the state of Michigan.

But we were no longer listening. Or I wasn't. I'd had no idea it went so deep: my father in tears; his evident contempt for me. I wanted the sounds to go away, but they would not. I had eavesdropped and I had heard him. I had *heard*. It was as if I'd stolen something from him and now it belonged to me forever. She lay quietly, watching me, her eyes bright and mournful. My confusion was complete. I vaguely remember the screen door slamming and, later, her father returning to the house. We sat in silence for many minutes, my father's words repeating themselves in my brain; I was numb, unable to sort out my feelings. I did not know what to think. She said, "Something like that happened to my father about a year ago. I was in the kitchen, I heard him upstairs —" I shook my head sharply; I didn't want to hear it. I'd heard too much already. I didn't want to listen to anything of a private nature between her and her father. It was midnight when we crept out of her room and down the stairs. Her father was asleep in the big wing-back chair, a half-empty highball on the table beside him. All the downstairs lights were blazing. He was snoring gently, his face slack. Whiskey fumes filled the room. I smiled, though there was nothing comical about it. She moved quickly to his side and took the glass of stale whiskey and put it on another table. The resemblance between them was striking; I had not noticed it before. In repose his face was almost feminine, and the look around his eyes was identical to his daughter's.

We quietly left the house and stood on the front lawn, out of the light. A breeze had come up and it was chilly and very dark. We pressed against each other, I could feel goose bumps on her arms. I could see the streetlights at the corner but nothing beyond. She looked at me, then smiled apologetically, her eyes lowered. She said, "Really, he's helpless. Helpless since his wife died. It was odd because they did not seem to've needed each other in life." I was not listening to her. She said she wanted to drive me to the hotel but she didn't drive. She'd never learned, no one had taught her. She was twenty years old and a nondriver, and that was unheard of. It's a long way, she said, maybe twenty blocks. I told her the truth: I didn't mind.

We walked off to the corner and it was like entering a tunnel. I was entirely absorbed by what I'd heard, my father's words mingling with the image of Sandra's body; her beauty was breathtaking. I thought, What was there about this country? This hard place in the heart of the nation. The carapace of control was so thin. It looked hard as iron but the looks were deceptive. Everything beneath was confused and in turmoil, dry on the outside and wet underneath. My father *in tears.* I could hardly believe it. His disappointment, the ragged edge of his emotions; I had always thought of him as a stoic. There was just his voice, gone to pieces, and the thickening atmosphere. I had always thought of him pursuing a line of duty.

"This place," she said. "It's surprising sometimes."

Something, perhaps it was the dark street and the prospect of a twenty-block walk, had made me cautious. I wanted very much to be alone and I did not want or need the help or sympathy of anyone. I said, "Yes."

She said, "It's all right."

I said, "No, it isn't." I was angry at her father.

"He's tired, he's been campaigning for — what? Two months, three months? They get worn out —"

"Three months," I said. I wanted to remain with the obvious explanations.

"Well, there you are."

"It surprised me," I said slowly. "I thought he had reconciled himself . . . I knew it meant a lot. I knew that. But I thought he was stronger . . ."

She paused a moment, looking at me. "Why should he be? You're not, I'm not." Her voice was very clear in the darkness. "Why isn't he entitled —"

"Defeated," I said. I was talking to myself now, still with the obvious things. "He sounded defeated."

"That's cruel," she said sharply. "That's the cruelest thing I've ever heard. Don't you understand anything about these men?"

"No, I'm not cruel," I said. I was honestly bewildered. I thought I had merely stated the truth.

"You don't understand anything about them." She put her hands on my shoulders. "They're trying to break out, same as we are. They know it isn't working, none of it. With my father, it's the Reds. With yours, it's you. Same difference. No difference."

"I don't have anything to do with this," I said thickly.

She sighed, exasperated. "Yes," she said. "You do."

"No," I said. "Definitely not." I took her hand. I wanted nothing more than to be away from there. It was so dark I could barely see her face, or the outlines of her body. But I was able to see her expression in my mind's eye, her clear sad eyes and the downward sweep of her eyebrows. I wanted to be away from that street and the house, and the man asleep in the wing-back chair.

She smiled and kissed me lightly. She said, "The Reds. You. Subversives. Problems to be solved. Think of it that way, will you?"

I told her I would write.

She smiled, then laughed. "Be good," she said.

We were at the corner. I was to follow her street straight into town. The hotel was in the center of town. The street sloped and I could see little puddles of light for perhaps six blocks; then the street curved down and away. Light filtered through the bare branches of the trees. It was black as hell, the blackest night I've ever seen. We kissed in the dark, leaning against the rough bark of a hickory tree and feeling the chill. Her body was wonderfully soft and supple. Then we broke and she turned away without a word and walked back up the street to her house, her arms hugging her body to ward off the cold. Indian summer was over.

♦

I did not leave Dement for another year, and when I did I went to Washington. Sandra and I saw each other twice afterward and we corresponded for a while and then gave it up. The episode in Bloomington remains an isolated event. Sometimes when I think about it I am not sure that it happened at all. (But I know it did.) Three years later I was married and when I explained it to my wife she said that everyone had a similar episode in the past, and ambiguous memories about it. She said that collapse was inevitable because the relationship was too intense; each is heavily dependent on the other and the dependencies do not fit. They almost never do. Too taut, exactly like a rubber band; it's pulled too far and it snaps. Expectations are too high. I said that it had been an enchanting experience, at least one half of it had; I said I would not trade that half for anything. She smiled sympathetically. Just see that it doesn't happen again, she said. Then, seriously: Passion wears out, you know. It doesn't endure. It can't be maintained; it exists only as a peak among valleys. We shall see, I said lightly. An odd fact: I never thought to inquire about *her* "similar experience," who he was and what she made of it, and she never thought to volunteer.

My brothers live in Dement still, managing the agency. This is a characteristic of the Midwest, small businesses handed down from father to son. It is particularly true of insurance, the law, and medicine. Of course, it is a reach for immortality, the agency or law firm or practice outliving and overwhelming the family serving it. The business acquires a weight and personality and growth of its own, often more formidable than the family. No wonder that the office is casually referred to as "the plant." In Dement the mortality rate was about fifty-fifty into the second generation. Attorneys are consulted to keep the businesses alive, control exquisitely balanced among families and generations. Usually the sons do not have the singleness of purpose of the fathers, or the stamina. The times intervene. The attorneys speak of these businesses reverently, as necessary keystones of the civic edifice. Dement, one of them explained to me once, was very much an insider's town. "Those of us here who run things, we don't have to finish sentences . . ." He wanted to see that Dement remained an insider's town.

Lewis and Sons Insurance was one of the rare ones. My two brothers worked hard and expanded the business, and today it is three times as large as it was when my father died. My brothers and I do not communicate often, because there is considerable bitterness between us. Our father bequeathed the agency in thirds, which means that I share in the profits though I do no work for the agency. I have had to hire an attorney in Dement to see that my interest is protected, and that the profits are distributed equally. My brothers have managed to increase the business each year but the profits do not grow; they are stable because the salaries and expense accounts rise. Last year, my share of the swag was ten thousand dollars. Meanwhile, Brother Warren bought a condominium in Fort Lauderdale and Brother Bill a thirty-five-foot Chris-Craft. Each of them takes seventy thousand dollars a year out of the business. They say (through their attorney), We're doing the work, we'll reap the profits. I say (through mine), Fine, as long as I get the ten thousand per annum, no less. This is a situation common in family businesses. Dividends, as everyone knows, are fully taxable to the corporation and to the individuals receiving them. It is the most expensive way to extract money from a business, and therefore it is not often done. The preferred method is to establish "consultancies" or bogus titles through which a family member can receive a salary. However, that is not desirable for me. Regularly, once a year, I get a letter from my brothers' mouthpiece urging me to "do something about this." Excessive taxation of corporate profits threatens the health of our capitalistic system, the attorney says. "We would hope you would use your position in a constructive way."

They have tried on numerous occasions to buy me out but I refuse to sell. For reasons I do not entirely understand, I want to keep a foot in Dement. The family has been there for four generations and I have not been anxious to cut the last cord. The only way I know to keep a foot in is to retain the stock, come what may. (Also, they have not offered me a fair price.) I return once a year for the formalities of the board of directors' meeting. There are five of us in attendance, I and my two brothers, the corporation counsel, and my uncle, who is eighty-two and in failing health. It is a stiff, formal ceremony that never consumes more than thirty minutes. President Warren Lewis confines himself to a recitation of numbers: new accounts and dollar volume at the bottom line. Details are scarce. All motions are proposed by the attorney and seconded by Treasurer Bill Lewis and passed unanimously by those of us at the table. They have the votes and they know it; I know it too and am resentful. We meet in the conference room at the agency; suspended on wires over the door is a ghastly portrait of the founder, my father, his light eyes wide and staring as if at a vision or apparition. His last years were spent playing golf and the artist drew him in a white shirt against a bilious horizon, a suggestion of fairways. President Warren sounds remarkably like the old man, and in his middle age has even come to resemble him (he is big). Afterward I have lunch with my brothers and their wives and the attorney and his wife and my aged uncle, and then I am driven to the Dement airport to take the commuter flight to O'Hare and then a jet to Washington.

For some years I have been a congressman from a district in upstate New York.

◆

Somewhere (in fact it is Lecture Twenty-three of the General Introduction) Freud describes the artist as one who desires "honor, power, riches, fame, and the love of women" but lacks the ways and means of attaining them. Frustrated, he attempts to satisfy himself by making fantasies which, according to Freud, represent repressed infantile longings. The great analyst then goes on to describe the artist's "puzzling ability" to reproduce his fantasies so persuasively that other disappointed souls are — consoled. I believe that the aim of art is consolation, and it is the aim of politics as well; the artist and the politician are brothers, and their situations essentially ironic. Freud: the artist "wins gratitude and admiration for himself and so, by means of his imagination, achieves the very things which had at first only an imaginary existence for him: honor, power, and the love of women." Similarly, the politician, his "program" and his "image." Thus, we win *through* fantasy that which before we could win only *in* fantasy. The way back from imagination to reality is art. I found Lecture Twenty-three in my last year at the university and have never forgotten it. Inspired by Freud's promise, I planned for myself a career as an artist. But I did not have the temperament for it, and it soon became clear to me that my life would be public. I wanted to touch people and be touched in return; that was how I explained it. I wanted things out front where I could see them and I had no taste at all for reliving, if only through memory, my rather ordinary childhood. Tom Lewis the child lives still in Dement. Tom Lewis the man is a Washingtonian.

Politics is a delusive trade. In his secret heart a successful politician believes he is truly loved. Not merely supported or well liked but loved. He is father to a constituency of children, and while some of the children may be obstinate or disobedient, none of them is beyond salvation. When a politician loses an election he cannot believe it is because he's disliked. No. He was denied full access to the electorate; he was not permitted to make himself fully understood. The press

was hostile and his opponent spread outrageous lies and falsified
issues. Even if he wins, a small voice wonders about those who voted
the other way. Why did they do that? Why did they reject me? This
is the small voice in the heart of every politician which says that if
there were money enough and time to reach every voter the result
might be . . . unanimous. It is absurd on its face, to invest so much
with the promise of so little. Except one is impregnated with history,
true and false. The ghost of Lincoln hangs over the shoulder of every
serious American politician. To console a nation! "To free from the
sense of misery." One conceives oneself suspended in an ineffable
state of melancholy, balanced between the truths of Freud and Lincoln. Is is not necessary therefore to find a code of conduct that will
not slander either side, or defame oneself?

Honor, power, riches, fame, and the love of women — my press
secretary and I call it the hots. That's the moment in a speech when
the words begin to burn and the audience moves in close, feeling the
rhythm. A passionate speech requires a passionate audience. It can
happen at any time, anywhere, but usually it happens at a rally, when
you're preaching to the converted. Shirt sleeves up, you throw away
the text and give it to them hard, aiming low. You step out from
behind the podium, reaching, no barriers between you and them, and
beat time to the music. You are one with them and the energy is *felt*,
flowing both ways, a reciprocal current. It happens only a few times
in any campaign.

The first time I ever saw it was in 1966, my first run for the House.
Robert F. Kennedy, then the junior senator, came up to help me out.
It was a hot day in early October; we rode in a motorcade from the
airport to the civic center for a rally. The crowds were enormous and
downtown the motorcade slowed to a crawl. The senator ordered the
car stopped and grabbed a portable bullhorn and stood on the hood
and shouted an impromptu speech. He filled the air with fire and wit,
drawing cheers and laughter at the same time. Sweating, roaring into
the bullhorn, he created a prizefight atmosphere. This was fifteen
rounds, he was the world champion, and I was the protégé. *Give me
some help down there!* he cried. *The nation needs Tom Lewis! We've
got to have him!* Then he began to laugh out loud. *Only Tom and I
can save the Republic from Republicans! Isn't that what you want?
Only Tom and I stand between you and the party of Harding, Hoover, and Nixon!*

It was outrageous and the crowd loved it, roaring back its approval. Kennedy waved his muscular arms and the crowd waved

back. I knew then that I would not lose, and when he got back in the car, smiling happily, flushed, I told him excitedly that he'd done it; the campaign was won. He shrugged and turned away, reaching to shake someone's hand. Hands were everywhere around us. He said that one speech didn't make a campaign. That one did, I said. I groped for words: It was electric, high-voltage. He smiled mischievously. "It isn't electric," he said quietly. "Electricity has nothing to do with it. It's sexual."

My opponent never recovered from that day, unseasonably warm, in early October. I believe that if our elections were held on the first Tuesday in September, our politics would be transformed. August would be the decisive month. The August heat would demand an altogether different style. In the August heat Nixon never would have been elected. I've never seen him in shirt sleeves in a fairground or union hall; he had no idea how to work a crowd in the heat. No idea what to do with the hots if he had them. But our elections are not in September, they are in November. One suits one's style to the seasons. Of course it is necessary to be in tune, to understand the nature of the dreams and nightmares of the population. That is something that has preoccupied me for twenty years, since Bloomington. The apparatus of control is fragile, and the people require consolation.

I worked for a congressman for ten years, first as intern and then as his legislative assistant and finally his administrative assistant, and when he retired I ran to succeed him and won. It was an arranged retirement. He supported me, and that (along with Senator Kennedy) made the difference, and even today I consult him on serious political matters relating to the district. He knows all the closets and all the skeletons in them; a great man for detail. I am entirely secure now; the last time out I had no opposition at all. (My victory may be said to have been unanimous.)

Since my election, my wife and our two children live in the district, in the house she grew up in; her father, my predecessor and patron the congressman, lives down the street. The house, his house, was his present to us the year I ran for his seat and won. It is a large Victorian house in a neighborhood of other large Victorian houses. Weekdays I live alone in a small apartment near the Capitol. I am home virtually every weekend, so that is in no way a hardship. My weekends home follow a predictable pattern: I arrive Friday night, hold open house in my office on Saturday morning, visit friends on Saturday night, and on Sunday we all have lunch with my in-laws. His health is not

good, and I believe that in his heart of hearts he wishes he were back
on the Hill. Gail and her mother cook and the old man and I talk
politics. I ask his advice on legislation and then I bring him up to date
on all the congressional gossip, particularly that relating to his old
friends. George Davies was a particular kind of Washington legislator, a figure more of the last century than of this one. His weekends
were spent in the Library of Congress, and his fund of Washington
knowledge was prodigious. He could name the artist who drew the
two murals in the Lincoln Memorial (Jules Guérin), describe with
quick wit the decades of quarreling that delayed the construction of
the Washington Monument, and digress for hours on the contradic-
tions of the American political system. In other words, a proper
Washington bore, but a bore with style, and I remain very fond of
him. This family, her family, is now mine as well. I feel closer to my
father-in-law than I ever did to my own father, though we are very
different men. He is extremely shrewd, an old man who knows what
he wants.

I like living alone in Washington. My apartment is pleasant and not
expensive, and quite private when I have guests. I have a hideaway
office in the Capitol building itself to which I return nearly every
evening after dinner. I love the old big-domed building, echoing at
night, with its marble floors and pompous statuary and distinctive
aroma; it is a government aroma, the damp smell of old paper and
tobacco. Or, as a friend of mine puts it, "the smell of drift and
inaction." I have never bothered to learn anything about the building,
its length or its height or the identities of the architects. These are the
sorts of facts that fascinate my father-in-law, and the other senior
men. I am interested only in the effects, the largeness of the chambers,
the pomposity of the design, and the silence at night. It is a comfortable building if you belong to it, and overwhelming if you don't.
Those of us who work after hours in the Capitol building form a kind
of fraternity. It's a fraternity of inside men who know and respect
each other regardless of party; a thoroughly masculine world.
    I'll have dinner and return to the office and work for two hours on
correspondence and legislation and then prepare a stiff Scotch and sit
at my desk, feet up, and meditate. My office in the Rayburn Building
is ceremonial, photographs and flags and certificates of one kind and
another. The hideaway office is for work only, except for a small
bookshelf containing the New York edition of Henry James. That is
a legacy from my past, but a legacy that is always with me. I have
read all the novels and short stories and Leon Edel's biography, and

I regard the master as an old friend. I freely concede that this is odd; the world of Henry James is miles away from mine. However, the atmosphere in Washington has been rancid for years; to be precise, for ten years, from the moment I became a congressman. It will take a generation to cleanse it. I live and work in Washington and do not feel obliged to read about it in novels. I expect I am somewhat disappointed and stale, and in that I reflect the city. At any event I prefer the Europe of Henry James and I connect with his rhythms: he writes of ordinary men in extreme situations.

I have not read any of his books lately because I have been studying my "image." The assistant majority leader is due to retire this year and there has been some speculation that I'll be put forward to succeed him. There is no obvious candidate and the leadership is determined to avoid a brawl. We are trying to prepare the battlefield from behind the scenes. I won't get the job because I'm too junior, but I'll work to get it, though in the circumstances there's a limit to what a man can do for himself.

The image is this. Hardworking Tom Lewis. Thomas Giles Lewis, forty-four, a ten-year veteran of the House, strong with the unions, respected by businessmen, moderate-liberal. No firebrand as an orator, but in the House of Representatives that's evidence of maturity. "His name is attached to no specific piece of legislation, but scores of bills over the years bear his fingerprints." A family man, well liked on both sides of the aisle. "Clean." The shrewdest of the reporters wrote that "his commitment to the House is genuine. He seems to lead two lives, one in Washington and the other with his family in the district, and he appears to be uncommonly successful at it." I would say middling successful, but then I'm a party at interest. Reporters, so secure in the cocoon of their professional neutrality, are especially fond of the word "commitment." They do not appreciate the double meaning. (Reporters are like Germans: they are either at your feet or at your throat.)

The image is accurate in all important respects. I do a politician's work and am paid for it and am obliged to defend myself and my record every two years, which is more than I can say for newspaper reporters. Still, I am bemused — perplexed, perhaps — by the image, the grand march of verified facts. Legislation supported and opposed, issues joined or avoided; men defended or abandoned. This C.V. discloses quite a lot; quite enough for a voter to make an informed judgment.

These thoughts are common among politicians, narcissists all. We scorn the image one moment and embrace it the next. But it is always with us, a shadow variously cast, a permanent doppelgänger. The night I thought seriously about my image I also thought seriously about Dement. Brother Warren had made a new offer, the most generous yet; my lawyer urged me to accept. I sat in the hideaway until midnight, drinking Scotch and doodling on a yellow pad and thinking about my image, the leadership, Dement, and the various women I had known. My mind roamed among the four. What would it be like to dispose of Dement? My third interest in an insurance agency? At midnight I decided to call Gail. The telephone rang half a dozen times before she answered, groggy and irritated at being awakened. We talked a moment of this and that, how she was, how the children were, how I was, how her parents were. Then there was silence between us.

I have always hated the telephone, an unfortunate circumstance, because I'm on it about two hours a day. I like to watch people when I'm talking to them. Faces disclose more than words, and now I tried to visualize Gail lying in bed, her head buried in the pillow, the telephone receiver held askew to one ear.

She said, "Where are you now?"

"I'm in the hideaway."

"It sounded like it, your voice is always friendlier when you're there rather than the Rayburn. What are you doing there at this hour?"

"Working. Having a drink."

"You don't sound like you're drinking," she said.

"And thinking," I said. I suddenly thought of my father. What would he have to say about my political career? What would be his advice? He would say, without doubt, "Slow down." Those would be his first words to me. The next two words would be "Watch out."

"Anything new?" She meant with the retirement of the assistant leader. I said there wasn't. She said, "When will you know?"

I pictured her in the second-floor bedroom, her night light on, puzzled by this call. I said, "A couple of weeks. They're sorting it out now. It'll take time." She yawned and smothered the yawn with a giggle. I said, "I'm going to Dement at the end of the week," and listened carefully for her reply.

"Dement?" She was silent a moment. "Tom, I don't want to go to Dement."

I said, "I'd like you there."

"Well, why? I've never gone before. You've always gone to Dement alone."

"I'm going to accept the latest offer. It's a pile of money and I'm going to take it and run. Sell my share of the agency, and cut that cord at last. It could be embarrassing, having an interest in an insurance agency." That was only half true. "It would be a help to me if you were there. I'd appreciate it, Gail. Really."

"Tom, it's impossible."

I said, "Two days. Thursday and Friday."

She was not happy and listed the things she had to do before the weekend. It was a long list. "I'm sorry, I'd like to. But it's too much."

I said mildly, "Shit." I knew I could persuade her.

"I *am* sorry," she said. "Go to bed now."

But I didn't. I hung up the telephone and sat silently for another hour. I made a fresh drink and reflected that the largest decisions were often made in the most casual ways. One way or another I had been associated with the agency all my life. But it was time to move along now.

◆

My wife and I were married two years after I went to work for her father. She had gone to George Washington University and then worked for a congressman from Indiana, her godfather, in fact. (As later the congressman's son would work for *her* father.) We fell in love right away, almost the day we met, which was a month after I went to work in her father's office. The courtship was smooth, though she kept delaying the wedding date. She said there was no hurry, and of course there wasn't. But she anticipated problems between me and her father.

I was fascinated by the centeredness and continuity of her life. She was a true Washingtonian, though she'd not actually grown up in the city; she'd lived with her mother in the district in upstate New York. But her father had been in Congress for twenty years and he shared everything with her. He and her mother kept their distance; she was the link between them. It was a congressional family, the old man consumed by his work; table talk between him and his daughter concerned politics and little else. She had a profound sense of the town, though for her it was always the Capital, pronounced Warshinton. Perhaps she took it too seriously. She said she would never live there as the wife of an elected official. Her words: Elected Official.

Her parents' arrangement was ideal. She would prefer not to live in Warshinton at all, but to live "at home," as her mother did. Warshinton was a transient town of shifting alliances. There was too much movement and commotion, and while she understood it, and loved living there as a single person, she did not want to be on the premises as a congressional wife. Any more than her mother had been.

Of course I wanted very badly to be an "elected official," and the two years of our courtship were thick with discussion and argument about *where*. Dement was out of the question. I did not care to pursue a political career or any kind of career in Dement or anywhere else in Illinois. It was the Congress I wanted. I wanted to be one of four hundred and thirty-five *congressmen*. Why? Perhaps I felt there was safety in numbers. But I did not believe it would ever happen. The House seemed unattainable to me. Elective office was surely beyond my grasp; I had no money and no "base" and no proven ability. Eventually I put "elected official" in the back of my mind and began actively to cast around for something else. I was at loose ends in all ways, believing the prize forever beyond me. Meanwhile, I picked away at my job, ADC to a father-in-law. I knew it would not last. A year after Gail and I were married it became clear to me that he had plans. Without any formal agreement between us it was understood that I would be his successor. The timetable would be of his own choosing. But increasingly I would accompany him on trips back to the district, occasionally filling in for him at a Rotary Club lunch or a Chamber of Commerce dinner. These appearances were successful. Each year he delegated more of his authority, but no one was more surprised than I when, in 1964, he told me he would announce his retirement early in 1966. I would have to fight a tough primary, but if I was energetic, "we would win." I would win with his help. My father-in-law was a man of the old school, and I had not worked for him for ten years and lived with his daughter for eight without knowing how his mind worked. I knew there would be a condition and I waited for him to spell it out.

"Give her up," he said.

We were sitting in his office. It was late at night and no one else was around. I flushed, muttered something, and looked away. His words were not angry and they carried no hint of threat, but he was not pleading either. He had advanced a simple statement of fact.

"That's the quid pro quo."

"Hell, George," I began.

"No, that's what it is. And not tomorrow and not next week. Right now. Tonight."

"She's just a friend," I said.

He smiled. "Then it ought to be easy."

"Well, it won't be easy."

"Call it what you want. I don't want to hear any details. I know most of them anyway. That's the bargain."

I was silent for a moment. He leaned back in his desk chair, staring at the ceiling. Then he lit a cigar, rolling the tip in the match flame. He pushed the cigar box across the table but I shook my head.

"You know I love Gail," I said.

He just looked at me sharply. "We'll leave Gail out of it."

"I just meant —"

"I know what you meant," he said.

My mind was racing. "It isn't what you think. I don't know what you've heard." I said, "This town is full of gossip. You know how this town is, you have a friendship —" I said, "Anything is open to misinterpretation, but I certainly —" Then I looked at his face and I knew I had made a mistake. George Davies was not a fool and did not like to be taken for one. I moved my hand as if to erase the words from the air. He looked at me and nodded slowly. Then he leaned across the table and spoke directly, his words cold as frost. He said he wasn't interested in morals, mine or his. He was not a priest, he was a politician; and he was a father and grandfather. He knew there was nothing he could do for the long term, but he had an obligation to his family. If in two years I decided to renew this . . . friendship . . . there was nothing he could do about it. But he was betting that wouldn't happen. He said, "I've watched you closely. You're smart, you're loyal. You are going to make an excellent member of this House. You can go as far as you want to —"

"With your help," I said.

He nodded. "With my help." He said it was a business arrangement. It was an entirely private transaction and I could accept it or not, as I chose. That was my business. But he would expect an answer first thing in the morning. A fait accompli, one way or another. He said, "You think it over." Then he looked at his watch, put on his hat, said good night, and left the office. I sat stiffly in the visitor's chair, his cigar smoke all around me, and listened to the door close and his footsteps retreat down the marble corridor. Then I called Jo and told her I would be there for dinner.

. . .

Gail was visiting her mother in the district. In those days she went back for a long weekend once a month, and it was during one of these absences that I'd met Jo. We were introduced at a crowded cocktail party; our host described me vaguely as someone who worked on the Hill. She asked me what I did on the Hill. I told her in as few words as possible, and understood after a moment that she had no idea what "the Hill" was. She lived entirely apart from political Washington, then and later. She listened to me politely, nodding and asking what she hoped were the right questions. I said finally, "You don't give a damn about any of this, do you?" She shook her head. No, she really didn't. I said, "Does the phrase 'House Ways and Means' mean anything to you?" No, she said. Sorry, it doesn't mean anything at all. Then, smiling: "I really didn't understand much of what you were saying a minute ago. I gather you work for a congressman. What do you do for him?"

"Legislation," I said. "And political business back in the district." She nodded, apparently satisfied. I said, "The congressman is my father-in-law."

She said, "Your poor wife."

I was startled. "Say again," I said.

"It must be awkward for her."

"Why would it be awkward?"

She looked at me strangely. "Well, what happens when there's an argument? Whose side is she supposed to be on? She's sure to offend someone, no matter what she says. Your poor wife, she's walking through a minefield."

"We don't argue," I said.

"Not at all?"

"Well, it's the office. It's business —"

She laughed and touched my arm. "Passing strange. That's all I ever did. Argue with my mother-in-law. We could make an argument out of anything, the weather, sex, religion, the competence of clerks at Marshall Field's —" She explained that she and her husband were separated. He was a lawyer in Chicago; she'd come to Washington because she had friends here. She sculpted; in fact she had a show at one of the local galleries. She reached into her purse and fished out a business card and handed it to me. It was the address of a gallery near Dupont Circle. Come tomorrow at five, she said. If you can stand bad sherry and the local art mob. Then she shook my hand and was gone.

I arranged to stop by the gallery the next day. Of course, I knew no one there and was ill at ease until she took me in hand and explained what it was she was doing with her sculpture. It made as much sense to me as my explanations of the Hill did to her. Her pieces were constructed of papier-mâché and were circular and all of them were white. The walls and ceilings of the gallery were white and the effect was disorienting, her white globes against the white walls. Each globe had a piece cut out of its skin, revealing the interior. In some extraordinary way the globes seemed reflective of her. I did not understand what she was doing but I knew it was genuine.

I took her to dinner that night and told her I had once contemplated becoming an artist. She smiled; I think she thought that artists were born and not made. They did not, in any case, "become." She asked me why I didn't. I said I believed there were inside men and outside men and I was an outside man. "Except professionally. Professionally, I'm an inside man."

"That's very clear. I'll remember that always."

I was laughing. "I knew you'd find it helpful," I said.

"Actually," she said, "I do understand what you mean. I'm a little surprised that I do. But I do."

I found myself reminiscing about the Midwest, Dement, and my father's campaign for lieutenant governor. I found I had near-total recall, the memories clear and sharp and funny. I could not stop talking; it was as if a door in my mind had swung open. "Let me tell you about Freud's Twenty-third Psalm." I embarked on a comic fantasy, connecting the episodes of my life to her papier-mâché globes: plunging through the diverse entrances to the empty spaces within, all the empty quarters of my mind. I loved making her laugh.

"They're not empty," she said.

"Unexplored," I said. "A wadi of the mind."

"No, no," she said urgently. "That's a mistake. The shape of the space defines it. That's what it *is*. Put in there what you want to, it's the shape that matters. That's what you have to know in your heart. The dream fits the shape." She was using her hands now, cupping them, describing arcs; I watched her, enchanted. I nodded gravely, then laughed. "That one of yours, the globe near the door? The shape of that one, perfectly seamless and nothing within. Hate to tell you, but it looks like Wilbur Mills."

"Inside or outside?"

I thought a minute. "Both ways."

She grinned happily. "Tommy," she said. "Who is Wilbur Mills?"

"A powerful chairman," I said.

"Like Mao?"

I laughed. "There is no difference between them at all," I said.
We became lovers that night. I remember walking to her house
from the restaurant, holding hands, walking head to head, our shoulders touching, ducking into a dark doorway, then resuming course.
Her house was a revelation to me. An empty birdcage hung from the
ceiling of the living room and reproductions of the Baroque portrait-
ists decorated the walls. There were no rugs and very few pieces of
furniture and the effect of the space was austere, though wonderfully
softened by the portraits — a melancholy prince, a soldier, a young
woman in repose. Our footsteps echoed on the hardwood floors.
Thick cushions were scattered here and there. A full bookcase and a
tiny white player piano sat side by side. One of her globes rested in
front of the fireplace, the center of attention. Fresh flowers were on
the mantel. I felt I had known the room all my life and was just
returning to it, although the objects in it were foreign to me. She put
a record on an old red Webcor and drew the curtains and opened a
bottle of wine. Then she looked at me, smiling shyly. "It's all right,
isn't it." She meant the room and it was a statement, not a question.
She said, "It's mine."

There was a month of craziness, a high-wire act of late night telephone calls and telegrams, two letters a day, clandestine meetings in
roadhouses, afternoons in motels, arranged encounters in art galleries, and one weekend in New York. From the beginning we agreed it
was a lunatic affair and would have to end. We had no future, our
lives were different, and there were many too many complications. I
was a married man, et cetera, and she was a woman of character, et
cetera. But I did not truly believe it. When we were together excitement carried us along and all doubts vanished. I was spellbound by
the moment, ignoring the precariousness of the affair; I believed that
somehow it would solve itself. I refused to think beyond the moment,
unwilling to disturb in any way what we had found together.

At the end of the month I had to visit the district on business and
when I returned she was beside herself. She said she could not continue. She said she was incapable of maintaining a frenzy. There was
enough frenzy in her work, she did not need it in her life. It was all
wonderful but insupportable. Her life did not work in that way. She
couldn't sculpt and was worried all the time and was being driven
out of her mind by guilt. This was an entirely different Jo. I tried to
joke and jolly her out of it; I was so happy to see her again I did not

listen carefully. But her mind was made up. She was firm: this was it. I did not understand what "it" was. I said I couldn't bear to be without her, not to have her in my life in some way; if that was what she wanted, I'd leave Gail. Gail and my work were part of another life altogether. No, she said; she couldn't bear that either, not yet anyway. But that was my own decision and she did not want to be a part of it. She said, Leave me out of that. She was miserable because she didn't know what to do. What were the choices? Always before there had been choices. This was a problem with no solution. But something had to change.

Jo said, "You. You've got to figure something out."

"I will," I promised. I was eager for responsibility. I would take charge and devise a strategy.

"Now. Right now."

"All right," I said and kissed her. I had no ideas at all.

She smiled sadly. "Because I am going nuts."

We spent a fortnight apart and I considered the possibilities. I was not thinking clearly because it had all happened so fast, and was so new to me. I was unchained for the first time in my life, amused and delighted in spite of the dilemma. I meditated, listening for echoes; I heard clamor. I am cautious by nature: I do not move quickly. I am accustomed to delay and obfuscation. I have learned that often the best and wisest course is to do nothing and wait for a harmonious solution to present itself. I believe the only way to control events is to let them play, intervening at the decisive moment. But the forces at work must be seen clearly and all I saw was a warm and amorphous haze. Nothing in my life had prepared me for this. I felt my own compass swing on its axis and was content to let it swing. I felt my chains snap and fall away.

It was exhilarating: whatever happened, life would never be the same. One's vision was forever altered and enlarged. Forever there would be dates remembered, specific times and places that would be with one always, memory's shadow. A life had changed direction. I believed there was no obvious way to "play" it; it was a throw of the dice — Einstein's random universe, perilous and unpredictable. I knew that Jo was obliged to see it differently. Jo loved complication; her life was a series of conscious choices. But the risks were not hers, they were mine. I explained that to her and she smiled (not unkindly), replying, "You have no idea of the risks that women take."

She listened very carefully. I said what men always say. I explained that I would need time, perhaps six months' time; there were practical considerations . . .

Saying nothing for a moment, her face a mask, she then began to
talk about her work. There were now two things in her life, me and
her work. I had to understand that they were . . . "poised." She said,
"I would not give up my work in order to have you. I would not give
you up in order to have my work. It is not a comfortable place for
me, but there it is. I'm on a knife's edge and I wish it were different
but it isn't." She paused, struggling with the words. "You cannot
expect too much from me in this. It is really your play. *But I will not
be toyed with.*" She gestured at one of the globes. "Do you know
how long I've studied and how hard I've worked in order to reach
the point where I can create that? I have been working at it for fifteen
years, fighting everyone . . . I don't know yet what you hang on to.
That's what I hang on to. That's the visible effect of my life." All of
this was said very slowly and seriously. "I do not mean to be anyone's
creature. I did that once and it didn't work out. How can I explain
this to you? I do not put my work first. But I don't put it second,
either. The two, you and my work, are equals. And separate —"
    I said, "In balance."
    She nodded. "Yes, I don't talk about it much, except to you. Men
are not conditioned to take a woman's work entirely seriously, no
matter what it is. In their tour through the maze that's a fact that's
neglected. Sad but true."
    "Nonsense," I said.
    "No," she said. "It's not nonsense."
    We talked most of the night, laughing often; the language of sex is
laughter. We concluded we could meet once a month. In between
times there were to be no telephone calls and no letters and no (she
was smiling) telegrams. The telegrams, she loved those most of all.
She had them all, plus the letters, in a shoe box. Yes, she said finally,
of course we can try it. Perhaps it'll even work for a while. But no
more daily frenzy. She couldn't eat or sleep but most of all she
couldn't *work*. I agreed to all conditions (my own work had never
gone better). Of course she was right, but I loved the commotion and
excitement and abandon of it, life running at full tilt. I had never had
that before. I described it exactly as I felt it, the words tumbling over
themselves.
    "I understand," she said gently.
    "Really?" I was pacing up and down in front of her.
    "Really. It's the same with me." Then she smiled, amusement fi-
nally bubbling over. "Except that it's different."
    I moved to the window and stood looking into the empty street
below. Soft early morning light had slipped in unnoticed. Across the

street a man in a dressing gown appeared on his front stoop and picked up the newspaper, unfolding it and glancing quickly at the headlines on page one. His expression was grave; this was the first news of the day, negotiable currency for today's transactions. I had to smile, it was so familiar: a Washingtonian and his morning newspaper. The man in the dressing gown seemed completely unaware of his surroundings. He peered at page one and grimaced. Then he turned abruptly and walked back into his house, closing the door smartly behind him.

The street was empty again but I continued to look into it, diverted by the long line of spare, monotonous, Federal façades. This was a very old and formal part of Georgetown. Two-hundred-year-old eagles crouched fiercely in horseshoe arches above lacquered doors, the eagles wrapped in Old Glory. I thought it an odd district for an artist to live in.

I heard her voice from the bed. "I couldn't continue living on a string, even when I know you're at the other end. People can't live like that." She smiled, her mouth turning down at the corners. "Doing themselves no favors. *I* can't."

I was avoiding the hard question. "I really believe we are one. One heart, one soul. I've believed it from the first —"

"No, baby," she said. "We are not one. We are two." She said, "Sometimes we are one. We are one sometimes when we are together and occasionally when we are apart and thinking the same thoughts. Otherwise, at those other times, we are two. Two persons. Separate." She looked hard at me, wanting to continue.

I continued for her. "And sometimes I am with someone else."

"Bravo," she said.

I corrected myself. "Most of the time."

She nodded slowly, wanting it understood.

I looked at her. "And that is intolerable."

She shook her head no. No, not intolerable. "But it doesn't make us one, either."

In that way the six months became a year, and the year became eighteen months.

I left the congressman's office that night of the ultimatum and drove slowly down Pennsylvania Avenue to M Street and then up to Prospect, where she lived. I was thinking of her, not what I would have to say to her, but of *her*. Jo laughing with her mouth turned down and her head cocked, a lock of auburn hair curling over one eye, her fingers describing arcs in the air; Jo in her shapeless sculptor's smock and black tights, explaining that she had a stepfather who had a stepfather. She called her stepfather "Step" and her stepfather's step-father "Step-step." Her laugh, low and subtle and suggestive; her anger, her turbulence, her unexpected passion. She was now as much a part of my life as my eyes and ears. I told her once that she was my sixth sense; that if we were ever separated for any reason I would return like a transmigrated soul to my former state, insurance man in Dement, Illinois. I would be just like everyone else, and so would she. There would be nothing unique about us at all.

She'd said to me once, "I can see into you. The part I love is on the inside. I don't understand the outside. In some odd way I think you're miscast. What is on the inside doesn't agree with what's on the out-side. I cannot see you as a representative of anything. You are real to me only when you're here, in this house. I saw you the other night on television. Some congressional thing, it was just a glimpse and I couldn't connect with it. With you. I thought, Here is the man who shares my bed and all the thoughts I have. A man I dream with, a cheerful man who laughs with me naked in bed. This other man is a serious man in a white shirt and a blue suit. Not the same man at all, I said to myself. Then I started to cry and I cried on and off all night. Not for me. For you."

We almost never talked politics at her house, though from time to time she'd ask me to explain something she'd read in the newspapers. She would listen to my explanation and shake her head, bemused. Occasionally her indifference would irritate me. But of course that was part of the attraction. Sometimes I talked about one of my cur-rent projects whether she wanted to hear about it or not. She was always polite but I knew her mind was elsewhere. Only once did I fully engage her interest, and that was when I told her about the hots, which was then only an idea and not a fact of my life. She said she understood that all right. How many people went into politics be-cause of the hots? Not too many men, I said. Most men went in for reasons of personal ambition, meaning power, money, and fame. I didn't know about the women; I'd always assumed with women that politics was a substitute for something else. What about you? she asked me. I said I wasn't sure, I'd have to campaign first; I suspected that it would be the hots, but I wouldn't know for certain until I'd done it. But I knew I wanted to be a representative, an outside man.

I wish now that I had told her more about my professional life, what I did during the daylight hours. I mean details. But our life together was grounded in a different world, an interior nighttime world that was closed to the outside. She had no doubts whatsoever that I would get what I wanted. She said, "It'll happen. It'll happen for sure. It's the way you've defined your space, or had it defined for you. I suspect your family defined it. Anyway, it's a compulsion. You're like a speculator plunging to protect his investment."

I'd said, "Don't I have anything to say about it?"

I remember her low laugh. "Don't you wish you did?"

"Well, you're in the same situation."

She looked at me sharply. "No. I arise from disorder. You arise from order."

I said, "The result is the same."

She lifted her shoulders, a noncommital comment. She said, "You can't imagine my life."

I said, "I know your work well enough. It's singular. Your own creation."

She smiled at that. "Yes," she said softly.

How I loved to watch her work: I'd curl up in a chair and read and she'd sculpt, talking to herself, complaining, exhorting, criticizing, humming music, occasionally looking at me, reciting odd bits of poetry. I'd listen to the performance and then become attracted to the black tights she wore when sculpting. We made love in the afternoon, listening to Vivaldi, *Four Seasons*, the Summer movement. It was there in her studio on Saturday afternoons that I discovered Henry James. On Saturday afternoons in the house on Prospect Street the books fit perfectly with the music, my mood, the white globes and black tights, the warmth and serenity of the room, and her vivid presence.

I drove to Prospect Street, parked in the alley, and let myself in through the back door. She was upstairs and called down: she was on the telephone, she'd be a minute. *My mother,* she whispered hoarsely. I made a drink and leaned wearily against the sideboard. I had avoided thinking about the congressman, but all that came back now with a rush. I could hear his careful voice and perfect sentences, and his cigar smoke still clung to my suit. Then the memory ebbed. I stood very still, sipping my drink, staring into the blackness of her back yard garden. I could barely make out the crowded rosebush, the blossoms hanging like bells from a jester's costume. I switched off the kitchen light and the entire garden came alive in the moon. A night bird hammered noisily nearby, competing with the roar of a cocktail party two houses away.

Then she was in the room and I kissed her and we stayed together a long minute in the dark. She took my hand and led me into the living room. The curtains were drawn and the radio was on, turned very low. The empty birdcage swung on its axis. It was bright, four spotlights blazed from the ceiling. She said, "Look."

It was a new globe; this one was five feet in diameter.

"This is the new one?" She nodded. I looked sideways at her. "You're sure it's big enough?"

"Very funny, come here." She wanted me to see the opening. There were in fact two openings, one square and one rectangle; they seemed to be cut at random but I knew she'd worked out the size and placement on a slide rule.

I was stunned by it and muttered something admiring. I said quietly, "It's a breakthrough."

She said, "I think so." She was standing back from it, her knuckles to her chin, her elbow in the palm of her hand. Her face was glowing with pleasure. She leaned toward her creation as if she were taking a bow, running her fingers along the two openings, feeling the rough texture. "Feel that," she commanded. "You'll notice that it's concrete. In case you don't know it, that's hard to do. It's *very* hard to do. Many structural problems. But I love it and I'm really and truly happy with it." Then she laughed. "Of course, it may not be sold because it may never be moved. When they brought it here from downstairs they asked me if I'd taken structural soundings. Of the *house*. They thought the house might collapse, clunk. It took four of them to move it . . ." She laughed again, giddy with excitement.

"It's wonderful, Jo. It really is."

"Do you really like it?"

"I really like it," I said.

"Well anyway," she said. "It's new. It certainly is new."

"The size —" I began.

She nodded. "Yes."

"Why two openings?" I wanted to keep her talking.

She looked at me, bubbling over with excitement. "Oh, it's very symbolic. High symbolism." I laughed and she touched my arm, suddenly serious. "It was an idea. I'd never made two openings before. It's a whole new idea about space. It has no special meaning that I can understand. It's just that from the moment I started working on them, the openings, I knew it was right. They're where they ought to be." She moved around to the far side of the globe. "Look at it from this angle." I followed her. "And from this one." She got down on her knees, looking up. "And from down here, where you can just see the edges of both of them . . ." She paused, considering what she would say. "It's *correct,*" she said at last. "Whether or not it's successful, it's correct. Size and placement." She backed away from it now, her face set. "I want it shown in a room all by itself. A perfectly bare room, wood floors, bone-white walls. A fairly large room. I don't know yet whether the room should be square or rectangular. But the piece should be free-standing and located near a corner. People will have to *approach* it, as if it were a sovereign. As people come closer to the globe they should become almost hypnotized until as they get very near they will cease to see anything else and will contemplate *it* only. They will become one with the whiteness and the roundness. If they are looking at it properly, they will imagine the openings begin to expand and spread like an eclipse of the sun. Expand and expand until of course there is nothing at all. They are left with an idea of an idea: the opening becoming the thing itself. If they're *really* looking at it, it'll be an overwhelming experience. They'll never forget it, it'll be in their memories forever, staying with them, the fondest memory they have, a memory as vivid as something special recalled from childhood or earlier. It's a celebration of possibilities. Infinite possibilities, no limits on what can be attempted or achieved." She paused and smiled broadly, consciously breaking the spell.

I was shaken. It was the most direct and explicit she'd ever been. A celebration, she'd said. I said nothing; my mind was racing over her words. She took my hand and squeezed it.

"That is, if I can ever get it out of here in one piece. If it can be moved." She was racing for cover now. "I'm going to put a good fat price on it."

I let her go. I said, "You ought to. No price is high enough." I thought, No price was high enough for her. I nudged her. "A breakthrough piece demands a breakthrough price."

"Five thou," she said. "How much is that in francs?"

"I don't know. I think it's twenty-five thousand francs."

"Well, twenty-five thousand francs, then."

"Why francs?"

She turned away from me. "Because they've offered me a show in Paris."

I took her by the shoulders and massaged her gently. "That is sensational," I said.

"They asked me three weeks ago; it would mean I'd have to go for at least six weeks. And to tell you the truth, I want to go. For six weeks or longer. Making this thing has emptied me. I have poured myself into concrete and I feel a little crazy, that's to be honest with you. I want to go to Paris and go a little insane. With you. Maybe you could arrange it. We two —" She looked at me nervously, biting her lower lip. My heart turned over. "I pity anyone who has never been crazy in the soul." Then: "I've got to have all this stuff crated by next week, it's going over by ship and I'm going with it. But what about the new piece? It'll cost a fortune —" She giggled.

"Do it anyway," I said. "The hell with the cost, do it and up the price another five thousand . . . francs."

"Would you come?"

I retreated, moving my shoulders like a ballroom dancer, yes-no, maybe, perhaps, nothing's impossible in an uncertain world. I said, "It'll be hard."

"Oh, sure," she said. "But there are ways." She looked at me slyly. "I read something the other day about junkets. Isn't that what they're called? Congressional junkets at taxpayer expense?"

I laughed; she really was wonderful. She'd read one of the annual exposés in the newspaper. "Jo, that's the kind of thing that congressmen get defeated for."

"But you're not a congressman, you're staff."

I said, "I will be."

But she did not catch that. "Think of us in Paris. I'd have the show and we'd do the gallery drill, the opening and the stuff that goes with the opening. Parties, interviews. You could —"

"I could coach you on the interviews."

She smiled. "We'd hang around Paris. We'd fool around." She laughed out loud, imagining how it would be. "Then we'd go south. We'd take my winnings and just *go*, rent a car. We'd go south —"

I said, "The famous artist and her consort."

She looked at me. "Is that sarcasm?"

I looked back, surprised. "No," I said truthfully.

She moved away and cocked her head, pointing at the new creation. "I've got to call it something, it wants a name . . ." She took my arm again. "This gallery in Paris, it's the best one, everyone says so." She stroked the globe again, unable to take her eyes off it. Its whiteness and haughty, regal roundness dominated the room, an imperial presence.

I wanted to get everything straight. "Why didn't you tell me before?"

"Well," she said stiffly. "We have our rules. We established our rules and I follow them. No calls, no letters or telegrams. And I wanted to make certain that it was sure, that it was locked up, this show. It's damn bad luck to *talk* it, you know. You can talk good news to death. At first I could hardly believe it, you know how pessimistic I am." She was silent a moment. "But mostly it was the rules. Our rules that we have established in order that we may live in some kind of orderliness without unwanted surprises." She looked at me eyes-on. "You know, save the whales."

She could always make me laugh. I said, "Jo."

"And I didn't know about you, whether you'd like it or not."

That hurt. "Honey," I said. "How could I not like it?"

She gave me the same look as before. "We'll be apart for longer than we ever have," she said. "Since this began. If you can't escape, and I suppose you can't. I suppose that isn't possible." She stopped talking and looked at me. "You won't, will you?"

I ignored the verb. "No," I said.

"Probably the most we'd have would be a week, ten days. For this particular celebration." She was looking out the window now, into the street, her face stretched into a smile; it resembled the formal mask of comedy. "Why not?"

That text was prepared. I thought, How can I? How can I disappear in Europe? There has to be an explanation for journeys abroad. Some explanation, however thin. I said simply, "It isn't possible." And I added, "For all the good reasons that you might imagine."

"Well, there's nothing to be done, then. It was such a good idea. I don't like to think about it."

"Neither do I." Just then I thought I had the first warning of her strategy, the manner in which she intended to stand in her own defense. She wanted precise bearings, nothing neglected. I wondered if we had each begun to take on the characteristics of the other.

She said, "Perhaps it's best. This is my business after all, there'll be quite a lot of business to be done in Paris. It isn't entirely pleasure, it's business as well. Business is separate. You said it once: one never argues about business." Her face was turned away from me. "Do you think it's best? I won't quarrel with you and I won't force you, but do you think it's best?"

I answered from instinct, "No." I looked at her and knew she understood. And I was wrong about the other; her characteristics were her own.

She said crisply, "I do." She turned off the overhead spotlights and suddenly we were in darkness. Her creation disappeared though its effects were still radiant. She said, "Come on, then." We walked back into the kitchen. It was perfectly still, the cocktail party nearby had ended. A dry breeze touched us through the open window. She was smiling her formal smile. We were both on soft surfaces, searching for a secure footing, trying to locate the high ground. She said, "That's out of the way now. We won't talk about it again. Make me a big drink, tell me about your day . . ."

I relaxed, staring into the gray garden. I said, "Come on, you don't have to say that. You don't give a damn about my day." I was thinking about her show in Paris and what it would mean to her, and was dismantling my defenses as she was dismantling hers.

"I give a damn about you," she said. "You, your day. What's the difference?"

She knew better than that. But I was certain now that we were on safe ground and that there would be no ill treatment or malevolence. We approached the window together, as close in our emotions as that first night on the streets of Georgetown, but still we did not touch. "There is no difference between them at all," I said at last.

◆

During those last minutes together I had forgotten absolutely about the fait accompli. I had not thought about that or about my wife and child or about my work. There were just the two of us and the life we had together, and the persistent avenging voice that told me this was a fresh turning and that she was obliged to go one way and I another. We had been together for more than a year and now we would have to be apart. What we had did not exist beyond the house on Prospect Street, it did not exist in Europe or New York City or any other place. We existed half slave and half free, and that was apparently the way we were meant to exist. It had worked, against all odds; but it would work no longer. To accompany her I would have to reject the others: not merely move away but consciously *reject*. I would have to tell them that they were not good enough for me, and that I would have to have this other.

I suddenly saw all the forces of my life with an awful clarity and knew the truth of the things she'd said. I had always thought of us as equals, "one," and abruptly we were no longer equals. We were what she had always claimed, "two people," "separate" — and everyone knew that separate was not equal. Except we had done such a good job, the casualties had been very light. I had always believed that casualties must accompany any good thing. The better the thing, the higher the casualties. She'd said to me, *It's a celebration of possibilities . . . no limits on what can be achieved or attempted.* I knew that song intimately and I believed it was a solo; I knew it was. Standing at last in the garden, both silent, I was able to tell myself that I was no prize. Those words came very easily and of course were consoling. No doubt it was all for the best, you think you are so wonderful it's impossible for her to live without you; you think she'll collapse under the intolerable pressure of being alone or with someone else. Without your wise advice and tender counsel to guide her through her days. A minute or two of that was enough. The whales could not be saved. I believed that Paris would have taken us onto heights too high and vast and rarefied. We could not live there. I could not. I felt I had watched a gorgeous comet flash across the heavens, its sublime light immeasurably out of reach. But the comet was not her. It was us.

I called the next day. This was a breach in the agreement but we both knew the agreement was dead. It had expired and there was no renewing it. She said she would be leaving at the end of the week, not in two weeks as she had supposed. She'd spoken to her agent that morning and they were anxious to move along. The globe would go with her on the *France,* and it would be the centerpiece of the exhibit.

I did not want to leave unfinished business.

I said it would be a wonderful show.

"It would be fun sharing it."

I said, "More than fun. *Much* more than fun. Anyway, I'm there in spirit."

"*D'accord* to that."

I said, "Maybe you deserve this one alone."

She said slowly, "Maybe I do at that."

"A limelight," I said. I remembered her the first night in the gallery, patiently explaining about the globes, and later her agreement to have dinner. She chuckled and fell silent and I knew suddenly what it was that I wanted for her. Whatever it was she wanted for herself, that was what I wanted for her. I wanted an enormous success, something huge and tangible; acclamation from the demanding French. A sold-out show, a globe in the Louvre. I wanted it big, too big for her to handle right away; she needed a swelled head. I began to laugh. "I know what's in store," I said. "What you're going to get." I could feel her grinning along with me and my voice caught. "It's come to me in a hot flash. You'll get — honor, power, riches, fame, and the love of men."

"My God, all that?"

"Each one," I said. "At once."

"What about you, cornball? What do you get?"

"Me too," I said gently. "The same things. Exactly the same things."

I heard the breath go out of her. "Yes," she said.

There was dead air between us then. Neither of us dared speak. I watched a secretary's fingers skate over the keyboard of the typewriter, and the receptionist hand a document to a messenger.

I said finally, "I'll be campaigning." That was the unfinished business.

"Oh," she said. She began to talk about something else, then stopped. "You mean, you're going to run."

"Run like hell," I said.

"When did that happen?" Her voice slipped a little.

"You know when," I said. Then, "The old man is stepping down. I'll run next year but the groundwork begins now." She was silent, I could hear nothing over the telephone. "Jo?"

"Does Gail know?"

I stammered for a moment, struck dumb. She never mentioned Gail, ever. "*Does Gail know?*"

I said, "Her father may have told her."

She said, "You haven't spoken to her."

"No."

She said slowly, "I didn't feel like being the last one in on this particular bit of information. Now. What did it have to do with last night?"

"You're going to follow it all the way down, aren't you?"

She said, "Yes, I am."

"It didn't have anything to do with last night," I said. "It doesn't have anything to do with Paris." She began to reply but I rode over her words. "Nothing," I repeated. "Not anything."

"All right," she said.

"No, not all right. Not all *right*."

"Gail didn't know?"

"No," I said. "And if she had, it wouldn't've made any difference."
She laughed quietly. "No difference at all."

I said, "None."

She said, "I'm going to name the globe after you."

I said, "I hope to hell."

"Tom," she said.

"It fits," I said, "and I'm honored." The buzzer sounded then; there
was a quorum call on the floor. It was one of the amendments to a
health care bill. The congressman emerged from his office and
pointed at me, the gesture reminiscent of a baseball coach signaling
the bullpen. He wanted me to come with him to the floor. I looked at
the telephone receiver, winking at my father-in-law, indicating I
would only be a moment.

"Best luck in the campaign," she said.

"Best luck in Paris."

. She said, "Let me know what happens. Particularly — well, you
know what particularly."

I said, "You too. The show. Tom."

"I will."

"Best luck in Paris," I said again.

She said, "Best love."

The congressman was standing impatiently at the door, jiggling the
coins in his pocket. He looked at his watch, then at me again. He
jerked his head: Come on.

I said, "Best love," and we hung up together.

Jo's show in Paris was a great success. The critics were unanimous in
their praise, displaying both puzzlement and delight, an excellent
combination in those times (and these). I sent her a long telegram the
day the show opened and received a letter in return. She said it was
fun to be a success in the City of Light. She remained there a month
and then four more months and finally returned to Washington
briefly to sell her house and collect her things and move back to Paris
for keeps. We did not see each other; I was addressing a Rotary Club
in the district.

But I kept my promise. The day after Kennedy came to campaign I
cabled her in Paris. *Hots are real,* I said. *But periodic, like the atomic
tables.* Then a paraphrase from Freud, *The way back from imagination to reality is art.* (The hots shepherd me, I shall not want.) I gave

her a brief account of what Kennedy had said, and predicted that I would win the election. That was ten years ago, and the last I heard Jo was still in France, living quietly in the country with a French academic.

◆

I flew into Dement in the early afternoon, beguiled as I always was by the flatness of the land, rectangular fields marching off to infinity. There was drought. The fields were various shades of gray, pockmarked here and there by oases of trees. Each field was plainly demarcated, as if it were a separate miniature nation; they were a thousand tiny nations in a vast dry continent. The city itself was triangular, its buildings low, its streets straight and even, curveless, fixed. The captain ordered us to extinguish all "smoking materials," and the de Havilland eased down, its engines sighing.

I looked for the family house but could not locate it among the trees, the hickories and maples and oaks. The town had grown in a year; Brother Warren had written me that it would be eighty thousand people before long. He said that once it was eighty thousand it would be no time at all before it was a hundred, if they could stop the rot downtown. If they couldn't stop it, they'd simply annex the surrounding countryside; the cat was skinned either way. Brother Warren spoke of a new golf course and three or four new restaurants and a new playing field for the high school. There was some talk about a community college but the city council could not agree on financing. Warren asked me were there any federal programs that Dement could plug into, payment on the come? Ask your congressman, I said. Lewis and Sons was prospering along with the town; it was now the largest insurance agency in a four-county area. Everyone was doing well and would continue to do well, if only the boom could be maintained.

I cinched my safety belt and the aircraft floated down, correcting its balance. The small field was clogged with private Cessnas and Pipers, and a few sailplanes. Skydiving and gliding had become quite the sports in Dement. A mile to our port side I watched a sailplane dip its nose and fall, gathering speed, then bank and rise, soaring beautifully. I wondered what my father would have thought of payment "on the come."

I turned to my wife, who was dozing, her head resting gently against the Plexiglas window. Her face was set; even in sleep she was facing the world stoically. I thought that she had gotten better-looking over the years. She did not look young, she looked exactly her age, forty-one, and she had put on weight, as I had. But she was a good-looking woman — now as then, except now she had character, a stamp, a mark as definite as an artist's brushstroke. I could recognize her in a crowd a hundred yards away, by the tilt of her head and her walk and the way her arms swung. I nudged her and she came awake blinking, her face still in repose. I asked her if any of it was familiar and she said it wasn't. Just the shape of the town in the middle of the fields, a triangular habitation . . . It was ten years since she'd accompanied me to Dement. She asked me who would meet us.

No one, I said. I'd told them I didn't know what plane we'd be on. I said I had political business in Chicago and didn't know when I'd get away. I'd let them know when we were settled at the hotel — except I intended to leave on the late commuter that evening. I wanted to avoid an overnight. There wouldn't be any hotel. I said to her, "I had an idea that we'd rent a car at the airport and have lunch together at a place I know."

She looked at me. "You seem almost happy."

"I am," I said.

"I always imagine you approaching Dement with dread."

"Do," I said.

"Well?"

"Well, this is different."

I collected a Chevrolet at the airport and we drove to the Wayside. My wife cautioned me twice; I always drive faster in the Midwest. I obeyed her warning the second time, just as I obey her instructions to have my hair cut, to make an appointment with the dentist, to have the car repaired, and to come to bed when it is late; she obeys me in similar matters. At other times we do not obey each other, though the warnings are spoken anyway. It was nearly two o'clock when we arrived at the restaurant, and the parking lot contained only about a dozen cars. She looked at the building, whitewashed brick with a red tile roof and an enormous neon sign: STEAKS CHOPS SEAFOOD COCKTAILS. It was years since I had heard a drink called a cocktail. She began to laugh. "This place, one of your poisonous roadhouses . . ." Her taste in food is more refined than mine.

I said, "A steak as thick as a gravestone, a baked potato the size of a shoe."

She said, "Good God!" Then: "I suppose you're going to have a martini."

I said, "Damn right. You, too."

She said, "I'll have a kir."

I shook my head. She would never get Dement right. I said, "The Wayside does not serve kirs. They don't serve them even if you call them *blanc cassis*. You'd better have a martini, it will improve your disposition." I said, "You can have it on the rocks, clean." She made a face. "Or straight up. You can say, 'Silver bullet up, olive and twist.'"

She said, "Wonderful. How about a weak Scotch? Do you think they can manage that?"

We were talking quietly in the foyer, waiting for the maître d' to seat us. I looked left into the bar and saw half a dozen men shooting dice for drinks. At the far end was a party of three women, their rugged heads close together, talking quietly. The women had apparently come from the golf course; they wore hats with golf tees stuck in the brims. Neither party seemed aware of the other, and the bartender stood poised midway between them. When the maître d' came he looked at me queerly, knowing he knew the face but unable to connect a name to it. When we were seated and he'd handed us menus I put out my hand. "Tom Lewis," I said. "Wife, Gail."

Well, *Tom*, he said. It had been too long. Four years, five. We chatted about the town and the weather. The growth and the drought. Then he left to fetch us drinks and when he returned we resumed the conversation. He said, "I suppose you're here for the dedication next week."

I shook my head. What dedication?

"Jesus Christ," the maître d' said. "Those brothers of yours. I suppose they were wanting to surprise you. A school is being dedicated to your father. Lewis School now, it used to be called South School. Remember?"

I remembered. A red brick building on a barren patch of land. A dusty baseball diamond and an iron jungle gym next to the ravine, and in the boys' room initials carved into the wooden partition between the toilets: TL.

"We all miss your father," he said, lowering his voice. "The one that's in there now." He shook his head. "No good. No damn good at all."

"Dead fifteen years next July," I said.

"Well, the firm has done real well." I nodded. "Your father would have been proud, all right. It's a fine thing, the school. You ought to go look at it, you couldn't recognize it. New addition." A customer on the other side of the room waved at him and jiggled his hand. The check. He turned to go.

"I'll look at it," I said.

My wife turned to me. "Did your father come in here often?"

"Sure," I said. "Every lunchtime for twenty years. Sat over there." I motioned toward a remote corner. "Had a schedule. He'd lunch with one friend on Monday and another on Tuesday. Always the same friends, same day of the week. Every week. Very orderly, my old man seemed to like that. Gave a shape to the week, he said."

She smiled. "You do the same thing."

"Correct," I said.

"It's funny, patterns in families. Fathers and sons and mothers and daughters."

I said, "This isn't a bad drink."

"I wonder if your grandfather did the same thing."

"Yes," I said. "He did. Every day, except it was with his wife, because he was a farmer —"

"And *his* father," she said. "I wonder if they were all in revolt against each other. Each following the same pattern —"

"It's so good I might have another."

"I wish I'd been a psychologist," she said suddenly. "That's really what interests me. I went to college and I had babies, that's what I did. And I was not a bad student. I could be working on the Hill now. That's where the serious work is being done," she said. "Social science, one or another of the soft sciences." She mentioned two pieces of pending legislation. "You know, they had to farm out some of the research on that. There was no one on the committee staff capable of doing it, they didn't have the expertise —"

"Two more," I told a passing waiter.

We left the restaurant at three, my head buzzing from the drinks. I never drink at lunch; even a glass of beer makes me sleepy. We had an hour and a half to kill and I decided to take her on a short tour of the town. We went first to the house where I grew up, and then to the elementary school nearby — South School, now Lewis School. It was familiar to me but remote, the land around it less barren now; all of it was smaller than I had remembered. The neighborhood had not changed, but the school had a new steel-and-glass addition, with a square plaque to the left of the entrance: my father in bas-relief. He had been mayor the years I'd attended the school, a frequent speaker on Flag Day and Lincoln's Birthday and other national celebrations. The day the war in Europe ended he arrived breathless and called an impromptu assembly. I remember his first words: "We've licked the Axis." He led us in cheers and a brief prayer and the Pledge of Allegiance. Then he hurried off to perform the same rites at the other schools. But not before he'd dismissed us on "this historic occasion." We all rode downtown on our bicycles to see what was happening; to see a historic occasion observed in Dement. But downtown was quiet, almost solemn; people were waiting for the end of the real war, the war in the Pacific. MacArthur's war.

The old schoolhouse was red brick and five stories high. I remembered how the wooden floors creaked, and the musty smell of the building, and the forbidding inner sanctum of the principal's office. School regulations were strict and authority and discipline absolute. Most of the teachers were spinsters and dry as old bones. There were only two male teachers; one taught shop and physical education and the other taught seventh grade.

The seventh-grade teacher had been wounded in the Pacific in the war, though none of the wounds was visible. At this time the war was still being fought, though no part of it seemed to touch Dement. This teacher, an ex-marine, was our only personal connection to the war. The class routines were in no way unusual, except the period devoted to arithmetic. He would carefully recite the lesson during the first half of the period and write questions concerning it on the blackboard. We were required to answer the questions during the second half. While we wrote he moved to the large windows overlooking the baseball diamond. The windows had shades with long black cords. He would take one of the cords in his fingers and begin to play with it, first twirling it like a lariat, then fashioning a noose, and finally tying knots in it, knot after knot, knot upon knot. It was a long cord and he was able to tie scores of knots, each building on the last until the cord was a hopeless tangle. We would watch him from our desks, bent over the oblong yellow work pads; alone of the teachers he required us to call him "sir," and in turn he addressed us by our last names, girls too. We watched him surreptitiously but he never turned around or acknowledged our presence in any way. The class remained very still; there were no disorders of any kind. He tied the knots and then untied them, his fingers working by feel alone; his hooded eyes were far away, staring into the playground, his expression blank. He finished untying the knots at precisely the moment the bell rang and would abandon the cord, leaving it dangling, kinked and gnarled and uneven, and would move to his desk to accept our papers silently. Then he would say "Class dismissed" in a thick voice and we would leave with a rush, anxious to be gone; it was the last class of the day. We would leave him at his desk with the papers.

He was at the school only one year, a small man with light wispy hair and china-blue eyes; he did not look the way we expected marines to look, even ex-marines. He had a face that was too small for his head. I remembered him vividly, standing in front of the window and staring into the playground, his fingers working by rote on the cord. God knows what his thoughts were. Of course he seemed very old and worn then, but he was probably in his early twenties, twenty years younger than I am now.

I parked in front of the school. I wondered what had happened to that seventh-grade teacher with the faraway eyes, where he had gone and what he did now. A casualty of war, I supposed; the school board determined that he was ill, unstrung, "not in control," and therefore unsuitable as a seventh-grade teacher. I heard it said that he was "not a good example." There was some commotion about it in the town but no one was prepared to cause trouble for the war effort, or embarrassment to the teacher. So he was fired quietly. To us at that time he was merely baffling, his behavior strange but never threatening; to my certain recollection, he never raised his voice.

"Do you remember his name?" Gail asked.

I said I had no idea.

"Poor man," she said.

I said, "They fired him."

She shook her head, angry. "I don't like this place at all."

"It's a small town like any other," I said.

"No it isn't," she said quickly.

I wanted to explain Dement to her, to find some way to convince her that the people there were no different from anywhere else. I meant no meaner than anywhere else. It was simply that the norms were narrower, and perhaps that accounted for the dreams or fantasies of people like me; it was one way out. But it was unforgiving toward outsiders, no question of that; at times I was certain that the root of it was envy, at other times as convinced of the reverse.

She put her hand on my arm. "I didn't mean to be harsh," she said.

I smiled. "Not to worry."

"But it's so *closed*, so self-righteous —"

I shrugged, staring out the window at Lewis School, the plaque, the playground.

"— and as a matter of strict fact this place reminds me of her."

I stared at her, astonished. She never mentioned Jo, except one night years ago. We had talked about her in retrospect, calmly and rationally — too calm and too rational for either of us, but that was how it had gone. Later there were tears. I think we were both afraid of heat then; we did not know where that would lead us or with what result.

She said, "For years I thought it was a reaction to this place, here, where you had come from and what you'd been taught to expect. What you had been taught to believe was rightfully yours, or anyway *possible.* But you believed that passion came only in fantasy, not reality, and when the reality happened . . ." Her voice trailed away. Then, "I was not real to you. Maybe you thought she was the fantasy but she wasn't. I was." I began to reply but she interrupted. "That was the explanation that was easiest for me, that it was Dement and Dement's attitudes — you think you hated it, how do you think I felt? Feel. If it had not been for Dement there would have been no Jo. Jo would have happened long before, an extension of that other one. What was her name? It would not have been a threat that it took *my father* to solve. And that idiotic Freudian business, that was all tied up with Dement too. The one played off the other and the result was her." She put her hand to her mouth. "All those expectations and the means to fulfill them denied. Forbidden."

Gail lit a cigarette, exhaling in a rush. Ten years later the memory was still fresh, explicable now as it had not been that night. She smiled suddenly and I saw in her smile a flash of youth; Gail as she had been when I first met her. She said, "Of course I wanted to distribute blame. It was either Dement or it was me, and I was not eager to believe that it was me. Of course it could have been you, just you. You yourself. But I was not anxious to believe that, either."

I said, "It wasn't you."

She said, "Well, then." I put my arm around her shoulder but she did not yield right away. She was lost in her own painful memory.

"Look," I said, "I have what I want."

She looked at me. "All of them?"

I said, "All that I need."

She smiled then and I could see tears in the corners of her eyes. "You're not all that famous."

"I have plenty of honor."

♦

"Or rich, either."

I laughed. "Will be, after today."

She turned away and ran her hand through her hair. She moved closer to me, though we did not touch. "And not very damn powerful, either."

"That leaves the last one," I said. "One to go."

She said, "I do not understand you at all, sometimes."

I said, "Stick to the strict facts."

"I mean to," she said.

"Come on," I said at last. "I'll show you the rest of the town." I put the car in gear and drove away. I do not remember everywhere we went that afternoon. I was on the west side of town, so I must have driven to the country club and the sprawling subdivision beyond. To the west the town gave way to farmers' fields, the fields decorated with billboards. I drove into the country a bit, then turned and headed back downtown. I was half asleep, driving slowly and cautiously through the unfamiliar streets. Then I was in the vicinity of the high school and made an abrupt turn to cruise by it. Where the Dement Township High School had been was now an apartment complex, and I remembered suddenly that five years ago it had been torn down and the land sold and a new consolidated school built closer to the center of population. I stopped the car and looked at the apartment building, another severe rectangle built (I supposed) with Title IV funds. I thought, Someone made a killing. Or no, not a killing; a massacre. I smiled; looking at this town gave the phrase "living off the land" new meaning. I knew that Lewis and Sons carried the insurance on the apartment complex, since Treasurer Bill was an early investor. The building, five years old, was already shabby and down-at-heel, and FOR RENT signs dotted the property. The old high school had been built like a fortress; it had taken months for them to demolish it . . .

Well, I thought, it was not the Parthenon or even Lever House. All it had to commend it was a certain congruity with the town; it belonged. I remembered the governor in 1948, shy and hesitant in the gymnasium, groping for some vision he could lay before the hearts and minds of the citizens of Dement. I remembered the speech as a discussion of ideas and men, of the civilization that had resulted, and of the unquiet future. Ideas that had endured, men who had not. The importance of the land, fidelity to it; the beauty and challenge of the nation's principles, and fidelity to them. The gorgeous future, if. And the various threats of alien ideology. I remembered the restlessness and hostility of the audience; this was not a Chautauqua they enjoyed. It had occurred to them by then that land was no longer "the land" but "property," and that subversives were everywhere. They did not need to be lectured about their responsibilities, or promised bliss and ecstasy at some future political time. They wanted praise and reassurance now: not for what they did, but for what they were. To be told — what? That no sphinx would move in their lifetime. That the future was under control as long as they cleaved to what they were, and refused to budge. This one, striped-tied, who stood before them, so high-minded; he was an apostate, and could not be trusted.

I drove downtown and met with my brothers and my uncle and the two attorneys. It was very amicable; there were jokes. The attorneys conducted the final markup of the contract, speaking as if the principals were not in the room. They reviewed the contract line by line while the rest of us sat in silence, listening. Then each turned to his client and nodded. Everything was in order. All the conditions had been met, both men were satisfied. My brothers signed. I signed. Two secretaries signed as witnesses. A certified check was handed me by President Warren and I put it in my wallet without looking at it. Then we shook hands, strained smiles all around, and prepared to depart.

Warren said, "The *Trib* had an item about you the other day. Said you had a shot at the leadership of that place. A nice item, considering."

It always surprised me when any reference was made to my work by anyone in Dement. I said, "It's a long shot."

"I don't know how the hell you take it down there," Warren said. "Goddamned Washington." He shook his head as if to rid himself of a stubborn small pain. A man would have to be crazy to live in Washington, the muggers and the politicians and the bureaucrats, the filth. "Well," he said, "don't forget your friends and relatives."

I said, "Not a chance, Warren."

"Dad would've been proud."

I shook my head. "'Fraid not. No, I think he held Washington in minimum high regard."

Gail looked at me and spoke for the first time. "Is that true?"

I laughed and said it was.

"Times do change," Warren said.

I said, "He wouldn't've."

Warren grinned widely, eyebrows aloft; he looked more than ever like the old man. "It's the goddamnedest thing," he said. "When Dad was alive he wouldn't have anything to do with city insurance. You know, public buildings, casualty, fire, and so forth. Pension plans. No profit in it and a lot of risk, that was the way he felt. Well, now" — he began to laugh — "now it's exactly the other way around. Man would sell his soul for a government contract. That's what it's all about, the bluest of the blue chips." He looked at me, smiling. "Everything changes, Brother Tom." I took Gail's arm and moved to go, but he put his hand on my shoulder. "You come back now. Both of you."

I said, "I may come back for the dedication. By the way, you ought to've told me."

He nodded his big head. "Those idiots in City Hall. I'll talk to them, you should've been notified. It's a hell of a thing, the old man deserved it. What he put into this place, twelve years of his life and not much recognition, I mean nothing material. Tangible. Not much to show for it except this." He meant the agency. "Which has not done badly, if I do say so myself." He paused and lit a cigar; then he replaced his hand on my shoulder. "The thing that makes me proudest is that he created the conditions for the boom. It was a hands-off administration, his. The old man believed in progress and no interference, bless his heart. I don't know what the hell he'd think if he saw the shape the country's in now. But he set the climate in Dement, excellent labor relations, strong banks, no problems with the zoning or with the minorities and only the usual problems with the politicians. He would've done fine if he hadn't gone haywire at the end with the Springfield thing. That was a mistake."

Warren grinned, the memory somehow comfortable. "This is a hell of a town. You made a mistake, Brother Tom. You should have stayed. Bill and I, we're going to run this place someday. You could've had a hand in it." He laughed loudly. "We damn near run it now, matter of fact. You ought to trot on over and see it, Lewis School. Dad's name on that school, highly appropriate."

Then: "You know, you look tired. You ought to take a vacation, do the rest of us a favor, ha-ha-ha. They ought to declare a vacation in Washington six months of every year, give the country a chance to get on its feet." He rocked back on his heels, expansive now, the cigar protruding from his fist like a gun barrel. "Seriously, you look beat. Any time you want you can have the condo in Lauderdale, just give me some warning. Doesn't cost me a nickel anyhow, it's a write-off. You know what the old man said, 'In a heavy rain, you need a shelter.' Christ," he said. "Christ, I'm sorry to see you out of the business but it's better all around. Hell, it's no secret; you never had the taste for it, Dad knew that. God, Bill and I; ah, the *fun,* Tommy, *the fun of it!*"

Bill had joined us and Warren threw one of his huge arms around Bill's shoulder. The two of them stood grinning, their bodies in motion, arms around each other. Warren shook his head, eyes glittering. Then he cleared his throat. "Now look, you come back here. This is where you're from, after all, you come back here and see us now and again, get yourself in touch with the real people. Listen, we want to see you both any time" — he was looking at Gail now, beaming down at her — "I know how difficult it is and how involved you are there, in the East. But you name the time, we want to see you back here in Dement. Certainly you can spare some time for us."

Warren's telephone rang and his young secretary reached across her desk to answer it. "Your people are here, not there. They're here, right? Right?" The secretary motioned to him and he picked up the telephone, cradling it in his hand. I was moving to the door, Gail ahead of me; I thought, What a performance. I was already thinking about the lights of the capital, the long slow descent over the Potomac. I would have to rush, hurry like hell, but I thought I could make the last flight from O'Hare. Warren watched us, his hand cupped over the black mouthpiece. He moved his thighs and smiled. I waved at him and opened the door. "Look," he said. "I'm sorry."

We took off to the south, then banked around and flew over Dement, heading northeast to O'Hare. I was watching the dials; it was a long time since I'd been in an airplane cockpit. Gail was in the rear, and I took the last empty seat, the copilot's. I asked the pilot about each dial, then turned my attention outside. The triangular city receded to port and I watched it go, moving back of me, the lights feeble now as we gained altitude.

My mind was suddenly crowded with images, the governor's benediction, the seventh-grade teacher of arithmetic, President Warren, Gail's matter of strict fact, Freud's Twenty-third Psalm; all of it crowded my mind, invading my imagination, the images confused. Then I looked back at the city, marveling at the lights abruptly blazing brightly to port. The perimeter of Dement was clearly defined, like the walls of an ancient city or the life of a man. There were no lights at all beyond the perimeter. The cockpit was dark except for the green glow of the instrument panel. The pilot was busy with the instruments. I stretched and craned my neck around, to motion to Gail two seats behind me. But she was turned away, her body slack; apparently she was napping. I stared at her a long moment — I had had the last one once, and might again. She stirred and our eyes met, caressing. Once free, anything was possible. She turned away. Passion, evidence of life. She closed her eyes. I looked down and the lights were still there, bright, burning, conspicuous as stars, and fixed forever.

1976

◆

# I'M WORRIED

# ABOUT YOU

◆

A T VERDUN it began to leak rain, staining the concrete of the monument, the Ossuaire. She insisted on taking a photograph of Marshall and Harry, who stood uncomfortably on the steps in front of the building. They were as gray as the day, dressed in floppy hats and trench coats. French tourists moved around them, apparently oblivious; one old man stood staring at the graves, wiping his eyes. Janine fiddled with the camera and finally snapped the picture of the men, who looked off to one side, casually, as if they did not know they were being photographed.

Later, the three of them went to the Tranchée des Baïonnettes, hustling because they were late; Harry had to catch a train. He kept looking at his watch while Marshall and Janine circled the trench. He knew the battlefield well. Look, he said finally. Look carefully in there. You can still see their bayonets pointed up. Killed where they stood, buried. See the bayonets?

It was true, the points of the bayonets poked through the soft earth, a grim iron garden. There was also a bent and rusted rifle barrel. It was a memorial to one of the great legends of the first war, members of the 137th Infantry Regiment holding the line, though bombarded and eventually interred by German artillery.

She said, You can't mean that the bodies are still there?

No, Harry said, looking at his watch. They have buried the men in the Ossuaire but left their weapons in place. It's to give you an idea of how it was in the spring of 1916. *La gloire. Mort pour la France.*

The goddamned French, he said savagely. This place is a monument to death.

Janine stood looking at the trench, shaking her head.

We have to go now, Harry said. My train.

I've been waiting for twenty years to see Verdun, Marshall said. I want to see Douaumont, and Fort de Vaux. Then we can go. You won't miss your train.

Inside Fort de Vaux, they stood next to one of the French 75s. On a sunny day there would have been a fine, clear field of fire. They stood silent a moment, oppressed by the closeness and thickness of the walls and the low ceiling, the dampness and the mass of the gun, silent for sixty-eight years. Fort de Vaux had been taken when the defenders had run out of water and ammunition; later, it was retaken. There were no graffiti on the walls and everything seemed to be as it was then. The rain had turned to a sporadic drizzle, almost a fog. Marshall looked at the fields below and imagined line upon line of German troops. He turned to his wife and said, Can you imagine the racket in here when the gun was firing? My God.

She said, I can't forget the old man at the Ossuaire.

At last they were en route to Bar-le-Duc, where Harry would catch his train. He had the schedule in his hand and was calculating whether it would be better to go to Metz or to Nancy. They were very late. The pavement was slippery and Marshall drove slowly, taking no chances; he did not know the road. Harry kept looking at his wristwatch and sighing. He was returning to Paris to have a farewell dinner with a girl. He intended to say good-bye to her at the dinner and break off their affair.

You can pass that truck, he said.

No, I can't, Marshall said.

Harry said, This is very stressful.

We'll get there in time, Marshall said.

I never should've come, Harry said. I should have stayed in Paris. Then he began to talk about the girl in short sentences, non sequiturs. Marshall only nodded, keeping his eyes on the road. He did not know the girl well; really, he did not understand what had gone wrong except that it was another busted love affair. There was a snapshot in Harry's Paris apartment, the girl in dishabille, sitting on a cocktail table. She was wearing one of Harry's oxford shirts, the shirt unbuttoned all the way down. She was sitting Indian-fashion, leaning forward, her head a little to one side. It was a low glass cocktail table and the photographer had been above her, shooting down; the result looked professionally made, grainy and slightly off focus. It looked like Harry's work. A cigarette hung from her lower lip, the smoke just visible around her head, a goofy smile curling around the cigarette. She held a champagne flute at an angle, so anyone looking at the picture wanted to cry out, Watch it! You're going to spill your wine! The whorish effect was comical because the girl was very well groomed, short hair, fine bones, and a cleft chin; a model's composed face. She was lovely to look at. It was just a snapshot stuck in a bookcase, but it caught everyone's eye. It made people, men mostly, smile when they looked at it.

The girl's name was Antoinette, and she came from a very old French family. Her great-grandfather, the viscount, was mentioned by Proust as a habitué of the many soirées chez les Verdurin. Harry said she reminded him of an earlier, happier, more organized time. She made him laugh. He called her Off-With-My-Head Antoinette.

He said, I'm worried about her.

Marshall said, We're almost there.

Harry said, As a matter of fact, I think that was the first thing I said to her in seriousness, the night we met: I'm worried about you. I was too. She didn't look well. She was mixed up with a bad crowd. And she still is. But the hell with it, it's all in the past. At my age you're happy for whatever you get, for whatever duration. And we had a great six months. These women today, they're too modern for me. But I came in at the end of everything — colonialism, the novel, decent movies, worthy women. And she's so goddamned young, only thirty-five. I kept telling her that. And that I couldn't ever be French. I'm an American and I don't want to be French. The goddamned French. So I'm going to end it tonight, and put myself out of my misery. Her too. She has a right to her own life, don't you think? Can't you hurry it up, Marsh?

Here we are, Janine said from the rear seat. Bar-le-Duc.

You two have been great, Harry said.

Marshall said, Good luck.

His hand on the door handle, Harry turned all the way around to smile nervously at Janine. His mind was still on Antoinette. He said, Were you surprised by Verdun?

She smiled back. She said, Surprised is not the word.

He nodded. Well, then, did you like it? A lot of people can't take it. And why should they? It's an ugly place that only a Frenchman could've designed. All that concrete, those crosses and the bayonets. But it's something that you have to see, once. It's where Europe died.

She said, I didn't *like* it, Harry.

He patted her knee with his free hand. You know what I mean, he said, sighing again, looking at his watch and then out the window. They were stopped at a traffic light. He said, This is ridiculous, we'll never make it. I'll have to go to Strasbourg with you. I don't know what'll happen to her, that's the thing. I just want to get it over with.

The train was in the station when they pulled up. Harry opened the door and flew out of the car. Marshall parked, and he and Janine strolled back to the platform. The train was already moving, Harry waving at them from the vestibule of the first-class coach. They watched the train disappear and then they turned and looked at each other. Janine closed her eyes. A great weariness came upon her, and she slumped against Marshall's shoulder. He sensed her mood at once, steering her firmly off the platform and into the waiting room and around the corner to the buffet. They drank one glass of wine and then another, and when at last they were on the road again, Janine realized she was tipsy. Her vision was blurred and she felt exhausted. She put her head back but was unable to nap. The snap of the windshield wipers and the whine of the little car's engine irritated her. It was gray and raining all over the place. Dusk was coming on. When Marshall lit a cigarette, she turned to him and said sharply, You're smoking too much. Why did we have to go to Verdun?

They did not make Strasbourg that night, choosing instead an auberge in a tiny hillside town near Nancy. It was almost eight-thirty when they arrived. Without a booking, Marshall wanted to secure a room immediately. The auberge was highly recommended, and popular on weekends. But Jan wanted to talk, to clear her head, to breathe deeply, to get the kinks out; really, she was tired of rushing. This was supposed to be a vacation, a *holiday*, their first in three years; it wasn't supposed to be a forced march, or a memorial service for the death of Europe. And Europe wasn't dead; it was only temporarily out of service, for the moment elusive in the darkness.

Your friend Harry, she began.

*Our* friend, he corrected.

Harry, she said, then didn't finish the sentence. Harry was Harry was Harry was Harry, and if he wanted to believe that Europe was dead, he had the right. She wondered why he hadn't added Europe to the list of things he had come in at the end of. She would listen to it, but she didn't have to believe it. She didn't have to *like* it.

They walked the few feet to the graveyard of the old church and stood looking over the stones into the valley. It was very dark now and no one was about; light rain obscured the view, and she wondered if there was a town and farmhouses below, or whether there was only forest. There was no light anywhere, but she heard the sound of rushing water. Something made her turn, and she saw a priest glide soundlessly from the side door of the church. Inside were the dim yellow lights of candles; a vigil. She might not have noticed him at all, except that the white of his collar glittered in the candlelight. The priest locked the door and moved down the path, picking his way. He was a portly priest, no stranger to the cuisine of Lorraine. He looked over at them, seemed to hesitate, and then went on.

Spooky, she thought. She turned to Marshall to say something, but he was distant. His mood reminded her of Harry on the way to the railway station — sighing, consulting his wristwatch, distracted, worried that he wouldn't catch the train, worried about Antoinette mixed up with a bad crowd. Marshall stood with his hands plunged into the pockets of his trench coat, looking like a sentry doing disagreeable duty.

It's chilly, Marshall said.

Yes, she said. It's good autumn weather, football weather, but nice, so quiet and dark. Let's walk just a minute more. She took his hand and pulled him along, past the graveyard to the road leading into the valley. There were silent, shuttered houses on either side of them, and she wondered if the town was a summer resort, like Edgartown or Wellfleet, unoccupied until the summer season. Then she saw a sliver of light behind one of the shutters, a dancing blue fluorescence; television. She turned quickly away.

It's time to get back, he said.

Just a minute more, she pleaded, one minute. She took a step forward. The road sloped down to the right and was lost to view. She wanted to follow it into the valley. She said, Isn't it great to be here? She heard him fumbling in his pocket and then he lit a cigarette, the match flaring and the smoke hanging in the heavy air. She was looking again into the darkness, listening to the rushing water and wondering where the road went. His hand was on her arm. She tried not to notice his impatience. She felt somehow that the place was enchanted and that her own life was entering a new chapter. No one in the world knew where they were.

Jan?

Shhh, she said.

He moved close to her and explained that they had to get things settled. He had to speak to the patron to see to the booking here, and get the luggage up to the room — assuming that there was a room — and find out about dinner. It was already close to nine, and the chef was no doubt temperamental. If the chef closed his kitchen down, well then, they'd had it. Also, he had to cancel the booking in Strasbourg. And Harry had made a reservation for them at that restaurant, whatsitsname, and it was important that they cancel that. Two telephone calls.

Gosh, she said. All in one night?

And I want a drink, he said.

All right, she said. OK.

He said, I hate these details.

She said, Me too.

But we don't want to be stranded, he said.

She said, Do you love me?

Yes, he said.

I love you, too.

He laughed and took her hand, and when they turned around, they saw the auberge, its lights rosy and welcoming through the rain. It was like a mirage in the desert, or an advertisement for gastronomic France — a pretty sign, and flowers in pots outside. Wonderful smells came from the kitchen. She suddenly felt very hungry.

They stood for a moment without moving. Marshall smelled escargots, and smiled to himself because escargots meant traditional cooking — heavy, rich sauces and large portions. He hated the delicate nouvelle cuisine.

This town, she said.

What about it? He pitched his cigarette into the street.

She said, It's insecure. It looks dead, doesn't it? Feels dead. An Ossuaire, and I've had enough of Ossuaires. No one's home in this town. Did you notice the priest, so furtive? Listen to the water, there must be a river in the valley. What a strange place this is. What's its name?

But Marshall had forgotten the name of the town.

She said, I'll call it Forlorn.

He said, It's late, that's all.

How did we happen to come here? she asked.

He took her hand and they began to walk. You found it in the Michelin, he said.

That's right, she said.

And a good thing we did. Good for you, finding Forlorn. We'd still be on the road, otherwise.

She opened her mouth to say something, then didn't. The odd thing was, this village in Lorraine reminded her of the town they lived in, an anonymous suburb north of Boston. In the suburb no one moved after dark, and the streets were always silent, blue fluorescence everywhere. They had lived in the same house for three years, and knew no one on their block; it was too much to call it a neighborhood. Of course, the shape of their suburban town was familiar; it held no surprises.

The next day they moved on to Strasbourg, and the day after that to an inn at Hirschegg in the Kleinwalsertal. It was a punishing drive, and they stayed at the inn two days, taking a long hike on the second day. The following afternoon they found themselves in Freiburg, where they dropped off the car. After lunch, they visited the cathedral, taking a seat quietly because a *son et lumière* was in progress. The narration was in German and they understood very little, so after fifteen minutes they left their seats and padded around the inside perimeter of the church. Then they left the way they had come, by the west porch, the one with the frieze depicting a princely Satan leading a procession of virgins; the *son et lumière* continued, in hostile, incomprehensible German.

Outside, in the shadow of the great cathedral, a crowd had gathered around a brightly colored Gypsy caravan. Two mute white-faced clowns, one grim and the other merry, were shilling for a circus due in Freiburg the next day. Marshall and Jan pressed close, watching the pantomime. The caravan was filled with animals, and these the clowns introduced one by one: a boar, a goat, a monkey, two hobbled doves, three roosters, a terrier, a black cat, a wee Shetland pony, and, finally, rats. One gray rat after another appeared on the steeple of a misshapen cuckoo clock in an alcove in the front of the caravan. The dour clown gathered them up and let them crawl on his shoulders and around his neck. He seemed not to notice his necklace of rats. He put the largest in his shirt pocket, its long snout moving this way and that, like a cobra's head. Meanwhile, the goat and the boar nuzzled each other, and the pony sat down with the dog. From its perch on a three-legged stool, the black cat eyed the doves. The monkey moved to the feet of the dour clown and he picked it up roughly, cradling it in his arms; the monkey's odor was pungent, and the rats ceased to move, except the shirt-pocket rat, whose snout swayed from side to side, sniffing the monkey. The cheerful clown reached inside the alcove and brought out a cassette, which he punched into the tape deck on the pavement. It was a Mozart concerto, scratchy, badly modulated. The cheerful clown began to hop in time with the music, while his confederate stood to one side, blank-faced, rats motionless on his shoulders.

When the dwarf burst through the little door below the alcove, the crowd laughed and cheered. Marshall gaped. The dwarf was the smallest man he had ever seen. He seemed scarcely larger than the monkey, yet he had a beard and heavy, powerful arms. The dwarf pirouetted once and crashed to the pavement, all this without a sound. The crowd cheered again, and the dwarf doffed his derby. The dour clown gave the dwarf a rat, which he placed in the crease of the derby. With a look of disapproval, the other clown shooed the black cat off the stool.

The doves waddled away.

The boar nudged the dog.

The crowd began to chant.

The cavorting dwarf embraced the boar, caressing it, muttering something into its ear, laughing soundlessly, then deftly plucked the gray rat from the crease of his derby and stuffed it violently down the animal's throat — though that may have been an illusionist's sleight of hand, it was so sudden and unexpected. The crowd gasped, delighted, then roared its approval. With a malicious grin, the dwarf released the boar and advanced on the Shetland, creeping really, moving on all fours like an ape, his hands scraping the ground. The roosters and the goat backed away and settled under the caravan, alert and wary. The two clowns stood off to one side, bored and weary, as the music ran down, now off-key, sounding more like Kurt Weill than Mozart. A strange nervousness swept the crowd; no one knew what might come next. The dwarf, sensing this, paused and turned his heavy head left and right, leering, the muscles in his forearms bulging — and in a moment had flung himself into a front flip, landing on the pony's tiny back. He crouched, his cheek touching the shaggy withers, looking for all the world like a professional jockey approaching the starting gate; the dwarf and the pony were in perfect proportion to each other. They looked like toys. The pony moved hesitantly, a step at a time, as if walking through a minefield, its eyes wide and terrified. When the dwarf opened his mouth and howled — the sound seemed scarcely human — the pony flared and stepped crabwise, moving in a circle around the other animals, which re-

mained rigid. The dour clown had moved surreptitiously to the front
of the caravan, and now began feeding the rats back into the mouth
of the cuckoo clock; show almost over. The dwarf was balancing
himself on the pony's back, and now laboriously lifted himself in a
handstand, to thunderous applause. The pony cautiously picked up
speed and the other animals retreated, scuttling under the caravan or
into the arms of the clowns. A single rat remained on the clock's
steeple. Still upside down, his eyes wide open, the dwarf fixed on a
point in the middle distance. He clenched his hands, digging into the
pony's flesh. The pony shuddered. Then the dwarf began to do something else, one-handed, and Marshall turned away.

He said, Jesus Christ.

Jan said, I think we are very far into Europe.

And with that, the great bells of the cathedral began to toll.

Marshall was sleeping badly. He would wake up at two or three
o'clock in the morning, the room cool but his body slick with sweat.
It always took him a moment to remember where he was, whether
this was Hirschegg or Nuremberg. The first few nights he thought he
was coming down with something, the flu perhaps, but after a week
he put it down to nerves, a kind of unease that he could neither define
nor suppress. He would lie awake for three hours, then fall asleep
and snap to punctually at nine. He had two books in his bag, one a
book of history and the other a novel. The history book was dense,
and he began with that after an hour's sleeplessness one night. The
preface to it was a lovely thing, the historian's memories of conversations with friends. He mentioned one particular friend, and the
many talks they'd had sitting beneath cedar trees at Souget, his
friend's house in the Jura. Marshall was beguiled by the preface, so
rigorous and civilized, and whenever he thought about the horrors of
war, he thought not about young children with their lives ahead of
them but about the two old men, two of the most learned men in
Europe, sitting beneath cedars on the lawn of a house in the Jura,
trading memories.

The book of history was so demanding that after thirty minutes
Marshall would put it aside, twenty pages read, and turn to the novel.
This was the novel about old Sartoris. On this particular early morning Marshall tried to enter the life of the page, the lines of type that
always reminded him of the formation of infantry regiments of the
nineteenth century. He allowed the lines of type to advance, and to
overwhelm him. It was necessary for him to open himself to any

possibility, to enter fully into the spirit of the transaction. He allowed himself to feel the heat and fragrance of the Deep South in order to come to know the novel's characters, and the great burden of the past. These were characters who seemed to have no future. They were in chains to the past, moored as securely as any vessel in a swift-running river. At the end of the hour, Marshall realized that he was not understanding what he was reading. He parsed the page a word at a time, the words not windows but mirrors, and the story not the novelist's but his own. Old Sartoris receded, and finally disappeared. Only the lines of type remained, motionless.

When he put the book aside and turned to look out the window, it was dawn, gray and uninviting; cloud cover shrouded Western Europe. His body was dry and he pulled the covers up, fearful of a chill; his nose was cold and his feet numb, and his mind thick with sleeplessness, though he knew he had been dozing while he read. Perhaps he had only dreamed the business about the two old men sitting under cedar trees, reminiscing. Outside, traffic began to move. He heard the clang of a trolley's bell and, far off, the hoot of an ambulance, *eine kleine Nachtmusik.* Except it was not night; it was dawn, six o'clock by his watch. He heard Jan turn and sigh in the next bed, then mumble something in German. Amused, he raised his head to look at her, concealed under the covers; her face was hidden, but her familiar hair was sprayed carelessly on the pillow. She knew no German, and in his muddled state he wondered if somehow he had wandered into the wrong room. Wrong room, wrong Fräulein. He looked out the window again and decided to take a long morning's walk while she slept. His clothes were slung over the chair across the room. He could stroll to the square and have a cup of coffee and watch the city wake up, read the *Herald Tribune* and catch up on the ball scores and the campaign, connect again to American time. But it was very gray outside; the streets were desolate. Turning over, Marshall fell asleep.

In Berlin they found a gallery that specialized in German Expressionists. They bought four posters: two of Beckmann, two of Grosz. The posters were exceptionally cheap, so on a spree they bought an Otto Dix lithograph as well. They spent two exhilarating hours in the gallery, wishing they had ten thousand dollars to spend instead of two hundred. How thin and flimsy and self-indulgent the American moderns seemed beside the prewar Germans. A little bit perverse, she thought, bringing these Germans to their quaint Boston suburb. Beck-

mann's thick black lines, Grosz's pig-faced capitalists, Dix's oppressed masses. But it was a way of retaining something of Europe,
and especially of Germany, which had come to mean so much to both
of them: a way to measure themselves, and their own time, and their
own country.

On the street again, the posters and the Dix secure in a cardboard
tube, they walked up the Kurfürstendamm to their hotel. The street
was thick with youngsters, teenagers of every nationality. A city of
children, he thought. A curt cabdriver had told them they were mostly
young men avoiding the draft in Holland, Scandinavia, France, and
the United States. Divided Berlin was the gathering place of the youth
of all nations, so eager to evade their responsibilities. Drugs were
cheap and plentiful. There was no discipline in Berlin.

Marshall said, There is no draft in the United States. The United
States is not at war.

Ach, the driver said, is that so? No military service at all? Then
why are there so many American young in Berlin?

Marshall had no answer to that.

Jan tugged at his arm as they walked up the great glitzy boulevard,
brilliant with light. For their last night in Germany, she thought they
should ignore the tyrannical Guide Michelin. They should trust to
instinct, find a place that looked cheerful and not too expensive, and
tuck into it for a feast. She tapped him on the shoulder with the tube,
grinning. Their luck had turned; how else to explain finding the gallery with its trove of German Expressionists?

She led the way, past the sidewalk troubadours, off the Kurfürstendamm, to a small, noisy restaurant. They ordered a bottle of wine,
sausages, and sauerkraut — specialties of the house. She was animated, talking about the first afternoon at Verdun, the drive to Bar-
le-Duc, and, later that night, the town she had named Forlorn. Some
of the details had gotten out of hand, but all in all they had done
well. Perhaps in the future they would plan a real itinerary, not leave
quite so much to chance. But it was difficult, traveling in a strange
country, not knowing the language or the customs.

She said, The other night you were muttering in German.

He laughed. I was? So were you.

In your sleep, she said. You talked.

I wonder what I was saying, he said.

The sausages and sauerkraut arrived, and they began to eat. He
was trying to remember the clowns in the square at Freiburg, and the
exact sequence in which the animals had appeared. She was silent,

her head bent over her plate. He said, What a menagerie! Narrative by the Brothers Grimm. Grosz could have done something with the clowns and the dwarf on the pony's back. He said, You were right when you said we were very far into Europe. Marshall signaled for another bottle of wine, then noticed that Jan wasn't eating.

He said, Is something wrong?

She said, The sauerkraut reminds me of my mother. She made such good sauerkraut, it was just the best sauerkraut, my mom's. Sorry.

She was crying. He leaned across the table to touch her hand and she looked at him, biting her lip, trying and failing to smile. Her hand was hot and damp. The noise rose around them, and they drew closer; it was as if they were in a cocoon, wrapped in hostile foreign voices. He murmured something to her, but she didn't hear. He said, You are my one and only. She made a little ambiguous gesture with her hand, pushing at her food with a fork. He filled her glass with wine and she raised it, toasting him, and drained it, every drop. Presently she began to eat and then, impulsively, leaned across the table, closed her eyes, and kissed him.

At the Café Einstein, where they went for a drink after dinner, she was pensive again, inspecting the room, scrutinizing the intellectuals. Conversation around them was low and intense. They were served cognac by a sullen Asian in black tie. Marshall wondered if he was Vietnamese; his English was flawless, idiomatic American.

She said, I'm sorry I was so mean to Harry. I didn't understand his life, the way he lives, what he has to cope with. He said he was an American and couldn't ever be anything else, but I'm not so sure. I think I understand him better now. This has been such an experience for me. I'll never forget it, ever. I feel as if we've been in Germany for a hundred years. I feel pushed back in time. I find myself remembering the strangest things, old emotions, memories. What was it that Harry said about Germany that I didn't believe?

Marshall looked up and shook his head. He didn't remember.

She said, This is the place where all modern history begins.

They were to meet Harry at his apartment, then go on to dinner. But driving in from the airport, Marshall had a sudden inspiration. It was afternoon in Paris, the trees turning and the weather warm. The French strolled hand in hand, animated, dressed in summer colors. He leaned forward and tapped the cabdriver on the shoulder and told him to take them to the Brasserie Flo. He wanted a plate of oysters and a bottle of Sancerre. They jumped from the cab with four pieces of luggage and settled around a table. Flo was crowded

and cheerful. The oysters arrived, along with the Sancerre. They ate
a dozen oysters apiece and ordered a second bottle. They were trying to remember the precise moment they had fallen in love; it had
been eleven years before, and they had both been married to other
people. He insisted it had to be the same moment, and she said
that was just like a man, an *American* man, searching for symmetry
when there was none. She offered a preposterous version of events
that had him roaring with laughter. She insisted that he had en-
trapped her, a kind of con. They were leaning across the table,
head to head, talking now in their private language, on familiar
ground. They remained that way for some time in the amiable,
boozy atmosphere of Flo. They had finished the second bottle and
knew now that it was time to go. But neither wanted to speak
first, to break the spell and reintroduce the old world of promises
and obligations. Knowing that, they looked up simultaneously
and winked at each other. Time for the check. Time to go meet
Harry.

They were very late, but in any event, Harry was not at home. He
had left them a note in his difficult, spidery handwriting. Make free
with the apartment. He had gone to Cyprus on assignment; it was
either assignment or assignation, hard to tell which. There was altogether too much commotion and turbulence in Paris. Too much anx-
iety, and the weather had been lousy, pissing down rain. However,
he and Antoinette had reached an accommodation; in fact, she was
with him in Cyprus, surprise, surprise. It turned out that the quarrel
had been the result of a simple misunderstanding, and he had taken
her to Kyrenia to sort it out once and for all. She was a good egg,
really, though a little off the wall. Wish me luck. There was a bottle
of champagne in the fridge. How was your trip? Do you like the
Jerries?

Marshall and Jan tumbled into bed, and it was after nine when
they rose and bathed. While Jan was still in the bath Marshall wandered into the kitchen and popped the bottle. It was warm in the
apartment, and he opened one of the kitchen windows. He poured
two glasses and walked into the living room, pausing at the bookcase
to look for Antoinette in dishabille.

He heard Jan laughing in the tub.

She called to him, Remember the German on the mountain in the
Kleinwalsertal?

He did, vaguely. They had taken a picnic into the mountains, leaving the hotel at noon, winding higher and higher along the macadam
path. The view was gorgeous. There were many hikers in lederhosen,

carrying backpacks and walking sticks, who looked at them with disapproval. They were dressed for a stroll on Boston Common. Marshall carried a plastic bag from the supermarket, with sausage and cheese and a bottle of wine. At midafternoon they left the path and began to strike for the summit, ascending through pastureland in lazy S curves. They stopped to eat, wondering whether to resume the climb or start back. It was then that Jan saw the German and called to him.

She was still laughing, recalling the conversation, a clutter of German, French, and English. No, the German had said, they must not go higher. The north slope was already in shadows and the snow six inches deep. He pointed at their shoes and laughed. They were not properly equipped for the journey. Heavy sweaters were required; darkness came quickly on the mountain, and with it the cold, and it was so very easy to lose your way. He produced a map that explained the difficulty. He said, Take the funicular, it takes five minutes. And you only have to hike one way and it's easier walking down than walking up. Or take the funicular both ways and save your energy. They shared their wine with him. He was an engineer from Darmstadt, on a hiking holiday in the Kleinwalsertal. Leaving them, he wagged a finger and pointed at their feet. Next time, bring boots! He strode away very confidently, descending, and in a few minutes he was an inch high, merging with the other hikers on the lower slopes, heading for the village in the valley.

She laughed again. He could hear her splashing in the tub.

He had forgotten all about the hiker, a large, good-looking German of the blond, Nordic type. He had given them sound advice. Marshall stood in front of the bookcase, two glasses of champagne in his hand. Jan called to him, but he did not answer. He felt the beginnings of a headache and looked at his watch. In fourteen hours they would board their plane for Boston. Seven hours across the Atlantic, then customs at Logan, and another forty-five minutes by train to the anonymous suburb — a tedious day. He looked around the apartment, depressed by its sudden familiarity. It was only a bachelor's pad, with the bachelor's fussy confusion of transience and stability, but its atmosphere nagged at him. His eye swept the bookcase — a pretty edition of Proust, Baedekers, histories of European wars, biographies of statesmen — but Antoinette's photograph was not to be seen. He searched and searched, then found it tucked between volumes four and five of Proust. He looked at her, a captivating off-focus European, a woman about to spill her wine. She had a carnival aura, a dangerous woman worth worrying about. That seemed to be what careless Harry desired. It was what made him laugh. No doubt he was attracted to her ironic glare and her bad crowd. Marshall stood motionless, staring at the photograph, stunned, knowing the most profound ambivalence.

Jan was in the doorway then, naked, dripping water.

He turned to face her, the headache beginning to tighten behind his eyes.

She said, Are you all right?

I'm all right, he said.

You look so sad.

No, he said, forcing a smile. I was just remembering us, a couple of middle-aged Bostonians, touring Europe. Thinking about Harry, and what made him laugh. Thinking about this apartment, thinking about us. Thinking about tomorrow.

Tomorrow, she said. Well, then, where's the champagne?

He said, You're drinking too much, and extended to her the hand that held the two glasses. She took one, sipped it thoughtfully, then drained the glass — and with a triumphant look that went back to the first day they met, she flung it with all her force into Harry's tiny fake fireplace. The glass exploded into bits, fragments everywhere, and he recoiled, surprised. *There,* she said, laughing. Isn't that what you're supposed to do at a celebration?

He said, What's the celebration?

Oh, Marsh. This is our last night! She laughed. And here I am, naked in Paris.

*La gloire,* he thought. He realized he was still holding Antoinette's photograph, and gently pushed it back between volumes four and five. He said, I found Antoinette.

I didn't know she was lost, Jan said, looking at him, grinning, giving a little toss of her head; droplets flew from her hair, catching the light, stardust. The glow from the single floor lamp accentuated the lines of her breasts and belly. She spread her arms wide and popped open the palms of her hands, an actress accepting the applause of a grateful audience.

But he was in another realm, forced there against his will; in the end, no two people could know one another, even if they loved each other and traveled well together. He thought of Harry and modern history, and remembered suddenly the trench of bayonets. He said, I hate the thought of going home. Maybe this is where we belong.

Not me, she said.

Yes, he said. That's right. Not you.

She said, There's always a limit to things, a time to say Enough. I'm ready to leave. We've had a fine time. We had a fine time this afternoon, and we're having a fine time now. Aren't we? But I want to go home. We're only visitors here.

He listened carefully but did not commit himself.

It's been a strange time, she continued. At Verdun I didn't think it was going to be so great. We didn't seem to know who we were and what we were seeing. It was all so alien, and grim. It didn't seem safe. Freiburg was so weird, and the mountain, the pictures that we bought, and the last night in Berlin . . . She turned, presenting her profile. His headache, forgotten these last few moments, returned. He stepped to her side and they stood together at Harry's picture window, looking out over the rooftops, sharing the last glass.

Really, she murmured. Do you want to stay?

Yes, he said. But his voice did not carry conviction and of course she perceived that, having lived with him so long, knowing him so well. Marsh always had trouble letting go. She put her bare arm around his waist. She said, I understand.

I know you do, he said.

Europe would always be here, she thought. But the idea did not console her, so she said nothing; in any case, it was true whether she said it or not.

1986

◆

# JOURNALISM

◆

SHE HAD A PATRON, and in that way advanced in the business exactly like any man. After an apprenticeship in North Carolina, she went to New York for a news magazine and then to Africa and the Middle East for a wire service. She remained very fond of her patron, an old-fashioned editor who'd refused to obey tradition and assign her to women's news. He understood from the beginning that she had not gone into journalism to describe women's clubs or marriages or charity balls. She was attractive and serious and somewhat shy, and the editor was not certain that she belonged in journalism at all. He thought, mistakenly, that she was fragile. But he trained her well in North Carolina and then recommended her to the news magazine.

She had wanted to be a historian and in the beginning entered journalism only to learn how things worked; impatient with theory, she was eager to learn the ethics of the street. To her surprise, she liked the milieu, its confusion and haste and chagrin and the instant obsolescence of yesterday's dispatch. After North Carolina and New York, she knew she would have to go abroad, because she wanted to cover politics and war, and she wanted to see at first hand the countries she knew only from books. In Africa and the Middle East, there were countless opportunities to witness politics and war, disorder and suffering, and no opportunity was ever missed. In time she became senior correspondent for the region, always traveling and often in danger. Her seriousness deepened, but her experiences did not make her either gallant or cynical, as they often did her male colleagues.

♦ She did not care for cynicism as an attitude and had no need for the protection it gave. She was determined to stay afraid and grinning.

She was a professional and intended to dominate the environment and in the privacy of her own heart was exhilarated by her success. She loved her work, and although she collected numerous offers from newspapers and television networks, she remained with the wire service; a matter of loyalty. Her years as a war correspondent gave her a hard sense of reality and of her place in reality's scheme. She need not have worried about fear. In the year 1972, a woman's group gave her an award for a series of articles describing the destruction of a village in a west African country. The citation took particular note of the effect of her pieces and concluded that through her courage and compassion she had advanced the cause of women in journalism. She was unaware of the nature of the citation until it was read to her at the banquet. She said then that she would be happy to accept the award on behalf of the dead and dying and the homeless. Then she turned to the president of the women's group and agreed that she had been fortunate to witness the particular war that had resulted in the destruction of the village. In order that she might win the valuable award and the honorarium that went with it, and be worthy of the citation; surely a small price for those thousands of dead and homeless to pay. Thank God they'd been present, willing, and accessible and available for interviews. She tactfully corrected the president's pronunciation of the name of the village. She said she hoped that before too long there'd be another war for perhaps another woman to write about, in order that the cause of women in journalism be advanced yet another notch. Thank you, thank you. God bless. The audience of women received these comments in shocked silence. She'd been so unfair, so savage and perverse . . .

"You didn't have to do that, Paige," the president said later.

"Yes, I did," Paige replied.

"You took it and twisted it —"

"Not as hard as I could have," Paige said.

The truth was, she did not believe that journalism advanced the cause of anything except her own understanding. It was for that reason that the women's award outraged her. Better that they give an award to male journalists, war correspondents, whose writing advanced the cause of men. She hated the idea of being a spokesman or spokeswoman or, God forbid, spokesperson of or for anything beyond herself, and agreed with Auden that no poem had ever saved a single Jew from the ovens; journalism's record was a little better, but not much. She understood that she had certain responsibilities as a result of the work that she did, so she had no objection to appearing at fund-raising rallies for refugees or other displaced persons. If her presence could guarantee a few extra dollars for a good cause, she felt obliged to comply. She'd speak, if called upon, or simply lend her name to a list of sponsors. They were always the same sponsors. She disliked the commotion that attended the rallies, but she believed that it was criminal to stand aside on grounds of temperament or of professional neutrality. In this world there were no neutral professions. Journalism was the least neutral of any of them.

Paige spent most of her professional life abroad in the company of men. She traveled with them in the war zones, because soldiers did not react well to women reporters working alone; they became imposters, self-conscious bullies or thin-lipped stoics or Don Juans unless other men were present to keep them honest. She believed she could not discover the truth about men at war unless she saw them with their own kind, at a distance; when she was alone with them, she was the living proof of the Heisenberg Principle.

In the various zones, the journalists behaved like a large and unruly family, and after the first few assignments she was accepted as one of them. She shared her notes with them and "covered" for them, as they did for her. It was obvious from the outset that she was no den mother or casual mistress either, yet being with so many men so far from home was unsettling to her. The love affairs that she had always involved men far removed from both journalism and the war. It was essential for her to keep the two parts of herself separate. The older correspondents beguiled her with their European manners and old-fashioned pride. Like journalists everywhere, they believed they could easily have been something else: soldiers, diplomats, ministers of the interior, novelists, innkeepers. They used their profession like a suit of armor. She thought of them sometimes as crazed medieval warriors, clanking around the battlefield in cuirass and basinet, invulnerable to the calamities they witnessed. They were not heartless men, far from it, but they saw themselves as recorders and nothing more and had contempt for younger colleagues who sought personal and professional involvement. She found herself personally closer to the older men, though of course intellectually she ran with the others (up to a point). She passionately desired change, by which she meant an end to the killing; she believed herself temperamentally a revolutionary, though she could never kill in the service of an idea. She knew that her affection for the older men was a contradiction, but because she was on the far side of thirty-five years old herself she had sympathy for anyone in early middle age who had spent his best years in combat zones. And the men had a certain gaiety.

Some of them were in flight from women and some from bourgeois respectability, and some were merely footloose adventurers. Journalism was a safe haven. They were men who understood and appreciated drama and mystery and who prided themselves on being dry. They did not like it when she praised their work. Yet late at night, when they were drinking, their emotions would come tumbling out in a torrent. It took only the smallest crack in the armor, a chance word or gesture (if it was late enough), and she would find herself listening to muddled tales of ruined love and opportunities lost; of loosened grips and lives gone to seed. The first time she listened to one of these stories she began to giggle, believing that she was listening to a *story*, a joke. Then she realized that the speaker was relating events he believed to be true, a part of his own personal history, lachrymose and melodramatic. These episodes were by turns hilarious and heartbreaking and without exception ironic in tone. They seemed to be able to deal with the facts of their lives only through irony: heroic gestures, commonplace ends. Most of the men were excellent storytellers with a sure grasp of idiom and a phenomenal memory for dialogue, their own and others'. The stories had been distilled by memory and were now more vivid than the originals.

The conversations were not one-way. She'd collected numerous amusing stories of her own, and while she was less operatic than the men, she was no less forceful. She found them sympathetic and intelligent listeners. Of course the longer she stayed, the more the stories, hers and theirs, tended to overlap.

But the men frightened her. She was physically afraid of them, sensing nascent violence. She knew that literally the last thing any of them would do was harm her; indeed, they protected her as they protected each other. She was afraid of an accident. She was afraid they would fall on her. She tried to avoid them in large groups, although that was difficult; they all traveled in a pack. When they were drinking, they had a tendency to surround her and pepper her with stories; at those times she felt under siege. Typically, she would be seated, and they would gather around her, looming over her chair. She was not a small woman, but she was delicate; and the men always seemed robust. A recurring nightmare had her surrounded by large men, who as if on signal commenced to fall like giant trees, crushing the life out of her. It would happen by accident; one of them would stumble and fall and they would all go down like heavy dominoes; there would be no escape for her, she would be smothered where she sat. She would not be discovered until later, like one of the wounded always left behind in any retreat.

She took care to avoid them when they were drinking heavily. Once in Cairo, one of them fell down a flight of stairs, an every which way slow-motion fall, flailing arms and drunken thuds down a dozen steps. Although there was a good deal of laughter and no one was hurt, she could not expel from her mind's eye the image of herself crushed beneath the huge body. In her mind's eye, Paige saw herself walking up the stairs and the man tumbling down toward her, the man out of control. She waited patiently for him; there was no route of escape in the narrow passage; there was no sanctuary at all.

She told an abbreviated version of this story one night to one of the younger men, who at first laughed in appreciation (assuming that he was hearing a joke). Then he turned serious, nodding with sympathy and understanding.

"It's sexual of course," he said at last.

She looked at him earnestly, her features softening; she was careful to arrange the expression on her face.

"You've been here too long, your time's up," the young man said. "Is that right?"

He said, "Sure."

She looked at him again, and a wave of compassion for the older men swept over her. How could she have been so foolish? She said, "It is not sex. It is fear. Do you understand fear?" He stared back at her, startled by her intensity. Her expression was benign, but her voice was cold. "That is when you are afraid physically. If you like, I will describe the difference between sex and violence, ecstasy and fear. Would you like me to do that for you?" She bent toward him, her taut face resembling a snake about to strike. But the young man was already rising, excusing himself, thinking that it was a tragedy when editors sent neurotic women to combat zones.

After that, she kept her fear mostly to herself. But there were moments when she was unable to do this. These were moments of terrible incongruity, when her world seemed to turn upside down. One night she and a friend, the wife of one of the correspondents, returned late to the hotel after dinner. It had been a pleasant dinner; they had not talked of the war at all. The others were in the lobby, sitting, when the two of them walked in, cheerful after a stroll through the darkened streets. All of the men stood up as they approached, their faces polite and composed; the wife nudged Paige, smiling, a silent comment on the good manners of these men. But Paige knew better. She knew right away that something was wrong. There was one moment of awful silence, and then one of them turned to the wife and said they'd just got word that her husband had been hurt. Paige moved to put her arm around the girl, but the men quickly gathered round, the largest of them reaching for her, cradling her almost. Then Paige caught a glance from one of them, and she knew that "hurt" meant "dead." After a moment, they all sat down again, and when the wife had stopped crying they told her what they knew. They told the story as they might write a dispatch. Each fact was given a source and its own special value. Conjecture was labeled as such. They all spoke in very low tones and assured the wife that everything possible was being done. Her husband was very popular, and they felt the loss as keenly as she did.

There was nothing more to be done. The embassy had been notified. Each man had rung up his best source in the government and appealed, as a personal favor, for verification, for any verified fact at all. Incredibly, the wife then reached out and touched each man — as if the men were talismans. They waited in the lobby until dawn, when the deputy ambassador called with a complete account. They had found the body, and it was being returned to the capital. For the rest of that day and the next, they remained at the wife's side. But Paige never forgot the moment when they entered the lobby, the men slowly rising, Paige knowing that something was greatly wrong.

She'd been abroad for seven years. She decided that the eighth year would be her last. She believed she belonged now in America. The eighth year was a horror; it opened with a letter from her mother: she and her father were separating after forty years of marriage. It was a terse letter, no details supplied. A month later a friend in North Carolina sent her an obituary notice; her old editor, long retired now, had died of a heart attack. Some weeks after that a close friend, a young American Foreign Service officer, was killed in Indochina. She was thirty-seven now and understood that there would be years like this one. She decided that the best way to get through it was to concentrate on her work, and to do that she needed a holiday. She arranged for a month's leave in Cyprus, intending to do nothing but lie on the beach and read. However, after a week, she found herself living in O'Ryan's apartment. He was one of the resident British journalists, a friend of a friend, the largest and most reckless of all of them, though he did not wear what she had come to regard as the usual badges of instability. He had not been wounded in action, was not divorced, and did not drink heavily. However, he had a high tolerance for pain and a jaunty attitude toward his work. He seldom drank, because he wanted his senses keen for journalism.

They knew each other by reputation but had never met. He'd worked the Far East and had only recently arrived in the Mediterranean. During her holiday, the cease-fire on the island collapsed, and she cabled her office that as long as she was there she might as well cover for them. She and the Englishman began to cover the war together.

You see, he said to her one night. We make an ideal team. I do the military, you do the civilian.

Oh, yes, she said. It's perfect.

I describe the search, you describe the destroy. We are the yin and yang of journalism.

Yes, wonderful, she said.

I can see us sharing the Pulitzer Prize or whatever it is they give you Ameddicuns.

Smashing, she said. Just what I've always wanted. But don't forget Stockholm.

I'd quite forgotten, he said. I do *beg* your pardon. Now look here. I've found this new village. You've never seen so many wounded people. Wounded and dead everywhere. They're preparing a new attack tomorrow, I've been assured of that on highly reliable authority. It'll be an especially heavy barrage. We can go to it. I've hired a car and driver, we can double-team the battle. How would that be?

Oh, *lovely*, she said.

I knew you'd like it.

I can't wait.

Car's hired for six in the morning. We get there by nine, watch the shooting till noon; we can be back to file in the afternoon. Rest of the bastards will be climbing out of the rack, or finishing their lunch drinks —

Will you be *armed?*

Bloody right I'll be armed. You too.

Well then, why don't we stage our own firefight?

No managing of the news, he said. We take the dead where we can find them.

How wonderful for us.

Now go to sleep, he said. We've got to be keen for tomorrow.

Is that really true, why you don't drink? To keep your senses sharp?

Certainly.

For journalism? You want them sharp?

Of course. Otherwise there's no point, is there?

I suppose not, she said.

I can already hear the sound of incoming.

Yes, I expected that you might.

And you, the cries of the wounded.

Go to hell, she said.

Yes, I can hear them in your head. The screaming. Inside your lovely head are all the casualties trying to escape. To escape their prison. That head of yours, it's Lubyanka or Flanders Field, depending on your point of view.

Go to bed!

I'm in bed.

Go to sleep!

Not before a good night kiss, he said.

No kiss, she replied. By no means a kiss. I'm afraid I might catch whatever it is you've got.

No, he said. You're immune. But you can give me a good night kiss anyway. A kiss from Paige, angel of mercy, journalism's nanny. You ought to show me the same consideration you show the damn casualties!

Screw you, she said, grinning in spite of herself.

That's what I've been waiting for! he roared, shaking with laughter and burying his face in her neck.

He was in many ways the worst of all of them. But he made her laugh. His nickname in the Far East had been Wretched Excess; at times she thought of him as a character out of Camus or Beckett. She believed he was the most thoroughly rootless man she had ever met, anywhere. He couldn't even be bothered to follow up on a story. Wretch was a man without a memory; each day was absolutely new, no dawn like any other; no one moment had any connection to any other moment. History was discontinuous, except of course for women; women marked the various stages of his life. In that way they were a convenience. The one thing to be said for Wretch was that he did not frighten her, despite the obvious and alarming fact that he was the most violent man she knew. He was the one man she had good reason to fear but did not.

She believed it was his sense of limitless possibility that enchanted her; he had a morning cheerfulness, a kind of rampant gaiety, that drew her to him. She thought he led an utterly seamless existence, his life and his work were one, each reinforcing the other. She'd begun her career with a search, and she knew she'd abandoned that search some time back. There wasn't any single detail of war with which she wasn't familiar. But her hard-won knowledge had gained her nothing. She had it all firsthand, and all she knew for certain was fear. Perhaps that was all there was to know. She had hoped that the details would lead her to some larger understanding — of herself or of humanity in general. She had hoped her experience would lead her to a General Historical Theory, something beyond cliché. For a very brief period, she thought she would find the answer in Wretch. Every morning they drove to a burning village, a village no different from the one the day before; similar casualties, identical acrid odor; "the stench of cordite." How many times had she written that? His enthusiasm never diminished; he charged from the car in the direction of rifle fire like a child chasing a pot at the end of the rainbow.

She asked him one day what he hoped to find.

He'd looked at her, puzzled. What was there to find? It was not a question of searching and finding or of hoping either. It was just describing what was there. *They* searched, you didn't. It was interesting, describing the search —

Interesting?

Of course, he'd said.

You never lose interest in it?

No, he said. Certainly not. It's what I do. What I've always done.

Why not? she persisted. Why don't you lose interest?

He'd shaken his head, exasperated. Stupid female questions.

Sincerely, she said. I want to know. And I want to know another thing. I want to know what you think you're doing. I mean, you write about it — OK. But then what? Do you see yourself improving matters? Or is it just personal?

*Christ*, he muttered.

No, really, she said. I want to know.

It's very simple, he said. Too simple for you. You don't grasp that I'm not like you. You like things complicated. That's the big thing with you. The more complicated, the better. The more complicated, the more depressing. You thrive on it! He was sneering now and his voice was rough. Anything *natural,* he said, you're not up for it —

Oh, *really,* she'd replied, stung. That wasn't fair, she was just trying to understand. She said, If you had any imagination —

He turned on her then, furious; she thought for a moment that he was going to hit her. But he rose from the bed, pale and shaking with anger, moving deliberately to the clothes closet. He began to remove her things, dropping each garment on the floor; then he pitched her suitcase on top of the clothes. He said, Go cry on someone else's shoulder. Take your bloody theories to someone else's bed. She wanted to reach out to him, but didn't, and in a moment he was gone, leaving the door ajar.

The next day she left Cyprus and returned to her base in Africa. She was glad to be home; all the old crowd was there and they welcomed her with open arms. The first night at dinner they asked her if it was true, they'd heard rumors, she and Wretched Excess O'Ryan . . .

It's over, she said.

There was a general sigh of relief; they were glad to hear it.

Strange to say, he drifted out of her life as easily as he had drifted into it. In retrospect, the entire episode seemed fantastic. She realized now how deeply she had hurt him with the remark about imagination, though she did not completely understand why. The thought of it stirred her to melancholy; but she was angry, too. What was there about him? Opposites attract, she concluded finally; live by the sword, die by it, et cetera.

In Africa a week, she found herself fatigued. She was seldom tired and thought that a good night's sleep was all she needed. That night, tumbling into bed, she knew that she would dream; she found herself looking forward to sleep, and to the dreams that sleep would bring. She thought she would try to transport herself to another time and place, assume a new persona altogether; falling asleep, she remembered that her birthday was next week. Thirty-eight years old; six months to go in Africa. Suddenly, just then, she decided that she would leave right away. She would cable the office the next morning and leave as quickly as she could arrange passage. She hugged her pillow and fell asleep, though she did not dream.

She woke on her birthday, understanding nothing. She was surrounded by white. White walls, a white net over her; she was clad in white, in a bed with white sheets. Her arms were chalk white, there was a white plastic band around her wrist. Then, slowly coming to, she understood she was in a hospital. She was frightened; what was she doing there? Still wondering, she dozed, then wakened, then dozed again. A nurse looked in, smiled, and left. She dozed. The nurse returned and moved to her bed when Paige's eyes fluttered. Seeing her eyes open, the nurse smiled broadly; pink teeth in a lean black face.

She would be all right now, the nurse explained in French. They were worried; Madame had been in a coma for almost a week. But she had responded to treatment. The nurse gave her a complicated name, apparently the name of the disease; a tropical disorder of some kind. Paige knew after a moment that this was not the nurse but the doctor. She was suddenly overwhelmingly grateful that the doctor was a woman. She began to cry; they were tears of relief. The doctor smiled distantly.

There were a number of men, colleagues apparently, who wished to see Madame, but perhaps not just yet.

No, she said.

Perhaps in two days or three.

Three days, Paige said.

The doctor smiled. Three days, then.

When will I be free to leave?

A week, ten days.

Paige smiled. Ten days, make it ten days.

The doctor shrugged. The beds were in demand.

I can pay, Paige said.

In that case, Madame, the bed is yours.

Three nights later they all came, the regulars. They brought with them bottles of liquor and mixer and a Scotch cooler of ice. They'd had hors d'oeuvres prepared at the hotel and passed these around. They brought a fistful of cables with them, messages from friends everywhere. It was a regular party; they joked and laughed for some time. They looked at her like jewelers examining a gem and told her she seemed quite fit for someone who'd been in a coma seventy-two hours before. And they were indelicate, as always.

You almost bought the farm, one of them said.

. . . the fellow in the bright nightgown.

She looked up, puzzled. What was that?

A joke of W. C. Fields's. That was what he called death, "the fellow in the bright nightgown."

Why? she asked.

I don't know, he said. I don't know why.

They all laughed again. The party was getting rowdy, and one of the nurses came in to disapprove. They waved her away. Paige was tired, but she did not tell them to go. She couldn't; these were her oldest, dearest friends.

It grew noisy. One of them bumped her bed and moved away, laughing. They were telling an old story now, hard for her to follow; it was a story about Wretch. She was getting sleepy, she was more tired than she realized. The drugs clouded her mind, she felt she was living in slow motion. Her bones ached. The nurse came in again and was told to leave. There was an argument, more laughter. Then a pause, and she saw they were all looking at her, knowing now that they'd overstayed their welcome. She was ill, she needed rest. They gathered around her bed, leaning down one by one to kiss her on the cheek, staring into her sad blue eyes. One of them touched her hair. She smelled the fumes of the whiskey and the smoke from their cigarettes. She moved her face on the pillow; they each kissed her in turn and mumbled their pleasure that she was all right, and that her illness was nothing permanent. Her eyes had been half closed, she was looking sideways at the door. Then she glanced up; their faces were above her, expressions blank, like masked surgeons in an operating theater. They loomed, large and misshapen. She looked away and they slipped out of her vision and she felt them all, every man, as a potential fallen; leaning over her, seductive, not anchored, teetering, not fastened to anything. If she was not careful they would smother her, one more random killing. She looked back, trembling. She was terrified now, beginning to go to pieces, fighting it, knowing it was only a matter of seconds. Then one of them moved, and when she flung up her hands to protect herself, he kissed her fingers and danced away.

1977

◆

# THE CONGRESSMAN

# WHO LOVED FLAUBERT

◆

T HE DEPUTATION was there: twelve men in his outer office and
he would have to see them. His own fault, if "fault" was the
word. They'd called every day for a week, trying to arrange an appointment. Finally his assistant, Annette, put it to him: Please see
them. Do it for me. Wein is an old friend, she'd said. It meant a lot to
Wein to get his group before a congressman whose name was known,
whose words had weight. LaRuth stood and stretched; his long arms
reached for the ceiling. He was his statuesque best that day: dark suit,
dark tie, white shirt, black beard neatly trimmed. No jewelry of any
kind. He rang his secretary and told her to show them in, to give
them thirty minutes, and then ring again; the committee meeting was
at eleven.

"What do they look like?"

"Scientists," she said. "They look just as you'd expect scientists to
look. They're all thin. And none of them are smoking." LaRuth
laughed. "They're pretty intense, Lou."

"Well, let's get on with it."

He met them at the door as they shyly filed in. Wein and his
committee were scientists against imperialism. They were physicists,
biologists, linguists, and philosophers. They introduced themselves,
and LaRuth wondered again what it was that a philosopher did in
these times. It had to be a grim year for philosophy. The introductions
done, LaRuth leaned back, a long leg hooked over the arm of his
chair, and told them to go ahead.

They had prepared a congressional resolution, a sense-of-the-

Congress resolution, which they wanted LaRuth to introduce. It was a message denouncing imperialism, and as LaRuth read it he was impressed by its eloquence. They had assembled hard facts: so many tons of bombs dropped in Indochina, so many "facilities" built in Africa, so many American soldiers based in Europe, so many billions in corporate investment in Latin America. It was an excellent statement, not windy as so many of them are. He finished reading it and turned to Wein.

"Congressman, we believe this is a matter of simple morality. Decency, if you will. There are parallels elsewhere, the most compelling being the extermination of American Indians. Try not to look on the war and the bombing from the perspective of a Westerner looking east but of an Easterner facing west." LaRuth nodded. He recognized that it was the war that truly interested them. "The only place the analogy breaks down is that the Communists in Asia appear to be a good deal more resourceful and resilient than the Indians in America. Perhaps that is because there are so many more of them." Wein paused to smile. "But it is genocide either way. It is a stain on the American Congress not to raise a specific voice of protest, not only in Asia but in the other places where American policy is doing violence . . ."

LaRuth wondered if they knew the mechanics of moving a congressional resolution. They probably did; there was no need for a civics lecture. Wein was looking at him, waiting for a response. An intervention. "It's a very fine statement," LaRuth said.

"Everybody says that. And then they tell us to get the signatures and come back. We think this ought to be undertaken from the inside. In that way, when and if the resolution is passed, it will have more force. We think that a member of Congress should get out front on it."

An admirable toughness there, LaRuth thought. If he were Wein, that would be just about the way he'd put it.

"We've all the people you'd expect us to have." Very rapidly, Wein ticked off two dozen names, the regular antiwar contingent on the Democratic left. "What we need to move with this is not the traditional dove but a more moderate man. A moderate man with a conscience." Wein smiled.

"Yes," LaRuth said.

"Someone like you."

LaRuth was silent a moment, then spoke rapidly. "My position is this. I'm not a member of the Foreign Affairs Committee or the Ap-

propriations Committee or Armed Services or any of the others where
. . . war legislation or defense matters are considered. I'm not involved in foreign relations, I'm in education. It's the Education and
Labor Committee. No particular reason why those two subjects
should be linked, but they are." LaRuth smiled. "That's Congress for
you."

"It seems to us, Congressman, that the war — the leading edge of
imperialism and violence — is tied to everything. Education is a mess
because of the war. So is labor. And so forth. It's all part of the war.
Avoid the war and you avoid all the other problems. The damn thing
is like the Spanish Inquisition, if you lived in Torquemada's time,
fifteenth-century Spain. If you did try to avoid it you were either a
coward or a fool. That is meant respectfully."

"Well, it is nicely put. Respectfully."

"But you won't do it."

LaRuth shook his head. "You get more names, and I'll think about
cosponsoring. But I won't front for it. I'm trying to pass an education
bill right now. I can't get out front on the war, too. Important as it
is. Eloquent as you are. There are other men in this House who can
do the job better than I can."

"We're disappointed," Wein said.

"I could make you a long, impressive speech." His eyes took in the
others, sitting in chilly silence. "I could list all the reasons. But you
know what they are, and it wouldn't do either of us any good. I wish
you success."

"Spare us any more successes," Wein said. "Everyone wishes us
success, but no one helps. We're like the troops in the trenches. The
administration tells them to go out and win the war. You five
hundred thousand American boys, you teach the dirty Commies a
lesson. Storm the hill, the administration says. But the administration
is far away from the shooting. We're right behind you, they say. Safe
in Washington."

"I don't deny it," LaRuth said mildly.

"I think there are special places in hell reserved for those who see
the truth but will not act." LaRuth stiffened but stayed silent. "These
people are worse than the ones who love the war. You are more
dangerous than the generals in the Pentagon, who at least are doing
what they believe in. It is because of people like you that we are
where we are."

Never justify, never explain, LaRuth thought; it was pointless anyway. They were pleased to think of him as a war criminal. A picture

of a lurching tumbrel in Pennsylvania Avenue flashed through his mind and was gone, an oddly comical image. LaRuth touched his beard and sat upright. "I'm sorry you feel that way. It isn't true, you know." One more number like that one, he thought suddenly, and he'd throw the lot of them out of his office.

But Wein would not let go. "We're beyond subtle distinctions, Mr. LaRuth. That is one of the delightful perceptions that the war has brought us. We can mumble all day. You can tell me about your responsibilities and your effectiveness, and how you don't want to damage it. You can talk politics and I can talk morals. But I took moral philosophy in college. An interesting academic exercise." LaRuth nodded; Wein was no fool. "Is it true you wrote your Ph.D. thesis on Flaubert?"

"I wrote it at the Sorbonne," LaRuth replied. "But that was almost twenty years ago. Before politics." LaRuth wanted to give them something to hang on to. They would appreciate the irony, and then they could see him as a fallen angel, a victim of the process; it was more interesting than seeing him as a war criminal.

"Well, it figures."

LaRuth was surprised. He turned to Wein. "How does it figure?"

"Flaubert was just as pessimistic and cynical as you are."

LaRuth had thirty minutes to review his presentation to the committee. This was the most important vote in his twelve years in Congress, a measure which, if they could steer it through the House, would release a billion dollars over three years' time to elementary schools throughout the country. The measure was based on a hellishly complicated formula which several legal experts regarded as unconstitutional; but one expert is always opposed by another when a billion dollars is involved. LaRuth had to nurse along the chairman, a volatile personality, a natural skeptic. Today he had to put his presentation in exquisite balance, giving here, taking there, assuring the committee that the Constitution would be observed, and that all regions would share equally.

It was not something that could be understood in a university, but LaRuth's twelve years in the House of Representatives would be justified if he could pass this bill. Twelve years, through three Presidents. He'd avoided philosophy and concentrated on detail, his own time in a third-rate grade school in a Southern mill town never far from his mind: that was the reference point. Not often that a man was privileged to witness the methodical destruction of children before the age of thirteen, before they had encountered genuinely soul-

less and terrible events: the war, for one. His bill would begin the
process of revivifying education. It was one billion dollars' worth of
life, and he'd see to it that some of the money leaked down to his
own school. LaRuth was lucky, an escapee on scholarships, first to
Tulane and then to Paris, his world widened beyond measure; Flaubert gave him a taste for politics. *Madame Bovary* and *A Sentimental
Education* were political novels, or so he'd argued at the Sorbonne;
politics was nothing more or less than an understanding of ambition,
and the moral and social conditions that produced it in its various
forms. The House of Representatives: *un stade des arrivistes.* And
now the press talked him up as a Southern liberal, and the Northern
Democrats came to him for help. Sometimes he gave it, sometimes he
didn't. They could not understand the refusals — Lou, you won with
sixty-five percent of the vote the last time out. What do you want, a
coronation? They were critical that he would not get out front on the
war and would not vote against bills vital to Southern interests.
(Whatever they were, now that the entire region was dominated
by industrial combines whose headquarters were in New York or
Chicago — and how's that for imperialism, Herr Wein?) They
didn't, or couldn't, grasp the paper-thin depth of his support. The
Birchers and the segs were everywhere, and each time he voted with
the liberals in the House he'd hear from a few of them. *You are being watched.* He preferred a low silhouette. All those big liberals didn't understand that a man with enough money could still
buy an election in his district; he told them that LaRuth compro-
mised was better than no LaRuth at all. That line had worked well
the first four or five years he'd been in Washington; it worked no
longer. In these times, caution and realism were the refuge of a
scoundrel.

The war, so remote in its details, poisoned everything. He read
about it every day, and through a friend on the Foreign Affairs Committee saw some classified material. But he could not truly engage
himself in it, because he hadn't seen it firsthand. He did not know it
intimately. It was clear enough that it was a bad war, everyone knew
that; but knowing it and feeling it were two different things. The year
before, he'd worked to promote a junket, a special subcommittee to
investigate foreign aid expenditures for education. There was plenty
of scandalous rumor to justify the investigation. He tried to promote
it in order to get a look at the place firsthand, on the ground. He
wanted to look at the faces and the villages, to see the countryside
that had been destroyed by the war, to observe the actual manner in
which the war was being fought. But the chairman refused, he wanted

no part of it; scandal or no scandal, it was not part of the committee's business. So the trip never happened. What the congressman knew about the war he read in newspapers and magazines and saw on television. But that did not help. LaRuth had done time as an infantryman in Korea and knew what killing was about; the box did not make it as horrible as it was. The box romanticized it, cleansed it of pain; one more false detail. Even the blood deceived, coming up pink and pretty on the television set. One night he spent half of Cronkite fiddling with the color knob to get a perfect red, to insist the blood look like *blood*.

More. Early in his congressional career, LaRuth took pains to explain his positions. He wanted his constituents to know what he was doing and why, and two newsletters went out before the leader of his state's delegation took him aside one day in the hall. Huge arms around his shoulders, a whispered conference. Christ, you are going to get killed, the man said. *Don't do that.* Don't get yourself down on paper on every raggedy-ass bill that comes before Congress. It makes you a few friends, who don't remember, and a lot of enemies, who do. Particularly in your district: you are way ahead of those people in a lot of areas, but don't advertise it. You've a fine future here; don't ruin it before you've begun. LaRuth thought the advice was captious and irresponsible, and disregarded it. And very nearly lost re-election, after some indiscretions to a newspaperman. *That* son of a bitch, who violated every rule of confidence held sacred in the House of Representatives.

His telephone rang. The secretary said it was Annette.

"How did it go?" Her voice was low, cautious.

"Like a dream," he said. "And thanks lots. I'm up there with the generals as a war criminal. They think I make lampshades in my spare time."

Coolly: "I take it you refused to help them."

"You take it right."

"They're very good people. Bill Wein is one of the most distinguished botanists in the country."

"Yes, he speaks very well. A sincere, intelligent, dedicated provocateur. Got off some very nice lines, at least one reference to Dante. A special place in hell is reserved for people like me, who are worse than army generals."

"Well, that's one point of view."

"You know, I'm tired of arguing about the war. If Wein is so goddamned concerned about the war and the corruption of the

American system, then why doesn't he give up the fat government
contracts at that think tank he works for —"
    "That's unfair, Lou!"
    "Why do they think that anyone who deals in the real world is an
automatic sellout? Creep. A resolution like that one, *even if passed,*
would have no effect. Zero effect. It would not be binding, the thing's
too vague. They'd sit up there and everyone would have a good gooey
warm feeling, *and nothing would happen.* It's meaningless, except
of course for the virtue. Virtue everywhere. Virtue triumphant. So I
am supposed to put my neck on the line for something that's meaningless —" LaRuth realized he was near shouting, so he lowered his
voice. "Meaningless," he said.
    "You're so hostile," she said angrily. "Filled with hate. Contempt.
Why do you hate everybody? You should've done what Wein wanted
you to do."
    He counted to five and was calm now, reasonable. His congres-
sional baritone: "It's always helpful to have your political advice,
Annette. Very helpful. I value it. Too bad you're not a politician
yourself." She said nothing, he could hear her breathing. "I'll see you
later," he said, and hung up.

LaRuth left his office, bound for the committee room. He'd gone off
the handle and was not sorry. But sometimes he indulged in just a bit
too much introspection and self-justification, endemic diseases in politicians. There were certain basic facts: his constituency supported
the war, at the same time permitting him to oppose it so long as he
did it quietly and in such a way that "the boys" were supported.
Oppose the war, support the troops. A high-wire act — very Flau-
bertian, that situation; it put him in the absurd position of voting for
military appropriations and speaking out against the war. Sorry, Annette; that's the way we think on Capitol Hill. It's a question of what
you *vote* for. Forget the fancy words and phrases, it's a question of
votes. Up, down, or "present." Vote against the appropriations, and
sly opponents at home would accuse him of "tying the hands" of
American troops and thereby comforting the enemy. Blood on his
fingers.

◆

LaRuth was forty; he had been in the House since the age of twenty-
eight. Some of his colleagues had been there before he was born,

moving now around the halls and the committee rooms as if they were extensions of antebellum county courthouses. They smelled of tobacco and whiskey and old wool, their faces dry as parchment. LaRuth was amused to watch them on the floor; they behaved as they would at a board meeting of a family business, attentive if they felt like it, disruptive if their mood was playful. They were forgiven; it was a question of age. The House was filled with old men, and its atmosphere was one of very great age. Deference was a way of life. LaRuth recalled a friend who aspired to a position of leadership. They put him through his paces, and for some reason he did not measure up; the friend was told he'd have to wait, it was not yet time. He'd been there eighteen years and was only fifty-two. Fifty-two! Jack Kennedy was President at forty-three, and Thomas Jefferson had written the preamble when under thirty-five. But then, as one of the senior men put it, this particular fifty-two-year-old man had none of the durable qualities of Kennedy or Jefferson. That is, he did not have Kennedy's money or Jefferson's brains. Not that money counted for very much in the House of Representatives; plutocrats belonged in the other body.

It was not a place for lost causes. There were too many conflicting interests, too much confusion, too many turns to the labyrinth. Too many *people:* four hundred and thirty-five representatives and about a quarter of them quite bright. Quite bright enough and knowledgeable enough to strangle embarrassing proposals and take revenge as well. Everyone was threatened if the eccentrics got out of hand. The political coloration of the eccentric didn't matter. This was one reason why it was so difficult to build an ideological record in the House. A man with ideology was wise to leave it before reaching a position of influence, because by then he'd mastered the art of compromise, which had nothing to do with dogma or public acts of conscience. It had to do with simple effectiveness, the tact and strength with which a man dealt with legislation, inside committees, behind closed doors. That was where the work got done, and the credit passed around.

LaRuth, at forty, was on a knife's edge. Another two years and he'd be a man of influence, and therefore ineligible for any politics outside the House — or not ineligible, but shopworn, no longer new, no longer fresh. He would be ill-suited, and there were other practical considerations as well, because who wanted to be a servant for twelve or fourteen years and then surrender an opportunity to be master? Not LaRuth. So the time for temporizing was nearly past. If he was going to forsake the House and reach for the Senate (a glamorous possibility), he had to do it soon.

LaRuth's closest friend in Congress was a man about his own age from a neighboring state. They'd come to the Hill in the same year, and for a time enjoyed publicity in the national press, where they could least afford it. *Two Young Liberals from the South*, that sort of thing. Winston was then a bachelor, too, and for the first few years they shared a house in Cleveland Park. But it was awkward, there were too many women in and out of the place, and one groggy morning Winston had come upon LaRuth and a friend taking a shower together and that had torn it. They flipped for the house and LaRuth won, and Winston moved to grander quarters in Georgetown. They saw each other frequently and laughed together about the curiosities of the American political system; Winston, a gentleman farmer from the plantation South, was a ranking member of the House Foreign Affairs Committee. The friendship was complicated because they were occasional rivals: Who would represent the New South? They took to kidding each other's press notices: LaRuth was the "attractive liberal," Winston the "wealthy liberal." Thus, LaRuth became Liberal Lou and Winston was Wealthy Warren. To the extent that either of them had a national reputation, they were in the same category: they voted their consciences, but were not incautious.

It was natural for Wein and his committee of scientists to go directly to Winston after leaving LaRuth. The inevitable telephone call came the next day, Winston inviting LaRuth by for a drink around six; "small problem to discuss." Since leaving Cleveland Park, Warren Winston's life had become plump and graceful. Politically secure now, he had sold his big house back home and bought a small jewel of a place on Dumbarton Avenue, three bedrooms and a patio in back, a mirrored bar, and a sauna in the basement. Winston was drinking a gin and tonic by the pool when LaRuth walked in. The place was more elegant than he'd remembered; the patio was now decorated with tiny boxbushes, and a magnolia tree was in full cry.

They joked a bit, laughing over the new Southern manifesto floating around the floor of the House. They were trying to find a way to spike it without seeming to spike it. Winston mentioned the "small problem" after about thirty minutes of small talk.

"Lou, do you know a guy named Wein?"

"He's a friend of Annette's."

"He was in to see you, then."

"Yeah."

"And?"

"We didn't see eye to eye."

"You're being tight-lipped, Liberal Lou."

"I told him to piss off," LaRuth said. "He called me a war criminal, and then he called me a cynic. A pessimist, a cynic, and a war criminal. All this for some cream-puff resolution that will keep them damp in Cambridge and won't change a goddamned thing."

"You think it's *that* bad."

"Worse, maybe."

"I'm not sure. Not sure at all."

"Warren, *Christ.*"

"Look, doesn't it make any sense at all to get the position of the House on the record? That can't fail to have some effect downtown, and it can't fail to have an effect in the country. It probably doesn't stand a chance of being passed, but the effort will cause some commotion. The coon'll be treed. Some attention paid. It's a good thing to get on the record, and I can see some points being made."

"What points? Where?"

"The newspapers, the box. Other places. It'd show that at least some of us are not content with things as they are. That we want to change . . ."

LaRuth listened carefully. It was obvious to him that Winston was trying out a speech, like a new suit of clothes; he took it out and tried it on, asking his friend about the color, the fit, the cut of it.

". . . the idea that change can come from within the system . . ."

"Aaaaaoh," LaRuth groaned.

"No?" Innocently.

"How about, *and so, my fellow Americans, ask not what you can do for Wein, but what Wein can do for you.* That thing is loose as a hound dog's tongue. Now tell me the true gen."

"Bettger's retiring."

"You don't say." LaRuth was surprised. Bettger was the senior senator from Winston's state, a living Southern legend.

"Cancer. No one knows about it. He'll announce retirement at the end of the month. It's my only chance for the next four years, maybe *ever.* There'll be half a dozen guys in the primary, but my chances are good. If I'm going to go for the Senate, it's got to be now. This thing of Wein's is a possible vehicle. I say possible. One way in. People want a national politician as a senator. It's not enough to've been a good congressman, or even a good governor. You need something more: when people see your face on the box they want to think *senatorial*, somehow. You don't agree?"

LaRuth was careful now. Winston was saying many of the things he himself had said. Of course he was right: a senator needed a national gloss. The old bulls didn't need it, but they were operating from a different tradition, pushing different buttons. But if you were a young man running statewide for the first time, you needed a different base. Out there in television land were all those followers without leaders. People were pulled by different strings now. The point was to identify which strings pulled strongest.

"I think Wein's crowd is a mistake. That resolution is a mistake. They'll kill you at home if you put your name to that thing."

"No, Lou. You do it a different way. With a little rewording, that resolution becomes a whole lot less scary; it becomes something straight out of Robert A. Taft. You e-*liminate* the fancy words and phrases. You steer *clear* of words like 'corrupt' and 'genocide' and 'violence.' You and I, Lou, we know: our people *like* violence, it's part of our way of life. So you don't talk about violence, you talk about American traditions, like 'the American tradition of independence and individuality. Noninterference!' Now you are saying a couple of *other* things when you're saying that, Lou. You dig? That's the way you get at imperialism. You don't call it imperialism, because that word's got a bad sound. A foreign sound."

LaRuth laughed. Winston had it figured out. He had to get Wein to agree to the changes, but that should present no problem. Wealthy Warren was a persuasive man.

"Point is, I've got to look to people down there like I can make a difference . . ."

"I think you've just said the magic words."

"Like it?"

"I think so. Yeah, I think I do."

"*To make the difference. Winston for Senator.* A double line on the billboards, like this." Winston described two lines with his finger and mulled the slogan again. "*To make the difference. Winston for Senator.* See, it doesn't matter what kind of difference. All people know is that they're fed up to the teeth. *Fed up and mad at the way things are.* And they've got to believe that if they vote for you, in some unspecified way things will get better. Now I think the line about interference can do double duty. People are tired of being hassled, in all ways. Indochina, down home." Winston was a gifted mimic, and now he adopted a toothless expression and hooked his thumbs into imaginary galluses. "Ah think Ah'll vote for that-there Winston. Prob'ly won't do any harm. Mot do some good. Mot mek a diff'rence."

"Shit, Warren."

"You give me a little help?"

"Sure."

"Sign the Wein thing?"

LaRuth thought a moment. "No," he said.

"What the hell, Lou? Why not? If it's rearranged the way I said. Look, Wein will be out of it. It'll be strictly a congressional thing."

"It doesn't mean anything."

"Means a whole lot to me."

"Well, that's different. That's political."

"If you went in too, it'd look a safer bet."

"All there'd be out of that is more Gold Dust Twins copy. You don't want that."

"No, it'd be made clear that I'm managing it. I'm out front. I make all the statements, you're back in the woodwork. Far from harm's way, Lou." Winston took his glass and refilled it with gin and tonic. He carefully cut a lime and squeezed it into the glass. Winston looked the part, no doubt about that. Athlete's build, big, with sandy hair beginning to thin; he could pass for an astronaut.

"You've got to find some new names for the statement."

"Right on, brother. Too many Jews, too many foreigners. Why are there no scientists named Robert E. Lee or Thomas Jefferson? Talmadge, Bilbo." Winston sighed and answered his own question. "The decline of the WASP. Look, Lou. The statement will be forgotten in six weeks, and that's fine with me. I just need it for a little national coverage at the beginning. Hell, it's not decisive. But it could make a difference."

"You're going to *open* the campaign with the statement?"

"You bet. Considerably revised. It'd be a help, Lou, if you'd go along. It would give them a chance to crank out some updated New South pieces. The networks would be giving that a run just as I announce for the Senate and my campaign begins. See, it's a natural. Bettger is Old South, I'm New. But we're friends and neighbors, and that's a fact. It gives them a dozen pegs to hang it on, and those bastards love *you,* with the black suits and the beard and that cracker accent. It's a natural, and it would mean a hell of a lot, a couple of minutes on national right at the beginning. I wouldn't forget it. I'd owe you a favor."

LaRuth was always startled by Winston's extensive knowledge of
the press. He spoke of "pieces" and "pegs," A.M. and P.M. cycles,
facts "cranked out" or "folded in," who was up and who was down
at CBS, who was analyzing Congress for the editorial board of the
*Washington Post*. Warren Winston was always accessible, good for a
quote, day or night; and he was visible in Georgetown.
"Can you think about it by the end of the week?"
"Sure," LaRuth said.

He returned to the Hill, knowing that he thought better in his office.
When there was any serious thinking to be done, he did it there, and
often stayed late, after midnight. He'd mix a drink at the small bar in
his office and work. Sometimes Annette stayed with him, sometimes
not. When LaRuth walked into his office she was still there, catching
up, she said; but she knew he'd been with Winston.
"He's going to run for the Senate," LaRuth said.
"Warren?"
"That's what he says. He's going to front for Wein as well. That
statement of Wein's — Warren's going to sign it. Wants me to sign it,
too."
"Why you?"
"United front. It would help him out. No doubt about that. But it's
a bad statement. Something tells me not to do it."
"Are you as mad as you look?"
He glanced at her and laughed. "Does it show?"
"To me it shows."
It was true; there was no way to avoid competition in politics.
Politics was a matter of measurements, luck, and ambition, and he
and Warren had run as an entry for so long that it disconcerted him
to think of Senator Winston; Winston up one rung on the ladder. He
was irritated that Winston had made the first move and made it
effortlessly. It had nothing to do with his own career, but suddenly
he felt a shadow on the future. Winston had seized the day all right,
and the fact of it depressed him. His friend was clever and self-assured
in his movements; he took risks; he relished the public part of politics.
Winston was expert at delivering memorable speeches on the floor of
the House; they were evidence of passion. For Winston, there was no
confusion between the private and the public; it was all one. LaRuth
thought that he had broadened and deepened in twelve years in the
House, a man of realism, but not really a part of the apparatus. Now
Winston had stolen the march, he was a decisive step ahead.

LaRuth may have made a mistake. He liked and understood the legislative process, transactions that were only briefly political. That is, they were not public. If a man kept himself straight at home, he could do what he liked in the House. So LaRuth had become a fixture in his district, announcing election plans every two years from the front porch of his family's small farmhouse, where he was born, where his mother lived still. The house was filled with political memorabilia; the parlor walls resembled huge bulletin boards, with framed photographs, testimonials, parchments, diplomas. His mother was so proud. His life seemed to vindicate her own, his successes hers; she'd told him so. His position in the U.S. Congress was precious, and not lightly discarded. The cold age of the place had given him a distrust of anything spectacular or . . . capricious. The House: no place for lost causes.

Annette was looking at him, hands on hips, smiling sardonically. He'd taken off his coat and was now in shirt sleeves. She told him lightly that he shouldn't feel bad, that if *he* ran for the Senate he'd have to shave off his beard. Buy new clothes. Become prolix, and professionally optimistic. But, as a purchase on the future, his signature . . .

"Might. Might not," he said.

"Why not?"

"I've never done that here."

"Are you refusing to sign because you don't want to, or because you're piqued at Warren? I mean, Senator Winston."

He looked at her. "A little of both."

"Well, that's foolish. You ought to sort out your motives."

"That can come later. That's my business."

"No. Warren's going to want to know why you're not down the line with him. You're pretty good friends. He's going to want to know *why*."

"It's taken me twelve years to build what credit I've got in this place. I'm trusted. The Speaker trusts me. The chairman trusts me."

"Little children see you on the street. Gloryosky! There goes trustworthy Lou LaRuth —"

"Attractive, liberal," he said, laughing. "Well, it's true. This resolution, if it ever gets that far, is a ball buster. It could distract the House for a month and revive the whole issue. Because it's been quiet we've been able to get on with our work, I mean the serious business. Not to get pompous about it."

"War's pretty important," she said.

"Well, is it now? You tell me how important it is." He put his drink on the desk blotter and loomed over her. "Better yet, you tell me how this resolution will solve the problem. God forbid there should be any solutions, though. Moral commitments. Statements. Resolutions. They're the great things, aren't they? Fuck solutions." Thoroughly angry now, he turned away and filled the glasses. He put some ice and whiskey in hers and a premixed martini in his own.

"What harm would it do?"

"Divert a lot of energy. Big play to the galleries for a week or two. Until everyone got tired. The statement itself? No harm at all. Good statement, well done. No harm, unless you consider perpetuating an illusion some kind of harm."

"A lot of people live by illusions, *and what's wrong with getting this House on record?*"

"But it won't be gotten on record. That's the point. The thing will be killed. It'll just make everybody nervous and divide the place more than it's divided already."

"I'd think about it," she said.

"Yeah, I will. I'll tell you something. I'll probably end up signing the goddamned thing. It'll do Warren some good. Then I'll do what I can to see that it's buried, although God knows we won't lack for gravediggers. And then go back to my own work on the school bill."

"I think that's better." She smiled. "One call, by the way. The chairman. He wants you to call first thing in the morning."

"What did he say it's about?"

"The school bill, dear."

Oh shit, LaRuth thought.

"There's a snag," she said.

"Did he say what it was?"

"I don't think he wants to vote for it anymore."

◆

Winston was after him, trying to force a commitment, but LaRuth was preoccupied with the school bill, which was becoming unstuck. It was one of the unpredictable things that happen; there was no explanation for it. But the atmosphere had subtly changed, and support was evaporating. The members wavered, the chairman was suddenly morose and uncertain; he thought it might be better to delay. LaRuth convinced him that was an unwise course and set about repairing damage. This was plumbing, pure and simple: talking with members, speaking to their fears. LaRuth called it negative advocacy, but it often worked. Between conferences a few days later, LaRuth found time to see a high school history class, students from his alma mater. They were touring Washington and wanted to talk to him about Congress. The teacher, sloe-eyed, stringy-haired, twenty-five, wanted to talk about the war; the students were indifferent. They crowded into his outer office, thirty of them; the secretaries stood aside, amused, as the teacher opened the conversation with a long preface on the role of the House, most of it inaccurate. Then she asked LaRuth about the war. What was the congressional role in the war?

"Not enough," LaRuth replied, and went on in some detail, addressing the students.

"Why not a congressional resolution demanding an end to this terrible, immoral war?" the teacher demanded. "Congressman, why can't the House of Representatives take matters into its own hands?"

"Because" — LaRuth was icy, at once angry, tired, and bored — "because a majority of the members of this House do not want to lose Asia to the Communists. Irrelevant, perhaps. You may think it is a bad argument. I think it is a bad argument. But it is the way the members feel."

"But why can't that be *tested*? In votes."

The students came reluctantly awake and were listening with little flickers of interest. The teacher was obviously a favorite, their mod pedagogue. LaRuth was watching a girl in the back of the room. She resembled the girls he'd known at home, short-haired, light summer dress, full-bodied; it was a body that would soon go heavy. He abruptly steered the conversation to his school bill, winding into it, giving them a stump speech, some flavor of home. He felt the students with him for a minute or two, then they drifted away. In five minutes they were somewhere else altogether. He said good-bye to them then and shook their hands on the way out. The short-haired girl lingered a minute; she was the last one to go.

"It would be good if you could do something about the war," she said.

"Well, I've explained."

"My brother was killed there."

LaRuth closed his eyes for a second and stood without speaking.

"Any gesture at all," she said.

"Gestures." He shook his head sadly. "They never do any good."

"Well," she said. "Thank you for your time." LaRuth thought her

very grown-up, a well-spoken girl. She stood in the doorway, very
pretty. The others had moved off down the hall; he could hear the
teacher's high whine.

"How old was he?"

"Nineteen," she said. "Would've been twenty next birthday."

"Where?"

"They said it was an airplane."

"I'm so sorry."

"You wrote us a letter, don't you remember?"

"I don't know your name," LaRuth said gently.

"Ecker," she said. "My brother's name was Howard."

"I remember," he said. "It was . . . some time ago."

"Late last year," she said, looking at him.

"Yes, that would be just about it. I'm very sorry."

"So am I," she said, smiling brightly. Then she walked off to join
the rest of her class. LaRuth stood in the doorway a moment, feeling
the eyes of his secretary on his back. It had happened before; the
South seemed to bear the brunt of the war. He'd written more than
two hundred letters, to the families of poor boys, black and white.
The deaths were disproportionate, poor to rich, black to white, South
to North. Oh well, he thought. Oh hell. He walked back into his
office and called Winston and told him he'd go along. In a limited
way. For a limited period.

Later in the day, Winston dropped by. He wanted LaRuth to be
completely informed and up to date.

"It's rolling," Winston said.

"Have you talked to Wein?"

"I've talked to Wein."

"And what did Wein say?"

"Wein agrees to the revisions."

"Complaining?"

"The contrary. Wein sees himself as the spearhead of a great national movement. He sees scientists moving into political positions,
cockpits of influence. His conscience is as clear as rainwater. He is
very damp."

LaRuth laughed; it was a private joke.

"Wein is damp in Cambridge, then."

"I think that is a fair statement, Uncle Lou."

"How wonderful for him."

"He was pleased that you are with us. He said he misjudged you.
He offers apologies. He fears he was a speck . . . harsh."

"Bully for Wein."

"I told everyone that you would be on board. I knew that when the chips were down you would not fail. I knew that you would examine your conscience and your heart and determine where the truth lay. I knew you would not be cynical or pessimistic. I know you want to see your old friend in the Senate."

They were laughing together. Winston was in one of his dry, mordant moods. He was very salty. He rattled off a dozen names and cited the sources of each member's conscience: money and influence. "But to be fair — always be fair, Liberal Lou — there are a dozen more who are doing it because they want to do it. They think it's *right*."

*"Faute de mieux."*

"I am not schooled in the French language, Louis. You are always flinging French at me."

"It means 'in the absence of anything better.' "

Winston grinned, then shrugged. LaRuth was depressed, the shadow lengthened, became darker.

"I've set up a press conference, a half-dozen of us. All moderate men. Men of science, men of government. I'll be out front, doing all the talking. OK?"

"Sure." LaRuth was thinking about his school bill.

"It's going to be jim-dandy."

"Swell. But I want to see the statement beforehand, music man."

Winston smiled broadly and spread his hands wide. Your friendly neighborhood legislator, concealing nothing; merely your average, open, honest fellow trying to do the right thing, trying to do his level best. "But of course," Winston said.

Some politicians have it; most don't. Winston has it, a fabulous sense of timing. Everything in politics is timing. For a fortnight, the resolution dominates congressional reportage. "An idea whose time has come," coinciding with a coup in Latin America and a surge of fighting in Indochina. The leadership is agitated, but forced to adopt a conciliatory line; the doves are in war paint. Winston appears regularly on the television evening news. There are hearings before the Foreign Affairs Committee, and these produce pictures and newsprint. Winston, a sober legislator, intones *feet to the fire*. There are flattering articles in the news magazines, and editorial support from the major newspapers, including the most influential paper in Winston's state. He and LaRuth are to appear on the cover of *Life,* but the cover is scrapped at the last minute. Amazing to LaRuth, the mail from his district runs about even. An old woman, a woman his mother has known for years, writes to tell him that he should run for President. Incredible, really: the Junior Chamber of Commerce composes a certificate of appreciation, commending his enterprise and spirit, "an example of the indestructible moral fiber of America." When the networks and the newspapers cannot find Winston, they fasten on LaRuth. He becomes something of a celebrity, and wary as a man entering darkness from daylight. He tailors his remarks in such a way as to force questions about his school bill. He finds his words have effect, although this is measurable in no definite way. His older colleagues are amused; they needle him gently about his new blue shirts.

He projects well on television, his appearance is striking; his great height, the black suits, the beard. So low-voiced, modest, diffident; no hysteria or hyperbole. (An intuitive reporter would grasp that he has contempt for "the Winston Resolution," but intuition is in short supply.) When an interviewer mentions his reticent manner, LaRuth smiles and says that he is not modest or diffident, he is pessimistic. But his mother is ecstatic. His secretary looks on him with new respect. Annette thinks he is one in a million.

No harm done. The resolution is redrafted into harmless form and is permitted to languish. The language incomprehensible, at the end it becomes an umbrella under which anyone could huddle. Wein is disillusioned, the media look elsewhere for their news, and LaRuth returns to the House Education and Labor Committee. The work is backed up; the school bill has lost its momentum. One month of work lost, and now LaRuth is forced to redouble his energies. He speaks often of challenge and commitment. At length the bill is cleared from committee and forwarded to the floor of the House, where it is passed; many members vote aye as a favor, either to LaRuth or to the chairman. The chairman is quite good about it, burying his reservations, grumbling a little, but going along. The bill has been, in the climactic phrase of the newspapers, watered down. The three years are now five. The billion is reduced to five hundred million. Amendments are written, and they are mostly restrictive. But the bill is better than nothing. The President signs it in formal ceremony, LaRuth at his elbow. The thing is now law.

The congressman, contemplating all of it, is both angry and sad. He has been a legislator too long to draw obvious morals, even if they were there to be drawn. He thinks that everything in his life is meant to end in irony and contradiction. LaRuth, at forty, has no secret answers. Nor any illusions. The House of Representatives is no simple place, neither innocent nor straightforward. Appearances there are like appearances elsewhere: deceptive. One is entitled to remain fastidious as to detail, realistic in approach.

Congratulations followed. In his hour of maximum triumph, the author of a law, LaRuth resolved to stay inside the belly of the whale, to become neither distracted nor moved. Of the world outside, he was weary and finally unconvinced. He knew who he was. He'd stick with what he had and take comfort from a favorite line, a passage toward the end of *Madame Bovary*. It was a description of a minor character, and the line had stuck with him, lodged in the back of his head. Seductive and attractive, in a pessimistic way. *He grew thin, his figure became taller, his face took on a saddened look that made it nearly interesting.*

1972

◆

# BURNS

◆

A NONYMOUS then, Burns joined the State Department in May
of 1959, the week John Foster Dulles died. He carried with
him a letter of introduction from his history tutor at Columbia, but
was never able to use it because the dying secretary was refused
visitors. Burns tucked the letter away, sad because he admired the old
man's Bourbon audacity (nothing learned, nothing forgotten) and
wanted to meet him; he disapproved of the *Weltanschauung* but liked
the *Geist*. He'd arrived in Washington with two suitcases and a half-
dozen cartons of books, all of them stuffed into the rear seat of a red
Volkswagen. An officer of the Foreign Service of the United States of
America. Diplomatic immunity. A black passport. He and a friend
from Columbia rented a small furnished house in Foggy Bottom,
within easy walking distance of the department, and the summer
passed pleasantly, without incident.

Burns was eager, trained in economics, and an accomplished lin-
guist as well: excellent German, French, and Italian, passable Russian. Intelligent, watchful, Burns had a thoughtful nature, and his
career proceeded logically and without sensation. The first year, he
was assigned to the European section as a cable clerk. Burns found
the State Department agreeable; he liked its stillness and atmosphere
of deliberation, quiet days broken only by the odd hasty moments
when the entire section would turn to, drafting instructions for an
ambassador or a memorandum for the secretary. The department was
a forest of hat racks, scholarly in its way; Burns was reminded of
low-keyed university seminars. That first year, he spent much of his

◆

time with the head of the German desk, listening to droll stories of
Berlin in the 1930s; the head of the German desk had known Doro-
thy Thompson and Christopher Isherwood and was a nimble raconteur.

The second year he was posted to Turkey, stamping passports, and
the next three years were spent in Bonn, in the office of the economic
counselor. These were rewarding and exciting years; Burns felt he
was doing useful work and was wise enough to take frequent holidays
throughout Europe. He saw all of Germany and the Low Countries
and most of Switzerland and France, and passed one Christmas in
Rome with friends. In somnolent Bad Godesberg he lived in a small
suite in the Yankee ghetto, the large bleak block of flats near the
embassy that the American government had built as a communal
residence. No living off the land! The staff hated its isolation. Burns
did not mind; he could walk to the Rhine, and he had a girlfriend
who lived on the Nibelungenstrasse. The ghetto was amusing in
its way, Mother America caring for her children, the government
surrounding you even as you slept; but the building was truly inele-
gant. The part of the job that he hated was the necessary contact
with traveling American businessmen, many of whom thought that
the State Department was a division of the U.S. Chamber of Commerce. Burns cultivated objectivity: he was no good at all out front.
    His record was excellent and studded with commendations. He
was discreet, reliable, and hardworking. By the time he left Bonn,
Burns knew most of the important older German labor leaders and
all of the unimportant younger ones. Burns was building for the
future, for the day ten years hence when he'd return. He got on well
with the younger Germans, finding to his surprise that he shared their
taste for the livid and the grotesque: gargantuan meals, carnival
sideshows, Grosz and Brecht, and the underground university theater.
Burns often filled in for the cultural attaché at benefits and openings, and at embassy receptions for visiting American artists and
writers. Through his contacts in the German labor movement and
his skillful analysis of the direction of the German economy, he
was brought into frequent contact with the deputy chief of mission,
a diplomat of long and varied experience. The DCM encouraged
his career and coached him in the ways of the department. Burns
particularly remembered one bit of advice, given late one night over
schnapps.
    "The department values loyalty, intelligence, and calm — in that

order. The Foreign Service is something apart from the run-of-the-mill American bureaucracy. Remember that. We are not action people, we are analysts. Leave the action to the pickle factory and the Pentagon, they are the ones with the resources (and the ones who'll evade the blame). Stay close to the bureaucracy," Burns was told. "It is an elite, and the better for it. Not as elite, mind you, as it was. But elite nonetheless. Study diplomatic technique. Read history. Always be cautious, always be firm . . ."

"Firmly cautious or cautiously firm?" Burns inquired with a flicker of a smile.

"Very," said the DCM.

Burns was surprised and disappointed in the fall of 1965 when he was ordered back to Washington and informed he was being loaned to CIA. He was told only that the agency had a major project under way which required the participation of many of their economists. It left them shorthanded, and meanwhile the State Department had been directed by Congress to cut its own budget. The loan would not be for long, perhaps no more than one year. Burns should think of it as a net plus, if not a clear advantage; he could have been transferred to AID. He'd been requested by name, and the transfer had the blessing of the department.

The first day at Langley he was shown his office, and it was not in the German section, as he'd been told.

"Here you are," the chief of section said. "Everything you'll need. Paper, pencils, slide rule, computer room down the hall. Filing cabinets there. Toilet down the hall and to your right. Staff meeting every day at nine, and sometimes again at six."

"I thought it'd be the German —"

"This is not the German."

"Yes, but I was told the arrangement."

"That is on another floor. That is on the third floor, quite different and apart from this. That is another section, something distinctly separate from what we do here."

"I know, but . . ."

"You can ask them about it. You'll get an answer. Perhaps there was a snafu. There sometimes is. Are. Snafus."

"Son of a bitch," Burns said.

"You were in Bonn?"

"Three years."

"Well, they probably thought that a change of scene . . ."

"But I am an FSO."
"You'll come to like it here," the chief of section said.

The first year at Langley was disagreeable in all but one respect. Burns watched the bureaucratic gavotte as it was danced by experts and learned lessons he never forgot. They were lessons in bureaucratic technique, and the uses of firmness and caution. At first, Burns told himself that these were lessons he wished he did not know, but he found out that once known they were impossible to ignore or forget; in the beginning, he thought it was like learning something damaging or unpleasant about a friend. The friendship changes, usually for the worse — and yes, yes, he knew it was naïve and unrealistic but it was the way he felt nevertheless. He found himself admiring the small ways a man moved ahead, the ways in which a man identified the winners and then placed his bets. There was no question of political or ideological conflict — the agency was too sophisticated for that; it was mainly a matter of technology and the skill with which a bureaucrat managed to force his ideas, and thereby gain a purchase on the future. In CIA Burns was able to learn with a clear and objective mind, because he was a man on loan; in time he would be returned to the State Department, where he belonged.

Burns had no ax to grind, but the department dawdled amid procedural inertia and the budgetary restraints imposed by Congress. Burns remained at Langley although he yearned for the security and familiarity of the Foreign Service, the satisfaction of fashioning American foreign policy; he felt himself an artist among artisans, made few close friends, and denounced (privately) the rules and regulations, which seemed to him frivolous when they were not corrupting. The spooks ran as a pack and considered him an outsider. But the job had its moments. Paper. He tried to explain it, his life inside the bureaucracy. Burns translated French documents relating to the economy of a small African nation, a small, *pivotal* African nation, in the vernacular of the Board of National Estimates. Every day the documents arrived in pouch, and Burns would translate them and summarize the contents. Some of them were official, some not; some of them were agents' reports. The précis went to the chief of section, who would include it in the running commentary on the economy and politics of the country.

"Think of yourself as Charles Dickens," the chief of section told Burns. "Writing a novel, a new installment every month. Odd turnings of plot. But a bold metaphor. Except that this novel goes on forever and forever, of course."

"A sort of *Pickwick Papers* in triplicate," Burns said.

"You've got it exactly," the chief replied.

The government of the small, pivotal African nation was fledgling and incompetent, and one week, the reports said, owned by the Russians, the next by the Chinese. Conscientious Burns received State Department cables as well (there were channels), and these he eagerly awaited, particularly the commentary of the chief political officer, a sardonic and witty diplomat who doubted everything, including agents' reports: "Buy the government? You can't even rent it for an afternoon." For the first two years the work was interesting, and even valid in a perverse way. The prime minister had committed "significant errors" in the management of his country's finances, and it was beguiling — often amusing — to try to put the pieces of fact together to make a comprehensible whole. Burns threw himself into it, juggling trade figures, cash flow, tax revenues, production, employment, resource management, inflation, and all the other classical indices of economic fortune. One afternoon he created an entirely fictitious Gross National Product, which he dropped in his out box on a lark. It turned up later in the National Estimate, and that worried Burns. At the time, the country was on the verge of collapse; indeed the statistics indicated the country had collapsed. According to the numbers, the bottom line as Burns called it, the country was bankrupt and not functioning — except that it continued as before, the vitality and innocence of the people defying all known economic laws, or anyway those laws that were promulgated by American economists. Burns conceived the novel idea that his statistics had nothing whatever to do with the situation. Novel to Burns, not novel to his section chief.

"You're learning," the chief said.

"Remember the GNP figure?" Burns was in the mood for a confession.

"Four hundred eighty-two point something-something million? Sure."

"It was all cock," Burns said. "Doesn't exist."

"Strange," the chief mused. "It seemed to fit in so well."

"Some of the figures were real. But I made most of them up. The GNP is meaningless."

"Yes," the chief said sadly.

"I'll play around with it again, if you'd like me to. Perhaps a new figure . . ."

"Please do."

"I suppose I shouldn't have said anything."

"It doesn't matter," the chief said. "So long as I know."

"Well, I'm sorry if it's embarrassing in any way."

The chief looked at him, surprised. "Why should I be embarrassed?"

Burns was nearing the end of two years in National Estimates, and most of his friends were overseas, some of them in Southeast Asia, where the wars were being fought, and their infrequent letters home made him long for the symmetry and rhythm of the State Department, anything real. He became nostalgic, recalling the details of his flat in the ghetto and the look of the Rhine at dawn, during his salad days in Bonn. He remembered the long talks with the DCM, and his satisfaction at filing skillful reports. Now he'd been passed by. One man he had known briefly in the embassy at Bonn had actually been a member of the working party negotiating the test ban treaty with the Soviet Union. His former roommate was ADC to the ambassador in Saigon, and that man was Burns's own age and grade. Other friends were in Europe or the Middle East, living well in Amsterdam or Beirut. Meanwhile, Burns reflected bitterly, he pushed paper at CIA and watched experts maneuver the bureaucracy. His polite requests for return to the State Department elicited polite replies, mere acknowledgments, no more.

In the evenings in Washington, home alone with his drinks and his dog, Burns would undertake National Estimates of his own life. A personal GNP, entirely factual and aboveboard. Big, bearish, awkward Burns, b. 1937 N.Y.C., father an M.D., mother a psychologist, "professional people." Medical talk at the breakfast table, mind-numbing Saturday afternoons at Yankee Stadium: good father, obedient son. But his childhood and adolescence were mostly blank, seventeen blank years until he entered Columbia University, became fascinated with economics and history, graduated with honors, and joined the Foreign Service. This became the central objective of his life, membership in the diplomatic corps and an understanding of the interplay ("the confusion") of politics and economics.The stress was on manipulation and management — of national interests, of alliances, of various political and economic crises, all of it huddled together under Reason and the Rule of Law. It was no place for an eccentric. Burns admired professional diplomats — men who were cool, collected, in control, rising to a geopolitical *crisis* (he liked the word — his doctor father first defined it for him as the point in the course of a disease when the patient either recovers or dies). He saw

himself as one of a dozen men in a small room, an anteroom in a
foreign chancellery (Belgrade? Helsinki?), conducting secret negotiations, ADC to a giant, Bohlen or Kennan, taking on the Russians,
and by sheer force of logic and remorseless dialectic, arguing them
back, turning their own deceptions against them. Forcing an agreement, and then a laconic cable to the department: NEGOTIATIONS
CONCLUDED . . .

But that was a joke now. What he had to show for eight years in
the Foreign Service were a few commendations, and some flimsies of
cables he'd sent. He had a Q Security Clearance; now he could read
intercepts from anywhere, from Havana or Hanoi or Pyongyang. And
he had a filing cabinet full of economic analyses of a wretched country that had, if the analyses were correct, collapsed. He had all those
things plus a flat stomach, owing in part to his noontime squash
games with an overweight colonel who was, similarly, on loan
to CIA. He did not know the colonel's job, and did not want to
know.

To an empty room, at midnight on a Monday night: "Celebrated
Diplomat. Superspy Burns, the hired gun. The cloak-and-dagger man
from National Estimates. A fast man with a document, that Burns.
Hard. Resourceful. Adroit."

Burns was a man of routine, at home as at his office. There were no
crises in his section of the agency, so he arrived home in Foggy Bottom punctually at seven each evening. He'd feed the dog and select a
recording with great care; a different recording each night. He prepared a shaker of cocktails, and at nine would put a steak on the grill
and frozen potatoes in the oven. He stood at the counter in the
kitchen, drinking his drink and slowly breaking lettuce into a salad
bowl. As the steak cooked, he selected his wine. The wine selected,
Burns moved to his bookcase for the evening's read. Something British, he thought, and ran his thumb along the spines of his books.
Disraeli. Cromwell. Melbourne. Yes, Melbourne — William Lamb,
alone and distracted at the end of his life, the affections of Victoria
detached from him and fastened on another. Melbourne, the quintes-
sence of controlled inaction. He prowled among the books, glass in
hand, then paused. He had not read his latest issue of *Revue de
Défense Nationale,* the authoritative guide to the thinking of the
French general staff. It was there now, arrived in the morning mail,
on the coffee table, unopened, waiting. He glanced through the table
of contents. Arms control. The Indian subcontinent. Ah. General

J. Nemo would bear careful evaluation: "Étude sur la guerre de Vendée (II)."

Burns smelled the steak and the potatoes and returned to the kitchen. He uncorked the wine and set it gently on the table. He'd set his place that morning, the knife, fork, and spoon on one side of the plate, the wooden salt and pepper shakers to his left, the white napkin folded just so, a fresh candle in the silver holder. Then Burns sat down with the steak and the potatoes, the salad and the wine, and began to read "Étude sur la guerre de Vendée (II)." Inside his mind, General J. Nemo competed with the memory of a candlelit dinner in Munich four years ago. The dinner was followed by visits to half a dozen nightclubs, ending at dawn. Burns finished in thirty minutes, then slowly washed and wiped the dishes and the silverware. He spoke to the dog and returned to the living room, where the backgammon board was waiting.

He carefully prepared his pipe with the tobacco purchased that evening and bent over the board, playing both sides, but mentally betting on white. He smoked three pipes, then lay back on the couch, thinking.

"Nemo appears to have got hold of something interesting in the new *Revue*. Pertinent to our own situation, it seems to me."

"I haven't seen . . . that number."

"I recommend Nemo and Mourin."

"Ah, Mourin. The historian."

"Some new insights into the Sovs on the subcontinent."

"How much time do you spend on that stuff?"

"Well, not much; I read it, is about all."

"Blast, I wish I could find the time."

"Important stuff."

"Burns, you're bullshitting me."

Every Friday night Burns and five others forgathered at one house or another to play poker or backgammon. Except for Burns on loan, all of them were State Department people. By civil servant standards, the stakes were high: at backgammon, a dollar a point; at poker, a ten-dollar limit. Burns, bearish over the backgammon board, was the big winner. He played a loose, conservative game — with occasional light and daring moments, when he felt the dice were right or when he found himself in untenable positions. He lived on the backgammon board, absorbing himself in the moves, studying probabilities, odds this way and that. Straitlaced men tended to be erratic at games, and Burns watched for the break, the wrong move when the dice were cold or the odds close, but not close enough. More interesting than chess, because the dice were thirty percent of it — all other things being equal, which they never were. The edge was in the double; he paid attention to the utility of the double. The psychological double or the administrative double or the deceptive double.

It was rather like diplomacy in that way, and as interesting, because Burns had learned the fanciful nature of world affairs. A carapace of madness, concealing the tortoise beneath; the revisionists saw it the other way around, but the revisionists were wrong. He inspected the men around the tables, all of them young like himself and ambitious in diplomacy; they had outflanked him, their careers were secure. The dice rattled, the counters flashed: doubled here, redoubled there. Acceptance. Refusal. Failure of entry. He played backgammon now as a substitute for diplomacy. Dulles was dead, had died the year he came to Washington. The letter of introduction hadn't been worth a damn.

◆

They knew *what* had happened; that was clear enough. They also knew, within limits, *how* it happened. They were less certain about the *who* and the *why*. But the government of the pivotal African nation had fallen, and the capital was now in the hands of insurgents. These were insurgents from the army and from the economics ministry, something of a queer alliance: the army officers were presumed to be reactionaries and the economists Communists. At ten in the morning they met in urgent session, representatives from the agency, the Pentagon, the State Department, and the White House. They met downtown in the Executive Office Building, entering underground. Burns was in on it, as the agency man closest to the economics ministry. They had tried to hash it out beforehand.

"Names, Burns, do you have names? You can bet your booties that the Pentagon will have names. Christ, they'll have a file on every colonel in that ragtag army. Half of them probably attended Leavenworth."

"I'll ransack the files."

"You do that, Burns. Do that right away."

But in Burns's section they had not concentrated on names. They had assembled numbers, numbers of bewildering variety and degree. They knew the names of the economics minister and his deputy, and the chief adviser to the prime minister. But these were not men who would participate in a revolt. These were men who were in the pay of others, or were said to be. So Burns went to the files and spent a feverish hour rummaging through them. The warning — the opportunity! — rang in his ears.

"Burns, we want control of this operation. If there *is* an operation. We've got men on the ground, we've got very good op-con. American interests are involved, and don't forget that. This is what the deputy director wants, and that is what we will have. But you've got to find the names. And give identity to the names . . ."

The meeting began slowly. Burns noted with satisfaction that there were two dozen men in the room, four or five from each agency. It meant there would have to be a second meeting. The Pentagon man, an army general, spoke first, and it was an astonishing stroke of luck, because he was inarticulate and ill at ease with the Gallicized African names. The deputy director scored a point straightaway.

"Our intelligence indicates that the leader is a major," the Pentagon man said. "Name's Hubert . . . Fooshing?"

"Ah yes," the DD said. "Ooo-bear. Foo-saw."

"You know him?" the Pentagon man inquired politely.

"Burns knows him," the DD said. "But we'll get to that later."

Rattled, the army general continued with his briefing. It was a disorganized briefing, but the names had been there. There were about two dozen names in all, mostly mispronounced. All the facts were there — ominous, compelling — but it required an effort of will to organize them. Burns saw the DD smile and make notes on the back of an envelope.

The representative of the State Department followed, and Burns sat back in his chair and listened. It was a *tour d'horizon*, the politics and economics of the country briefly, brilliantly, sketched. The geography and demographics of the country, its relations with its neighbors, its natural resources, its investments. There was a side excursion into cultural anthropology, a long reach back into prehistory for the national metaphors. Burns was dazzled; the State Department man had them in the palm of his hand. Finally, almost casually, he brought them up to the present moment, and the question of the American interest. This was done lucidly and skillfully, a history of diplomatic relations between the world's most powerful nation and one of the world's weakest. The diplomat stood at the head of the table, his hands in his pockets, speaking without notes. A low, musical voice: "The truth of the matter is this, gentlemen. The United States has no interest in this country. Sad, but true. Lamentable if the country falls to the Communists — Russians, Chinese, Cubans, whomever . . ." Burns noted the correct "whomever" and nodded in appreciation. "But in any serious analysis, not important. Too much risk against no gain. Gentlemen, let us leave them be. And remember the Armenian proverb: *A thousand men cannot undress a naked man.*"

He'd taken it all, ears and tail, hooves and bull.

The DD said nothing for a moment; Burns watched his jaw work. In the general conversation that followed the State Department presentation, he heard the DD mutter, "Oh fuck," but no one else heard. Now he was in a jam: he had to outmatch not only the diplomat's logic but his elegance of speech as well. Burns watched the DD rise, and pause for dramatic effect.

"I hope none of us falls into the trap of disregarding the fate of a sovereign nation simply because it is small," the DD said. "Or black. Or without resources. Or generally friendless in a hostile world. Or in the fist of revolution" — not bad, Burns thought — "its national identity not yet fully forged from the tangled threads of its own tribal history and the odious legacy of colonial exploitation. A nation without a center of gravity. A nation which looks to the United States of America for leadership . . ."

"Last month they burned down the embassy," the State Department man murmured, just loud enough to be heard.

"*They* didn't, the *Communists* did. And that's the difference. Easy for us here in the capital of the United States to shrug off this *minor*" — the word was spoken harshly — "country's agony, these *infaust* events . . ." *Infaust,* Burns thought: the DD was pulling every lever he possessed. There weren't a dozen people in Washington who knew what the word meant — except of course the diplomat, who nodded, slight smile.

Burns was anxious; the DD made a good case. He was pulling the levers available to him. The diplomat had not been specific; he'd given them a brilliant *tour d'horizon*, nothing more. Presently the DD lapsed into facts: so much American investment, the strategic value of the Nbororo River, the threat to peaceful neighbors.

"I think we ought to consider very carefully putting a team in on the ground. Civilians, no more than forty or fifty. But before we come to that, I would like Burns to say a word about the sort of men who run the economy of . . . this 'naked' country."

Well played, Burns thought. He rose, a tightness in his throat. The DD had them now; they could not ignore the facts. Facts were the

♦

DD's strong suit, and now he was calling on Burns to back him up. The DD looked at him, encouraging a strong response. Burns stared across the table at the diplomat, hands loosely clasped on the table. The diplomat's expression was benign; he'd made his case. That was the trouble with the State Department. They didn't *fight;* they were gentlemen. They didn't read each other's mail. Well, they deserved what they got, Burns thought. If they did not control events, events would control them. Laissez-faire had its limits. For Castlereagh, Chamberlain. Burns cleared his throat.

"There is no question they will expropriate American properties," Burns said. Then he named the economists, two who had received instruction at Lumumba University, Moscow; a third from Havana; two or three others who'd cruised through the L.S.E. "One of these" — he mentioned a name and an age — "has unusually strong ties with the . . . black movement . . . in the United States. So there is a domestic political spin to all this . . ."

The agency, at that meeting and at later meetings, carried the day. Forty men were dispatched up the Nbororo River in rafts. They landed and reported the town quiet. There was no shooting nor any signs of upheaval. The communications worked splendidly. In time, most of them returned. There was a different government, but no expropriations.

They were good about it. They wanted him to stay, to "pack it in" for keeps at the State Department and become permanently attached to the agency. They liked him. Burns did intelligent, careful work. Sometimes, when the problem truly interested him, he was brilliant. They indicated to him, but delicately, that his habits were somewhat bizarre — but fully within the . . .

"Ah, parameters."

"Of what?"

"Behavior, acceptable."

"Oh, yes."

"Look, Burns. If you will do no more than trouble yourself to get an M.A., preferably in your field, economics, the future here is very bright, very very bright. Limitless, really."

"Forget economics. How about this, something stronger? An M.A. in the diplomatic history of Europe."

"Not as good, but acceptable."

"The . . . Eastern religions?"

The personnel man smiled. There were already more ersatz Buddhists than the agency could comfortably tolerate. SEA Section smelled like an incense factory, gnomic sayings sprouted like tulips. No, definitely not "the Eastern religions."

"Too bad," Burns said.

"Look, if you're tired of Africa, we can . . ."

"I am tired of Africa, Africa is tired of me," Burns said.

"All right, we understand that. Like pinning Jell-O to the wall, no?"

Burns smiled.

"So let us turn elsewhere."

"The field," Burns said, and the personnel man shook his head. No, not possible. Burns was an inside man, an analyst from the inside; anyone could see that. Outside men were something else altogether. Burns wasn't one of those, probably wouldn't ever be.

The personnel man was encouraging. He tempted Burns. "Look. One immediate jump in grade. That's a couple of thou a year more for you. What will it be? Seventeen, seventeen-five. You have another income. You can move to Georgetown. Or Chevy Chase, and really go with the high rollers."

Burns was expressionless, though surprised. But of course they would know about the gambling.

". . . A couple of thou more a year."

Burns smiled bleakly; he had no need of money.

"And a change of venue." The personnel man mentioned two countries, one in Asia and the other in Latin America. The Latin American country was an interesting proposition, no doubt about it. Its economy had even less to recommend it than the African. But other aspects were more favorable. It was clearly a nation in crisis.

"Not exactly the Soviet Union, is it?"

The personnel man smiled and shrugged.

"Or Germany."

"You know the ropes here now. You know us, we know you. We all get along together. We don't have to finish sentences, do we? Saves us a lot of bother both ways, no?"

"I suppose it does."

"There's another compensation. If you take the LatAm job, you can go down there for six weeks, see the place yourself. Eyeball it firsthand. We'll set you up. We're very liberal about that sort of thing, as you know. On your way down you can stop off at Puerto Rico, Freeport . . ."

"For the casinos?"

The personnel man smiled.

"Who do you think I am, Nick the Greek?"

". . . Break up the return trip in Jamaica, Tobago."

"Six weeks, you say."

"More or less."

Burns mused: "It takes time to really get into these countries. They're complicated. The people, the statistics. It takes time to know what makes them tick . . ."

"This place is no Girard-Perrégaux, Burns."

"And when I get back?"

The personnel man explained the job again, and its title. The location of the office, and the men immediately above and below him. His superior would be a man sixty-one years old, near retirement. Burns would be in line. From there would come a shot at the secretariat itself, the board. If everything broke right, Burns would be on the front line, on the inside, at forty-five, forty-six years old.

"I've always thought about the field."

The personnel man said nothing and looked at the clock on the wall.

"Give me a week to decide?"

"Of course."

"I want to check in with some friends at State. Get another opinion. It's a radical move."

"State's agreeable," the personnel man said quickly.

"Oh?"

"Quite agreeable."

Burns shook his head. His old friend the DCM in Bonn was correct. Once he'd left the department, there was no returning. He'd left their files, become a memory attached to another agency. Others now competed for attention. It always happened in government; once you broke your career chain it was curtains, and you ceased to exist. You were elsewhere, no longer in their control. Burns supposed that the State Department suspected he'd picked up bad habits at Langley; they assumed no one ever *quit* the place, as indeed no one ever did. The procedures were different, and these would become habits that would divide his loyalties. That was the other thing they thought about, the loyalty of the man to his agency. That was critical, particularly if you were truly of the bureaucracy and on your way up, not an inner and outer, but a career professional man. If your loyalty was divided, there was no end of potential disagreement and therefore of conflict and strife. You were not a man whom they could count on in a crisis.

"I'll tell you in a week," Burns said.

"I don't understand this one thing," the personnel man said. "What exactly is your reluctance? You've a clear shot here."

"I always wanted to be a diplomat."

"Well, there's a lot of action here. More than the other place. You're doing essentially the same thing, analysis. It's just going into a different pipeline. And of course —"

"You know, the Congress of Vienna."

"— you're anonymous."

"That's the only thing that appeals to me," Burns said.

1972

◆

# NOONE

◆

THE EMOTIONS OF IT were fairly straightforward, and I don't want to make too much of them in any case, either way. She was crying on the bed, or it sounded like crying, and I was in my rage at the doorway. I had said the words so many times in my head that when I said them out loud, they sounded false. I told her we were finished, and I was leaving. She told me to get out then, and I did. After I slammed the door, I couldn't hear her anymore. I stood for a moment in the street, then began to walk down Dent Place to Wisconsin Avenue. I was walking very quickly, head down, looking for a taxi. The regular Yellow would arrive at eight, but I didn't feel like waiting for half an hour. My knees were shaky and I kept to the inside of the sidewalk. Then I collected myself and slowed up. My briefcase swung in rhythm, my footsteps even on the sidewalk. *Click click click click.*

I arrived at my office in thirty minutes; only a few people were in. The receptionist, one or two others. My secretary followed me through the small offices to the large one, bearing a cup of coffee. She remarked on the weather, hot, and the day, heavy, and handed me the appointments list and waited.

"Is Noone in yet?" I asked.

"Noone's downtown this morning. Back at eleven."

I nodded, irritated.

"At eleven, then."

"Shall I telephone?"

"No need," I said.
My secretary made a small note on her stenographer's pad.
"And hold all calls."

There were two meetings that morning. We were having trouble with
a transcript. I wanted State to agree to release an uncensored version
of an ambassador's testimony, and State had refused. Can't conduct
diplomacy in a fishbowl, the secretary said; not so much a fishbowl,
more a muddy river, I replied. He smiled. I smiled. *No, he said then,*
very politely, knowing he had the strength. The White House would
back him, so the thing was hopeless. That was where Noone was
now, at the State Department talking to their legislative man. Making
everything as difficult as possible for them. Like everything else, it
had its positives and negatives. I was getting solid publicity, and the
cause was a good one, which it isn't always. But the dispute had gone
on for a month, and people were tiring of it; some of my colleagues
on the committee were tiring of it. Noone and I agreed that there
should be one last press release, then forget it. An issue that became
a bore was worse than no issue at all. But others had come in behind
us, and the two meetings this morning were to let them down gently.
To tell them we weren't marching anymore, at least at the head of
the parade. This will sound fatuous, but it is true: I have always tried
never to let people down without warning them.

I have two offices, a public office and a private office. The public
office is very large, with a huge mahogany desk in the center of an
oval rug. The Capitol building is in the background, visible over my
left shoulder through the windows. *What a wonderful view,* the visitors say, and I smile, *Isn't it?* The desk belonged to my uncle when he
was in the navy; it is a beautiful object. He bought it in Honduras
and gave it to me when I first came here. The walls of this office are
crowded with pictures of me and my family, me and politicians, me
and military men, me and important constituents, and plaques with
my name on them. They are commemorative, of this and that —
Rotary, AUSA, AFL-CIO, the United Jewish Appeal. That sort of
plaque. The other, smaller, office is personal and difficult to find in
the maze of rooms in the Capitol. I have a small bar in the corner and
an old Underwood typewriter and a bookshelf full of mystery novels.
I have all of John D. MacDonald's sixty-odd books, plus Ian Fleming
and Ross Macdonald and the others. No photographs, no plaques. A
comfortable couch along one wall, leather chairs around the room,

◆ stand-up ashtrays, a government-issue desk. There is a seascape, a self-conscious impression of a slice of American coastline, Maine or California, Castine or Big Sur. I am in the smaller office now, waiting for Noone.

Gloria Noone is thirty-five, dark, compact, austere. She is divorced from a lawyer, and she pronounces her name *new-nee*. Before she came to work for me she handled public relations for a television network, and although she is ten years younger than I am, I trust her judgment and her instincts. I trust her absolutely when it comes to dealing with the press. We did not get on well at first, owing mainly to her unfortunate habit of correcting the smallest mistakes. In the first interview we fell to talking, for some reason, about Iowa. I was making a point about redistricting.

"In the eight congressional districts of Iowa . . ." I began, but she interrupted.

"There are seven congressional districts in Iowa," she said, and named the congressmen.

It vexed me, and she saw that, and smiled. Of course then I had to hire her.

She knocks, is in the room.

"How did it go?"

"Fine," I say. She is talking about Nancy, but I am talking about the meetings this morning. "They took it very well. They seemed pleased that we had gone along as far as we did. Kudos. We get kudos."

"I'll get the last press release out right away." She looks at me, bland as warm milk. "As long as it went so well, we might think about a press conference."

I smile. Score one for Noone.

"I'll concentrate on the secretary personally."

"You do that."

"Pompous bureaucrat. Another Wall Street fool."

I laugh.

She puts up a hand; she's steady, resolute. "Senator, we will get the last *ounce* . . ."

Gloria Noone is talking, and I am looking over her head. The room is small, so comfortable. Sometimes I think she is a touch paranoid: she had it swept for bugs. Of course there were none. But the knowledge gives me a strange satisfaction. We are absolutely private in this room. We have a code word for it. The Vatican. I have only had the office for two years; they gave it to me after my tenth year in the Senate. But now I never talk about confidential matters in the large office; it is as if that office were ceremonial. Noone and I and sometimes Walter Mach go to the Vatican in the evenings. We do our business there, over a drink. They are for me the best hours of the day, sitting and planning; scheming, Noone says. The day they gave me the key to the office, Noone insisted that I go inside and talk in a normal voice, and she stayed outside with the door closed, listening. She wanted to be certain that nothing could be overheard in the corridor. And it can't be, even when you shout. The soundproofing is gorgeous. When I call her paranoid, Noone smiles and says she is cautious.

She is silent now, waiting for me.

"Well, we are quits."

"Sorry about that," she says. She manages to make it sound both sympathetic and ironic. So I can go either way, and she can follow.

We are both quiet for a moment, and I see her pick up a pencil and begin drawing boxes. One box is fastened to another, a series of boxes slanting down the white paper. She shifts on her chair, sighs, and rubs the flat of her hand along her cheeks. She pushes her hair back behind her ears, then she looks at me, a long moment.

"Nancy *is* staying."

I nod.

"And you're moving out."

I nod again.

"Well," she says. "Well." Noone is carefully inking in the boxes she has drawn, turning the paper as she does it. Now she is using a felt pen, and the ink is staining her fingers. She is unconscious of that. "I think," she says, "a short, blunt statement."

"The shorter the better."

"Two sentences," she says. She has stopped doodling altogether and is staring at the pad. Then she says, "Due to irreconcilable family differences, Senator and Mrs. Hayn . . ."

"Christ, no," I say. "Jesus Christ, no."

Noone shrugs; I am angry. But the anger does not concern her. She is silent for a moment, then tries another approach.

I am a fatalist, and that has served me well in politics. When I am in a tight spot I try to remember that life is capricious. Life is unfair,

Jack Kennedy said. He could afford to say it, although he didn't believe it, really, and I do. He was more romantic than fatalist. Noone and I talked about fatalism once, just once. She said fatalism was for losers, and I laughed at her and called her Horatio Alger's mother. She looked at me as if I were insane.

There is a funny aspect to this. A month ago we looked for precedents and could find none. It isn't the sort of problem you can refer to the Legislative Reference Service, so Noone went personally to the morgue of the *Times*. I wanted her to find out how these problems had been handled in the past, specifically what was said, how it was explained. She drew a blank; perhaps the *Times* did not consider a politician's personal life news fit to print. So we are operating on our own instinct, because it would have been awkward to ask questions, even of close friends. The place is like a sieve, Noone says.

She tries two or three approaches now, and they are improving.

"Senator and Mrs. Tom Hayn have decided to seek a legal separation . . . well, no." She pauses, thinks, begins again. She is writing the statement as she recites it out loud. "Senator Thomas Hayn's office announced today that the senator and Mrs. Hayn . . . no." She begins again. "The senator *and his wife* have decided to seek a legal separation. Mrs. Hayn will continue to live in their Georgetown . . ."

"Unh-unh," I say.

"Oh, right. Dumb of me," she mutters. ". . . *their house in Washington, D.C.* The senator has moved . . ." She looks at me, her eyebrows up, inquiring.

"A downtown hotel," I say.

She smiles. "Right again. You should have my job."

I am thinking that after all I was right, and we should have prepared a statement in advance. But she argued against it, worried about a leak or the possibility of a misplaced piece of paper. We can work it up in two hours, she'd said. That would be a bad piece of paper to have lying around. I agreed finally. But now I don't see the need for all the detail, and I tell her that. I want a simple statement of fact. A one-line statement of fact.

"Tom, you have got to say something," she says. "You have got to give them more than the fact that you and Nancy are quits. So it has got to be in two sentences, and maybe three. This is not major news, but it is news. You have got to give them more than the blunt fact. If you don't, they'll know you're hiding something. They'll speculate."

"They'll speculate anyway."

"Of course. But if you give them something to chew on, the speculation will be built around that. I mean, it doesn't matter an awful lot what it is. What the extra fact is. I think that place of residence is the most neutral, and it fits; the impression is that you've nothing to hide. This is a family tragedy, politics be damned. That's the point we want to make."

Noone is at the bar. She fixes a martini for me and a Dubonnet for herself. She is lost in thought, worried now. The dining room has sent up sandwiches. There is no telephone, so we are quite alone. I smile when I think of that. It is the only office in Washington without a phone. If there is no telephone, Noone said, there will be no spur-of-the-moment, ill-considered calls. She prefers to conduct business face to face.

"How difficult is Nancy going to be?" She looks at me before she asks the next question, which I ignore. "How difficult was she this morning? Or was it last night?"

"I don't know," I say, which is the truth. We have been married for twenty years and have been in trouble the last ten. We are disconnected now, I don't know her feelings. I am preoccupied with the immediate problem, which is the statement; I have lived with the other long enough to know it is insoluble. "I honestly don't know," I say. "Depends in part on that son of a bitch." I mention the name of Nancy's priest, and Noone smiles.

"Rasputin lives," she says.

"The hell with that, Gloria," I say.

She is back to business again.

"You are going to have to take gas."

"Unavoidable."

Noone is thinking, very quiet now. She is circling the subject, closing off the routes of access. She is very thorough. "Think about this," she says, leaning across the desk, concentrating on her drawing. She is very slowly inking in all the boxes. "It might be advantageous to leak it. It might be better to get the word out informally, to prepare the state for it. Then, in two or three days, make the official announcement." She looks up. "I don't think I would recommend this course, but it's one possibility and we ought at least to consider it."

So we talk, and finally I shake my head. "It's going to come as a hell of a surprise. Best to come from me, this office, officially. Better that than rumors for a week, followed by an announcement. They'll have me in bed with every woman in Washington anyway."

Noone nods gravely.
"Have the kids been told?"
"Nancy will do that," I say.
"But Tom junior's in Europe."
"She'll find a way."
"It'll be a surprise," she says.
"No, it won't."
"I mean in the state, and that's the bad part. The surprise."
"The Knights of Columbus," I say, grinning.
"The Holy Name Societies," she says.
"Monsignor Shaw," I say.
"The cardinal!" she cries.
And we both laugh.

Noone has prepared three statements, and I am reading them now. She gave them to me on one sheet of paper. They represent three different "spins," she said. This is how they look on the paper.

1. Senator and Mrs. Thomas Hayn have decided to seek a legal separation. Mrs. Hayn and their three children will continue to live at the family home in Washington, D.C. The senator has moved to a downtown hotel.

2. Senator Thomas Hayn's office announced with deep regret today that the senator and his wife have decided to seek a legal separation. Mrs. Hayn and their children will continue to live in the family home in Washington, D.C. The senator has moved to a downtown hotel.

3. Senator Thomas Hayn's office announced today that the senator and his wife, Nancy, have decided to seek a legal separation. Senator and Mrs. Hayn emphasized that their decision came most reluctantly and was made, finally, in the best interests of the family. Mrs. Hayn and their three children will remain in the family home in Washington. The senator has moved to a downtown hotel.

I choose the third, naturally.

I am thinking of adding a single sentence: "There is no question of a divorce," but Noone is against it.

"The word looks terrible on paper and raises questions," she says.

"But it will be the first question they ask." I want to know how Noone intends to handle this particular inquiry.

"Of course. And I will answer it: 'There is no question of a divorce.' It will give them a second story, which they will have to have. There will be other questions about the children and their ages and Nancy and her age and so forth." She stops, smiles. "Thank God, there's no need to clear the statement with her."

I look up, startled. I hadn't thought of that.

"Not to worry," Noone says. "If she objects to a decision made 'in the best interests of the family,' then she's on the hook and you're off it. There's one thing in our favor. These stories are really awkward for them to pursue. The locals will be reluctant anyway, and you're not so famous that the nationals can really bird-dog it. If they do, it looks like a vendetta. Unless, of course, they smell real scandal." She smiles. "Then anything can happen."

"Thanks for all the good news," I say.

Noone is pleased; the statement has just the right tone, melancholy but dignified, she says. "When I talk to them privately tonight, I will stress the family tragedy aspects. I will not talk politics with them at all. I will tell them that you have gone away for a week. Tom, I am not going to close any doors." I return her stare. "It isn't unheard of. You will take gas, but attitudes have changed now. Even back home. I could foresee circumstances . . ." She does not finish the sentence. She types a clean copy of the statement on the old Underwood and leaves to return to the big office. Perhaps she is right; she is a smart woman. Times change. But I am feeling a little melancholy myself. If I'd been a Protestant, there'd be no trouble, or anyway less trouble. I think about that for a moment, then turn it around. If I'd been a Protestant, I would not be a senator.

The statement is typed and Xeroxed; it will be given to the press at eight or nine tonight. I leave the small office and walk across the street to the large one. Everyone is gone now, except for Noone. I look in on her and motion for her to follow me. She does, eagerly. We march into my office, and she places the call.

I talk to His Eminence.

His Eminence talks to me.

Because the question is lying there, palpable, a shadow between us, I try to reassure him. "John, I want to tell you personally that there is no question of any divorce or remarriage. Nor any third parties either. That is definite."

The old man grunts and says that he is glad to hear it.

But he doesn't believe it.

"You have let me down," he says. "You have let me down badly."

While I am talking, trying to explain the situation, I am watching Noone. She is taut, excited; she seems to me like an athlete before a game. I cannot tell what she is thinking; her mouth is set in a hard thin line.

She'd insisted that Walter Mach not be brought into this, and I reluctantly agreed. I used to think that she and Walter were close, but now I am not so sure. She didn't want anyone brought into it; otherwise it would look like a council of war. "Bad atmospherics," she explained; "too political." She catches me looking at her and smiles slightly, distracted; she is perched on the edge of the big desk, her hand under one elbow, concentrating on the conversation. Her hair falls wonderfully over her face; she turns now, and her mouth and eyes are obscured. Her left leg swings free, describing a circle. The cardinal is silent, and there is nothing to do but say good-bye and hang up the telephone. I have known this cardinal since he was a bishop. I am in politics largely through the early patronage of this cardinal. We were friends.

Noone listens for two clicks, then puts down the extension phone.

"Pretty frosty," she says.

"Balls like ice cubes," I say absentmindedly.

"That bastard," she says. "With *his* record."

"Well, he is an old man."

"But he won't help."

"Why should he?" I ask.

We make six other calls after that.

I am walking down the Capitol steps. Very theatrical: it is raining softly, and wisps of steam rise from the still-hot pavement. The late-working secretaries are going home now, and I watch their bodies move. I am walking with another senator, and he nudges me, nodding at a miniskirt ahead of him. He shakes his head, grinning. *Quiff quiff quiff,* he murmurs. I laugh.

Noone is still in the big office. She said she would make selected calls to selected members of the press. Different men, different spins, she said. Not to worry. I leave her at her desk, her hair freshly combed, new makeup on her cheeks, two packages of cigarettes next to the telephone. Coins lie atop the cigarettes. She is excited, anxious for me to be gone so that she can begin her telephoning. Straight-faced, I say that I think I'll wait and listen to the first call, see how it goes. She shakes her head quickly, *No*. She would be inhibited with me on the extension phone. It is better if she does it alone. This is her job, she says. The reason she is paid twenty-eight thousand dollars a year.

"Twenty-eight five," I say, and her humor returns.

"It's cheaper than a trip to Rome," she says.

I know her friends, so I know where to look tomorrow. I mean which newspapers and which network. They will be very interested in this story because I am on all the short lists for Vice President. They will say this will take me out of the running, and they are right, although Noone will not believe it. I tell her she is crazy, she had better set her sights elsewhere. A Catholic separated from his wife, three children.

"I can live without the vice presidency," I tell her.

"There are seven congressional districts in Iowa," she says, and begins dialing.

1971

◆

# PRIME EVENING TIME

◆

H E TOLD HIS WIFE that the most important fact of his war
duty was that he'd survived it. He made the statement once in
Hawaii, when they were reunited, again in San Francisco, when they
deplaned, and several times in the car, driving from the West Coast
to the East. On the remainder he was silent. She hated the war,
although she was very proud of him, and did not insist on details.
The details would only depress and frighten her and she told him that
she would rather not know them.

He was an infantry captain, and in the course of three years in the
war zone had won a Bronze Star, three Silver Stars, and, finally, the
Medal of Honor. He looked at the last with a certain ambiguity,
because he'd won it while leading a company of men into an ambush.
Possessing natural skills, he'd performed creditably and did not know
until a week after the firefight that his CO had put him in for the
Congressional, the highest decoration an American soldier could receive. He'd gotten it a year later, somewhat to his embarrassment.
The captain did not grieve, however, because his Bronze Star should
have been a Medal of Honor; in that action, he'd managed to save
lives, perhaps as many as twenty or thirty lives, and his company had
all but destroyed an enemy battalion.

In Washington they wanted him visible, so they made him a staff
assistant to the chairman of the Joint Chiefs of Staff. After his tours
in the war zone, he accepted the assignment with pleasure, because
he'd have an opportunity to meet the men who actually made policy.
Soon to make major, the captain assumed that his future with the

army was secure; he'd done three tours in the war, and that was enough.

The captain kept his wife separate from his work. For all she knew about him he might have been an insurance salesman or a dentist, except of course for the uniform that he wore, and the telephone calls at odd hours. Their life centered on casual things, the house in the suburbs, their army friends, the occasional holidays south. The captain did not carry work home with him, and in fact it was mostly military trivia, nickels and dimes. The captain shuffled papers from one box to another and attended daily meetings, spear carrying for senior officers. He wrote reports and conducted briefings for distinguished visitors, including members of Congress. The captain was "known," in an imprecise way; from his bearing and his correct manner, visitors rightly assumed him to be one of the army's bright young men. From time to time he was trotted out on display by the army public relations office, so he was not surprised one morning to receive a telephone call from the chief of information, an elderly and argumentative colonel whom he'd known in the war.

"Do you know Charles O'Brien?"

"I don't know him," the captain said. "But I listen to him."

"Well, his network is doing a special on war veterans. War heroes, according to O'Brien. He tells me it's going to be a sympathetic show — that's the word he used, 'sympathetic' — on combat troops. Very favorable to the army. No cheap shots. Now he's particularly interested —"

"Negative," the captain said. "Respectfully, sir, negative."

"Wait a minute. O'Brien is not a prick. I've known him on and off for years. I knew him in the real war. He's the anchorman and this thing is going to run in prime evening time." The colonel's voice dropped. "He showed me a list of our people that they want to interview. It's going to be all army, mostly infantry. No sailors, no fly boys. All army, do you understand? Now this list. It's a hell of a good list, and your name is at the top of it. Because you're such a hell of a war hero."

The captain sighed.

"O'Brien specifically wants you, hotshot. And he did not come to me with the request. He went straight to the old man, and the old man said that if he wanted you he could have you. Old man's orders."

The captain thought a minute, knowing now that argument was useless. "I knew some of them overseas, and I didn't like them except for one or two."

◆

The colonel snorted with contempt. "As far as I'm concerned, they're war criminals. They're the enemy, and a concentration camp is too good for them, but O'Brien's something else." The colonel's temper flared and subsided. "O'Brien's all right. He's a different echelon altogether."

"Sure. You bet."

"Anyway, I'm sure you can work it out. I'm sure you can come to terms with it in your own mind. Because it's orders."

"Thanks, Colonel."

"Any time, Captain. I'll tell the old man that you're delighted and honored to participate. That you're a good soldier. That you want to do your part for the army's image."

"Yes, sir."

"In front of about thirty million people, give or take a few. That's the audience in prime evening time."

"When will they be around? When does it start?" The captain's voice was hoarse and confused. He'd been obliged to deal with correspondents when he won the Medal of Honor, and a couple of them had managed to slice him up. The war lover, an animal. One of them made him sound like Goebbels.

"Next week, week after. They want to get this thing 'in the can,' as they say, before the current offensive is ended." The colonel paused and chuckled softly. "You see, it has news value. They want to run it while there's still a lot of action overseas. While the casualty figures are still high."

"Christ," the captain said.

That night, having a drink with his wife, the captain worried the problem. He told his wife that the television people never got anything straight, and it was very difficult talking about what they wanted him to talk about. It was not something that was easily articulated; you either understood it or you didn't and there wasn't any satisfactory explanation. The other thing was that he was back in Washington now and wanted to forget about the war. He was not ashamed of it or bored with it, but it was another part of his life and he wanted to get on to other things. He was proud of what he had done, and very proud of the Medal of Honor. But it was an emotion he preferred to keep to himself. His wife, not understanding the motivation, thought that he was being selfish.

"If it'll help the army, why not?"

"I suppose," he said glumly.

"It can't do any harm."

"Yes it can," he said sharply. She looked at him, startled. "It's hard to explain."

The truth was that he believed they were *his* medals, honorably earned. They were *his* experiences and, when it came to that, *his* survival. The medals were part of his own history, they were evidence of things seen with his own eyes. Burned in his own memory. All these things were personal, and the captain thought that he was entitled to keep them to himself.

So his wife was partly correct after all.

They recorded two preliminary interviews and then arranged a shooting schedule. The interviews had gone so well (or so they told him) that O'Brien decided to build the entire show around the captain. Others would be interviewed, but the captain would be the centerpiece. They'd sent two reporters to conduct the preliminaries, one to ask questions and the other to operate the tape recorder. They taped the entire interview but the reporter took notes anyway. Then they fixed the first day's shooting, and when the captain learned of its location he immediately telephoned the chief of information.

"Do you know where they're doing it, Colonel? Do you know? Did they tell you?"

"They told me," the colonel said.

"Arlington," the captain said, his voice incredulous and furious at the same time.

"O'Brien's idea." The colonel was beyond surprise.

"But *Christ!*"

"Well, that's the way they want it. And they've got the old man's blessing."

"Perched on a tombstone, I suppose."

"No, actually not. We've got a copy of the shooting script. Minus your lines, of course. Just a general outline. They're going to shoot you standing, with the gravestones behind you in a long line. I was worried about it, too, but the way they're doing it will be kind of I'd guess you'd say heroic. Not depressing, but heroic."

"Oh, I see. Heroic."

"Well, dramatic."

"Dramatic-heroic."

The colonel laughed and said nothing.

"Colonel . . ."

"That's showbiz, baby."

"But they can screw me up."

"No, they think you're a natural. Good-looking, modest. Intelligent, a warm and positive personality. Reserved, a good voice. A model soldier. They're going to tout you as the chief of staff of the future."

"How will that set upstairs?" the captain asked after a moment.

"Don't worry, the old man thinks it's outstanding. He's taking a personal interest. He and O'Brien are on the phone every other day. The old man himself is going to do a short interview at the end of the show."

"So he's not angry in any way."

The colonel laughed. "I never knew you to have problems with generals."

"It's the first time I've been involved . . . in this way."

"Yes. There's one other thing. I've arranged a briefing for you this afternoon on one or two suggested topics. Now, they're going to get into the conditions over there, and your response to that will be positive. If they ask about equipment, your response to that will be *very* positive. And it would be well for you to suggest that there's been a lot of bloodshed. You know, so the dinks can be free. Got that?" The colonel coughed. "Other than that, you're on your own."

"One of your guys will be there, I hope. To monitor."

"Unh-unh," the colonel said. "That was one of the arrangements with O'Brien. No PIOs at all, not even me. Just you and the cameras and the microphones and the reporters."

"In the graveyard at Arlington."

"You'll figure a way. Bye-bye, General."

"Yes, sir," the captain said.

They decided to film at dusk, three successive days, since the light was right ("moody") for only about an hour and a half. The first day, they staged a military funeral that would be barely visible, blurred, through the camera's lens. That would be in the background, with the gravestones in the middle distance and the captain up front. They told him that they intended to edit the sound track so that there would be no questions, only answers. Anyone looking at the film would assume that the captain was talking spontaneously, not responding to a reporter's interrogation. Charles O'Brien hoped for an impression of stark and melancholy drama. A Stephen Crane short story, he told his reporters and cameramen; spare, deeply sympathetic, *and no irony*.

The captain arrived the first afternoon wearing his suntans, with

only two ribbons: the combat infantryman's badge and the para-
trooper insignia. He'd brought along the others in an attaché case, in
the event they wanted him to wear them. The assistant producer
called O'Brien in New York to ask him about it, and O'Brien said
that the captain could wear what he wanted. O'Brien said he liked
the idea of a minimum of ribbons. It gave the impression of soldier-
liness: lean, austere, modest, manly.

They began to film in the late afternoon, the captain standing next
to a Civil War gravestone. The main camera was only ten feet from
him, it obstructed his view of the cemetery. A second camera was
located on a bluff a quarter of a mile away. This camera would give
them a long shot from time to time, the captain and his suite of
technicians almost invisible among the gravestones; then the long lens
would pull him into focus very slowly, the captain's tall figure becoming gradually more prominent, the distance between the lens and the
man foreshortened. The audience would feel isolation and loneliness.
The camera's lens was a quarter of a mile away but the man's voice
was up close, a disorienting conjunction of distance and intimacy;
O'Brien thought the combination would be stunning, if the captain
spoke the right lines. The reporter stood behind the close camera and
one of the enormous lights, feeding questions.

"How did you come to join the army, Captain?"

"Do you intend to make it your permanent career?"

"Can you describe the military life?"

"How many medals do you have, Captain?"

"Well, sir, there are the Mickey Mouse medals that everyone gets.
Good conduct ribbons, campaign medals, this medal and that. The
important ones that I have are the three Silver Stars, the Bronze, and
of course the Medal of Honor."

"How did you get the Medal of Honor?"

"Sir?"

"The Medal of Honor. What did you do to win it?"

"Well, sir."

The reporter motioned to the cameraman to cut and walked over
to the soldier. "Captain, this is kind of embarrassing. But I think it'd
be better if you didn't say 'sir.' What we're after here is an even flow,
just a guy standing on a hill talking about the war and the way people
fight . . . the wars. What separates the good soldiers from the bad.
What it takes, or doesn't take, to win a Silver Star. Why one man is
good at it and another not. Just what makes a soldier, in other words.
Just a nice easy flow, natural, and don't become disconcerted if the

camera moves away. Most of this will be a voice-over, your voice heard while the scene the viewers are watching is the long row of gravestones or the funeral over there. We're thinking of splicing in some battle footage, all of it, or some of it, in slow motion . . ." The captain tried to concentrate on the words that came so smoothly. The reporter had a deep voice and enunciated carefully. "We've got a bit of film of you in the war zone, and we'll splice that in too. You know, a little *cinéma vérité*. Very effective. But your words are going to carry the scene, it's what you're *saying* that will make the impact. So the objective is for you to be as relaxed and natural as you can. Now just go ahead, about the Medal of Honor."

"Well, it isn't the easiest . . ."

"I understand." The reporter was sympathetic, his voice soothing. "But we can edit, cut, and fit. Don't worry, it's fine so far. You ready?"

"Now?"

"When the red light's on. Now."

"Medal of Honor's the highest award a man can win in the military service . . ."

". . . but this is very, very difficult to put into words. I guess you begin with an enjoyment of the physical life, comradeship with other men, that sort of thing. I guess it's partly a test, you're testing yourself against yourself and against others. That's one part of it, you want to excel, and of course there's no tougher place than a battlefield. It's no football field. You make a mistake and it's not only your own life, but if you're an officer, a leader, it's the lives of other men. The responsibility is enormous. I don't know of anything, any other field of endeavor, where it's any greater . . ."

"Excellent, Captain. Really first-rate. Talk a bit more about the responsibility. Were you ever in a situation where a decision of yours cost lives?"

"Certainly. Any decision you make in battle costs lives, in one way or another."

"Talk now about the most important decision you ever made. How you came to make it, and so forth."

"Well, that's interesting. That's a good question. It was in my third tour . . ."

The captain found that after a while he forgot about the television cameras and the reporter. By turning his face slightly to the left he presented a profile and avoided the light. As he talked he looked over the Civil War gravestones and the big oak trees beyond. He developed a technique of pausing, just before he ran out of words. He'd pause for five or six seconds, then resume his monologue. He found that it had a strange, hypnotic effect on him, as if he were reading from an invisible script; he never skipped a beat. After the first session, one of the cameramen told him it was the best thing he'd ever filmed, and by "best" the cameraman meant "genuine."

The captain discovered that it was possible to slide over details that halted the flow of language. These were unimportant details. In retelling one anecdote he'd misplaced the scene of the action. In another, he'd slightly underestimated the number of dead. In a third he mispronounced a man's name. None of these slight errors had an effect on the overall theme.

"It's strange," he told his wife after the second day's filming. "But I sort of like it, it's interesting to do."

"Why not? You like what you're good at."

"Well, I was opposed to the whole idea. Those press bastards. But it's important that the public understand these things, things about the war. They're important. There is a war on, after all, and the public ought to understand what it means to actually fight it. As opposed to just talking about it. And if I can be of help in that, well and good. They reckon that thirty or forty million people are going to watch this show. Anyway, this is the way it's done now. And O'Brien is a hell of a guy."

"I'm glad you don't hate it," she said.

"Well, it's a technique, like everything else. I was stiff in the beginning, but then I warmed up and it went off all right. The trick is to ignore the camera. Just talk as if the camera wasn't there."

"Did Charles O'Brien tell you that?"

"No, I just picked it up. It happened. If you work it right you can blot out the camera and the lights and the people who go with it. The paraphernalia, the cameras. Out of your mind. They take my notes and put them on a TelePrompTer, and when I fall short of words I can look at that and get a clue. But I almost never have to. I've one or two tricks of my own, and if those fail then I can sneak a look. It's the damnedest gadget, I wish I had one at the briefings. But the cameraman on the project, Joe somebody, said it was the best thing he'd ever filmed."

"Darling!"

The captain smiled and shrugged. "That's what he said. I don't know if he meant it, but he said it."

"*What* did you talk about?"

"He's supposed to be a great cameraman." The captain sighed. "One of the best." He watched his wife sitting in the armchair, absently leafing through a woman's magazine, her feet tucked up under her. Her habit in the evenings, after dinner. The television set was on, its sound turned low. He wanted to tell her more about the filming, the look of the cemetery at dusk, the language the technicians used. He saw her looking at him, puzzled.

"What did you talk about?" she repeated. "What is it that you're saying to them?"

He smiled. "This and that." She nodded. "The Medal of Honor, one or two other things. You know."

"Your army life."

"My life, period," he said.

"Yes," she said. Then: "I think it's wonderful."

"Well, I wasn't going to mention this. But O'Brien said the same thing after he saw the rushes."

"I guess I'll have to watch the show," she said.

"How does your wife fit into this life?"

"She's a good wife."

"But how does she feel about the war?"

"Well, that's my job. Like most women, she doesn't like war. But she understands that soldiering is my business. She understands that." The captain paused for a moment and looked to his left, down the long line of gravestones. The light was failing over the Potomac, and he could faintly hear the sounds of traffic on Shirley Highway. A private jet inbound to National Airport descended over the cemetery. "She was very proud when I got the Medal of Honor. Very, very proud." He raised his voice slightly: "We never talked about the circumstances of it. I guess she read about that in the papers, and of course there were several different versions. It was pretty hairy. This is not to say anything against the nation's press, but they were like the blind man and the elephant — you know? She never asked me directly about it, though, and I never told her.

"She never *asked* you?"

"No." The captain shook his head.

"Well, what did she say when you got the news?"

"She said it was wonderful. There were ceremonies, you know, and interviews and so forth." The captain described the parade in his hometown, the rows of Boy Scouts and American Legionnaires. The mayor, the members of the city council. And the ceremonies at the White House, where the President himself read the citation.

The reporter muttered to the assistant producer to make certain that the camera with the long lens was filming the captain. He wanted the camera to bring him into the middle distance, still a long shot but enough to make him visible, in profile among the gravestones. He motioned for the close camera to move back and give the captain room to walk.

"What did she say when the ceremony was over?"

"I don't remember. We had tea with the President and the secretary of the army, and then we went home. There were two others in the ceremony. One air force and one marine, as I recollect. But noncommissioned officers."

"Did you wonder about that at all?"

"What? The noncoms?"

"No, no. Your wife. Let me read part of the citation right here." He heard the familiar words and phrases, formed in the stilted language of the military: "conspicuous gallantry . . . at great peril . . . took command." When the reporter was finished, the captain was confused. What did they want him to say? He was standing apart from them now, and the reporter had to raise his voice to be heard. The captain began an answer, talking rapidly.

"Sorry, Captain. You're talking too fast. Take your time. No rush."

"Well, she was concerned about my safety, of course. But this is all in retrospect, all after the fact. Like any wife whose husband is in a jam. And we were in one *serious* jam. She was happy that I got out of it, that's all. I don't think she concerned herself with the details, they were pretty grim. Why should she? By the time she heard about it, the action was over."

The reporter waited a moment before answering: "No reason at all."

"She's a damn fine wife."

The reporter was silent, letting the tape roll. He knew the long-range camera was focused on all of them, the camera and the lights, the captain standing a little apart. A tiny group of men on the grass among the gravestones, like a matador and his *cuadrilla*, the reporter thought. The captain looked solemn; the microphone would pick up his breathing. This was a long minute, a long still scene: the reporter stared at the captain, who had turned his profile to the camera. This soldier had picked up the tricks very quickly. But the reporter was surprised to notice that the captain's hands were trembling.

"Do you talk about it at all now?"

"No."

"I see. It's a dead-letter issue, then."

"It was a couple of years ago, more than that. It was three springs ago. The afternoon of the twenty-second of April. Three in the afternoon. I was going to write her about it, all the details, but then I didn't. As I've explained, it was all available in the newspapers."

"Accurate and inaccurate."

"Mostly the latter," the captain said with a smile.

"What did they get wrong?" The reporter wanted to put the interview back on the track. He wanted to get the captain back to his wife.

"It's hard to explain, sir." The captain paused, and shifted his feet. "It's very confusing, a battle. Nobody ever gets all of it. The after-action reports are only half right, even the people who are there know only their own part. It's all just details."

"Well, your own part then. Just that part."

"It's a long time ago."

"But it must have been a critical moment. In your life," the reporter said, and added: "and your wife's."

"Well, she wasn't in the war."

The reporter was silent now, knowing from experience that the captain would have to speak. The camera and the lights were intimidating. It was impossible to ignore them, for the same reason that it was impossible to ignore a ringing telephone. The experts were able to avoid it, but this captain was no expert. Knowing that the cameras were rolling, an amateur would feel forced. The reporter decided to keep still, to wait patiently until the captain picked it up again.

"This was my second tour."

Silence.

"I was commanding a company then."

Silence.

"There were a hundred and forty of us, it was an understrength company. This was in the highlands. Near a river, I never could pronounce the name of it. Our mission was to sweep through a valley."

Silence.

"It developed there was a whole lot of enemy dug in along the trail. Which was mined and booby-trapped, although we didn't find that out until later. It was at the end of a long day. Very hot."

The reporter was giving instructions to the far camera, to move in on the captain very slowly. A millimeter at a time, bring him into close focus so slowly he would fill the screen before the audience was aware of it. No voice-over this time, he wanted it entirely natural; he wanted the actual scene, as the captain was speaking the words.

"We bumped them and they hit us."

Silence.

"We call that a meeting engagement."

The captain smiled and the reporter turned away, as if he were speaking to the cameraman.

"As you read in the citation, we lost about two dozen killed and wounded. We were out on our own, there wasn't anybody else. There was just our unit and theirs. Might've been on the moon, or any other uninhabited or undiscovered place. I couldn't raise headquarters on the radio, so we had to stick it out with no help and no advice. For about an hour we were orphans."

There was another long silence while the captain put his thoughts in order. The reporter nudged the assistant producer and whispered in his ear, "Hands." The other nodded and told the cameraman to focus in tight on the captain's hands, which were fluttering at his side.

"They lost upwards of fifty men, when the air strikes and the artillery were over. I'd crawled into one of their bunkers with my RTO and we directed the fight from there."

"So you were out on your own," the reporter said.

"I've explained that."

"What did you think about during that time? Did you think about home, or . . ."

"I was trying to stay alive."

"Yes, but during the pauses . . ."

"There weren't any," the captain said.

"So you didn't think about anything other than your position, where you were, and what your job was." The way the reporter phrased it, the question sounded critical.

"I thought about my wife," the captain said stiffly.

The reporter smiled; he thought he had it now. He wanted to move in gently, without alarming the captain.

"She was living where?"

"In Hawaii. We had an apartment there."

"And you'd been apart how long on this tour?"

"About six months. I was due for some leave."

They were taking simultaneous pictures now, tight shots from the close camera and the panorama from the camera on the bluff. They would edit later. The reporter had motioned the captain away from the gravestone, and now he was standing alone about twenty yards distant.

"Yes, it was about six months," the captain said.

The reporter could feel the moment moving away again. The soldier had his hands in his pockets and was staring at the ground. "Was this an inspiration for you?" the reporter asked. "Knowing you'd be off on home leave soon?"

The captain shrugged.

"Knowing that you'd be able to see your wife in Hawaii or wherever?" He signaled the close camera to move in tight, to fill the lens with the face of the captain. He wanted the camera to focus on the man's eyes. "When you thought about your wife, what exactly did you think about?" The reporter watched his man very carefully; he was working as delicately as a surgeon. But he was almost there. The reporter pressed again: "Did you think about . . ."

"I thought about survival," the captain said.

Silence.

"My survival."

"And?" the reporter asked quickly. But the soldier said nothing. He was standing at attention, still as stone, staring levelly ahead of him. His jaw muscles were tight. "And then what, *Captain?*"

He seemed in a trance, his eyes were blurred and in motion. He turned to the reporter and opened his eyes wide, as if seeing him for the first time. He shook his head and murmured, "Nothing." The reporter waited, gambling. A moment passed, then the captain straightened. It seemed a very great effort for him to do so. He looked at the camera and smiled crookedly. He talked directly at it now, as if it were a human being. "I killed half a dozen men. It was an action that was over in two hours and a half, and we had help from a lot of fine people. We damaged the enemy. After we got hit, they were outstanding. They put in air and artillery, and then they flew in some choppers to take us out. That was all there was to it. They flew us back to base camp. That's the end of the story."

"But you —"

"There's no more to it," the captain said.

"But you were talking —"

"Nothing," said the captain.

The reporter nodded slowly and motioned for the assistant producer to cut the far camera. There was no need for it now; they had all they could use. They had more than enough for a dozen special programs. He had been on the edge of something, and he'd almost made it good; but now it was gone for keeps. This surprised him, and he was not often surprised. But the captain had slipped the hook.

He turned away to say a word to the assistant producer, and then looked back at the captain. He was still standing, his profile to the camera, staring down the long row of graves, talking quietly. His voice was smooth and steady, the voice of a confident soldier. He was standing at ease, one hand in his pants pocket, the other resting lightly on a weathered marble tombstone. The captain was ramrod straight in the spine, and as the reporter looked at him he could see a small, tight smile on his lips. What a son of a bitch, the reporter thought; what an arrogant, insensitive son of a bitch. Then he nodded at the assistant producer to get the far camera rolling again. The captain evidently had more that he wanted to say.

1973

# A GUIDE TO

# THE ARCHITECTURE OF

# WASHINGTON, D.C.

◆

THE DAY after the election he took five of them through the Oval Office and all of the rooms in the West Wing. They were polite and attentive, but a little cold. Candler understood and didn't mind. He thought they looked very young and would improve with age; give them four years in the West Wing and they'd age quickly enough. Candler showed them everything, from the location of the coat closets to the safes and special communications equipment. He explained that many of the pictures on the wall were personal and would leave with the men who owned them. All of this was carefully taken down by the one with the notebook. There was no question that this new crowd would want a thorough house cleaning, which was entirely understandable. The old man told him to expect that and be courteous about it.

Candler filled them in as best he could on the way the White House was run. Who had which offices, and the lines of authority each to each. It was a pointless exercise, because the staff followed the whim of the top man, and no staff was like any other. But there were certain practical considerations, and Candler understood those after eight years. The six of them made desultory conversation for thirty minutes, then got up.

"See you later," one of them said with a smile.

"Any time," Candler replied.

He showed them to the door and watched them walk away down the asphalt drive. They looked like college boys in their tweed coats and careful manners. He knew one of them slightly, from a conversation they'd had before the election. The old man had told him to offer his services to solve a financial problem and he'd done that, only to be refused. No thanks, they'd said; we can handle it. We appreciate your interest, and your boss's; but no thanks. This was the new crowd, and they were very jealous about that. Also they were the new crowd running against the record of the old. Same political party, different generations.

Candler watched them go and felt no regrets. Eight years was long enough, and he was tired. His work was done. Candler thought he would go to Sun Valley for a month and arrange to be back in town just before the inauguration. He hadn't missed one of those in sixteen years. It signaled continuity, an orderly transition. Then he'd go back to New York and begin his book. And after that — time would tell.

The five men had walked down the asphalt and were now standing on the sidewalk in Pennsylvania Avenue, looking back at the White House. Measuring it for size, Candler thought; thinking about the offices. The offices in the basement, the ones on the second floor, and the *real* ones. The ones next to the Oval Office. He grinned, knowing *exactly* what they were thinking.

Then he turned and hurried back inside.

He listened to Billingsly's innocent drawl, the one that had deceived two generations of lawyers. "Tell me again," Billingsly said. "What is Oldfield offering?"

"The usual guarantees. The front money, the fringes. For the usual services, and these are specified. It's a tight contract. I told them who I could bring in with me, and these are very, very good clients. Top-of-the-line people. But the thing is this. They won't talk about the other stuff. 'We'll take care of that when it comes up,' they said. Of course they want me to stay public. They don't want an invisible man."

"No."

"And that's all well and good, they're good people and all that. Except that the guarantee isn't all that high. It's high enough, but it's nothing exceptional . . ."

"How high?"

". . . and they've been slipping lately. They were hurt when the judge died. To a certain extent, they're living on reputation."

"How high, Paul?"

"A hundred and a half, plus a percentage. Of course they're counting on me to deliver."

"Any problem there?"

"No, none. As I said, these people are top-of-the-line people." There was dead air between them, and Candler lit a cigarette. They had plenty of time, there was no hurry. Candler heard his friend breathing heavily into the telephone. He switched buttons to the squawk box so that he could talk from anywhere in the room. "None at all," Candler said.

"It's a good offer, Paul."

"Fair, not good."

"When I began it was eight dollars a week and you walked to court and all the fees went into the hands of the senior partners. But I was twenty-five then."

"And I'm forty-one."

"And I'm seventy." Billingsly paused. "What are your options?"

"Christ, I'd like to get back into the game. Tom, I'd give my left nut to get back into it. But there isn't any entry. They're all new people now. Hell, some of them I don't even know. The guy there that has my old job, Christ, he used to be the attorney general of Christ, *Idaho,* or some damn place. I don't even know their names, where they came from. New crowd entirely."

"I know what you mean. Same thing happens every time the big man dies or is defeated. They bring in the new brooms, but the last time we had this kind of situation was Coolidge and Hoover. I mean where there was an election, a definite stop and start. I remember what happened then. They —"

"Hell, we didn't have a *government* then. All we had was guys sitting in offices. Not a government, the way it is now." Candler lit a cigarette. "Well, back to the problem at hand. What do you think of Oldfield's offer?"

"He's your ticket of admission, Paul."

"What do you really think of it?"

"I think it's a pretty good offer. That firm's right for you just now. You've got to think long-range. Oldfield must be older than I am, and his kid is a horse's ass. The judge is dead, but they've got five or six others in there who know their way around. Damn well. It's still a quality outfit, and your going there could make a difference. The front money's not all that important in the last analysis. You know good and well that they can't get the sort of business you can, and that no one in that place has got your contacts. Just leave the contract open-ended. That's my free legal advice. Write it for a year, then renegotiate."

"Fisher got more," Candler said.

"Well, yes."

"More front money, and a guarantee he could move on damn near anything he wanted, any time he wanted. He got carte blanche."

"Of a certain kind. But we've been through this before, and you've got to accept it. You've got to remember who Fisher was and what he did. And how he did it. The kind of exposure he had. You know the truth and I know the truth, but Fisher's new employers don't know it."

"Those were great days," Candler said.

"Screw the great days. This is right now."

"Well, Fisher got his name on the door. Davis, Davis and Fisher. The son of a bitch. I'm surprised he didn't make them reverse it. Fisher and Davis. Or maybe just Fisher and Partners."

"He's no novice at writing contracts."

Candler was silent for a moment. Then: "Maybe I ought to wait until the book is out."

"He was more visible than you. That was just the way it happened, nothing to do with you or with him. You were too damn stiff with the newsies, Paul. Fisher wasn't, and that made the difference. The *Time* cover, all that horseshit. Everybody thought after a while that Ted Fisher was running the government, when in reality it was you." The old man barked a laugh and they were silent again. Candler stared morosely at his drink. He switched off the squawk box and picked up the telephone receiver.

"Maybe if I wait until the book is out, maybe then . . ."

"Paul, the book is *now*. Your chips are *then*. The past in this case is more important than the present. Everybody is friendly as hell, but you've got to put yourself in their shoes. They're not buying an author, they're buying a lawyer. Historians are a dime a dozen, Presidents' lawyers aren't. Now I know it's a fine book. But what you're giving Oldfield is the past. That's what you've got on the table, that's your ante. You know where to go, he doesn't. You know the passwords, he doesn't. You know the graveyard, and he hasn't a clue. That's your little secret. You can win the Nobel Prize with that book and it won't matter a damn to Oldfield. Believe me that."

"The book will get attention."

"Yeah, attention will be paid. But you're not getting this job through the *New York Times*."

"So you're saying this to me: go now."

"Absolutely, unless you've got something better. The longer you wait, the more you've got to contend with memory. Memories fade. It's all on the instant now, and you've got to strike while you're hot. You've been with that book for two years, and you're already a former. Am I right? How do they identify you? Paul Candler, former special counsel to the President. Right? Am I right? And it's an ex-President."

"Right."

"So you have a problem."

"I guess I didn't tell you that I let out the word that I was available if they wanted me."

"You did *what?*"

"Well, I did."

"Christ, Paul."

"It took about a week for the word to come back, through a third party. They said they'd like to talk about it sometime, but there was nothing just now in the White House. They wondered, though, if I'd consider chairing a . . . study group." Candler listened to Billingsly's impatient breathing. "This was to be a presidential commission to do with auto safety. Me and about four hundred other distinguished citizens. To find out for Mr. and Mrs. America if driving is good for you. You know, there'd be me and the president of some third-rate university, a sports hero, a defeated politician, some women, a writer down on his luck. A retired Supreme Court justice — hell, that could be *you* except you're not retired. But don't worry, I'll pass your name along. I'll tell them that Mr. Justice Billingsly is ready and willing —"

"Paul Paul Paul."

"All right, a mistake."

"For a smart guy, you sometimes do the damnedest things."

"But it's done now."

"Never never never never never."

"Right."

"I would have done that for you. I see them all the time. I mean I see quite a lot of them, including the Man. That's the sort of thing that has to be handled with great diplomacy, because they don't know what's behind it. Those Midwesterners, they're suspicious as hell. It's the sort of thing where you deal face to face, after the initial contact. I would have done that. Pleased to do it. Why didn't you ask me about it, before you went ahead? Look, some of them are top-notch people. It's a mistake to think they're all opportunists."

"Right right right."

"Are you serious? Did they really ask you to chair a study group?"

Candler thought he had been too flip, that he'd made himself unnecessarily vulnerable. But if he couldn't trust Billingsly, there was no one he could trust. "Yes, I'm serious about the study group. The President himself suggested it, they said. The President himself would be honored. Delighted. Very pleased. By the way, they call him the Man." Candler was silent, waiting for a reply. When there was none, he went on: "The Man wants this. The Man wants that. The Man says this. The Man believes."

"Yes, I know that."

"I was going to reply that I'd be pleased to do it. My experience in settling railroad strikes, negotiating with the Cubans, strong-arming the oil men — let alone that Canadian business — that eminently qualifies me. Rich experience, put to good use."

"Well, they think they've got an identity problem over there. They want to separate this administration from the last, and that's why there are so few holdovers. For better or worse, Paul, you're identified with the *ancien régime*. So am I, for the matter of that. But they can't do anything about me, I've got my job for life. I'm sorry to tell you this, but the book won't help. It'll just serve to reinforce their paranoia about . . . loyalties."

"But Tom, the old man's almost dead. How can you have loyalty to a dead man?"

"It's who you're identified with. That's your problem just now. And it won't go away, not until the second term at least and maybe never. Well, not *never*. But it's something you've got to face up to."

"Yeah, I suppose. I suppose." Candler put the squawk box on and went to the bar to mix himself a fresh drink. Talking with Billingsly depressed him. He said over his shoulder, "Well, Fisher seems thick enough with them."

"I suppose you know why."

"Unh."

"You *do* know why."

"I've heard," Candler said carefully.

"The meeting at the club."

"Right."

"Seven figures, Paul. And Fisher was the broker for that. Hell yes, he's in tight. You can't ignore that kind of help. And he spends a lot of time with the newsies, which doesn't hurt any. And it develops that he and the Man share a passion for . . . duck hunting."

"Oh Christ," Candler said.

Billingsly was silent for a moment. Then he added: "I hear on pretty good authority that he'll be offered Billy's job . . ."

"Deputy secretary of *defense?*"

"Right."

Candler stood at the bar, absently moving ice in his glass. He reached for the bottle of Scotch and filled the glass to the brim. He sighed. Forbearance. "When?"

"End of year."

"But I keep reading about a campaign for governor."

"No, that isn't going to happen. They took some polls and it showed up very badly; he's got a carpetbagger image. And as a matter of fact, he's a lousy politician. He knows that, and the talk about running for governor was a screen to keep his name out front. He wouldn't make a politician any more than you would."

"I don't know about that."

"I do. You and Fisher, you're inside men."

"You know a hell of a lot about what's going on, Tom. You sound like you're in pretty tight yourself." Candler paused, aware that he'd overstepped himself. "Sorry, Tom. I didn't mean that the way it sounded."

"No problem."

"It's just that Fisher irritates the hell out of me. I saw him a couple of weeks ago on the street. We went up to his office and had a drink. Biiiiig corner office, a carpet up to your eyeballs. Two telephones, a lot of soup can art on the walls. And that one photograph on the desk, of the old man before he got sick. 'To Ted Fisher. Loyalist first last and always.' That was the inscription. Nice."

"Has Oldfield showed you around their place?"

"Yes. And to answer your question, my office there would be about a third the size of the one I had at the White House. Now that's a strange thing. A hundred and fifty thousand dollars a year guaranteed, and they give you an office the size of . . . an assistant to the deputy assistant undersecretary of . . . what? The Commerce Department. Some Daumier prints go with the office. It's got a view of another building, directly across the street. But if I strain I can see the East River, at an angle, looking left out my window. It may be a mistake to go to New York with Oldfield. Wouldn't it make a lot more sense to stay in Washington?"

"Fisher didn't."

"No."

"I think it makes more sense to broaden your base. And those New York lawyers. They're a little awed by Washington. They don't *know* it, not the way we do, and they're a little afraid of it. They're afraid of it and patronizing about it, all at once. Oldfield's outfit is old-line, and they're probably being deliberately casual. But that'll stop when they have a serious problem and you can solve it for them. That'll stop right away at that time."

"New York's a pain in the ass."

"Well, you force yourself, Paul."

"A hundred and a half makes up for the discomfort."

Billingsly coughed and said casually, "Did Fisher talk to you at all about his plans? Did he say anything?"

"No. I got the idea he was going to make money for two or three years, then engineer a re-entry. That's why I'm surprised at your news. But we're pretty cautious with each other, there's still some hard feeling. Not on my part, on his." Candler laughed a short, quick laugh. "Know anywhere I can scare up seven figures?"

"So he didn't say anything specific."

"Not to me."

"Well, wait it out."

"Sure. And I'll go to work for Oldfield, and we'll spend a lot of time reminiscing about the old man, and then he'll start to ask me the questions. 'What really went on at the meeting in Ottawa?' Or, 'Tell me the straight story behind the oil deal, did Big Clint really say what they said he said?' Or he'll buy me a big lunch at the Harvard Club and we'll have a drink or two and some fine wine and he'll say, just about the time the cigars come, 'Say, Paul, I was talking to old X today and it turns out he's got a problem with import quotas.' Or with the FCC or the NLRB. Or someone from the White House is leaning on him and isn't there a way to do a quiet end-around? And I'll say, 'Don't worry, I'll look into it.' And I will, and maybe I can do something and maybe I can't, and the client won't be any the wiser and we can hike the fee a couple of hundred percent, and he can be a big man on the golf course back in Cleveland by saying he's hired Paul Candler to solve his Washington problem. Wink. Smile." He paused, listening to Billingsly's breathing. "Tom, I want to be where it's happening. I know what to do and how to do it. I had the place in the palm of my hand. I'm good at it, what I did for the old man. No one could come in cold and move a man around like I could. I couldn't put it in the book because the book is supposed to be about the old man, but it was *me* who sealed the oil thing. *I* negotiated. *I* set the terms. The old man gave me blanket authority, and I took it and the thing was settled to everyone's satisfaction. It never broke in the press, and it never will. I let Fisher and the rest of them massage the press, and they did a hell of a job. And got their names in the paper. Well, I've hinted at the oil deal in the book. Anyone who reads between the lines can guess at the truth of the matter." Candler heard Billingsly laugh. "Or part of the truth anyway."

"Yes, I was about to say."

"So now I'm out in the cold. Fisher's in, I'm out."

"Look at it this way. You'll make some dough for a couple of years. Then you'll come back in."

"The old man was some man to work for," Candler said. "Remember that look, the over-the-eyeglasses look? Just a glance across the desk. *Now you take care of this, and I want it done right.* Remember that, Tom? And we went off and did it and didn't bother him again until the thing was done. Just *did* it, with no questions asked. And no publicity either."

"Absolutely."

"I loved that old man."

"We all did. Do."

"That's where it is, you know. That's where it counts. Up against that, Oldfield and Wall Street are Dubuque." Candler took a long swallow of his drink; the squawk box was still on. "But it's the old frontier now, that's for sure. And Fisher's playing bagman for the new crowd." Candler swirled ice around in his glass, standing at the bar with his back to the telephone. A habit he picked up in the West Wing, strolling around the office while he talked into the telephone.

"Paul? You know I never really thanked you for letting me see the galleys of the book. And agreeing to the changes. It would have been awkward as hell for me."

"I understand. I don't know how the passage got in there in the first place. It was careless research."

"Well, you know I appreciated it."

"Yes."

"Well, I guess that's it."

"All right, Tom. One last thing. I want to just pursue this for a minute, if you've got the time. *What if* you took it up in a private way with your friends back there. Casually, no big production. You say to them, Paul Candler wants to get back into the government. He knows it's hard for you. But he'd like to work in the White House again. He thinks he can be useful to the President, and he's willing to take on damn near any assignment. Troubleshooting, speech writing, anything . . ."

"It's a hard nut, Paul. What did you do about the auto safety thing?"

"Oldfield represents about half of Detroit, so I said I'd be delighted to take it on. When Oldfield heard about that, he was pleased as hell. That announcement won't be made for three or four months, so there's no problem either way. What do you think about talking to them? You can say you're not speaking with my explicit authority, necessarily, you're operating on assumptions. You can say I'm bored with life on the outside."

"I could do it all right," Billingsly said slowly.

"Well, good."

". . . except for the other thing. They *know* you're interested. You've brought your name to their attention. They know you're out there. I'd leave it to them now, and what I'll do is put in a word for you. I mean a very good word. Paul, they're hard as rocks right now."

"Well, hell. No hurry. We'll talk about it again soon."

"Right, we'll do that. Meantime, you think about Oldfield."

"You think definitely that I ought to take it?"

"I do. No question."

"In a couple of years, I ought to make half a million dollars."

"That's the spirit."

"Yeah. I'll buy some duck blinds." They were silent for a moment, the conversation almost at an end now.

"Take care, Paul."

"Give my regards to Fisher, if you see him before I do."

"You bet."

"And I ought to see you next month when I get in town."

"Just let me know."

"And speak to the Man, next time you see him."

"You can count on it," Billingsly said.

Candler cradled the telephone and turned back to the bar. He remembered everything, and he knew his life wouldn't ever be the same; he knew Billingsly too well and understood all the nuances. He remembered the black Mercury sedans, with the telephones and the reading light in the rear seat. He was up every morning at seven sharp, swinging into the big circular lobby at a quarter to eight. He remembered the silence of the lobby, and the wan light from hidden lamps. In the early morning there were always one or two visitors seated on couches, nervous men waiting for appointments, who put down their newspapers when they saw him. It was as if they felt newspapers were an unnecessary frivolity, a sacrilege in his presence, something profane.

He remembered the two guards at the door and the old Negro

receptionist at the desk near the far end of the room. There were different Negroes at different times; he could never keep them straight. He'd pause, it always seemed an eternity, then stride swiftly to the corridor that led to his own office; he felt the others watching him, following his progress. From the corners of his eyes he'd notice the old man at the desk struggle to his feet, looking at him with large watery eyes, and glide like a bird, soundless, to the corridor entrance. He'd wait there, ready to be of service — who knew if Candler had a message to be delivered, someone summoned, something fetched? Candler never did, and the old black man would then offer to take the briefcase for him. Candler'd shake his head, no; grimly, no. His fist tightened around the briefcase handles as he swung by the Negro with a nod and a muttered good morning.

Then, safely inside the sanctum, he'd relax and stroll down the hallway to his office and the morning's business. Before he did anything he checked the appointment book to see what was scheduled. What was public, what private, and what personal. Then he checked the Oval Office to see if the old man was in. To see if there was anything special that day. Anything that needed doing. Anything at all.

It was the office, not the man. That was what the historians said, and for once the historians were right. Oh, what a place Washington was when you were there on the inside. Right in tight, near the Oval Office, where it happened. He'd been there for eight years, an assistant, a President's man. Now he was on the outs. He hated being on the outs more than he hated anything. For a President's man habit died hard, and suddenly he was afraid.

1973

◆

# D.

◆

THE HOT WEATHER affected her badly and finally she collapsed. For a month or more she'd felt edgy and distracted, and one afternoon all of her defenses crumbled at once.

A friend found her weeping in bed and called an army ambulance to take her to a private hospital on the outskirts of the capital. After a brief examination the doctor diagnosed exhaustion and melancholia and ordered her to bed for a week. He gave the head nurse prescriptions for half a dozen vitamins and drugs, including two potent tranquilizers. He did not inform the patient that he was giving her tranquilizers, because he suspected that she did not believe in them. There was no direct evidence for this — just a doctor's intuition. He told the nurse to keep a close watch on the girl, because he thought she might be approaching a nervous breakdown. He was not entirely sure of his ground and stressed that a breakdown was only one of several possibilities, and that if it came, it would be due as much to physical causes as mental ones. The girl was really very run-down.

The doctor explained all this to the friend, the young man who'd found her and summoned the ambulance. He omitted the part about the breakdown on the theory that it was personal and that the friend did not need to know about it. It was no more than a doctor's supposition, anyway. "She doesn't take care of herself, that's obvious," the doctor said. "It's important to do that here, in this climate. The food, the water. We'll put some vitamins in her. How old is she?"

"Twenty-six, I think. I don't know that vitamins are her problem, however. She chews vitamins like candy, a dozen pills a day. Her faith in vitamins is unshakable. Do you think it's serious?"

"I don't think so. I think she's exhausted. How's her mood been?"

"Depressed," the man said. "Everyone's depressed."

"*Tiens*," the doctor said with a grin.

The man smiled, warming to him a little. "Sorry, I don't speak French. Your English is excellent. Idiomatic."

"I learned it in the United States," the doctor said. "My father was a diplomat." The doctor had attended medical school in Washington when his father was political counselor in the French embassy. Later the father was sent to Indochina as an adviser to the French general staff. "We were here in the early days of the war, and when they threw out the French administration, he went and I stayed." The doctor waved his hand — a weary gesture embracing the countryside, any of the anonymous communities outside the hospital compound. "They have no prejudice against doctors," he said.

The man nodded, politely, and moved as if to go. He did not want to listen to another personal history, and he'd taken a three-hour chunk out of his workday. "Well, is there anything more I can do?"

"Bring her books and magazines, things she enjoys. Not many visitors, though. Is she married? I suppose not. Being here."

"No, not married. She's unattached."

"How depressed was she?"

The man was standing in the doorway, looking at his watch. "I think she was pretty depressed, Doctor. She's been here for two years and was set to go home, and then she signed up for another tour on the spur of the moment. That was last month, and she's been understandably depressed about it ever since. She knows now that it was a mistake — everyone told her so at the time. But she doesn't like to make mistakes. Nobody does."

"Do you both work in the embassy?"

"No. She's a photographer. I work in the embassy. She free-lances pictures — she's very well known. You've probably heard of her. She signs her pictures D. Everyone calls her just D. Well, I must go."

"I see," said the doctor with a flicker of a smile.

"I'll look in later," the man said, and was gone.

The hospital was not air conditioned, and all the windows were thrown open to the hot weather. Because the buildings were situated under large shade trees, the rooms were really quite comfortable. Slowly turning ceiling fans moved the still air.

D.'s room was large, and from the window next to her bed she looked out over a wide lawn with narrow hedges, and benches where the patients sat. She'd always meant to do a picture story on the hospital. The patients were mostly American civilians. There were a few French and an occasional local, if the local was rich enough to afford the fees or too important to be turned away. The hospital was adequately equipped and decently maintained, and it was always assumed there was a subsidy of some kind, probably from American Intelligence. There were rumors that the doctors occasionally treated important enemy cadre as a hedge against sabotage or extortion. But that was nowhere proved except in the negative: it was a fact that the hospital had never been touched in any way by the war and existed as an island of neutrality, a collection of anonymous buildings on the outskirts of the capital.

The first day in the hospital D. slept for eighteen hours straight, but when she awoke she felt no better. Her skin was clammy to the touch and she was shaky. She felt robbed of her energy and ten years older and she didn't know what was wrong. She explained this to the doctor, who listened attentively but said nothing to relieve her mind.

"Look at my fingers," she insisted. She held her hands out, palms down, and they watched the slender fingers tremble.

The doctor raised his eyebrows but said nothing.

"I feel like that on the inside too. Particularly my stomach. My appetite's shot. Oh, damn," she said brokenly. "Sometimes I feel like crying. I feel like crying right now, for no reason. Damn, I hate it so."

"It's all right. There's no law against it."

She smiled thinly. "You mean you give your permission? I can cry right now with no loss of face?"

The doctor perched on the edge of her bed and took her wrist in his hand to check her pulse. His expression was very serious. "I think I might even prescribe it."

"Oh, a good cry. Let the little lady have a good cry — right?"

"If she wants," the doctor said, looking at her squarely for the first time. He was concentrating on her pulse, which seemed steady.

She smiled, looking at his fingers on her wrist. She thought he was probably nicer than he sounded. "You mean I can cry right now?"

"Absolutely."

"Well, I guess I will." The girl laughed and began to cry. Large tears rolled down her cheeks and hesitated on her chin. She made no sound. She turned her face to the wall. With her free hand she covered her eyes.

"Your friend told me you were a photographer." He watched her head nod slowly. She was not crying now but her face was still turned away. "You're very well known. I should've heard of you."

"Top of the trade," the girl said matter-of-factly. "I photograph for a lot of French magazines. *Match.* And *Elle.* Also the French *Vogue.*"

"It's been years since I've seen *Elle,*" the doctor said.

"You don't know what you're missing."

"Yes I do."

She dropped her hand from her eyes and looked at him. He still had her wrist in his fingers and was counting.

"Before I came over here I was a fashion photographer. There aren't very many women fashion photographers. Most of my assignments were taking pictures of men."

"That's very unusual," he said. Her pulse was irregular now.

"Well, that's what I do here too. Take pictures of men. My picture file, a couple of thousand snaps of green men. Men dressed in green. Long, short, tall and all of them green. They're like plants wilting in the heat. They all wilt sooner or later. Think of it — a thousand pictures plus. I have a snap for every conceivable occasion. I send them to my agent in New York, and when news magazines are doing a spread they can select the pictures they need. The pictures are all there on file, so an editor has only to taxi across town and go through the file cabinet. By the way, that's green too."

She was silent for a moment, and the doctor thought that she had fallen asleep. He released her wrist and stood up, appraising the small figure in the bed. But her head turned and she looked at him, tears still in the corners of her eyes, wide awake now.

"Why don't you come later and we can have a drink before dinner? A glass of wine — isn't that supposed to be good for the spirits? It's just a bore, being here alone. I think my friend brought me some white wine."

He was looking at her, no longer thinking of her pulse. "I can be back at six."

"Don't forget."

"I won't forget. Would you like some cheese?"

"The cheese in this country is terrible."

"You'll like mine," the doctor said. "I have a private source of supply."

"All right — wine and cheese. And I'll tell you more about my snaps."

The doctor laughed and wrinkled up his face in an exaggerated grimace. "I can hardly wait," he said.

He liked her. She reminded him of his daughter in France. D. was twenty-six, eight years older than his daughter, but they had the same assured outlook on life. Very dry and beautifully made, D. could have been a fashion model herself except that she was petite. But she had a startling, direct look to her, and large brown eyes that seemed to take in everything. It did not surprise him that she was a photographer. The doctor thought that she was in no way frail, which made the facts of her illness all the more puzzling.

The preliminary tests were inconclusive — a high white-cell count and an irregular pulse, temperature a steady ninety-nine degrees. The doctor thought she was suffering from a low-grade infection of some kind, complicated by simple exhaustion. She was underweight and her eyes were too bright and her skin was dull. With all this she maintained a kind of bravado — as if her vitality were merely in hiding and at any moment would reappear.

On the evening of the fourth day in the hospital he decided to tell her he could not diagnose her illness. He couldn't make a positive diagnosis of a physical problem. He'd assembled symptoms, not causes.

"I thought at first you were having a nervous breakdown. I don't think that anymore, although you're obviously upset. I shouldn't be telling you this, really, but perhaps if you knew it yourself . . ." His voice trailed off. "What makes it puzzling to me is that you're not a neurotic."

She smiled because he pronounced the word with a French accent — *noo-row-teak*. "How do you know that?"

"Hunch."

"Well, you're right."

"It was your attitude."

"Well, the pills aren't helping any. I don't feel any different when I take them."

He said, "No, I can see that."

She was propped up in bed, her drink balanced on her knees.

"Have you ever thought about going home? Back to America?"

"What's a nice girl like you doing in a place like this?"

"Exactly."

"This place, it's a cliché. I couldn't say anything you'd believe, and you'd be right for not believing it. It's embarrassing for me to say, it's so dumb." She waited for him to answer but he said nothing. "Well, it's part of our time, isn't it? Where else would one want to be? While this was going on and you were a photographer, would you want to be photographing models for a fashion magazine?" She raised her eyebrows and shuddered, laughing. "Besides, I just extended my contract. This is a binding contract, although obviously if I stay sick, I'll have to go home. I'm counting on you to prevent that. I've never reneged on a contract. In my work you have respect for contracts and for deadlines. And it doesn't matter that I've already been here on and off for two years. That doesn't matter a bit — no Brownie points for that. I've signed a contract with a magazine and I intend to stick by it."

The doctor was amused. He wondered what it was about Americans and their contracts. One dedicates and defines one's life for a piece of paper. Signed by oneself. It offended his sense of logic and brought to mind the cheap patriotic talk of politicians. He thought it would be simpler for this girl to acknowledge her feelings of guilt.

D. said, "This war is the opiate of the people."

He snorted.

She laughed in spite of herself. The doctor was having none of it. Well, there was no reason why he should.

"You ought to withdraw," he said. "Kick the habit."

"I will if you will," she said. "You who've been here — how long?"

"Eighteen years."

"Well. Fancy that."

"You remind me of me," he said after a moment. "That's what I did the first year I was here. I signed up, and then I signed up again. I had a different answer for every person who asked me why. Before I knew it, I'd been here five years. The sixth year, my wife took my daughter and left. Later I was supposed to meet her in the south of France. But it never happened. I acquired a financial interest in this place. One thing and another. I've been here all these years. This hospital."

"Are you glad?"

"Glad? I never thought of it that way."

"Well, are you sorry you didn't follow your wife?"

"No — that was over. She married a dentist a few years after arriving back in France. She's happy, the child's happy. There wasn't much of a life for them here."

"But you. There was a life for you," she said, pressing him.

"Of course."

"I can't conceive of living here with a family."

The doctor smiled. "Neither could my wife."

She balanced the wineglass on her knee and frowned. She said, "I was living with a man here, but he left. Now, that was odd because it happened without warning — usually there's a warning signal. One morning he announced he'd had it in the war zone and was going home and to hell with the consequences. He worked for a research outfit, very hush-hush. There was something in his contract about mental stress and strain. He copped a plea on that and they sent him home. He was here one day and gone the next. I drove him to the airport and he promised to write but he never did."

"You didn't follow?"

She looked at him a long moment, surprised and irritated. "Of course not."

"Sounds a little like my wife. One morning she announced that the country was going to hell and she didn't intend to go to hell with it. She was very *French* — do you know what I mean by that? She was seriously chic and enjoyed conversation. She liked to travel. She liked to shop —"

The girl giggled and touched his hand. "Isn't that funny? I haven't been shopping in a year. *Shopping* — that was something my mother did. I haven't bought a dress in a year. I don't own a hat except for my steel pot. I haven't bought any jewelry in two years and I can't imagine buying any ever. I bought a Nikon in Hong Kong, but that was business. *Shopping.* That's a scream. Why, I don't even collect half my income. It's banked for me in New York."

". . . so I booked her on Air France to Paris and she was gone in a week, furniture to follow. I didn't see her or my daughter for a year and a half because we were very busy then and I couldn't leave the country. One has responsibilities. So I stayed, and my wife remarried."

"I remember, now that I think about it, that six months ago I bought a cashmere sweater in Hong Kong."

"A few years ago I lived with a woman who sang in one of the nightclubs. But she tired of the life here, too, and left. She made quite a good income before leaving. She was very careful with money. Of all the women I've known here, she was the most agreeable."

All this was said intently and swiftly, the words bright with nostalgia and amusement. They spoke as if time were running out on them and they had to get everything said at once. Their voices were low and intimate, their eyes focused elsewhere. Now they were silent, sipping wine and watching the darkness come. From somewhere on the hospital floor they heard rapid steps, and then it was silent again.

The doctor said, "In this country one does not lack for people." At times he felt the country was like a waiting room in a clinic. It was a place where people came to pause and wait but never to live. Never to put down roots. He imagined a faded waiting room with run-down décor and out-of-date magazines, the walls soiled, the floor scuffed.

"I was going out with a colonel, but his tour ended and they sent him home. He's at some base in the States now. Nice man. There was the colonel, the researcher, and one other who's still here. That one just *ended,* bang." She waited for a reply, some exchange.

"One becomes caught up," he said.

"One does."

He raised his glass and smiled. "Regrets are awfully damp, don't you think?"

She shook her head, waving his words away with a flick of her wrist. "Oh no, I have no regrets. Why should I have regrets? I'm twenty-six; I enjoy my work here. I don't *love* it, as some of them do, but I think it's important and I like to do it. I'm good, by the way. My friends in New York thought it was a lark when I came here. '*Vogue* goes to the war' — that kind of thing. They all thought it was just another lark, but it wasn't." She was silent a moment, remembering things her friends had said about her. "I found that once I was here, I had to stay on." She smiled sardonically. "And that had nothing to do with the contract."

"It's easier to stay than to go — that's the diabolical thing. And it gets easier the longer you're here." He was conscious of sounding like the voice of experience, middle-aged and world-weary, almost cynical.

"For a while I lived at the hotel, but then I got a flat. I decorated the place and that may have been a mistake — temple rubbings, bronze Buddhas. Our equivalent of college pennants, I suppose. But it's home and it's convenient, and I'm attached to it."

He nodded, understanding what she was saying. He'd lived in a hotel for two years following his divorce. As a transient he could work himself to exhaustion. He was working eighteen hours a day until one murderous afternoon when three of his patients died on the operating table and he walked into the waiting room and saw twenty more. He understood then that there would never be enough hours

in the day to care for all the casualties, and that evening he checked
out of the hotel and found himself a small flat in a quiet neighborhood. Now he worked from sunup to sunset, only vaguely bothered
by his atrophied ability. (He had no time to read the truly advanced
medical journals, and it was years since he'd been inside a first-rate
hospital.) When the sun went down he went home. If there were
patients in the waiting room, they were told to come back tomorrow.
Sundays he worked on the hospital accounts.

He asked her, "Do you take days off?"

She looked at him strangely. "Well, not often. Every three or four
months I take a vacation. But when I'm here I work. I hustle. There
are more pictures here than I can ever take."

It was dusk and patients were strolling in the park. They wore blue
smocks and clogs and strolled in twos and threes around the gravel
paths. They walked very slowly, as sick people do. It was quiet outside, the light failing behind the shade trees, indistinct shadows reaching across the lawn. A soft breeze stirred the curtain. The doctor had
had too much wine and felt light-headed. He'd intended to return to
his office to check x-rays and then meet a colleague for dinner. But
he'd stayed on, talking to the girl, fascinated by her and wary of her
at the same time. He'd stayed with her while she ate her supper,
discreetly moving to the window when the nurse came at seven to
clear the tray and give her an alcohol rubdown. Now it was eight,
and he was tired and hungry and no longer sober.

"I must go," the doctor said.

"No, please don't."

"It's late. I've x-rays."

"We're having such a good time. Are you sad, all this talk about
the past?"

"No," he lied.

"It's like a reminiscence. Only a little bit damp. I like it. I like it
that we connect and it's not necessary to spell everything out."

"Yes and no," he said. He finished the last of his wine, thinking
about the singer, the one who had come and gone. She had been very
careful with her money, not so careful with his.

"This hospital. It's yours, isn't it?"

"Only partly. It's owned by a group — most of them are French."

"But you're the head man." She looked at him, smiling. "You
know there are rumors. I've heard that you treat enemy in here.
Important enemy, wounded or whatever and unable to get back to

their own base hospitals. You treat them anyway, the same as anyone else. Me."

"A charming story," the doctor said.

"And true."

"No comment, *rien*," he said, laughing. "This is an ordinary hospital. We have nothing to do with the military authorities."

"I can see that."

"We heal whoever comes to our door."

"I believe it." She was thinking that she would do the picture story when she got out of the hospital. But it would be necessary to get snaps of them actually in the operating room. It would make a dandy story, quite a coup. She wondered if she could talk the doctor into it. "Let me photograph it sometime," she said playfully.

"Yes, the next time General Giap comes in for a tonsillectomy I'll tell him you're here. D. from *Vogue*. *Vogue* wants to do a cover story on you, *mon général*. D. wants you in your fatigues and then in your black pajamas on the operating table." He began to laugh.

She protested, "I was joking!"

"No more jokes," he said. "You see the problem?"

"Yes-I-see-the-problem."

"I think you need another week here — seriously."

"I suppose so." She was no longer thinking about the picture story, concentrating instead on staying awake. She was drowsy from the wine and lulled by the doctor's voice.

"You're exhausted. I know you've been working too hard. It would not surprise me if you were working right now. You're depressed and it's had its effect on your body. All these things are connected . . ."

"Yes, *Doctor*." She did not feel depressed at all.

He smiled, knowing she found his bedside manner ludicrous. "You've been shaken up — you move around too much. You'll be all right, but you need rest. Sleep."

"I've been sleeping for a week," she murmured. Then, softly: "I'm having such a good time."

"It's as good as any place."

"Better."

He fell silent. It was awkward for him. He'd lived alone for so long, living in his work. The hospital rooms were as familiar as the rooms of his own flat. He knew their dimensions, the look of them at different hours of the day; those he'd slept in, those he hadn't. There'd been so many sick and wounded. This girl was not dangerously ill, only run-down and depressed; her nerve was fine.

"You're enchanting," he said in French, so softly that he was certain she could not hear. He didn't want her to think him foolish. The situation was banal. If anything was to happen, he wanted it to happen naturally, with no forcing. He repeated several other phrases in French to himself.

She looked at him and smiled. She moved toward him and put her cheek in his open palm. She felt his rough skin and kissed his wrist. He wore a battered brass bracelet that had turned his skin green and smelled like an old penny. She wrinkled her nose and pushed it back and forth on his wrist. She pressed his hand close to her cheek, and he bent down and caressed her hair with his lips. Then he had her face in both his hands, holding it lightly as he would a child's. His hands trembled slightly, but he did nothing to correct or disguise their tremor. His eyes shut tight, he put his face next to hers, very carefully so that his beard would not scratch her. He tried to erase his memory, to force the past from it. He wanted to live in the present as she did. They stayed like that a full minute, and when the doctor got up to leave it was all he could do to take his hand away from her skin. In a daze he leaned over and kissed her, hearing her gentle breathing.

"Tomorrow night," she said.

He smiled at her, nodding slightly.

"You're so good."

And you, he said in French.

"Please stay. Stay with me here." Her speech was slurred.

He shook his head and told her she was almost asleep as it was. She needed sleep. He'd be back in the morning — eight o'clock, as always.

She raised herself on one arm and brushed the hair from her forehead. "I want to ask you just one thing. Just one — something silly. Will you tell me? You won't hold anything back?"

He nodded, encouraged by the expression in her eyes.

"What kind of drugs are these?" She held up two bottles. "They aren't vitamins. They're bitter and they're the wrong size."

He said, "They help you sleep. They're harmless. Don't worry about them. I sometimes use them myself."

"They're tranquilizers, aren't they?"

He nodded.

She handed him both bottles and shook her head firmly, a quick shudder. She said, "No tranquilizers. Take them back. Give them to someone who needs them. No offense — there was no way you could've known. But I don't want *them*."

. . .

♦ He accepted the bottles. Both were more than half full; she could not have taken more than a couple of pills. He stood by the door, looking at her; she was flushed and smiling and determined in the big bed. She glanced away, her hand touching her cheek. She was almost asleep. He put the bottles in his pocket and backed out the door, still looking at her. In the hallway he paused and slumped against the wall, so tired, smiling privately and thinking to himself in French. The girl was formidable, a treasure. He looked back at the door, closed now. No, she didn't need tranquilizers. She didn't need them now. He'd understood that from the beginning. His doctor's intuition was exquisite, as always. So young — her vitality was returning; she'd be well in a week, and off to photograph her multitudes of green men. He shook his head sadly. What a run they could have had.

1974

# THE SHORT WAR OF

# MR. AND MRS. CONNER

♦

CONNER'S WIFE was French and self-possessed, a tart, petite
woman who cared for the amenities. Though she'd spent many
years in the United States, she spoke with a distinct accent, complete
with Gallic pout. Not a woman to suffer in silence, she made it very
clear what she thought of life in the zone. "This terrible place, these
dreadful people." Of all of us there at the time Conner was the only
one who'd brought his wife. The other wives either lived in Hong
Kong or Bangkok or had been left at home; a few of them refused to
come at all. The reason usually cited was the children.

Conner and his wife had no children. They were going to have one
later, after Conner's transfer from the zone. No one wanted to raise
a child in the middle of a war. Conner believed, and encouraged his
wife to believe, that the magazine he worked for would send him to
Western Europe when his tour was over. That was the usual procedure, Paris or Bonn a tangible expression of gratitude for the years a
man spent reporting the war. Conner was a serious and resourceful
war correspondent.

They lived in a small but well-appointed villa in a residential section of the capital. Conner had rented the villa at a time when most
of the rest of us were living in hotels. He explained that there was no
reason to live in a hotel when one could live in a house with an
adequate kitchen and servants. There was no reason for a man and
his wife to live like transients when in fact they were residents. He'd
promised his wife that much. And he'd seen what had happened to
"hotel wives" when their husbands were in the field reporting the

war. He did not want to subject his wife to the ennui of a hotel. He felt obligated to make their living arrangements as pleasant and natural as he could; hence the villa and its two servants.

Once a week Mrs. Conner would organize a dinner party. Those of us who were unattached looked forward to them because Mrs. Conner set a very fine table. In the beginning she behaved no differently in the zone than she would have in Paris. She'd quickly located all the best markets and wine shops and it was not at all unusual to arrive at the villa and find it soaked in the aroma of blanquette de veau or gigot roti. There were always two kinds of wine and a fine brandy later. The evenings at Conner's tended to be noisy because the food was excellent and the company always stimulating. Conner himself prepared the guest lists with some care. There'd always be one or two journalists, a middle-level army officer (usually a colonel whom Conner'd met and liked and wanted to cultivate), the CIA station chief and his attractive assistant, a foreign diplomat, and any unattached Western girls who happened to be around. There were always three or four of those, journalists or embassy secretaries. Conner and I had been friends for ten years, so I was more or less permanently invited along with the CIA man, who was usually good for a crumb of information late at night after brandy.

Dinner at Conner's was unlike dinner anywhere else in the zone, among our circle. It was planned; the menu was planned and the guest list was planned. There were fresh flowers on the table and a servant to mix the drinks and Bach on the stereo. Conner's wife would begin to prepare the meal at six, intending to sit down precisely at eight. But it never worked out that way. Someone was always late or didn't show up at all. This was not due to rudeness or thoughtlessness, just the situation. It was usual to get caught in the field without transportation or any reliable way to telephone regrets. Promptly at eight, Conner's wife would become nervous and count the guests. One or two were always missing. She'd wait fifteen minutes and then a half hour and finally we'd all sit down. "Jamie, the deen-ir will be ruined." "Nonsense, baby; it'll be delicious, formidable; it always is." "But what can I do, when people don't arrive when they say they'll arrive?" "It'll be fine." "It's impossible to plan anything here, nothing's compatible . . ." Of course the meal was always excellent and none of the rest of us even noticed the absentees or late arrivals. The first part of every meal was spent assuring Mrs. Conner that the veal was succulent and the wine delicious.

. . .

She was brought up in Paris, the only daughter of a prominent banker. They were a cultivated family and widely traveled. She'd spent two years at the Sorbonne and a year at a university in the United States, and when Conner met her she was working part time at the French consulate in New York. She thought his life looked very romantic and anticipated many years of travel.

When Conner was abruptly transferred to the Detroit bureau of the magazine, they decided to marry, though they'd known each other only a few months. Conner was thirty-five and a bachelor and instantly enchanted by her good looks and her sense of order. He believed she would bring a sense of arrangement and logic to his life; he thought it was time for him to grow up and cease being a nomad in the service of a news magazine. He was tired of girlfriends, he wanted a wife. As for her, she had a dour side; he felt that his own sense of fun would loosen her up.

They were in Detroit for a year and then moved back to the main office in New York. They were there another year and then transferred to Washington. Detroit, New York, and Washington were not Mrs. Conner's idea of "travel." When he was asked — ordered, really — to become the magazine's correspondent in the war zone, she was torn. Pleased at leaving America, she was apprehensive about living in the middle of a war. A very stupid war. A war that her countrymen had had the good sense to lose a dozen years before. But still it was foreign and friends told her that the capital retained some European ambience; indeed it had once been known as the Paris of the Orient. On the whole, friends said, it would be a welcome change from the brutality of American cities. And of course there were wonderful places nearby, Singapore and Bali to name two. Beyond that, there were very interesting people in the zone. A number of foreigners came through the capital to monitor the progress of the war. It was not at all unusual to have a drink on the veranda of the hotel and find Moshe Dayan deep in conversation at one table and John Steinbeck at another. Friends were optimistic. Who knew, one night she might induce André Malraux to her table. French was spoken everywhere, so she would have no trouble getting on with the local people.

But what she did not know and what her friends did not tell her, because it was so obvious, was that the zone resembled a prison. It resembled a prison because that was all anyone ever talked about: prison personalities, prison conditions, the duration of one's sentence, "the situation." And of course it was a war, and no one bothered to explain that to her either.

It was difficult for her because she never left the capital. At that time there was savage fighting in the countryside, and while most places were theoretically "secure," one could never be absolutely certain. She attempted to ignore the war and build a life as if it didn't exist. There was something oddly touching about her efforts, and a number of us tried to rally round. Of course there were others who wrote her off as a selfish bitch with no political consciousness, but I believe that was unfair. She was not American, she was French. The war had nothing to do with her. Those of us sympathetic to her wanted to see her succeed, I suppose in the same way that inmates of a mental hospital are pleased when a fellow patient is "cured." We believed that her efforts were doomed, but that made her attempt all the more gallant. Of course everyone was extremely fond of her husband, who was always cheerful and an excellent raconteur.

So she attempted to ignore the war and one way she did it was to assemble her dinner parties with care. She desperately tried to organize them in such a way as to lead conversation to other subjects: literature, art, what they were wearing in Paris, sex, religion. Anyone might at this point object: If that were true, why then invite journalists, army colonels, and spies to your table? The answer is that we were all there was. There wasn't anybody else, except for the occasional visitor — who was also there, one way or another, because of the war. She believed that by some trick or the force of her personality she could compel her guests to talk about *la réalité* — by which she meant real life, a life which had nothing to do with the situation in the zone.

Conner, on the other hand, was exhilarated by it. He was appalled by it, hated it, loathed the killing and the waste — and was exhilarated. It was not uncommon at the time. He spent two weeks of every month in the field, though as a concession to her he no longer accompanied the front-line troops. He knew he was doing first-class work and at the end of two years was the premier correspondent in the zone. He was forty and knew it was now or never. He tried to explain this to her and she replied that she understood. "J'comprends, Jamie. I understand, I *understand*." And it was true, she did. But she could not sympathize.

One night everyone arrived at the villa on time and sober. There was the usual crowd plus someone unique, a Frenchman, the owner of an art gallery in Paris. He was a Frenchman very much opposed to the war and was in the zone to collect children's art. He wanted to assemble an exhibit to tour Europe, the proceeds to go to orphans' relief. However, he was discreet in conversation and did not push his extreme views. He perceived very quickly that ours was a closed circle and that those of us who lived there had no interest in listening to the opinions of outsiders. We called them tourists. But Conner's wife was excited because she thought she could steer the table talk away from the war and onto neutral ground. She was eager to hear about life in France.

The Frenchman gave her an opening when he said he'd recently been in Biarritz, buying for a private collection.

Mrs. Conner turned to her husband, her eyes alive and glittering with memory. "Oh, Jamie, do you remember in Biarritz the casino? How much did you win?"

"A hundred and ten dollars, five hundred francs," Conner replied. "I had an unbeatable system. Five francs each on four numbers, thirty-one, thirty-two, thirty-three, and thirty-four. And I was smart enough to quit while I was ahead." He was looking at her, smiling. "You were my good luck charm."

"We drank champagne afterward. I remember, it was Pol Roger. Remember the crowd, Jamie. The demimonde . . ." For a few quick sentences, she lapsed into French. "Remember, we met those two who were off a yacht."

Conner explained, "We stopped off on our way out here. That was two years ago; it seems like yesterday."

She winked, smiling at the Frenchman. "It seems like two years ago to me."

I could see what she was trying to do and I wanted to help. I have never been inside a gambling casino in my life, but the subject looked promising. "There are wonderful casinos in the Caribbean. There are one or two in Puerto Rico which are very small, stakes not too high. And there's always the possibility of running into a Mafia type. Gun in a shoulder holster, that kind of thing."

She immediately interrupted, putting her hand on my arm. She didn't want to hear about the Mafia, or about guns. She turned to the Frenchman. "What did you do in Biarritz? Did you go to the casino? There's this wonderful restaurant, at the airport of all places. A specialty of seafood. But the casino —"

"No," the Frenchman said.

"One of these days Jamie and I are going to take a tour around the Mediterranean. When we get out of this place, that's the first thing we're going to do." She was talking very fast. "If we ever do get out of this place that's the first thing I want to do. All the old places, the old haunts that I knew before I was married. We will have several months of holiday time by then." She laughed harshly. "At this rate, perhaps six months . . ."

The CIA man, silent until then, spoke up. "You and Jamie ought to go to Macao. Very easy to get there and there's plenty of gambling on the ships. The casinos are all afloat. But the tables are run by the Chinese and they're hard cases. You won't win anything but it'll be fun. You can go over by hydrofoil, stay the night, and return the next day to Hong Kong. Macao still looks like a movie set; it's theoretically under the control of the Portuguese but the Chicoms really run it. It exists because they permit it to exist."

The Frenchman looked down the table. "Why is that, Monsieur?"

"It suits them. A little smuggling, some banking, a window on the West. It doesn't do them any harm and they find it useful. Of course they can shut it down any time they care to. Interesting ride from Hong Kong, you can run right along the Chinese border. Can actually see the mainland."

The Frenchman grunted but did not pursue the conversation.

Conner's wife looked at me with the expression of a woman drowning. I said, "Macao is to Biarritz as Charlestown racetrack is to Ascot."

Conner turned to the CIA man and said slyly, "I understand your people picked up a couple of Chinese in the last offensive."

The CIA man raised his eyebrows, as if that news came as a surprise to him.

Conner's wife smiled at the Frenchman. "I know you don't care —"

But the Frenchman had turned away and was listening to Conner and the CIA man. Conner said, "These Chinese were weapons experts, according to my information. Government troops killed one of them, your people have the other. That's the first time we've had any hard evidence of Chinese involvement —"

"They only talk about the war here," she said to the Frenchman.

"— documents left no doubt who they were or what they were doing." Conner smiled and sipped his wine, gazing steadily at the man from CIA. "I was told that there were quite a lot of documents."

"Anything's possible," he said. "I'll check it out."

Conner continued, "Incredible we haven't seen more of it." He looked up then, and smiled brightly at his wife. "Baby, this dinner is delicious." There was a chorus from the table, everyone assuring Conner's wife of her triumph. I looked at her, knowing she'd lost. I said, "It's the best French restaurant in town."

There was a brief pause; then suddenly the conversation became general. It revolved around the question of the Chinese and whether they were actively assisting the revolution. Conner was pressed to cite his sources, but he refused. Every few moments the man from CIA would nod and chuckle and mutter something gnomic. After ten minutes of this I looked over at Conner's wife. She was sitting straight as a soldier, staring at her food, picking at it, her lips a thin red line. To her left the Frenchman was leaning down table, absorbing every scrap of information. By then we all assumed he was something other than the owner of an art gallery. The talk rose in a crescendo, the wine bottles went around the table. Laughter was loud and frequent. From the Chinese we drifted to a discussion of the newest American assault rifle. I gave an account of my latest journey to the Delta. One of the American girls disclosed that the ambassador was ill with dysentery . . .

Mrs. Conner left the table directly following dessert, which of course was sublime. A pear drenched in kirsch.

That was the last dinner party for some time. Conner told me later that his wife pleaded with him to stay away from the war that night. Please, she'd asked; do it for me. But he couldn't, though he tried. The question about the Chinese was so natural to him, it just popped out. He proposed elaborate justifications, but he knew he was in the wrong and felt bad about it. And it was not the first time and he felt bad about that, too.

He suggested halfheartedly that she take a flat in Bangkok, but she refused. What would she do there? That was just a slightly safer version of the zone. She had no friends there. What would be the point? For a time he tried to involve her in the life of the community, and to that end she taught a class in English at one of the private lycées. But she found the children tedious and undisciplined and decided she was not a teacher after all. Of course she was bothered all the time now by the heat, and the new evidence of war: refugees were crowding the capital. Her conversation, never light, was now a monody of complaint.

One night the three of us were dining in the Chinese quarter. They'd been picking at each other all through dinner, and finally she turned to me for support.

"Hank, you tell him. Please, you know what our life is like. We've been here almost three *years*."

"Two and a half," he said.

I looked at Jamie, who'd been listening with a bored expression on his face. I liked his wife and was one of those sympathetic to her, though one's sympathies were wearing thin. But I knew better than to start advising her husband, my friend, on his career. "You've got to leave me out of it," I said.

"It won't be long," Jamie said. "A year, six months. Then it'll be over. Then we can live the life of the haute bourgeoisie in Paris. I'll get you a flat on the Avenue Foch. Isn't that what we both want, a flat on the Avenue Foch?" He looked at her evenly.

"Why then?" she demanded. "Why six months or one year? Why not now? Now. *Maintenant.*"

"Because I'm not finished," he said.

"What will change in six months or a year?"

"I'm not leaving in the middle of it," he said stubbornly.

She said, "This war will go on for a decade."

"No," I said. "Not a decade." Then I laughed. "Two decades."

"Do you know," she said. "Did you know I had my purse snatched in the market? I didn't tell you that, Jamie. Hank. That was last week, I still have the bruise on my arm." She extended her arm and we both looked at it. "It frightened me. So now I send the servants to do the marketing. And the food is not so good, they don't know good meat from bad. And they steal the market money. Ten percent, twenty percent is stolen. I am told it is the custom here. So now our food is less good and it costs twenty percent more. The wine, all of it is Algerian . . ."

She talked on and I stole a look at her husband. He was not listening and I knew why. He had just returned from a long and very bloody offensive. He had not told her about it. Probably he had not told her for the same reason that she had not told him about the purse snatching. He was saving it.

"War is hell," he said dryly.

An American woman might have flared, and come right back at him: that is unfair. It is unfair and unreasonable to be sarcastic. It is not fair to say that to your wife. But she didn't say any of those things. I think she was beyond sarcasm. She just looked at him and replied, "I am not accustomed to this life."

"You think I am?" He looked at her incredulously. "You think *they* are?" He meant the victims, the casualties of war.

"That is the point," she said with impeccable logic. "None of us are."

A month later they left for home leave, six weeks in Europe. Jamie told me that it was a nightmare because all his wife could talk about was the war and how dreadful their living conditions were. How frightening their life in the capital. How difficult to obtain even the simplest staples of life. He took her to the finest restaurants he could find and made a determined effort to be attentive and cheerful. He was prepared to forget the war for a month but she was not. He admitted to me in amazement that it was as if they'd switched roles. For that month he wanted nothing to do with the war and all she could do was remember it in every detail.

They took a motor trip through the south of France but life was not satisfactory there either. She complained that the Riviera was crowded and expensive, and there were too many American tourists. In that way it was exactly like the zone, except of course there was no shooting.

Finally late one night he suggested that they split. Just a temporary split. A separation, really. She could stay in Europe and he'd return to the zone for the remainder of his tour. It was impossible now for them to continue living together.

"It's like living on a battlefield," he said, laughing at the irony. They were lying in bed in a small hotel near Cap St. Jacques. A midsummer night's breeze fluttered the curtains, and moonlight gleamed on the Mediterranean.

"If you wish," she said stiffly.

"I don't 'wish' it at all," he said, the familiar irritation rising. "I don't 'wish' it, for Christ's sake. I don't see any other solution. If you see another solution, tell me what it is. Do you want to go back?"

"No," she said.

"Well?" He smiled in the darkness.

"It is not what I expected," she said. "This marriage is not what I expected."

He said, "Things seldom are."

"Well, then. There's nothing more to be said."

He walked to the window and looked out at the soft night, considering the changes in his life. He'd sublet the villa and move into the hotel. There would be no difficulty supporting her, although it would dent his savings account. Better all around, he thought. He

◆

could devote all his time to reporting the war and perhaps in the last six months he could secure his future forever. He had a hunch that after six months the war wouldn't be worth reporting. She was better off in France, he was better off in the zone. They had no children, the damage was minimal. He thought of a military after-action report: minor damage, light casualties. Perhaps later they could put it together and he could have the kind of life he'd always wanted. The war was one kind of order and a family was another. At the beginning of their life together in the zone they'd had a bit of fun. But she couldn't adapt. That was the trouble, it all came down to that.

The next morning he rose early and walked down to the port and bought a newspaper and a coffee and sat in a café. He was reading the international edition of the *Herald Tribune*, deep into an account of the latest offensive, when he felt movement behind him. It was she, looking bright as a new coin; she was smiling, as if she'd forgotten about the talk the night before. She was wearing her bikini and looking beautiful and fresh as the day he'd met her. She leaned over his shoulder, all smiles, and then froze. She saw what he was reading and pulled back. Her face went hard as iron and she turned on her heel and marched back to the hotel, packed her bags, and was gone before noon.

He told me later that that was the final irony; he'd only bought the paper to have something to read. He was just skimming it, not really thinking about the war at all. But perhaps it was a compulsion, like that night at dinner. He conceded that something in him wanted to dominate the war, and to do that he had to immerse himself in it. He knew that it was careless of him but that was the way it went. It was the way he was.

And the odd thing was that when he returned to the zone he stayed only three months, not six, and the magazine did precisely what he expected them to do. They sent him to London with a vague assignment to write about personalities. He set himself up in a flat in Chelsea and reported show business for two years. Show business, the art market, sex, religion. When I saw him last I asked him if he ever saw his wife and he shook his head. Never, he said. She lived in Paris. Oh, once he saw her picture in one of the French magazines. She was hanging on the arm of some count. He laughed; some member of the minor nobility. He looked at me. What the hell, he said. Probably some count who'd never done anything in his life, never worked; never accomplished anything. Some idler, a *paresseux*, who didn't know the score.

Much later that same night he admitted he was sorry they'd never had a child. The child might have saved it. The child might have bound them together, given him the order and logic he wanted so badly. And given her a *raison d'être*. But the zone was no place for children.

1976

# JOURNAL OF A

# PLAGUE YEAR

◆

IN THE AFTERNOON the shooting stopped and the dead were lying under the rubber trees on canvas stretchers. There were eight dead and an aid tent nearby with a dozen wounded. It was hot and very still. The grove of rubber trees was situated on a flat plain, inland from the sea; the plain was littered with military machinery. Naval gunfire was still falling, and they could hear the explosions a mile or two away. Soldiers were sprawled under the trees, smoking dope and drinking beer and talking quietly. Someone had a radio turned to AFRTS, and the soldiers' heads nodded to the beat. They paid no attention to the dead, who were covered with green rubber ponchos; the dead blended into the vegetation, and after a while they were scarcely noticeable at all. They might have been men sleeping, unless you looked closely at their hands, which were rigid and gray.

She noticed that their boots looked new, hardly worn at all; two of the rifles had not been fired; they had full clips and were still on safety. She wrote these details in her notebook. She had no desire to see the faces, but she wondered if the dead had head wounds, and whether the wounds were gunshot or shrapnel. The colonel had told her they had run into snipers, and the wounded men in the tent confirmed that. The colonel said he had never seen such accurate sniper fire, and his lead element had lost a dozen dead and wounded in the first few minutes. They had been moving through the rubber trees on line, and had taken all their casualties in the first half hour. Those included the company commander and his RTO. It took a while for the company to regroup and understand where the fire was coming from. Officially, the report read that they had bumped an enemy battalion. But hell, the colonel said, it could have been just a few enemy; five or six snipers, who'd been very cool and deliberate about their business. Sniping, he said; that was a tactic that one way or another dated back to the Peloponnesian Wars, Athens and Sparta. There was nothing new or different about sniping.

She stood a little distance away taking pictures, framing the shot to catch the dead in the foreground and the soldiers relaxing in the rear. She shot a dozen pictures in different focuses to make the ironic point. There were a number of ways to get various effects: blur the foreground and sharp-focus the rear, or vice versa. Or use the depth of field to pull the entire picture in sharp. She practiced with different settings, regulating the light and shade, although everything would depend on the darkroom and how it was handled there. Not that it made any difference; they seldom printed her pictures.

Someone handed her a can of beer and she sat down, cradling the camera. The dead were at eye level now, and she took the camera and shot the rest of the film, shooting with the boots in the foreground. It was a disgusting and witless business, but she was there for a purpose, and she thought she ought to get all she could. Just then she knew that someone was looking at her, and the vibrations were not friendly. Without glancing up she put the camera away, stuffing it hard into her rucksack and staring straight ahead. After a moment or two she shifted her eyes, and saw a soldier staring at her. The soldier's face was hard with hatred. After a minute, he looked away. Then she got up and walked away to find the landing zone, and a helicopter that would take her back to Division.

That night they were all drinking in the third-floor suite and quite early she left with another journalist to have a nightcap and then go to bed. They had one or two drinks; the journalist wanted to talk about his love affair with an airline stewardess. He was wondering if he should ask his office to extend his tour. His paper sent their correspondents on six-month tours; the assignment was passed around the office like a penalty.

"See, she's based out of Hong Kong and I could work at least three more visits there if I'd apply for an extension. Christ, I'm really in love with her. Fallen for her, you know?"

"I'd reapply, then." She was thinking about her story, the fight that afternoon. She could write the story around the interviews with the wounded and the colonel, folding in some description of the grove of rubber trees and the dead. She could write it from the point of view of the enemy.

"I hate this goddamned town, and the war that goes with it. This crummy hotel and the money-grubbing people." He took a long swallow of his drink, staring at her over the edge of the glass.

What did you say to that? It was better in the field?

"She's something, look at this." He handed over a picture of a very blond girl in a bikini. "This was taken on one of the beaches in Hong Kong. She's nice, no? She's a swinger, that's really what she likes to do in life. It was a hell of a lot of fun in Hong Kong. We went shopping. I got a Nikon and some threads. Three fittings in three days." He paused, smiling. "You ought to find a man."

"Is one lost?"

"Something permanent for a little while."

They sat quietly, drinking the last of a bottle of Scotch. It was near midnight; she thought she ought to be in bed. She wondered whether to write the story that night or in the morning. She thought it was better to write it fresh, with no complications. The other started to talk about his stewardess again, how she had changed his life. He said she was uninhibited, that was the best part about her. The voodoo princess from BOAC. He was very relaxed and happy, sitting back in the big chair. All the rooms of the hotel were similar: same beds, same furniture. A stereo set in the corner, freshly laundered fatigues hanging on a hook near the door; military gear, knapsacks and canteens. She felt pleasantly tired; it had been a strain, making three airplane connections from the field. They finished the last of their drinks and she got up to go.

"She's a hell of a girl."

"Al, you're the envy of your friends."

"Why don't you stay?"

She laughed and stepped into the silent hall and walked down to the elevator. She was excited at the thought of writing the story in the morning, two pots of coffee in the room. She'd take three, four hours writing the story, then have a long and languid lunch. No, not the elevator; there was a better idea. She walked down two floors and knocked on another door, after listening quietly for a moment and hearing music from within. The door opened a notch.

"It's me," she said.

"Back from the wars."

She leaned against the doorjamb, and smiled.

"It's late," he said.

"Ten minutes of talk," she said. "Then I'll go."

The door opened wider and she walked in. He climbed back into bed. She was carrying two note pads, and she put those on the night table. Then she stretched out on the bed and kissed his elbow. He smiled and touched her cheek. He was reading one of Céline's books, the book open and lying on his chest.

She was suddenly very sleepy. "I don't know how you can read novels of that kind, here, in this place. The place is crazy enough without compounding it. I think one's reading ought to be very highly structured. Sears catalogues. The Book of Genesis. Shakespeare's sonnets. Captured enemy documents. Céline will drive you crazy. Everything that's in Céline is present here as well. There are a number of very important concepts here that Céline has not begun to touch."

"Invincible ignorance," he said.

She yawned, very sleepy now.

"You would be better informed if you read Céline."

"Crazier," she mumbled.

"Did you get a good story today?"

"Unh."

"Make notes? Did you get to the bones of the myth? Did you count the dead? Did the dead count you? How many puzzled expressions today? Any fanciful explanations?"

"Thought about you," she said. Her eyes were closed; she could feel his palm. She was almost asleep. He was speaking very softly to her, touching her head and her neck. She moved closer to him, dreaming about him. She dreamed they were in bed together, making love. She dreamed he loved her, they loved each other. She was dreaming before she was asleep.

When she woke in the morning he was gone.

◆

In the fall she went home on leave, back to Washington. She found Washington nervous and agitated, though the weather was gorgeous. It was a poisonous atmosphere, and she endured three Washington dinner parties where she was lectured on the war. They had all the textbook answers, orders of battle, force levels, kill ratios, free fire zones, A and B levels of pacification, endurance estimates, morale factors — all of them classified. Washington was harsh and metallic, edges everywhere. She received three cables from him. She stayed with friends and watched television programs in the evening, news reports from the war zone. It was peculiar, seeing her friends on television, watching them doing their stand-ups with gunfire in the background. Seeing the streets of the city, more familiar to her now than any American city, she bored her friends with travelogues. Her paper obliged her to deliver lectures, and she found she could not talk persuasively about what she had seen. She had no powers of recall. She could write about it, but she could not talk about it; the emotion was something within. The lectures were a failure except for one television appearance when she spoke from notes. Reading the notes afterward, she decided that what she'd said were lies. She related these episodes to him in a long letter that took her most of the morning to write; it was difficult to connect their lives.

But in Washington they thought it was fantastic, what she was doing. Fantastic. They thought she made a difference, made them uncomfortable in the Department of Defense. The trouble with Washington, they said, was that it was too comfortable. She reached them with her war stories, she was way down deep.

"Whatever they're paying you, it's not enough."

"It's enough," she said.

"No, really. It's fantastic. Are you going to stay for long? Six months more? A year? You ought to think about a return to America, and reporting from Capitol Hill. They're crying for women now. You could write your own ticket. Do such a good job. I don't know how you stand it, where you are."

"Invincible ignorance," she said.

"Oh, we know how it is. You don't have to play that role with us. We know how it must be, or perhaps we don't. Perhaps we can't conceive. But you're well read."

She was confused; two or three of them were talking at once. For a lunatic moment she felt like one of those Japanese soldiers who are found on Guam or Saipan or somewhere, holding out twenty-six years after the surrender. It put her off to be told that the stories were being read, although, of course, she knew that; but it was better knowing it at a distance. It seemed to her that people were looking over her shoulder. She took a drink from a passing waiter and backed away.

"God," one of them breathed. They were being very solicitous, kind in their way. But it was an invasion, and what was she supposed to say?

"If you're telling the truth in your stories, then it must be the most dreadful place. Crazy. I mean, crazed. Don't you hate the war?

Though it's exciting, of course. It's a hell, it must be sixth or seventh circle. No kidding now, just how bad is it? On the other hand, you must be making a bundle."

"I'm the happiest I've been," she said.

◆

She made her way west, cabling him from San Francisco. She gave him her flight number and time of arrival. She was enthusiastic, flying into the city; she'd decided that if she was so valuable and fantastic, then she could fly first class. She was going to stop in Tokyo, but decided against that. She would come in straight as a die from Southern California, reading books and listening to tapes. A bottle of wine, no sleep, sunrise over the Pacific. There was plenty of time for thought, five miles above the Pacific Ocean. She was sorry now that she'd left the war. Washington had given her nothing; home leave was a misnomer. She had to be arch about it, and tell them that she did not relate to the environment. Everything in Washington was pale by comparison; there was nothing to be seen with the eyes. It was antiseptic. Washington was insincere, it had no structure, its life was loose and at odds. He'd asked her to buy some books for him in America, and she had those in her carry bag. It was a gaudy assortment: Robbe-Grillet, Bernard Fall's latest book, *Bleak House, Black Mischief, A Sentimental Education,* the short novels of Henry James. She wondered how Henry James would relate to the environment, how Henry James would handle the five o'clock briefing. Follow that through: it was a turn of the screw removed from the Home Counties and Pall Mall. It was a pleasure buying the books, and having them with her.

In a rumpled dress, swinging the carry bag, she alighted from the airplane in heat of a hundred degrees. She stood to one side at the base of the ramp, searching for him in the crowd. The other passengers swept past her, construction foremen, diplomats, army officers, people who in one way or another were involved in the war. She didn't see him on the tarmac; strange, because he said he'd be there. She walked toward the waiting room, sad, searching with her eyes. She was anxious to see him, and slightly panicked now; she'd thought there was something formidable and intimate about his meeting the airplane. The place was entirely familiar to her.

She saw him then, standing alone against the wall of the waiting room, staring straight ahead, puzzled. He looked at her, then past her. His eyes floated past, his hands were in his pockets. She walked up to him, smiling — and when he saw her he gave a little start, and grinned shyly. He shook his head, as if he'd awakened from a nap. She kissed him, unaware that anything was wrong.

"I've got your books."

"Oh, good."

"They're in the carry bag, all of them. I couldn't get one of them in French. All they had was the English."

"I don't mind."

"But the rest of them are here. James and the others." She opened the carry bag so he could see the books.

"Well, how was it? Did you like it? I'm sorry about the cables, but I was worried when I didn't hear."

"I didn't like it at all. If it's news to you, *they're* the ones behind bars, in straitjackets. I'm glad to be back. To be here with you."

The passengers were moving past them; there was a long line at customs. He motioned to the bar in the waiting room. They were in no hurry, and it was useless to try to accelerate the customs process. Customs proceeded at a deliberate pace.

"I've got a car outside. Let's have a drink, then go through the line."

"It's *so* long, I'll get in line now."

"It's an hour either way."

"Maybe there'll be someone that we know. You wait. I'll go through now."

He saw small beads of perspiration on her forehead and cheeks. She hated the heat; it affected her badly. He dried her forehead with the back of his hand, and kissed her again. She smiled and gripped his arm. He kissed her again, more gently, then drew away. She looked weary, tired, and drawn.

"Are you all right?"

She smiled brightly and nodded. The heat.

"No, seriously."

"I'm on pins and needles," she said, still smiling.

"Let's get a drink."

"No, I'll go through the line. I'll be very quick."

He shrugged. "Sure. When will the war end?"

They didn't talk much in the car, and later, in the hotel, they circled each other, wary. They made love very roughly. He was not with her, and she knew then that something was very wrong. She pressed him for explanations, but it was useless. He said it was impossible to explain correctly, so he would not explain at all. He looked at her strangely, as if he'd expected someone else; usually so cheerful, he did not smile at all. The next day he moved out of their hotel room to an apartment near the cathedral. He said that life was confusing, and she wished him good luck on that. She had her work, but she was sorry just the same. He was as much a part of her life as the work. But she was stoic about it, there being no real alternative; she would stay busy and would not lack company. Mystified, she let him be, to work out whatever it was.

◆

Circumstances drew them together again. Much later, when he'd tried everything to get her back, and had been successful in a temporary way, he told her about the morning at the airport, and what had happened later. She didn't want to hear about it particularly, but he told her anyway. He said he could describe it, but not explain it; the emotions were complicated. He said he hadn't recognized her. "You were someone else altogether. I didn't recognize you until you were five feet away, looking me in the face. I saw you standing at the bottom of the ramp, but I didn't know . . . who you were. Three weeks was a millennium. You were a stranger. I didn't know what to expect. Until we were face to face, and I saw you smiling at me, I didn't connect. I knew that it had to be you, because you were looking at me in a special way, and when you spoke I recognized your voice. You looked like you ought to look, and then you kissed me. But your face was unfamiliar. Were you different in some way? I thought so, but I didn't understand it. You were a stranger, so later when we were together it was like being with a stranger. And to have that, after everything that had happened before. You: a woman casually picked out of a crowd at an airport, a woman in a slept-in dress and an old carry bag. A beautiful woman bringing books, neither young nor old. I could've died. In a week or two, I knew you again, but it was a different acquaintance. I remembered all the things we'd done together. But that morning at the airport, the surface escaped me."

She understood him. To her sorrow she knew exactly what he meant. "This place has no memory," she said. "If anything leaves, it's forgotten, and if it returns, it has to begin again. No memory, no loyalties."

"No moving parts," he said.

She shook her head and sighed. "It was pretty bad in the hotel room."

"I'm sorry about it," he said.

"I know."

"I didn't understand."

She gave him a rueful little smile. "How could you?" she asked.

They lived together on tiptoe, quietly and conservatively, stepping lightly, under strain. They reported to each other as they reported the war, at a distance. They became oddly domesticated, as toward the end of her tour she began to avoid the battlefield. She avoided small units, and except for one week with the navy never left the city for more than two days at a time. She knew what to expect in the field; there was nothing more to say about the dead. There was neither virtue nor innocence nor anything else except paradox; even irony, her most reliable weapon, was worn out. She took her evidence, the scenes and the dialogue, from radio operators in colonels' tents. Interviews in hospital wards. After-action reports. Ex post facto accounts. Briefings. She knew all the colonels now, and two or three of them were at pains to alert her when a major operation was under way. She convinced herself that the war had moved into a political phase, and that the battlefield story was less important than the political one. Coincidentally, this happened to be true. But she was still wonderful at what she did, supplying immediacy and drama to the episodes of the war. That did not change, though everything else did.

At length he left for America, and they maintained a sporadic correspondence. She reported on activities in the provinces, he on the atmosphere in Washington. These were detailed, factual letters, suitable for a collection. She would write the letters as carefully as she wrote her newspaper articles, and assumed he did likewise. But nothing was the same after the afternoon in the airport. She didn't know whose fault it was, or if it was anyone's fault; but there were no more dreams in any case. She remembered his words often, and they were troubling. She had always thought of herself as a stranger — and what if that were true after all? Where did that leave her?

1973

◆

# CEASE-FIRE

◆

A T THE END of the day we gathered in McDonough's room. The
games of bridge began in his air-conditioned sitting room, then
moved to the balcony when the sun went down. From McDonough's
balcony we could see all the points of interest, the embassy and the
Presidential Palace and the lately abandoned United Nations Command Post. The games lasted for an hour or for eight hours, depending on the way the cards fell. Dummy was expected to watch the city
below, looking for suspicious traffic and listening for sudden noise.
But the island was quiet. The cease-fire was holding, thanks to Ned
McDonough and me.

We played bridge on a wrought-iron table on the balcony, and
when the game was interesting McDonough would call room service
and we would eat in. We were tired and had lost the taste for long
hours in the hotel bar and late, muddled meals with the ladies and
gentlemen of the press. At the table were McDonough and me, General Grandoni, and the general's aide-de-camp, a Pole named Molz.
We drank beer or lemonade, complained about the weather, and
discussed the situation on the island. McDonough turned up the volume on Brahms and we spoke softly, in German so that Molz could
understand. We four got on fairly well; everyone wanted to see the
negotiations succeed so that we could leave the island. Even Molz
was cooperative.

Grandoni was the secretary general's personal representative. He
and McDonough met with the combatants every afternoon. Molz
was present as amanuensis. I was the inside man, verifying the viola-

◆

tions and interpreting the protocol. In the beginning we were a team of twenty specialists and a battalion of Yugoslav troops, the peace-keeping force. But now there were just the four of us, Grandoni the chairman, McDonough the negotiator, and I the lawyer. Molz had no function, but he was a Communist and it was important that the delegation be balanced. In the evenings around the bridge table we would discuss the afternoon's meeting and set an agenda for the next day. Grandoni, Molz with him like a shadow, would leave for the Swiss embassy at seven to cable a message to the secretary general. Then, alone, McDonough and I would decide between us what would be done the next day; the words McDonough would use and in what order and with what inflections. We made an odd pair, McDonough an Irish radical and I a pragmatic American. However, he was more radical than Irish and I was more American than pragmatic.

Radical, in the sense that he went to the roots of things. He was the least self-deluded man I have ever known, and it is no contradiction to add that he was a romantic in his own fashion, a high-bouncing lover and patron of the arts. McDonough accompanied me some-times to the small museum near the marketplace. I took tea with the curator most days in the late afternoon, finding him valuable in a number of unexpected ways. He was an anthropologist and enjoyed retailing legends of the island's glorious past. He wished us success in our negotiations but doubted that anything permanent could be achieved. He believed that his island was cursed, a concept that ap-pealed to Ned. One afternoon on impulse I gave him a personal check for three hundred dollars. For the new dig, I said. Smiling bleakly, murmuring thanks, the curator tucked the check away in his vest pocket. Magnanimous, Ned said when we left. What do you think that'll get you? A ticket out of here? Is it a talisman? I nodded. That was exactly what I thought, or hoped.

I amused myself in the early mornings by writing lengthy letters to my wife, describing my colleagues and the atmosphere on the island. Two weeks ago I did something I have never done, with my wife or with anyone else. I wrote her a long pornographic letter. Diana, surprised but game, tried to reply in kind but her letter was clumsy and self-conscious and at the end she appended a postscript, news of the children. Then yesterday she called and said it was time I de-manded to be relieved; six weeks was too long and the island was now quiet. She said she was better in the flesh, which was true, and that she and the children were lonely without me. I warned her that one did not "demand" anything from Niccolò de Grandoni, count, patriot, warrior, and personal representative of the secretary general. General Grandoni followed instructions to the letter and we four would remain on the island until the assignment was concluded. Probably four more weeks, I told her. But why didn't she come for a long weekend? No, no, she said; that was impossible. She asked me why McDonough couldn't do what I did. I began to laugh, because I'd told her a little of McDonough's temperament. I said, Not a chance.

That night at eight the general returned from the Swiss embassy, mustaches bristling, with the news that he'd spoken personally to the secretary general at a golf club in the county of Westchester. He, Grandoni, was to return immediately to New York. I was to return to my base in London. The feeling inside the secretariat was that our mission should be downgraded, "made inconspicuous," and therefore an encouraging sign to the combatants. McDonough began to laugh but Grandoni silenced him with a look. "You and Molz are to remain," Grandoni said. "Indefinitely," he added maliciously. Molz sat with a satisfied expression, examining his boots. After a few more words Grandoni and Molz departed.

I saluted McDonough with the glass of lemonade and he began to chortle softly. He was sitting with his feet on the balcony railing, looking into the square below. He picked up his discards and began to sail them, one by one, into the night. "Dumbest damn thing I ever heard of. In forty-eight hours this place will explode. Again." He continued to pitch the cards over the balcony. "Now what am I supposed to do? With you gone, I'll have to take up womanizing again. As an alternative to gin rummy with Molz. It's disgusting."

I said, "Remember that girl —"

"Sonia," McDonough said. "And she's gone. I checked."

I had not been thinking of Sonia. "Sonia was trouble."

"Ned McDonough would rather die of trouble than die of boredom." The last of the cards flew into the night and McDonough slapped his palms, satisfied. I stood and looked over the balcony. No one was in the square, but a few of the cards were still floating in the thick night air. "Well," I said. "We did good work."

"Not so bad."

"We did very good work the first three weeks."

"Once we shook Comrade Molz," McDonough amended. "We made a hell of a team."

I said, "I'm not anxious to spend another minute here. But this is premature. They've made a mistake. And it's a pain in the ass for you —"

He shrugged, gazing across the darkened square. "It's no matter to me whether I stay for another week or another month. Weeks, months; it's all the same to me. I'd just as soon be here as anywhere." We both smiled. "And it'll be interesting even so, even with Molz. Maybe especially with Molz."

"I'm glad to be going," I said bluntly. He asked me if I was laying over in Athens and I said I was. There was a long wait between planes. I was impatient to get to my room and pack. If I caught the midnight plane to Athens I could be in London by tomorrow evening. McDonough smiled strangely and reached into his desk and brought out a single key on a silver chain. "You can have my flat for the night. No one's there. I haven't seen the place in months. I'll give you a note for the concierge and you can leave the key with her when you leave." I took the key, surprised; McDonough had said nothing about a flat in Athens. "Damn nice flat, I've had it for years." He reached for the pitcher of lemonade, then thought better of it and poured us two cognacs. The night was warm and the lemonade tepid. "Time for Ned to return to his old haunts," he said. "And it is most definitely time for a new companion." Suddenly I was sorry to leave him; I suspected that he and Molz would make a destructive combination. We sat and talked for a while and then I went to my room, packed, checked out of the hotel, and left for the airport.

Of course the flight was delayed. I sat in the airport bar, watching mechanics tinker with the landing gear of the 707. It was not a sight to inspire confidence and I was inclined to return to the hotel and take a morning plane. But I was sick of that particular Hilton, it seemed to me that I'd spent half my life in Hilton hotels. Men do travel in diverse ways. I have a friend who takes an attaché case containing nothing but personal effects from his bedroom at home. This friend believes that if he duplicates his own bedroom in a hotel he will be less tense and lonely, and perhaps he is; he says he is. I travel with three suitcases of clothes, though I think of my trips as interregnums; they are parentheses in my life (though my wife believes the reverse). The particular work that I do is specialized and technical and requires concentration and I would rather not be reminded of Diana and the children and my house in St. John's Wood. I bring nothing personal except my worn copy of Walter Lippmann's *A Preface to Morals,* which I read when I become discouraged. It is really about politics, not morals, as indicated by the title to the first chapter: "Whirl Is King." On the road I tend to be all business, except at those times when I encounter men like McDonough. Thank God it isn't often; they're magnets to men like me. Laughter and excitement follow them wherever they go, or seem to, their lives buoyed by luck and privilege. In a way they resemble royalty, envied and resented by turns. The relationship is political: if McDonough were a government, he'd be overthrown. I envy his anarchic life, no possibility ignored. His life seems to me a work of art, a created thing, and I am aware that that says as much about me as it does about him. He told me once that he viewed his existence as a romance, meaning something removed from ordinary concerns, a life with no ties or duties or special loyalties to anything except himself and his work.

He'd found a girl in the bar of the hotel the first week. We called her Anne of the Thousand Days, an evidently rich and certainly comely heiress from Fitzgerald country who filed intermittently for the Voice of America, making the Troubles sound like a drunken lunch at Tuxedo Park. Of course she and McDonough had friends in common, and one of these turned out to be an old lover of Ned's. It was as if they'd discovered a mutual godmother, and Anne of the Thousand Days knew immediately that Ned would "do." The VOA recalled her after three weeks, so the affair languished, though naturally they corresponded. McDonough corresponded with women everywhere; no post was satisfactory unless it brought scented letters from women. It is reasonable to suppose that this confident life had flaws; most lives do. There was after all no family and no one person he was bound to; he had made few promises; his life lacked essence. And what would happen to him when he was old? A work of art, whether portrait, sonnet, or symphony, had an end as well as a beginning: a last brushstroke, a fourteenth line or coda. Anne of the Thousand Days, like the others, slipped out of his life as easily as she had slipped into it. Of course I never asked him if at times, late at night, he yearned for a home and family. It would have been like asking Bakunin if really, truly, he wouldn't, honestly now, rather be a businessman. No, he would not. Would anyone? Would I?

The plane left at three A.M. I spent the last hour in the airport bar with one of the stewardesses, who confided to me that the difficulty was not with the landing gear but with the pilot. He had not arrived and a search was under way. But I was not to worry; this happened frequently and the delay was never more than a few hours. I replied quickly that it didn't matter to me; three hours, six hours, it was all the same. I was going home and my conscience was clear.

I did not sleep at all on the plane, and approaching Greece in a brilliant sunrise, I found myself ravenously hungry. Throttling down, the plane shuddered and I watched the sunlight play on the water. Athens was a marvelous city. I reflected that my work tended to take me to second-rate countries; but there was always a first-rate city nearby. Nearly always. I had been in most of the second-rate countries of the world, and nearly all of the first-rate cities, always on business . . . organization business. Inside the terminal I paused at a newsstand to buy the papers and a magazine and a postcard, intending to send the postcard to McDonough. Then I looked at the flight schedules. The next plane for London was at noon. There were others at three and at five-thirty. I stood looking at the departure times, then went to fetch my bags. Outside, surrounded by luggage, light-headed in the early morning coolness, I looked for the stewardess. We had agreed to share a cab downtown, she to her hotel and I to Mc-Donough's flat. She waved from an ancient Mercedes and as we moved away from the terminal I thought suddenly that it would be wonderful to drive to the port and have breakfast, a full *carte* of fish and wine, a dessert, and strong coffee. I felt like celebrating; it was not a morning to sleep through. We could sit in the café under an awning and watch the boats put out to sea. The stewardess was easily convinced and I told the driver to take us to the best café at the port.

She was petite and trim in her blue skirt and white blouse, and her appetite was healthy. She was not indifferent to wine and we drank two bottles of Roditis. I described my six weeks on the island, making them sound more amusing than they were. Not mentioned were the museum or the marketplace or Grandoni or Molz or Anne of the Thousand Days. The stories were of McDonough and me, two raffish businessmen at play. She said she hated the island, the tension at the airport; half the flights were delayed for one reason or another. I confided finally that I missed London and was happy going home. I had enjoyed the island but was anxious to return to my normal routine. In the last analysis, I said, the island's Troubles were of no lasting significance. "The situation is hopeless but not serious," I said with a smile. She smiled back. "Except for the women and children, of course," she said.

By nine we were both yawning. The sun blinded us, the waters of the harbor flashing like diamonds. I had shed my coat and tie and was sitting in shirt sleeves, sweating. The café was crowded now and we sat with our backs to the water. She looked at me and said she had to get some sleep. I paid the bill and hailed a cab, wondering whether she would come to McDonough's flat with me. Inside the cab I turned toward her but she had pulled away into the corner of the seat, her eyes closed. I stared at her a long moment, hoping her eyes would open or her face give some other sign of life. Finally I decided that negotiations would be long, complicated, and probably unsatisfactory. I touched her hand and when she stirred without reply or answering pressure I turned away, suddenly angry, believing that I had somehow been cheated, or had cheated myself. My light-headedness returned when she opened the door and got out, saying goodbye with a tight smile and a polite wave. I thought it was just as well.

McDonough's flat was only five minutes from her hotel. The concierge was out and I walked up the three floors and let myself in with the key on the silver chair. The wine had made me languid and I leaned against the doorjamb, looking into Ned McDonough's deathly silent apartment. I put my bags down and listened in the darkness a moment, and then I switched on the living room lights. The room was comfortably furnished, indubitably a man's room — but that was not what astounded me. The walls of the living room and every free surface were crowded with photographs. They were photographs of McDonough, a woman of his own age, and various children, singly and together. A sideboard accommodated three photographs, and an end table four. They covered the walls, photographs of every conceivable shape and size. I moved forward in the silence, looking more closely, peering at them. I saw a handsome family at play, McDonough with his arm around a young boy on a porch swing, McDonough and the woman smiling together, their arms linked, pointing; the picture was off-center; it had no doubt been taken by a child. There was McDonough and two children on a boat somewhere; McDonough holding an infant; the woman and a young girl (unmistakably mother and daughter) on a beach; a rowdy birthday party; standing with fishing rods on a wooden dock; in a loaded station wagon. There were photographs everywhere, some of them overexposed and out of focus, like those in any family album. I was dismayed because it was obvious from the first moment that this was McDonough's family, preserved in frames. I felt as if I'd been caught looking through his wallet or diary. The photographs were entirely private; excruciatingly so, for they revealed nothing to an outsider. It was like looking at a military atlas of an unfamiliar war: the outlines of the struggle were visible, the sides advanced and retreated, ground was gained and lost — but what was at stake? Who were the combatants? There were a man, his wife, and the children.

The youngest boy was self-conscious. The oldest boy looked like his father. The girl was pretty like her mother. McDonough had never hinted at any of this and it was then that I remembered the peculiar smile when he'd offered me the key to his flat, not visited "in months."

I wandered into the bedroom, still feeling a trespasser. The closet was filled with men's suits and on his bureau was a formal portrait of his wife, this one obviously made by a professional. She was a tall woman with wide-set eyes and long dark hair. I turned away in confusion, then looked back at her; she had an alluring mouth. McDonough's wife was wearing a man's shirt and khaki pants and her thumbs were hooked into her belt. She was staring straight into the camera's lens. I took off my shirt and trousers and went into the bathroom, grateful that there were no photographs on the tiled walls. I stood in the shower and soaked, my thoughts muddled. I had gone from high gear to low in thirty minutes. I decided to call Diana right away and tell her I would take the noon plane. She always met me at Heathrow.

I went straight to the telephone from the shower. The housekeeper answered after one ring. No, Mrs. Lyons was not at home. She had tried to reach me yesterday and again this morning but the Hilton did not know my whereabouts. Mrs. Lyons was concerned, it was an inconvenience. I listened to all of this with mounting irritation. At any event, the housekeeper said, my wife had received an urgent message from America. Her brother was ill and she had flown to New York to be with him. She intended to return on Monday or at mid-week, depending. It was apparently not critical, but it was serious. I said nothing. Diana's brother was an invalid. Their parents were dead and brother and sister were uncommonly close. Diana and her hound, I thought bitterly. I asked how the children were and the housekeeper replied dryly that they were fine, of course; both of them were at school. I gave the housekeeper the telephone number of Ned's flat. In case Diana called home she was to relay it, please. But I would call her myself later in the day, in New York, at the clinic where her brother lived. The housekeeper asked coldly when I was returning to London. I said I'd let her know and hung up.

I looked into the kitchen and opened the refrigerator. It was well stocked, unopened tins of orange juice and a bottle of milk and plates of ham and cheese and eggs in a wire basket. *Damn,* I said aloud, remembering the stewardess and how she looked in the back seat with her eyes closed. I was breathing the iced air of the refrigerator and trying to think clearly. No point now to take the noon plane. I was tired and feeling the aftereffects of the wine and sleeplessness. I wished I'd negotiated with the stew after all. I backed out of the kitchen and went to the window, the curtains drawn against the sun. I felt surrounded by McDonough's family, the pretty woman and the children and their life together, all of it mysterious. I thought of Ned and his suite at the Hilton, and the late night bridge games; it seemed a world away. I pulled apart the curtains and stood looking into the street below, burning in the sun; the street was white as an eyeball and deserted. I could see my reflection in the glass and that was in no way reassuring. My face was drawn and lined and I needed a shave. No, I thought; I needed sleep. A long sleep now, and rational plans later.

Well, hell; the poor bastard. Diana's brother had polio when he was a child. His recovery was nearly complete when complications developed. Then his mother died and a month later his father was killed in an auto accident. He was thirty now and lived in a private clinic on the East Side of New York, a young man who quickly attracted sympathy and just as quickly repelled it. He possessed a sharp and savage tongue; loathing himself, cursing the cards he'd been dealt, he chose to blame his sister. He crooked his finger and Diana jumped always. And he always managed to crook his finger at rotten times.

I stood staring into the street, then shook my head and went on into McDonough's bedroom. I avoided looking at the walls or at the woman in the picture frame. I took off all my clothes and stood there a moment, my socks in my hand. Sleep, I thought; a long sleep. I muttered a brief apology to Diana for beating up on her crippled brother. The poor bastard. Then I balled one of the socks and threw it as hard as I could against the wall. It made a soft sound, *thuh*, and caught on the edge of a picture frame and hung there weakly.

The curtains in the bedroom were open a crack and, waking, I saw it was still daylight. My head hurt and I was sweating and still disoriented. I lit a cigarette and lay still for a moment. Then I heard a noise somewhere and climbed out of bed. A radio was playing very softly. I padded into the living room, where the curtains were open, admitting stark afternoon sun, creamy and hot. I followed the sound of the music into the hall and then into McDonough's narrow study. The light, so brilliant that it blinded me looking into it, came through French doors leading to a tiny balcony. The doors were open and I stood in the sunlight and looked at the girl on the balcony. She lay as if in fire, heat waves rising around her, a mirage. She lay on her stomach, her body brown except for a narrow pale stripe across her back and another across the rise of her buttocks. A transistor radio rested between her feet. She was fifteen feet away but I could see the tiny hairs in the small of her back move in the soft breeze, rising and falling with her breathing. Her head was turned away from me and the sun flashed off a pea-size gold earring. I was slick with sweat standing in the sun, but she was dry, appearing cool and fresh in the appalling heat. I stepped back into the darkness of the hall and stood watching her, perfectly framed in the French doors. It was like looking at a portrait in a gallery, and wondering if by watching it you could make it come to life.

I did not know whether to advance or retreat. I had no idea who she was, except she was not the woman in McDonough's photographs. That woman was dark and big-boned and this one was slender and light. She raised her arm then and I took a quick step backward, quietly so that she wouldn't hear me. I didn't want to alarm her, she would believe that the flat was deserted. I walked into the kitchen and pulled a towel around myself and put on water for tea. Then I noticed my suitcases in the hall. It was obvious she knew that I, or someone, was there. I walked back into the study but by then she was on her feet, dressed, looking at me and grinning. She was very beautiful with the sun at her back.

I said, "Sorry."

She made a nervous gesture with her hands. "It's too hot."

"I'm making tea," I said. "We can have some iced tea." Then I put out my hand. "I'm Wylie." She murmured a name I did not catch and moved out of the light into the hallway. We both retreated into the kitchen.

She said, "I come up here sometimes after work, to lie in the sun and read."

"You're American," I said.

She made a face. "Canadian."

I smiled. Canadians were always touchy. "Well, I'm sorry."

"My mother was American. You were half right."

I turned away from her to fetch a large pitcher. I filled it with ice, then dumped four teabags into a china pot. The water was almost boiling. I got a large lemon from the refrigerator and a knife to cut it with and two tall glasses. I put the sugar next to the pitcher. She watched me fussing with these things and smiled widely. I had placed

the glasses just so on the countertop and now she moved forward and
with her forefinger gently touched one of them out of line. She had
the smallest hands I have ever seen.

"Do you work with Ned?"

I said, "Sometimes." The water was boiling and I poured it into
the pot. We stood a moment, ill at ease, not speaking, watching the
pot. Without thinking, I moved the glass back into line.

She said, "I'll turn on the air conditioning." I followed her into the
study. It was so hot I imagined the books melting on their shelves, a
library by Dali. She brought the radio from the balcony, closing the
French doors and drawing the curtains. Then she moved behind the
leather chair and turned on a window unit. Presently I felt cool air
begin to circulate in the darkened room. She dropped onto the couch
and I went back to the kitchen for the tea. When I returned she was
sitting with her head thrown back, eyes closed. She reached for a
glass, took a long draft, and smiled contentedly. Then she said, "Oh!
You had a telephone call." I had completely forgotten about Diana
and the flight to London. I looked at my watch, it was five P.M. She
said, "I guess it was your wife." She looked at me, amused. "Is it a
secret? She didn't actually say. First she asked me who I was. When I
said I was a friend of Ned's, she asked who Ned was. When I said
'McDonough,' she said 'Oh.' "

I thought that was odd, Diana knew who McDonough was. I
waited but the girl said nothing. "Was that all?"

"She gave me a number for you to call in New York."

I nodded, looking at her. "What exactly did she say when you
announced you were a friend of Ned's?"

"She didn't say anything except 'Oh.' She said you could call Diana
at that number, if you could spare the time."

If I could spare the time. I could hear her voice, the clipped mid-
Atlantic accent that came with ten years in London. The accent would
amplify her annoyance. "Maybe," I said. "Maybe you could charac-
terize her tone of voice for me." We both looked at the telephone on
the desk, the receiver crooked in its holder.

"I'd guess." She took a sip of tea. "Just the smallest bit hostile."

"Did you say I was in?"

"I said you were asleep."

"Good Christ," I said.

She touched the corner of her mouth with her finger. "It had the
virtue of being true, what I said. I'd looked in on you, a man in a
deep snooze, dreaming . . ." She grinned and drank tea. "What

could Diana have thought? Perhaps she thought you'd gotten loose in wicked Athens. Could she have thought that?"

"A distinct possibility," I said dryly.

"Does it happen often?"

"It never happens," I said.

"Well, then." She looked at me with her wide eyes and smile, and lifted her shoulders. "Well, then, it's a bagatelle."

"Should be," I said. "But isn't."

She looked at me closely. "It *never* happens."

"Hardly ever," I lied.

She picked up the telephone and handed it to me. "You better call her, bub. Sounds serious. The number is on the pad."

"I know the number," I said. Diana always stayed at the same hotel. I began to dial and she rose and picked up her glass and walked slowly out of the room, leaving me to deal with Diana alone. Guilty husband, possessive wife. I called to her, "You don't have to leave." She looked at me from the doorway, curious. I said lightly, "Sit down. Finish your tea." I had been married to Diana for eighteen years and any business between us could be conducted openly. I did not want this girl to think she had the power to interfere with my private life. I put my feet on the coffee table and waited for the connection to go through. But Diana was not at the hotel and would not return until late that night, New York time. That meant she was unreachable for another twelve hours. I left an affectionate message and hung up.

She lay full length on McDonough's soft couch, not moving, and I sat back and watched her, amused. Nothing about her reminded me of any of Ned McDonough's women. He'd spoken of French and Italian women, a Greek woman, and an assortment of Americans. But they were not this one, I knew that. This one was self-possessed and provocative, and I sensed a quick and subtle intelligence behind the assurance; she was not, I was sure, a part of Ned's *haute monde*. This one was undisguised, she wore no makeup, and was dressed in a plain white shift. She looked at me now, suppressing a smile, knowing that I was assessing her. She'd asked, Do you work with Ned? And I'd replied, Sometimes. She seemed to understand right away that Ned's life and mine were not similar, and she'd asked no more questions. I thought I ought to tell her that Ned was the man at the table and I was the man in the back room. What was there about my life that would appeal to her? I devised cease-fires that held. Truces that endured. I relaxed and sipped my tea, enchanted just looking at her stretched out on the couch, her hands one over the other on her stomach. I wondered who she was really, and what she was doing in Ned McDonough's flat.

I said, "Tell me about the pictures."

Her eyes popped open but she did not look at me. "How well do you know Ned?"

"Well enough, " I said. "But I didn't know he had a family."

"They're in the United States." I said nothing, waiting for her to continue. "He doesn't talk about it a whole lot."

"He doesn't talk about it at all," I said.

"Then I won't."

I looked past her to a picture of Ned and his wife at a table in a nightclub somewhere. The photograph was grainy and off-focus, and I wondered when the picture was made. Ned and his wife were grinning gamely and toasting each other with champagne. I said, "Very mysterious."

"He hasn't seen them for years."

"His wife remarried?"

She shook her head, meaning *no* or *I don't know;* it was hard to tell which. She said, "How about yours?"

"She wasn't in," I said. "Won't be in until late tonight. You heard the conversation."

"Wasn't listening," she said. Then, smiling: "What do you suppose she's up to, in wicked New York?"

"Being wicked," I said.

"You don't believe she's up to anything?"

"Doubt it," I said.

"Well, you're probably right." She arched her back, staring at the ceiling. "What do you *do?* Actually *do,* when you're working with Ned?"

"I make cease-fires."

She began to laugh and her hand flew to catch my knee. She shook her head, spilling hair over her face. She was still laughing when she asked me if they were difficult to make. I replied solemnly that yes, they were extremely difficult to make. She sat up now, cross-legged on the couch, grinning. How long did it take to make one? I said it was a quotidian affair that depended . . .

"On a number of factors," she said.

"More or less," I said. "It's like making a suit of clothes."

"Ah," she said. And were the best ones made of natural fiber, silk or wool, or the synthetics? Rayon, polyester, Dacron. Did you ever make a double-knit cease-fire? One that would never wrinkle or crush or tear — one that would hold its press for a generation?

Actually, I said, the skins of rare beasts were the best. Endangered species. Ocelot, alligator.

So they are expensive!

I said, "Invariably."

We were both laughing now. She was bouncing on the couch, her skirt hiked up in her lap, her eyes bright as gems, and her small hands describing each new thought, as if she were conducting an orchestra. The questions kept coming between bursts of laughter. "I understand it perfectly," she said finally. "You and McDonough, I suppose your offices are on Savile Row. McDonough and Lyons, purveyors of cease-fires to H.M. the Queen. But what I want to know is, Who's the tailor and who's the salesman?"

I said, "I am the inside man."

"You make it and McDonough sells it."

"That's it."

She threw back her head and laughed. "McDonough takes the measurements and you cut the cloth."

"Exactly."

"And they last?"

"Most of the time. Sometimes. Sometimes not. It varies. Sometimes he screws up. Sometimes I do."

"How long has this one lasted?"

"The island? Eight days. Assuming that nothing has happened in the twelve hours I've been gone."

"How —" She put her hand to her mouth, giggling again. "Will you please tell me how you got into the business of making cease-fires? I assume there's no school for that, no Oxford or Cambridge or Sandhurst. I assume there's no institute located on Savile Row." She came off the couch and sat on the table in front of me; I could smell her hair, and the light scent she wore. "Please," she said. She was leaning toward me now, her green eyes staring into mine.

"What are you to McDonough?" I asked her.

"Friends," she said impatiently.

"You're not —"

"We're not lovers."

"Well," I began doubtfully.

"You're spoiling the mood," she said irritably. "You're just spoiling the hell out of it. Now stop it, and tell me."

I smiled. "I'm a lawyer."

"Right."

"I worked in New York."

"Yes."

"My law firm did some work for the organization."

"Bull!" she said loudly. "Those are things I don't need to know. I don't need to know them and don't care about them. I mean *why?* Tell me *why?*"

"I'm good at it. Some men make furniture. Some make money. Some are mechanics, doctors, soldiers. I'm good at this." I shook my head. "How the hell do I know?"

She smiled encouragingly. "Better."

"Look," I began, taking her tiny hand. She wore no rings, or any jewelry except the one gold earring.

"We can get to that later."

"Well," I said thickly. "What do you want? Do you want me to make a cease-fire for you? I've never done it for individuals. I usually work with *nations,* you understand. Sovereign states . . ." I wanted her to laugh again.

She asked, "Is Ned good?"

"Forget about Ned a moment."

"Is he as good as you?"

"He's good," I said. Then: "We do different things." She looked at me, her head cocked to one side, waiting. "Not as good as me," I said finally. She laughed and took two cigarettes from the box on the table, lit them, and handed one to me. "Look," I said again. She arched her neck, her face inches from mine. She murmured, "Um?" I put my hands on her shoulders, dizzy now with the smell of her. "Look, all this —"

"Much better," she said.

"Look," I said. "Do you want to go to bed or not?"

She smiled brightly and stood up, looking at me through cigarette smoke. Smoke hung between us and she waved her hand, dispersing it, still smiling, her head thrown back as if stargazing. "Ned told me that you were not seducible, but from the moment I saw you I knew that he was wrong."

◆

We did not make love right away that afternoon. The fiery sun disappeared and the air, cooling at last, became velvet. I opened the window in McDonough's bedroom and we lay together, talking. We were lying face to face and she said she wanted me to talk because she liked my voice, accentless and ragged. I did not know what was behind her, I was seeing only her surfaces. I began to talk aimlessly, fastening finally on a gangster I'd once had for a client. But somewhere in talking about that, perhaps it was the memory of the *mafioso* in my office, fingers clogged with diamond rings, I shifted direction and described my own career as an actor. I acted all through high school and college, *Boy Meets Girl, Misalliance, Winterset.* What I loved about acting was that, alone among the arts, it never let you witness what you created. A writer or painter sees what he does; an actor sees only the effect. Standing stage front I loved watching the audience, its attention or lack of it, its laughter or tears, and of course the applause. There was always applause, even for the most disorderly productions; at amateur theatricals no one is so churlish as to withhold applause. But it was not noise that exhilarated me, it was the expressions on the faces of those out front — watching, something I could never do. I suppose this was the first hint I had of what I would do with my life. That's to say, it was the *effect* that mattered; the result. The roles that interested me were the ones that made the play go. I loved the ensemble. I did not have the taste or talent for the Big Scene; it occurred to me much later that I didn't have the ego for it. It was a paradox; my amateur acting convinced me that whatever I did with my life, I would do it behind the scenes. I would be the one who made the thing go. An inside man, contemptuous of celebrity, measuring his life in result.

She said, "I don't believe a word of it."

I said, "It's true."

"You saw too many Gary Cooper movies when you were a kid. I know your kind —"

I had to laugh at that; maybe she had a point. Gehrig, not Ruth. "And you?" I asked. "What about you?"

"I went to McGill for a year, dropped out for a year, went back for a term, and then dropped out for good. I worked for an insurance company and last year my father died and left me a little money, and here I am. And here I intend to stay until the money runs out."

"You're a very beautiful girl," I said.

She ignored that, occupied now with tracing a line from my collarbone to my toes. She said, "No, not beautiful. But sometimes I am daring. And sometimes that is beautiful." Then she asked me if I was satisfied with what I did, making cease-fires. I said I was and asked her if she was satisfied, living in Athens.

She nodded. "Very satisfied."

"It suits you?"

"Um," she said. "But you. You might've been a great actor."
I said, "I can't see it."

"Well, not now. You don't have the face of an actor. It's a fine face, but it's not an actor's face. And you don't move like an actor, or talk like one." She put her hand on my chest. "And you're really happy now? Working behind the scenes with your organization, making cease-fires?"

I said, "Of course." Then: "Yes, seriously. I am." It was easy to become damp or sentimental about it, but it was true. I was a man lucky enough to have saved lives. I know that thousands of human beings are alive because of my efforts, pursued quietly and with no fanfare. In my line of work one success outweighs a dozen failures. The truth is, my career has encouraged idealism so long as I kept my expectations within limits. I am proud of who I am and what I have done, though I understand that it has taken a personal toll. Everything exacts some price. I asked her, "Where did you live in Canada?"

She slowly disentangled herself from me and lay spread-eagled on the bed, staring at the ceiling. "Saskatoon. Do you know how far from the back of beyond Saskatoon is? As far as you'd ever want to be, for sure. And cold. You do not know what cold is until you have waited for a school bus at six-thirty in the morning in the month of January. The trees creak in the cold. You're bundled in four layers of clothing . . ." Then she began to move in rhythm to some tune she was hearing. She closed her eyes and began to whistle, almost soundlessly. Her hips pulsed slowly, her skin smooth as ivory and glowing in the fading light. I put my hand on her stomach, thinking her as singular and mysterious as the country she came from. I thought of her as teeming with life.

"Tell me more," she murmured. "Tell me about triumphs and disasters, stage center in a high school gymnasium. Tell me everything you can think of, and what went before." I listened to her voice, soft as fleece, and watched her mouth. And I began to talk, inventing stories, pausing every few moments to look at her, eyes half closed, mouth parted. Then the pauses were minutes long, and electric. Her arms went around my neck and held. I tried to look behind her eyes into her dreams. We lay together, tingling, kissing for minutes, holding hands like children. She opened to me and then we were making love in earnest and when it was over I was almost sorry.

I said to her, "Tell me about Ned."
"Ned is Ned," she said.

And I replied, "None of that." I gestured at the walls around us, the pictures of Ned and his family. The wife; the children; the house; the station wagon; the sailboat; the picnic; the portrait on the bureau. I asked her, "All that. What happened to it? Where did it go?"

She said, "They went home. They live in the United States now. She's an American born and bred. The children are being raised as Americans. She and Ned did not get along. Ned would never discuss that part. He moved out one day. He doesn't see them often and I've heard him talk about them only once. One night he got very drunk, and if you know him well you know that's uncharacteristic. He said she wanted to tame him and he wouldn't have it. It went against his nature. I think he hypnotized them out of his life, understanding that he could not live with the knowledge of his family split in two. You talked about him as the outside man, the one who sells the goods. Ned believes there is no Humpty Dumpty so shattered that he cannot put it together; *talk* it together if he can meet with it face to face. She'd meet with him all right but she wouldn't give. Anything. It's the way he's made, he walked out when some part of him understood that he would have to remake himself for the marriage to go. And he wouldn't do it. Ned puts one hundred percent into everything he does, whether it's working with you or making love to me."

"You said you weren't lovers."

"We're not," she said. "We never were. There's more than one way to make love and Ned's an expert in at least three of them."

"But abandoning your children —"

"He didn't, in his terms. Ned." She began to smile, hugging her knees. "Ned believes himself a hero. He believes that it's better that his children see him as a hero than as an unhappy husband, unable to come to terms with his wife." She smiled again. "A mere woman. Ned believes in setting examples. The exemplary leader, you know? And he understands that he has only one life and it's necessary to win with it. He believes in that just like you believe in cease-fires. And the pictures in this flat remind him of his promises. One trouble was, he married a woman just as tough as he was; maybe tougher."

I remembered suddenly a talk I'd had long ago with Diana. Marriages progress (I'd told her) exactly like a negotiation. First, general agreement on a few fundamental principles; next, the grappling with details. I thought then that the first two years of a marriage were critical; they were time spent defining the territory and the emotional range. Later on, there were fresh talks but the points under review were minor. There were adjustments of boundaries, restrictions on

propaganda, agreements to move certain gun emplacements; but the
fundamentals did not change. In that way marriages were similar to
crises like Berlin or Cyprus or Palestine; negotiations only ratified an
abnormality. Diana thought it a bleak analysis and did not apply it
to us. I said, "What exactly did Ned say when you talked to him?
And when did you talk to him? And why?"

"Last night," she said. "He calls me at odd times just to talk."

"And what" — I touched her forehead — "did he say about me?"

"He said you were dust wunnerful." I turned away laughing. She
was a marvelous mimic. "He said you were using the flat for the
night. I asked him who you were and he told me without getting
into specifics. You two are very circumspect about your work. You'd
think you were at Los Alamos, making atomic weapons. It's very irritating. He said you were up for some fun, but I was not to get any
ideas."

"Because I am not seducible."

"The exact words."

"But you knew that wasn't true."

She said, "It was the heat."

"This morning," I said, "I was disoriented. I didn't expect to find
a portrait gallery. And this afternoon I didn't expect to find you.
Things were not normal. And you're right about the heat."

"That's the way, in Greece. Ned thought it would be a grand thing
if I came over and made you breakfast. He said that I'd come as a bit
of a shock to you but that you'd like it once you got used to it. And I
did come early this morning, all prepared, but you weren't here."

"Plane was late," I said. Then: "I took the stewardess to Piraeus
for breakfast, and then I took her to the hotel and came here. And
the apartment was empty. Except for the damn photographs. Ghosts
all over the place."

"How did you and the stewardess get on? Was she chummy?"

"She was Swiss."

"I'm glad, dear."

I laughed; her words carried a wife's tone and nuance. "She
wouldn't say it that way, Diana."

"How would Diana say it?"

"I don't know. Not that way."

"Did you want to go to bed with the stewardess?"

"I would've," I said. "If it had been easy. I wasn't interested in
making a campaign out of it." I looked directly at her. "I wasn't
kidding this afternoon when I said it didn't happen. It doesn't. But

Ned was dead wrong about the other." She looked at me without expression. "I haven't been through the preliminaries in so long —"

"Your wife must love that," she said dryly.

"— until today, with you, it's been a long time."

She said, "I think you're going to be very complicated."

"We'll be complicated together. We can carry each other's baggage."

She gave me a strange look, then smiled. "It's almost four in the morning. Call her now. I'm going to take a shower." She rose slowly and walked to the bathroom door and disappeared inside. I waited until I heard running water, but the room was still filled with her; her scent and spirit.

This time the connection was made. Diana sounded chilly over the telephone. Her brother had had a breathing seizure but he was all right now. She thought she would stay a few more days, returning to London on Wednesday or Thursday. Where are you? I replied that I was still in Athens but preparing to leave. I'd been up all night because the plane was late. But the housekeeper was on duty at home so there was no . . . immediate need. Who was the girl? she asked. A friend of Ned McDonough's, I said. Does this girl have a name? I realized that I had not caught her name. I had no idea what she was called. I laughed and said I didn't know; she was one of Ned's girlfriends. Diana heard something false in my voice because she said she had to go then. A late supper with friends. I told her to cable me in London when she was arriving. She said she would when she knew. Then I said, The hell with London. Meet me in Paris. We'd have a long weekend in Paris together. She was silent and I could hear the hum of trans-Atlantic wires, and the splash of the shower in the next room. There was a very long silence. Then I said it didn't matter, we could meet in London on Thursday or Friday and go on to Paris the next day, or not at all. Up to her. Yes, she said, that sounded less complicated and more convenient from her point of view. I agreed, it was easier for me, too. I was mad as hell by then. She said she'd cable me her time of arrival when she knew it, and rang off. I sat a moment, thinking, and then I went to the bathroom door and opened it. She was washing her hair and whistling softly. I reached into the shower and turned off the water and looked at her a moment.

"I don't know your name."

"I said it but you didn't hear it," she said with a laugh. "It's Virginia."

"And I don't understand about Ned's wife. And the photographs."

She stood dripping, blinking at me. "Wylie, it isn't like the tide tables or a mathematical formula. It isn't easy to know. Life isn't always symmetrical. Marriages aren't. She left. And he saved all the pictures, maybe in the same way you keep a foreign-language dictionary even though you no longer use the language. Maybe *because* you no longer use the language." She looked at me shyly, her arms covering her breasts. "That's the best I can do."

I said, "OK." Then I leaned into the shower and kissed her wet face and turned on the water. I had always thrived on complexity.

I have a friend who maintains that the virtues of marriage are visible only to people who have a profound sense of the future, and have seen successful marriages up close. His own parents had a very happy marriage. This friend believes in the marriage vows, particularly the one pertaining to adultery. He is forty-five, a stockbroker, and one of the nicest men I know. He says that restraint and fidelity pay "dividends" later on. Besides, the thought of an illicit love affair scares him to death. The thought of putting his wife, himself, and another woman through a "scene" appalls him. But beyond that he has a vision of the future and the vision sustains him. He sees his children grown up and fortunate and he and his wife living quietly and productively in a temperate zone. He believes that when he is sixty, he and his wife will look back on a betrayal-free life and rejoice. He is betting that the market will rise. I suppose in his own way he is betting on a counterrevolution. Charlie anticipates a day when, retired, he and his wife are sitting at the bar of the country club after a round of golf. They are sitting with other couples, friends, of their own age. Everyone has a drink too many and something is said and suddenly one of these couples begins to go at each other. Anger, tears; it is an awful moment, a resurrection of some ancient offense. I believe my friend lives as he does in order not to have a moment like that when he is sixty. *Au contraire,* Charlie wants to look back on good times. He believes that a secure present depends on a virtuous past. Good times depend on good memories.

It is difficult to recount an upright Presbyterian life without sounding smug, unless you are writing about a saint or a hero, and my friend is neither. Charlie has a habit of laughing at mutual friends who live on the margins. *Him?* Charlie will say. *Him?* — speaking of a middle-aged friend lately seen with a girl, twenty. *Him?* — meaning that the standards of girls, twenty, have fallen since Charlie left the field. There's a note of regret in his voice but he does not waver.

◆ Whatever Charlie's personal life is really like, I cannot imagine that it is meaner or more brutish than the lives of these friends who live on the margins, or mine. All the evidence supports the worth of his view, though none of us can foresee the future and that is the heart of the matter. I once tried to joke with him about his theory, making sarcastic mention of dat ole debbil temptation — and to my surprise he agreed. He agreed it sounded mediocre and priggish and one could scarcely talk about it without gagging. But that did not make it false. One must *resist*, he said heatedly, and for a moment I imagined him — incongruously, for we were lunching at his club on Wall Street — as an old Bolshevik on the barricades. I was forced to smile because the image came to me fully furnished, and I saw him in cloth cap and corduroy jacket and blazing red banner, this fastidious broker picking his way through the chef's salad and sipping white wine. He mistook my smile for condescension and immediately fell silent, embarrassed and irritated. I quickly explained to him about the image I'd had and when he heard me out he smiled and agreed that it was apt, though odd. He said that was exactly what he felt like, an old Red lamenting the death of the true faith.

"Christ," he said, laughing. "I'm an ideologue after all. Old Charlie, they'll never believe it in the locker room." We changed the subject then and talked of this and that, my business, his business, but after a few moments we were drawn back to our middle-aged marriages. We never talked in specifics; I am not comfortable in the confessional and neither is he. But at the end, as he was paying the check and we were preparing to leave, he said an extraordinary thing. "Of course, once you clear away the underbrush, women's liberation and hedonism and the rest of it, the heart of the problem is the death of romantic love. Marriage can't sustain it. Could once maybe, but not now. Maybe it never could. And we both know that we're romantic animals. If you don't get it one place you'll get it another. Try to suppress the impulse and you'll dry up like a prune. Indulge it and you'll end up in a motel somewhere with a teenager." He carefully signed the check and put it in the center of the table, the pencil placed just so across it, diagonally. "There's nothing in the contract that says it has to dry up, but it does — and I have a hunch that the reasons are identical to the ones that keep the marriage together. Civility, compromise, and a suppression of rage. People like you and me, we can't live in an atmosphere of perpetual turmoil. We're not made for it, so we find ways around it. I suspect that it makes us feel manly and capable to yield. I think that when we do that we hear the voices of our fathers, who were living in another epoch altogether. And of course we believe that nothing is perfect. That's a lesson we understand perhaps too well. We're reasonable men. My wife" — he smiled and pushed his chair back — "began to gain weight ten years ago. Not a lot, but it gathered around her hips and I didn't care for it. I told her so and she looked so hurt I never mentioned it again; I said, in fact, that probably I was wrong. Next day she began to tax me about smoking in bed, and we were at war for a week. But ah, Wylie. What minor complaints! What feathers on the scale! And I could give you a dozen more and you could match them, feather for feather. In some strange way it sustains me, seeing all these feathers as feathers. Keeping them firmly fixed and in perspective." He stood up and looked down at me, smiling, his eyes bright. "Every week I send my wife a dozen roses." We began to walk out of the club; it was now three o'clock and the place was all but deserted. But he had one last thing to say, so we paused in the center of that vast room, surrounded by mahogany tables and polished silver and white-jacketed waiters standing at attention out of earshot. "So we carry over one life into another. I broker my life as I broker stocks. I've sold long, believing that the market will rise. You," he said, "have done the same thing. You've negotiated a cease-fire."

I was thinking of all that, waiting for Virginia to come out of the shower. *Every week, I send my wife a dozen roses.* It was a wonderful thing to be able to say, twenty years times fifty-two weeks of roses. Charlie was playing Trotsky to Ned's Stalin, and what did that make me? A modern man, an uneasy compromiser, I suppose I was — Khrushchev. Making my accommodations with the decaying West, sometimes ludicrous, but shrewd. It depressed me thinking about it, so I thought about Virginia instead. Virginia of the green eyes and smooth skin and tiny hands, and brilliant laughter. Virginia from the outside; I did not know yet what was inside. Just looking at her was enough to destroy the habits of a lifetime. All weights and measures and the awareness of time itself were redefined. Weigh it against twenty years of roses — and which was the feather on *that* scale? At lunch in his club Charlie and I had barely mentioned sex, that Geneva Conference of mediation and barter. When he'd spoken of the death of romantic love he'd meant more than sex; he'd meant elation and optimism and heat. Amazing sometimes the way one . . . clung. I'd said to Diana once, Let us never negotiate out of fear. But let us never fear to negotiate. I thought it was funny and laughed. She thought it wasn't funny and didn't laugh. She'd said evenly, "I am not a nation.

♦

I am a person. A human being with grievances, and I do not believe
that 'negotiation' is the word we should be using." And she'd walked
to her dresser and taken a book out of the top drawer and handed it
to me, and left the room to spend the night on the couch. The book
was a sex manual and in those days they were not easy to find. They
arrived by mail in a plain brown wrapper, and not from the Book-of-
the-Month Club, either. I read it with the attention that Metternich
might give a high school test on the diplomatic art. However, in the
end we did negotiate — what else was there to do? And my life followed the pattern of my work. Truce followed cease-fire and peace
followed truce. But the two sides did not disarm. Far from it. The
weapons were still there, whole arsenals of them. But they were not
used. The threat of use preserved the peace.

"What did she say?" Virginia was in the bathroom doorway,
drying her hair.

"That she won't be back until Thursday or Friday."

Virginia said, "Well, well." She perched on the edge of the bed, still
ruffling her hair; little drops of water sprayed my shoulders. I said,
"She was not friendly." Virginia nodded distantly, watching me.
"And I don't think we have to discuss the matter further."

"Don't we?"

"No."

"I don't know," she said. "I'll let you know. I don't think I do,
though. Why would I?" She looked at me with wide-open eyes and
the tension dissolved. She smiled fleetingly and lay down on the bed.
I was sitting up among the pillows and she was below me, legs casually crossed at the ankles, hands locked behind her head. I touched
her shoulder, her skin hot and damp from the shower. She smiled
again, deliberately, and turned away. Her cheeks began to redden
and she closed her eyes. Her hand floated above my stomach. She
was still smiling but trying now to disguise it. I gently moved her head
into my lap and kissed her forehead, closing my eyes in order to
imagine her; I wanted to see her in my mind only. She rubbed her
knees together, then looked up at me. "I'm sexy," she said with a
laugh. "I'm so damn sexy I can't stand it." She moved away and lay
looking at me. We were lying apart, not touching; but what she said
was true. You could see it, in her face and eyes and body. It was
tantalizing, looking at her. We kissed very gently and I could feel her
lips and face tremble. I was trembling, too, with a great joy and
release. Her spirit was flowering with desire, and inside me all the
parched places were flooding. I did not know those places still existed

and I gave myself over to them. I had not been conscious of them for a very long time, those empty places down the dark streets of my mind.

Later, when it was almost dawn, her eyes fluttered and closed. I had a terrible premonition that if I slept she would be gone when I awakened and I would never see her again. I touched her cheek and she moved closer to me and muttered something. She was almost asleep. I said, "Where do you want to go?"

She gave a little shake of her head. "Nowhere."

"I mean tomorrow."

She opened her eyes and looked at me, dazed. "What do you mean?"

I spoke very softly. "Let's go somewhere. You name it, anywhere. But not too far. Not out of this hemisphere. Not out of the free world."

"Anywhere?" She was waking now, slowly.

"Sure."

"Paris," she said.

I shrugged. "We can go to Paris any time. Paris is a common place."

"Commonplace to you, big shot," she said. "Not to me."

"OK," I said. "Paris."

"Have you spent a lot of time in Paris?" I nodded yes. "Not Paris, then," she said definitely. I waited as her eyes roamed the walls and ceilings and finally came back to rest on me. Her movements were languid, she was as fluid as a cat. I looked into her green eyes and she looked back. I thought I would help her out, so I began to name cities at random: Venice, Copenhagen, Nice, Amsterdam, Dublin, Rome. Then, joking, all the awful places: Birmingham, Bonn, Belfast, Mulhouse. She shook her head at all of them, she was thinking of something else. "There's one place," she said finally. "A museum I'd like you to see, if you haven't seen it. It's interesting, it would mean something to you. I know it would."

"Name it," I said. "We'll go there."

She said, "Barcelona."

It sounded all right to me. I had never been to Barcelona. "We'll go today if I can find a flight out of here."

"You're serious, aren't you?" I nodded. "This isn't some dumb joke that's been cooked up?" I shook my head. "We're going to go to Barcelona, I'll be darned." She sighed then, shuddering, and tucked her head into my shoulder. "I want to do it more than anything. I was there two years ago, alone, and loved it. One" — I could barely hear her now, her breath was light and hot against my skin — "dines very well in Barcelona. One" — her eyes were glazed and closing; I strained to listen — "loves very well in Barcelona." She pronounced it with the Castilian accent, Bar-thuh-lona. "And there's the museum, which I will show you. I will guide you through the museum, which I know intimately, and you will fall in love with it as I did." Then she was asleep and I gently put her head on the pillow and walked into the study. We had not left Ned McDonough's bedroom for twelve hours and it was strange to me, looking at our empty glasses and the two half-filled ashtrays. The flat was more ours now than Ned's.

I dialed Iberia and booked us two seats to Barcelona. Then I called the housekeeper in London and told her I would not be returning for a few days. I spoke to the children and they were well, unhappy at being awakened. I sat in the quiet room and watched the dawn rise over the balcony. When the phone rang I grabbed it right away. I didn't want it to wake Virginia. It was McDonough, "just checking."

"Well?" he asked.

"Well, what?"

"Did you meet her?"

"Yes. I met her."

"Is she there now?"

I paused a beat. "No." I could hear him chuckle. "We had dinner together and then she left."

"Right," he said. "Nice girl, no?" I said she certainly was. "I asked her if she'd go round to look in on you. Make sure everything was shipshape." I heard the chuckle again.

"Ned," I said, "you're all heart."

"Molz keeps me on my toes. Comrade Molz suggested I call Virginia, said it would do you good; nice Canadian girl." He waited for a moment, listening. "That's a joke, Wylie."

"Ha-ha," I said. "What's happening there?"

"Some firing last night. Nothing important, except of course it means the cease-fire is technically broken. We're not acknowledging that."

"Casualties?"

"One KIA, a couple of wounded."

My heart sank. "God *damn* them," I said. "They knew this would happen. 'Made inconspicuous.' Horseshit! It was absolutely obvious, you cut the team in half, take Grandoni and me out of there, it was like giving them a hunting license. And we both know what will happen now. There'll be a probe tonight in retaliation for last night, and one tomorrow night in retaliation for tonight, and so on and on." I hesitated, disgusted. "Does New York know?"

"Of course," he said mildly.

"Hell, I'd come back right away if I thought it would help —"

"No," he said quickly, surprised. "They know the facts, they'll deal with it. Don't worry, Wylie. These things come unglued all the time, you know that. I think we can contain it. New York understands the situation."

"But New York is not *capable* of understanding —"

"No, that's true," McDonough said equably. "But they are the ones in charge, alas." He rang off then and I sat for a moment in the leather chair, watching the dawn and wondering if the island would explode after all. Perhaps it was cursed, exactly as the curator had said. I hated to think about it and briefly considered calling New York myself. But I knew that would be a wasted telephone call. I was not on the scene; Ned McDonough was. Suddenly I wanted very much to leave Greece, and was happy that in six hours we would be on our way. I smoked a cigarette and returned to the bedroom and stood watching Virginia. She was lying on her side, one hand where I would be, the other tucked under her chin, her hair spread in a golden fan over the pillow. I was not sleepy and simply stood there a minute, looking at her, wondering if she was dreaming.

♦

We arrived in Barcelona at dusk and went immediately to the Ritz. We bathed with a bottle of champagne for company, then came downstairs to the lounge. There were only a few people in the lounge and from a ballroom somewhere drifted orchestra music, tea dancing. It was prewar music and the arrangements were Lester Lanin's. We talked about the situation in Spain. This was the period when Franco lay dying and Catalans were gathering in the streets, in suspense, hoping. We kept our voices low; it was discourteous to speak of the antichrist in the cathedral of the regime. We were excited, sitting at ease, talking politics, anticipating uncrowded hours; we touched each other continually, no point was seriously made without a caress somewhere. An outsider listening to our conversation would have thought it lunatic, though of course we thought each other wonderfully witty and lucid. I think I have never been happier; our faces were inches apart and we were oblivious of the surroundings. I was telling her Franco anecdotes when the music grew suddenly louder. The doors at the far end of the lounge opened and starched men and women began to stroll toward us to the lobby. I stopped talking at once and we turned to watch this extraordinary *paseo,* reminiscent of matadors entering the bullring in full regalia. The men were mostly middle-aged and dressed in swallowtail coats and white ties; some of them wore florid decorations on their chests. The women wore black gowns with gloves, pearls at their throats. Cole Porter's music followed them, *oompah-oompah,* and presently a young man and woman appeared, the woman in a white wedding dress and train and carrying a bouquet. They stood a moment, both of them slim as sabers, looking over the lounge and those of us in it as if we were animals at auction. Then they commenced their promenade to the lobby. They walked very slowly, silent and erect, paying no attention now to us. There was an atmosphere to all of this, these well-bred Spanish faces in no way representative of our era; it was an antique show. The men wore their hair plastered to their skulls and the women were modest to an extreme, displaying no flesh below the neck and careful with their smiles. In the lobby they stood with the bearing of royalty, in conversation with the bride and groom. There was no obvious hilarity. Conversation for a moment was patient, then one by one they began to leave. A *paso doble* filled the lounge now as more people filed past, heads high and expressions proud. I looked at them and wondered if there had been speculation concerning the old man dying in Madrid and what it would mean for Spain's *treinta y cinco años de paz.* Franco's *paz.* She said, "All Spanish believe in miracles."

In a moment they were gone, leaving no trace, and we were alone in the lounge, listening to the dance band. I thought of those confident citizens of the old regime and imagined a bright cavernous ballroom, waiters gliding by with trays of drinks, the dance floor deserted but the orchestra continuing to play. We looked at each other and laughed and I paid the bill and we left, threading our way through those still standing in the foyer. Every man watched Virginia. She murmured apologies in a demure voice as we moved into the courtyard. We began to walk in the direction of the old city, and our restaurant. She'd made the reservations; it was a small place she'd visited the last time she was in Barcelona.

"I won a beauty contest in Saskatoon," she said, "and that got me to Montreal for a week. In Montreal I fell for an artist, believing that I

could be his muse forever or for the season, whichever ended first. It
turned out he already had a muse, Mrs. Artist, so it didn't work out
entirely to my satisfaction, though I believe he remembers that week
to this day. He ought to. My father owned grain elevators in Saskatoon and when I won the beauty contest he almost disowned me. A
sinful thing, wicked. Beauty contest winners were 'hoors' in his opinion and as a matter of fact he wasn't far wrong. I was eighteen and
after seeing Montreal I decided it would be a good thing to go to
college. But the truth is, I'm not very studious or scholarly. There was
no one thing that interested me more than any other thing, so college
was a waste of time. And I hate to waste time. I do have an interest
in Canadian Indians but they are better appreciated in the field than
in a classroom. Facts don't stay with me but sights and sounds do;
emotions do. My relations with men in Canada were not letter-per-
fect, the first man I was ever really serious about was a separatist
from Quebec. My God, the meetings! We'd come home to the apartment after a movie and there'd be a dozen of them there, men and
women, and they'd stay all night, arguing; it drove me nuts. They
thought Quebec was the center of the universe and I knew it wasn't
because I'd thought Saskatoon was the center of the universe and I
found out soon enough that *it* wasn't and ditto with Montreal, the
Paris of North America. There is no single place in Canada that
qualifies except certain Indian habitations and you have to be an
Indian to know where they are. I have visited a few of them and
intend to visit more, sometime in my life. Anyhow, they bored me to
death with their ideological squabbles. They were then 'into' French
anarchy, which I always understood to be a contradiction in terms.
They were very cross with Camus because he'd had the bad luck to
be born in Algeria. I suppose this gibberish comes from being a part
of that great amorphous country, so loosely linked and so in thrall to
outsiders. It's so big, Wylie, and so unimproved. Well, if you discover
that Saskatoon isn't the center of the universe and then you find out
that Quebec isn't either, and you have an ironic turn of mind, like I
do, then you set out to discover what other places aren't. So I took
my inheritance, which was not large but not small either, and went
to Europe. That was a year ago and I believe that Europe isn't the
center of the universe any more than Canada is, but it comes a little
closer, and it's a lot more fun. And of the European cities I like
Barcelona best. It's an ancient city-state, like Venice or Genoa." We
were drinking coffee and looking at each other across candlelight. It
was nearly midnight but the restaurant was crowded and noisy. "It

was odd," she said. "My mother came from California but when she moved to Canada with my father it was as if her Americanness ceased to exist. Saskatoon devoured everything, it was the strongest culture I've ever been in. I mean by that the most definite, and the most exclusive. My mother never spoke of California except occasionally to mention her sister, who still lived there — lives there still — but whom she never saw. It was as if California were an unbridgeable distance from Saskatoon; it was the old world and Canada was the new. But she kept her United States citizenship, there was never any question about that. Though I have never felt the slightest bit American. Yankee." I lit her cigarette and she leaned forward, brushing my hand with her fingernails. "I have never had a relationship with a man that lasted more than a couple of months. I don't know why that is, unless it's a reaction to my parents, who lived as if locked in an iron embrace. My parents never to my knowledge spent a night apart from each other; yet they were not especially affectionate and the house was not what you would call merry. It seems to me now that whole evenings would pass without the exchange of a single thought or emotion. There were no transactions in that house. Maybe I thought that was the fate of durable marriages: clenched teeth and short sentences. But my dear father died one June and my mother died the following October, a heart attack if you like symbolism. She followed him everywhere, even into the grave. To this day it is impossible for me to say whether they were happy together or not and I'm not certain that the question is even relevant. They simply were. Together. Is the shore happy with the sea? I know that life in Saskatoon was very hard, particularly their early years together; it was little more than a frontier. They were married ten years before I was born and I try to imagine what it was like, carrying a child in that country. A Californian living in Saskatoon, a spinster sister living in California; both parents dead." She paused then, her eyes turned inward; she was grappling with her memory. "I suppose I have been promiscuous in my relationships with men. I've never thought much about my body or 'saving' it. I've been careful not to be taken advantage of, and let me tell you I've got a loan shark's eye for when I am. If it's an equal attraction, it's fine with me, and if the man's a gentleman." I smiled at that, it seemed such an old-fashioned word. I had not heard a woman use the word "gentleman" in years and I asked Virginia what she meant by it. "It's in the dictionary," she said with a smile. "You can look it up. It's surprising how many men aren't. However, it's only fair to tell you that despite the artist and the separatist and one or two others, I never had a completely satisfying sexual experience until I got to Europe and met a man of fifty-five who had spent his *life,* I think, in bed. Nice man, though odd. An easy man to be with, though he tended sometimes to order me about. I didn't mind it as long as we were equals in other ways. I seem to have an affinity for men older than I am. I think I'm attracted partly because of the baggage you carry around. At least, I am in the beginning. It's always difficult later on. I travel light and sooner or later you try to lay off your baggage on me, and I want to tell you now that it never works. Never. First place, I'm not eager to take it; second place, you never really let go of it. You just rent it out, like any chattel; you collect rent and retain the title. The odd thing about the fifty-five-year-old man was that he seemed to have less baggage even than me and of course in time he left, for a woman younger than I am. It was a liaison that was just about worn out anyway. It took me a week to get over it. I'm not made for broken hearts. That was a few months ago." I poured the wine while she lit a cigarette, silent now, looking at me over the candlelight. "Now you. I felt your presence yesterday morning when I was lying on the balcony. I knew you were there and I knew you were perplexed. Who is this girl? And I was apprehensive, too, though I was also being provocative. Ned had described you in very appealing terms. He said you were a man unaware of what was happening in your own mind but that he admired you, 'extravagantly,' he said, though you worried him. He said you had a weakness for the beau geste and naturally that tickled me, because I do, too. But it's a happy quality in men. Anyway, I can't say why these things happen but when I saw you, blinking in that godawful heat, looking at me in a nice way, appreciating what you saw but not leering or making some stupid remark —" She laughed suddenly. "It was a thunderbolt, a *coup de foudre.* Then in the kitchen you were so nervous. All the utensils had to be lined up, it was as if you were arranging a regiment for inspection. If you said sorry once you said it six times. It irritated me at first, you had nothing to apologize for. Then I realized that it was just a reflex action and then I began to wonder about *that,* but by then . . ." We both began to laugh and I leaned across the table and kissed her, holding her a long minute. Then I summoned the waiter and paid the bill and we rose from the table, prepared to return to the hotel.

I said, "So you won a beauty contest in Saskatoon."

"First prize," she said. "Blue ribbon."

I said, "I have baggage."

♦

"That's what Ned said."

"A portmanteau," I said. "And it's full."

"Well." She was smiling. She hooked her arm through mine and we began to edge between the crowded tables. "That's usually the way." I was leading and she came up against me, locking her arms around my waist. She said, "Maybe I'll buy part of it." I said, "It's all high-priced goods." She whispered the next words into my ear: "But I won't take anything on loan." In that spirit we hurried out of the restaurant and onto the street, bright at midnight.

I assume it is different now, but at that time, some months before Franco's death, it was not easy to find the Picasso Museum. The regime had a long memory, which the artist did nothing to appease. It took us thirty minutes to find the building, a handsome brick structure on a side street near the docks. She had not told me what to expect but her enthusiasm was contagious and whatever it was I was eager to see it.

The museum is organized on historical principles, beginning on the ground floor with Picasso's juvenilia. There are very few paintings from his middle period and most of the very famous paintings are in other museums in Europe and America. I have always put Picasso in a special category of genius and it startles me to remember that he was born two years after Stalin and two years before Joyce and was an infant when Darwin died. I was accustomed to seeing him in the pages of *Time* or *Life* working in his studio in the south of France or surrounded by young women on a beach somewhere, his satyr's stance and grin captured in four colors; a man to admire without reservation, and his life did not lack joy.

We began on the ground floor, walking slowly, hand in hand. There were drawings in school notebooks and on the backs of envelopes, and I was enchanted to see that even as a child he had love for the female body and spirit. Women and animals, his charcoal line was always strong and supple. We paused in front of a portrait of a teenage girl, this done when the artist was seventeen. It was the portrait of his sister. I wished suddenly that Virginia had sat for Picasso and I was looking at her, the open emotion of her eyes and mouth and the barely suppressed passion of her spirit; Virginia painted as she was now, in a plain white shift with the single gold earring and her hair careless. Virginia loose in white against a dark background. She touched my arm and we moved on, looking at the pictures on two levels, as art and as commentary on Picasso's life, because it was obvious that he was struggling with his own genius. There were periods when nothing seemed to happen, the artist content to occupy ground captured by others. Strolling through the silent rooms, I imagined Picasso's genius to be a ball of twine, Picasso chasing it like a cat, batting at it, trying to pin it down, ravel it, inspect it, and possess it. But it kept scooting away into awkward corners; he could possess it only a bit at a time. In one or two of the pictures I thought I saw something like despair. I turned to Virginia and she had a special smile on her face. I knew that whatever it was she wanted to show me, it would not be long in coming.

It happened then. We passed out of one room and into another and it was like witnessing a miracle. This was another order of experience altogether: *Woman with a Stray Lock of Hair, The Unbefriended, The Frugal Meal*. Picasso had found his theme and, standing in the doorway of that hushed blue room, dazzled and breathless, I thought only of a great army brought suddenly into battle, each unit behaving with discipline and courage, commanded by a supremely confident general. It was a stunning experience and when Virginia pressed my hand I could feel her own wonder and emotion. The pictures seemed to explode off the canvas, different from the ones we had seen in other rooms but connected to them, too. And this room was only the first skirmish, gloriously won but still a skirmish; Austerlitz and Jena were yet to come. We moved together trancelike from the blues to the roses and then, rounding another corner, to the center of our times. The artist had taken apart the world he created and put it together anew: physical forms, ideas, emotions, all history. The general had had himself psychoanalyzed by Freud and tutored by Marx and Einstein and was now a modern man, his art a definition of the epoch. I thought, foolishly, that it was like falling in love; the soul's door swung on its hinges. Nothing was concealed. We stood looking at the first Cubist drawings, then at *Las Meninas*, the maids of honor.

"What do you think? Doesn't it make you dizzy?"

"It makes me dizzy."

"What else?"

I said, "It makes me think of love. Loving. Being loved."

She said, "It's genius." We continued to stroll through the rooms and my excitement began slowly to drain away. The museum was filling now and there were visitors in every room, mostly Germans. I wanted to get away from it in order to think about it. I wished I had as clear a view of my own life as I seemed to have of Pablo Picasso's, or knew more precisely the quality of his resolve. Or the source of his inspiration; something beyond "genius." Where had he found his riotous music? I wanted to see my own life in periods of time, blue periods, rose periods; and understand the connections between them. I stood in the doorway looking back at the last maid of honor. Virginia said, "It's also egomania."

We stopped at the museum shop and I bought her a print of the portrait of Señora Canals. Then we were on the street again, wondering where to have lunch. Virginia said she had one last place to take me in Barcelona, but it was a sight best seen after a leisurely Spanish meal, four courses and plenty of wine. We could go where the meals were elaborate and the ambience cheerful because if I thought the Picasso Museum a wonder, well, wait until we saw and scaled this other . . . phenomenon.

I was glad to be in the sunlight again. My emotions were still in a turmoil and I was only half listening to her. I looked around at this unfamiliar city and wondered for a moment what I was doing there. What was I doing in Barcelona? And who was this girl leading me through history? We stopped at a newsstand on the corner and I bought a *Herald Tribune*. And we were crossing the street when the map and the headline caught my eye. SCORES FEARED DEAD. I stopped in my tracks and she took my arm to hurry me as the light changed. I stood dumbly on the curb and read the dispatch, a very short wire-service bulletin. The details were sketchy, there was an "incident" and "firing" which had turned into a "pitched battle" near a tiny coastal village. I knew the village; the reporter had misspelled it. As I read the paragraphs, my throat tightened and I felt physically ill. There was no mention of McDonough or Molz, only that the cease-fire had collapsed. Virginia was reading over my arm.

"Poor souls," I said.

"What does it mean?"

"That we begin again. From scratch. If they'll let us. Unless they find the killing too wonderful for words." Pedestrians were moving around us, annoyed that we stood on the curb. I put my hand on her waist and moved into a doorway.

"Why? Why would it begin again?"

"Because those *idiots*. In New York . . ." I didn't finish the sentence. I was sick at heart and there seemed nothing to say; this market would not rise. We stood for a moment; I was imagining McDonough and Molz trying to move between the lines, questioning their contacts, cajoling, pleading; they would have threatened except they had nothing to threaten with. I thought about all that and the many variations of it, and then I turned away toward the street. There was nothing I could do about the island. I was not there. I was here. I was in an unfamiliar city with an unfamiliar woman and I loved them both. The island was something else, inaccessible now; old baggage. I would not allow that to destroy this. They were separate parts of my life. I touched her cheek; she seemed more lovely to me than ever, standing in the shadows, her head tilted to one side, waiting. I kissed her once and then again and insisted we move along. I reminded her, there was one more sight to see. We could go to any restaurant she wanted, except that it had to be excellent and expensive. It had to serve Barcelona's greatest meal. Did she know of such a place? She nodded and I saw there were tears in her eyes.

"We're going to forget about all this," I said. She nodded again and tried to smile. I threw the newspaper into an ashcan. "Come on," I said, taking her by the hand. We began to walk rapidly up the street in the direction of the Ramblas. I wanted desperately to restore the earlier mood. This day was too crowded with emotion, and when I thought about it I was sad into my bones.

"Wylie?" Her voice was small. I stopped and put my arm around her waist. She felt weightless as she came up against me. I drew her gently to me and we stood a moment, saying nothing. Then I touched the tip of her nose and smiled. I was concentrating on her face, looking directly into her wet eyes and wondering if I could lose myself there. But my memory would not stop working, though I smiled and smiled. I realized then that I was squeezing her arm, hurting her. "That's better," she said sadly.

◆

Lunch consumed three hours. We began with drinks and then we ordered wine, three bottles, and followed the wine with cognac and coffee. I thought that by drinking we could banish all the blues and to my surprise I found that we could. When the drinks arrived I began to tell her a little about the island and the work that Ned McDonough and I had done. I thought that the way out of it was through it. I told her how good Ned was and briefly described his technique. She asked me for examples and soon we were both laughing quietly. Halfway into the second bottle of wine I was nicely tight and knew that she was, too. The island slipped into the background. We were talking of ordinary things when suddenly she asked about Diana. What kind of marriage we had, what Diana was like, and what we did together when we were alone.

I thought a minute, then said we were suited to each other and not all married couples were. Obviously, I said, it was not a hundred percent. But quite a lot depended on what you expected; her expectations and mine. She asked me to describe Diana and I replied that I wouldn't do that. *Ne kulturny,* I said with a laugh, though the truth was I wasn't sure I could do it. She said briskly that she understood that; it was all right. But she needed to know something. "The picture I have is incomplete." I told her that Diana and I were suited in practical matters and had been from the beginning. We agreed on the ways to raise our children and how to entertain and whom and how to live and where. We agreed generally about people. I have known too many couples who were unsuited in the practicalities not to know how important it was. Agreement in small things . . .

She glanced at me and laughed, not unkindly. "Important, is it?"

I said, "Very." She shook her head and mouthed no. "Is too," I said.

"Not small things," she said. "Big things. The primary passions. Maybe you can ignore them but I don't think I can. I know I can't. We can pretend they're isolated moments but we both know they're not . . ." She went on in that way a moment, spirited and confident, sure of her ground. I was enchanted listening to her, though I felt myself pull away by inches. No reason now not to open the portmanteau and display my wares. I said I had a cynical story to tell her. She didn't have to believe it but she ought to listen to it. These were two London friends, their story. These friends had converted the primary passions into an art form. Not for them the Saturday night special, and while they made no particular boasts about their private life, they made no apologies or evasions either. They had an exemplary sex life. The trouble was, that was all they had. It was the only thing they agreed on. They disagreed about children, friends, vacations, houses, books, wine, and how much money was required to keep it all afloat. Dinner at the Burnses' was an agony of sarcasm and dispute and by the time dessert arrived Burns was sullen (and often drunk) at one end of the table and his wife was triumphant at the other, or vice versa. And leaving that house (seldom after eleven P.M.), one did not care somehow if later they managed to agree on the anterior or superior position to commit sex, each moving the earth for the other in multiple orgasm; it would be like admiring two goats . . . I studied her slow smile and wondered suddenly what I was doing, defending the trenches of the Somme when my enemy possessed nuclear weapons. "Well," I said, beginning to laugh. "You have to know the Burnses to appreciate the nobility of the concept."

"What is that story supposed to tell me?"

"I don't know," I said. "Maybe that all Americans believe in miracles."

"I think that you are trying to tell me that the ordinary business of living. Is a firm that prospers. Isn't that it?"

I looked at her across the cluttered table. "It prospers until you fall in love."

She let that pass. "Describe the dividends. As long as we are pursuing this."

"They are not in excitement," I said. "Maybe they're in peace."

She said, "You can't believe that."

I looked at her closely, her face split by a thin ambiguous grin. How could she possibly understand the Burnses? They had been fighting for fifteen years, war was a natural condition; there had never been the slightest suggestion of disengagement. Diana and I had spent whole evenings wondering what kept them together, knowing that there had to be something besides sex. But there wasn't and we both knew it and the knowledge made us jealous and defensive. I was going to tell Virginia that it depended on what you were used to, or had become used to, and what you expected or were taught to expect or thought you ought to expect. But I didn't say that or anything like it. I said, "I used to believe it."

She was silent a moment, lost in thought. Then: "Do you know that there are only three intellectual pursuits in which people have performed major feats before adolescence? They are mathematics, chess, and music. Hard to say what connects them. A certain logic and order may. But there are no child poets, architects, or philosophers. I think it's because children are incapable of *desire*. It's different from just wanting something, you know. Desire and passion and ignoring limits in order to have them, or gratify them; *have* them, I think. They're so conservative, children; and of course they have no history to toss in the ashcan when it's required." She leaned across the table. "Is it really war and peace? That's what you were saying a minute ago." I shook my head; that wasn't what I meant. She said, "I don't want to have a war with you. But I don't think I like the sound of peace, either. Not the way you describe it. Sounds more like confinement than peace, and I find it childish. This logical, orderly confinement —"

"The analogy isn't correct," I said.

But she wouldn't settle for that. "It's yours, not mine. If it isn't war and it isn't peace, what is it? You've got to *say* it." Her eyes flashed and she leaned back in her chair, intent now. She said, "You've got to say it yourself."

"The analogy's wrong," I insisted. "It's an easy analogy and it's wrong."

"Then there's only one thing it can be. The story of your life."

I nodded. "If you believe the analogy."

"Please say it," she said.

"Cease-fire."

"Do you love me now?"

I looked at her, all defenses gone. "Of course."

She touched my hand and we rose unsteadily and made our way to the door and the bright afternoon sun.

Where else do you go in Barcelona? The Expiatory Church of the Holy Family, La Sagrada Familia. We sat in a café across the street and drank a brandy, staring at the church, the sublime achievement of Antonio Gaudí, begun in 1882 and still not completed. It will never be completed, there is not money enough or time in all the world to finish this building. It is to stare into a mirage, bony spires spinning into the skies, an immense Art Nouveau façade, the stone incurved as if sculpted by a river's current. We walked through the side entrance, stumbling here and there because our eyes were on the spires. There were only a few visitors and, in a corner of the unfinished nave, two artisans sculpting a stone, working carefully with hand chisels, two old men working one immense stone, one of an unimaginable number still to be carved and fitted. We stood close together silently watching them and it occurred to me that I could watch these old men for the rest of my lifetime or theirs; this was an infinite undertaking, at the end of the twentieth century the nave would remain open to the sky. Gaudí's monument seemed to me at that moment to represent time itself, an eternal becoming.

The stones curved, and seemed to drip. Stone figures stared down at us from fantastic perches, and the spires soared dizzily overhead. I felt blood and alcohol rush to my face, and nudged Virginia. I said thickly that we had not really needed the brandy in the café and she replied that it was best to see La Sagrada Familia while intoxicated, the blood boiling. It was a conception so cuckoo and magnificent and outrageous; it was not of this world, and therefore not best seen with a cold eye.

"I'm tight as hell," I said. She moved against me, her eyes on the cross atop the tallest spire. I dipped my hands in a helpless gesture. "All this . . ."

"Think about it," she said. "A primary passion. Nothing like it anywhere on earth. It derives from nothing, imitates nothing, suggests nothing, forecasts nothing. Nothing like it came before and nothing like it has come after. Absolutely its own kind, fully blown or fully flown . . ." She began to laugh.

I said, "You're tighter than I am."

"Medium tight," she said. Then, impatiently: "Come with me." There was an ancient elevator that traveled halfway up the main spire. A winding staircase went the rest of the way up. We got into the elevator and Virginia said something to the operator that made him laugh. I looked at my feet and noticed my suit trousers were unpressed and soiled at the cuffs and my shoes were dusty. She looked immaculate. We alighted at the highest landing and stood looking over the nave and presbytery, the great porches and smaller spires to the rear, and the city beyond that. She nudged me playfully and indicated the operator, still standing in the open doorway of his machine. "Give him a peseta, lamb." I gave him five and he thanked me and took the elevator down.

We were alone in the damp silence. She stood looking at the city below us, breathing fresh air in great gulps. She rocked back and forth, testing the wrought-iron barrier. Then she turned, flushed and grinning, and began to climb the narrow spiral staircase, beckoning me to follow. "The view's better from up here, you can see forever, everything . . ." She was out of sight almost immediately; I heard only her voice and her shoes scraping the stones. The stairway was enclosed, built into the stone walls, and black as a cavern. I said, "You go on." I was dizzy and very disorganized now, though I was standing fully two feet from the aperture. I looked out over the city, shielding my eyes from the glare of the afternoon sun. "Come on!" she cried, her voice faint now, disappearing as she climbed. I waited, afraid, standing back in the shadows. I did not want to follow her up the stairs. I realized then that I was trembling and forced myself closer to the railing. Looking down, I saw the city commence to spin and rearrange itself like one of Picasso's Cubist paintings. I shut my eyes and turned my face skyward, into the sun, praying for a breeze. I wanted to leave and looked around for the elevator but there was only the empty shaft. Birds wheeled and called above me. "Wylie!" Her voice came from a great distance and I could not locate it. "Here!" she cried. I craned my neck and looked up, leaning through the opening. She was fifty feet above me, waving from the highest window, her stomach pressed into the iron railing. She was balancing herself like a seesaw, smiling and waving. Her face swam in my eyes, high above me. I saw her fling out her arms and yell something and I turned away. I did not know up from down now and stood staring straight ahead, trying to get my bearings. Then I heard her familiar laugh, brilliant and sparkling above me. I looked up again but she was no longer there and my eye was drawn up the spire to a grinning Gaudí demon. Then she appeared, eyes alight, blond hair flying; she was balancing again on the railing. I knew then that she would fall and yelled to her to get back inside. Her laughter grew thunderously loud and she called, "Wylllllie!" I leaned far out, motioning with my hands; the spire began slowly to spin. The world was going to pieces now. I pushed away from the railing and scrambled up the spiral stairs. Once inside I could not hear her; the heavy stones muffled all sound. The passage was narrow and treacherous, the risers wide on the outside where they touched the wall but narrow at the spine. My feet kept slipping on the stones, though I braced myself at every step. I was gaining, and after a moment I thought I could hear her voice. The sound of her voice was indelible in my mind. I imagined her face and body as I climbed, trying to see her now in my mind's eye. I thought she was calling and I rasped a reply. I climbed as fast as I was able but the steps were much steeper and more precarious than I expected.

I was falling before I knew it, tumbling heavily backward, landing on my spine. Then I was doubled over and falling. I felt a sharp pain and then nothing but surprise and wonder. My feet were above me at a crazy angle when my head hit stone and abruptly I was falling in slow motion, tumbling gently into the darkness, deep silence surrounding me as I floated in rhythm, the stones turning above me like graceful figures in a ballet.

Time held. Virginia drifted in and out of my vision, at last coming close to me. Her mouth touched my ear and she was talking. There were tears in her eyes and on her cheeks. She dried her eyes on my pillow, then spoke a few serious sentences, her hand resting lightly on my chest. When I woke she was gone. Later, Diana arrived, looking different from the way I remembered her. I believe she stayed a few days, then returned to London; she did not bring the children. I saw Ned McDonough the next day.

He could tell me nothing of Virginia's whereabouts. I remember him sitting in a plain wooden chair in a corner of the room, reading. I would waken and we would talk a bit. When the nurse came in he joked with her in Spanish. He told me I would be fine if I took it easy and did what the doctors said and tried not to remember too much. I asked him to find Virginia for me and he promised to look but she was an elusive woman and he could not hold out much hope. There were many cards and cables from friends. Ned read me a florid Italian greeting from the count and warrior Grandoni, and an undecipherable message from Molz. He said encouragingly, When you get out of here you can go to Athens and use my flat, if that is what you want to do. I shook my head no. I expected to go to London; after all, that was where I lived. Diana and the children were there. He smiled doubtfully and made as if to go. I asked him finally if they had met, Diana and Virginia. He said that they had. And what was the atmosphere of the meeting? He paused before replying. "I would describe the atmosphere as 'correct.' " I wondered what that meant, in the circumstances. All of it was difficult for me to understand. He was at the door now, looking at his watch. I asked him what they talked about. I could not imagine what they had to say to each other. McDonough grinned and opened the door. "You, old boy," he said. "They talked about you."

"But why did she leave so suddenly, no word —"

"Wylie," he said, reproach in his voice.

"No explanation. No note, no nothing —"

"She knew you were on the mend. Of course she felt badly. I think she felt responsible."

I said, "That's cock."

He moved through the door, then paused. His smile was vintage McDonough, devilish and cynical and worldly. "It's the way they are," he said.

"Who?"

"The free spirits," he said. "All the Virginias. They only stay a little while but they always leave a trace." Then he reached into his pocket and tossed me a tiny box secured by a rubber band. Inside was the gold earring, the one that had flashed in the sun the first time I saw her on the balcony of his Athens apartment.

♦

I was in the hospital four weeks, then released. On crutches I stood in the Barcelona airport, wondering where to go. There were flights to all the European capitals and the islands. I thought that a week in Ibiza would be agreeable but it was the height of the season then and I did not relish dining in the evenings surrounded by German tourists and their children. So I flew home to London.

The house was empty, as I expected it would be. I put my bags in the hallway and wandered through the rooms, a stranger. It was almost three months since I'd been home. I wandered from the living room to the kitchen and finally into our bedroom, which doubled as a study. My desk was as I had left it; hers was bare. Familiar things were missing and her closets were empty. The children's room looked like any guest room, the beds carefully made and no clutter anywhere. The place was spiritless and looked to me as if no one lived there or had ever lived there. It was a house invented in someone's imagination, and then neglected. I looked through the dusty windows into the garden, badly overgrown but still recognizable.

I found the letter on the dining room table, addressed to *Wylie*, in her neat script. The letter said that she had returned to New York City, where she would stay until she found a place in the suburbs. She would take her brother out of the clinic where he had spent half his life; he would live now with her and the children, somewhere in Westchester. She did not know my plans but would like to, "for planning purposes." It would be easier for her and the children, especially the children, if she knew my plans. She hoped I was feeling better; I must have had a dreadful time of it. "I met your friend and I wish you luck. You'll need it." The letter was signed simply *Diana*. I stood in the center of the dining room holding the letter; then I let it fall. I walked slowly back to the bedroom. Everything of mine was where I had left it.

I made a cup of coffee and sat in the kitchen drinking it. After a period of time I returned to the bedroom. That night I tried a dozen ways to locate Virginia. There was no answer at Ned's flat and no listing for her elsewhere in Athens. I tried hotels at random, and Information in Paris and Rome and Belgrade and, for a reason that escapes me now, Helsinki. There was no listing anywhere. There was nothing at all; she had vanished. I have no idea what I would have said to her if I'd found her. Come back? Stay away? What happened that afternoon in Barcelona? What were we doing in Gaudí's towering spire? *What do I do now?* At length I gave it all up and lay down on the bed, aching. I ached in every part of my body. But sleep would not come and I lay awake until morning.

I went to work the next day but left at noon, exhausted. I did not return to the office for two days. When I went back there was nothing for me to do. A younger colleague had been assigned "temporarily" to the team on the island. I had my desk and my files and my secretary, but no assignments. My colleagues were extremely polite and deferential and I attended a number of meetings but there were no contributions for me to make. The circumstances of my accident were never discussed in my presence but were the subject of much office gossip, sotto voce.

Finally I was urged to take a leave. I had been back a month but it was obvious to everyone that I had not fully recovered, though I continued to arrive at my office each morning at nine. Then Ned flew in from Athens; they thought he was the one to convince me. He said that everyone was worried. You're the best in the business, he said, and we need you on the island but you've got to be fit. When I looked at him without expression he said he'd booked me into a small private hospital in Kent; "the best little hospital in England." He asked me if I'd talked to Diana and I said I had, three or four times since arriving back in London. She seemed happy in White Plains. The children got along well with her brother, the poor bastard, and vice versa. The brother was particularly happy to be out of the clinic. No, I said in response to his question, I did not plan to go to America. Ned's eyes shifted constantly and he seemed embarrassed. Then I remembered his flat in Athens, the photographs of the family I knew nothing about. I told him I was surprised that morning, coming upon his family. He looked at me steadily for a moment, as if appraising a combatant. "Know your enemy," he said quietly. Then, with vehemence: "You must know everything about them. Or I do. You don't. Isn't it strange, you don't need to know them at all." I allowed the silence to gather; the distance between us was immense. When I asked him about the island he looked away and shrugged. "About a hundred dead this week, both sides," he said. "That's fifty less than last week. I suppose." He smiled confidently. "That's progress, of course."

So I went to his private hospital in Kent. There was a French chef and wine with meals. I related my dreams and childhood memories to the resident swami. Each day I ransacked my memory and if nothing came (and frequently it didn't), I made something up. I remade my memory to suit myself and those imaginary connections were sometimes quite startling. Once I asked the good doctor if he thought I was telling the truth during our morning sessions. He looked at me carefully, expecting a trap, and said he always assumed his patients were telling him the truth. Why would they lie? I did not mention Virginia, assuming that he knew about her from other sources. This treatment was not supposed to be therapeutic. I was being analyzed in depth. You will go all the way down, the swami told me, until you can go no lower. But you can go lower and if you are brave enough you will touch bottom. When you touch bottom you will be well again, and in control. I felt no need to tell him that I had been there already, or what I had discovered. He looked at me pleasantly and asked if I thought the treatment was helpful. I smiled and said of course it was. It was like a gift. "I am sending myself a dozen roses a week."

I signed out after three weeks; that is, I packed my bags and left. I was sick of the smell of roses. Everyone knows that my sort of disorder does not rise from an unhappy childhood or some long-buried trauma, nor is it revealed in nighttime dreams or nightmares. Still less is it corrected by a self-administered caress. It rises from the collision between one's public and private selves. It is an accident of history, this head-on crash, and naturally there is noise and confusion and injury, as in any accident. I have come to believe that we are stars fixed to certain courses, and those are not necessarily in harmony with the times; and that is the difference between good fortune and bad.

According to a postcard, Virginia has been traveling in Canada, visiting Indians she says; she has no fixed address, and hopes to return to Europe next year. She writes that her inheritance is dwindling; she gave away part of it to a tribe in Saskatchewan. "I have restored their faith in miracles." At night in London I think of Virginia and me alone in Athens and Barcelona, and of that remote island and the cease-fire I devised. Ned informs me that the island is quiet and there is now a de facto truce. The combatants are courting at last. The agreement we had seemed splendid at the time, a document at once humane and severe; perhaps it demanded too much. I search in earnest for the causes of the violation. I return to the island next week and it is essential that I understand what went wrong. I am composing a new pact in my head, taking all the fresh facts into account. I am writing a lyrical protocol, spacious enough to allow for human nature and strict enough to end the killing.

1979

# A MAN

# AT THE TOP OF

# HIS TRADE

◆

H<small>E TOLD THEM</small> to hold all calls, except any that might come from her. There was no reason for her to call, but that was no guarantee that she wouldn't. She often called. Once several weeks ago she'd called and insisted on being put through, and there'd been an awkward five minutes while he muttered into the telephone and the others sat silently looking at their fingernails or otherwise pretending that they weren't listening. Of course, they couldn't hear what he was saying; he normally spoke into the phone in a guttural, a tone so soft that it couldn't be heard more than a foot away. That night when he asked her about it she'd laughed and said her only demand on him was instant access. When she was blue and wanted to talk, he'd have to listen. That was his half of the bargain.

His colleagues were due now, five of them. He'd had the chairs arranged just so, in a semicircle in front of his desk. Ashtrays within easy reach. Pads and pencils on the chairs. There was a conference room across the hall, but Stone didn't like it. The conference room was formal, and this discussion did not need formality. At exactly ten-thirty they had a radio hookup with Browne.

Stone lit a cigarette, thinking about Browne. He'd be preparing his notes now in the tank in the basement of the embassy, the lead-lined color-coordinated "module" sunk like a squash court below the foundations of the building. It was a completely secure room; Stone had helped with the design. Data banks lined one wall; the technology was phenomenal: computers scrambled the voice at one end and unscrambled it at the other, a fresh matrix for each transmission.

That had been the true breakthrough. The number of available matrices was virtually infinite, encoding and decoding accomplished in two and a half seconds. Stone had made a hundred transmissions from that same office before they'd made him an inside man. In his mind's eye he saw Browne sitting in the swivel chair, checking the control panel. He smiled; thirty minutes in the tank could seem a brief life.

Browne felt the same way. Their careers and personalities were similar in many ways; perhaps there was a pattern to their trade. They worked well together, always had; it was on Stone's strong recommendation that Browne had succeeded him as chief of station in C——. And he'd been excellent, though the station had declined in importance. However, that was no fault of Browne's; it was a reflection of changing times and attitudes and priorities. Now Browne was out too; this was his last operation. He could not see Browne as an inside man any more than he had seen himself as an inside man, two years ago. But Browne would adapt. He would be very good as an inside man, though he worried about the girl, Chris. When Browne left C——, Chris would go with him. Well, he was a professional. Stone and Browne were both professionals.

The buzzer sounded, and Stone picked up the telephone. The five of them were in the outer office, waiting.

They would have thirty minutes of discussion before the transmission. The split was two to two, with Otto on the fence as usual. All of them understood that the decision was Stone's, but if the disagreement was profound, they'd be obliged to file a dissent. They knew that Stone would want to avoid that. Stone did not like what he called "pieces of paper" circulating around the building. Stone had a passion for unanimity.

Stone opened the discussion. "The position is this. Browne has to have a definite go or no-go by eleven A.M. It's short notice, but it can't be helped. Everything in the way of transport is laid on. If the decision is go, Browne meets his man" — Stone looked over the tops of his eyeglasses, smiling — "under the clock at the Biltmore . . ." This was the customary euphemism; there was no need for these men to know where the meeting was taking place; that was an operational detail strictly under Stone's control. ". . . at noon. Browne and his man get in the car. There's a second car and a third car. Classic procedure, and we anticipate no difficulties. We've got an airplane that will have him in Brussels in three hours and at Andrews by tomorrow morning." He looked at his watch. "Comment?"

"You have no doubts about his authenticity?"

"Browne is completely confident," Stone said.

Otto asked, "And you?"

"I have doubts about everything. I always have doubts; that's one reason I'm here. But I've satisfied myself that he's genuine."

"What makes Brownie so sure?"

Stone hesitated a moment before replying. "Instinct."

"The approach came out of the blue, is that right?"

Stone nodded. "Over the transom."

"A week ago?"

'No, three days. And he wanted to do it now. Right now."

Jason McAlvin looked at Otto, then at Stone. "The procedure seems sound, and I agree that he's probably genuine. In the past we've gone on a lot less. But I think the main question is, What does he have? What can he give us? And the answer to that is, Military intelligence. Right?" McAlvin looked at the men grouped around the desk. "Well, we're quite up to date on that. I have a sufficiency of information. I believe that what we'll get from this man is corroboration. Useful but not decisive. I don't think he'll be able to give us much that is new. Perhaps a scrap here and there. But hell's bells, when you think of the effort that's going to go into it. *His* care and feeding for the next year, maybe two years. That's a lot of coin for small beer. What is he, anyway?" McAlvin shrugged his shoulders and lit a cigarette. "A colonel? We could no doubt get some cute details from him. Personalities, procedures. It's interesting reading, but in this case I don't think it's worth it. Worth the time, the effort, and the money. I recommend no-go."

"Browne thinks it's worth it," Stone said. "Very much."

"This is his last run, isn't it?"

Stone looked at McAlvin, a restless, fluid man; his wiry body seemed almost boneless. He'd never been an operator in the field. He was strictly an inside man. Stone said, "Yes."

"It would be a nice coup for him," McAlvin said.

Stone turned to Bricker and Stein, sitting impassively, listening to the discussion. Bricker spoke first. "It doesn't sound high-risk to me. My reaction is, why not? Even if we got just one nugget, it would be worth it."

Stein was doubtful. "Normally, in cases of this kind, I like to go with the man in the field. So long as everything else holds up. However, in this case . . ."

"What's different about this case?" Stone asked quickly.

"It's always a temptation . . . This is Browne's last operation. It's always a temptation to ride out on a big success. There hasn't been much happening in his area lately. Isn't that right? This is the first good news we've had from Browne in a long time. And what the hell, it's Jason's section. If Jason says he has all he needs —"

McAlvin interrupted with a wave of his hand. "You never have all you need. I merely meant to indicate there are limits."

"Well, either way. In fact, this operation sounds quite high-risk to me. High-risk versus a possible no-gain. Or no, not *no*-gain; minimum-gain. I'm a persuadable, but on the evidence so far I'm inclined to counsel no-go."

Stone turned to Carmichael, who had said nothing. Carmichael was the youngest man in the room by ten years, an economist by training; he was the director's man. "Bill?"

Carmichael said, "I'd like to hear what Browne says on the radio."

Stone had been aware of the white light blinking on his telephone. He picked up the receiver and tucked it into his chin, his mouth a quarter of an inch from the perforated black plastic. He heard her low laugh and then his name with a question mark. He said nothing. "I love you," she said at last and hung up. He waited a few moments before replacing the phone. In ten minutes Browne would come on circuit.

She turned away from the bedside table and walked downstairs to the kitchen to make another cup of coffee. That evil secretary of his; it had taken her five minutes to get by the secretary. "Is Mr. Stone in?" "Who is calling, please?" "Miss Morris." "He's in a meeting right now, Miss Morris." "Oh, my. A meeting." "I'm sorry." "I just wanted a very quick word with him." Silence. "It wouldn't take more than half a minute." "He'll be out of the meeting at noon." "But it is important." Silence. "Very." "One moment please," the secretary said, and put her on hold. Finally the connection was made, and she heard him breathing. She'd watched him talk on the telephone a thousand times and could see him now, his eyes focused elsewhere as he listened. He didn't say *anything;* that was typical. She'd asked him about that once and he'd apologized and explained that it was part of his telephone technique; he hated telephones, and when he used them, he thought of the old Down East expression: Better to close your mouth and be thought a fool than open it and remove all doubt. She did not understand how that pertained to her, *them;* but she'd let it go. He was very attentive in other ways. If he did not choose to be attentive on the telephone, that was all right. Still, a word now and again; a word wouldn't have hurt. She prepared a cup of instant and turned on the FM. Bach, they were playing Bach. The rhythmic logic of Bach enchanted her. She smiled to herself, then laughed out loud.

Browne's voice came from the receiver evenly and naturally. It was as if they were in the same room. He spoke for only five minutes, a complete report, concise and informative, no wasted words.

Stone looked around the room, satisfied. "Comment?"

Otto asked, "No doubts about authenticity?"

Browne's voice sounded a trifle bored. "None."

"And everything is laid on?"

"To a T," Browne said.

They were all silent a moment, watching each other. It was apparent that Browne had covered all the bases. Then Jason McAlvin cleared his throat. "One question. I didn't understand from your . . . presentation. How did he come to you?"

"He approached us. It was strictly over the transom, out of the blue. No cleverness on our part," he said disarmingly.

McAlvin said, "I know that. I know that, it was in the preliminary report. I mean exactly *how*. How the approach was made. And to whom."

"To a girl who works here in the embassy."

"Ah," McAlvin said. He paused, waiting for Browne to continue. But the radio was silent. McAlvin smiled. "Well, if it isn't demanding too much. One wouldn't want to pry," he said archly. "But where. When. And how."

Browne said, "Three days ago. In a café. A note. It's all quite genuine."

"And what is the girl's name?"

"She works for me," Browne said. Then he was silent again.

"Is that generally known? That she works for you?"

"I suppose the other side knows it," Browne said.

"The plot thickens," McAlvin said. He was doodling on his yellow pad, a series of connected boxes. He was carefully inking in each box.

Stone thought it was time to cut this off. McAlvin was making mischief, as usual. Stone switched off the receiver so the six of them could talk among themselves. "In what way does the plot thicken, Jason?"

"Well, these are facts I hadn't known. I thought our man had made a normal approach to one of the embassy officers. I hadn't known it was made to Browne's . . . secretary. Or whoever she is, Browne wasn't exactly precise. That changes the bidding, don't you think? He knew who she was, obviously he knows who Browne is."

"Be a damn poor intelligence man if he didn't," Stone said irritably. "He's a colonel of intelligence. That's the sort of information he'd have as a matter of course, for Christ's sake."

"Well, yes . . ."

"He made an approach to his opposite number. Not to Browne directly; he knows that Browne's watched. That would have been obvious and dangerous. So he goes to his secretary."

"Yes, indeed," McAlvin said. "That's slightly less dangerous than going to Browne himself."

Stone switched on the receiver and turned to McAlvin. "Put the question to Browne."

"We were talking here," McAlvin said suavely. "Why do you suppose the approach was made to your secretary? Isn't that a bit dangerous? Or stupid?"

Browne said, "It all seems quite straightforward to me. A classic approach, no surprises. It seems to me" — his voice showed signs of impatience, Stone thought — "that the authenticity can easily be established by you people there. Once we have the bird in hand. My assignment is to pick him up and get him out of the country. Which I am prepared to do. And give you my evaluation of his worth, which I am also prepared to do; have done, in fact. Let me go over the salient points again . . ."

"With all the details of the approach, please," said McAlvin.

The radio was silent; Stone knew that Browne was waiting for some sign or signal. Perhaps some sign of support. Stone said, "Proceed."

"The approach was made on the fifth of May. The girl, whose name is Chris DuPage, has a coffee in the same café every morning at nine . . ."

Stone was listening carefully; there was something new in Browne's voice. It was something irregular. He could hear it even through the scrambling and the metallic quality of radio transmission. There was a tone and timbre he couldn't identify. Browne was being too casual. Stone knew the approach had been made through the girl; it was not unusual, though it was risky. This was Browne's girl, the one he intended to bring back with him. She was a very solid girl; Stone had known her for years. He listened to Browne talk, and suddenly something else forced its way into Stone's mind. It was a hunch from nowhere, one question, just one, and when Browne had finished, Stone asked it. "Had they ever met before?"

"Not to my knowledge," Browne said slowly.

Stone was silent a moment, along with the others. He knew what that meant. It was lawyer's talk, and not responsive. Stone looked at the radio speaker, his expression betraying nothing. He said, "We'll get back to you." Browne started to protest, but Stone didn't wait for him to finish. He switched off the radio. The operation was dead. "We'll get back to you" meant no-go.

"What happened today?" She asked the question playfully, not expecting an answer. To questions about his work he seldom answered in any responsive way. Of course, she knew what he did but had no idea whatever how he did it or what was involved. She had no idea of the details of his professional life. But this time he surprised her.

"I had to kill one of Browne's operations."

"Brownie? But I thought he was on his way back."

"He is; this was his last job."

"What was it?"

"A defector. He'd picked up a defector."

She was astonished; he'd never disclosed so much before. Living with Stone was a continual surprise. More as a lark than anything else she decided to press him. "Why did you have to kill it?"

He shrugged and sipped his drink. "Brownie trimmed on me; he'd never done that before. There was no alternative, none at all. The thing began to smell. All you need is a whiff in an operation like that. One whiff, and you kill it."

"You caught a whiff," she said. "How?"

"Instinct." He lit a cigarette.

She looked at him. "Instinct?"

"Besides, this was just a marginal operation. It wasn't as if we were about to snatch Castro. This was just a" — he hesitated, smiling slightly — "third-level character. A bureaucrat. Useful to have, but far from necessary. Not necessary at all."

"Well," she said. She leaned toward him and plucked his cigarette from the ashtray and took a long drag. "Well, why did it smell?"

He said, "That's complicated."

She laughed, knowing he'd fall silent now. She had all she was going to get. From now on he'd turn every question with a joke, and finally change the conversation altogether. That was his habit. She said, "All the better. I like complicated stories."

"Well, it turns out that the contact was Chris. I knew that, but this morning I found out that she'd known him before. Known the defector. God knows how, or in what capacity. I *didn't* know that, and I should've known. Brownie should have told me. He didn't, and there was a reason behind that. The reason doesn't matter. It was enough that he withheld the information. That was enough to kill the operation."

She was fascinated and wanted to respond in such a way as to keep him talking. "But . . . it might have been innocent."

"I'm sure it was," Stone said.

"But if it was innocent . . . ?"

"He withheld, that was reason enough. Innocent or sinister, it makes no difference."

"You didn't *ask* him?" She was incredulous. He and Brownie had been friends for ten years. On the job and off it. They were as close as brothers.

"No. No point to that."

They were sitting on the back porch of Stone's house. He refilled their glasses with ice and tonic and stood looking into the garden. The roses were doing very nicely. They covered the board fence and drooped down to the flat bricks. He cultivated three varieties of roses, and one of the varieties was always blooming in the spring and summer.

She looked at him a moment, puzzled, not speaking. Then: "You really didn't ask him what it was about?"

"No, of course not. He'll be back here next month. I can ask him then."

"But the operation . . ."

"That's dead in any case."

She thought, What a strange world he lived in. A whiff of trouble. An "operation" abruptly "dead." No reconsideration. "In any case." He seemed to give no more thought to it than to the gin and tonic he was drinking. "Instinct," she said. "You said it was instinct. Is that all it is?"

"Informed by experience," he said dryly.

"And the experience . . ."

He said, "Informed by instinct."

She laughed, moving closer to him. "Oh, that's very helpful. May I quote that, Mr. Stone?" She looked at him a moment, wondering whether to pursue. No, that was useless. She was amazed that he'd told her as much as he had. On the other hand, she knew them both, Browne and the girl. She and Stone had seen a lot of them in the old days. The girl, Chris, had been particularly kind. "Was Chris trying to pull . . . something funny?"

"I don't know. I doubt it. You know her better than I do. What do you think?"

"I can't imagine," she said. "Chris was always careful in her work. Devoted to Brownie. I can't imagine her . . ." She let the sentence hang. "It'll be nice having them back here, won't it?"

"Yes," Stone said.

"Well," she said. "Thanks for telling me."

He said, "Thanks for the phone call."

"You didn't say anything."

"I was in a meeting."

"Well, you could've said, 'Thanks.' Or, 'Me, too.' Or just anything."

"I should've, you're right."

She said, "I feel lonely in the mornings. After you've gone to work. It's nice to hear your voice, I like it . . ." She told him then about the day she'd had, cleaning the house, talking to a friend on the telephone; two invitations for dinner, a doctor's appointment. Then in the afternoon she lay down for a nap and had a bad dream. She almost never dreamed in the afternoon, and that upset her. It was her old dream about walking up a ramp to an airplane, the ramp becoming longer and longer in front of her eyes. The stewardess beckoning. She shook her head and reached for his cigarette; it was a very scary dream. She had tried to call him again, but he was out of his office. The dream frightened her, and she had stayed in her room until he'd come home. She had a headache . . .

He looked at her, nodding sympathetically. He thought, What was there about him that attracted unhappy women?

1974

# DIETZ AT WAR

◆

Twice or three times a week Dietz wrote his children. They were informal letters that began Dear Girls and ended Much Love from Dad. He liked to describe the country and the hotel in which he lived, and at every opportunity he wrote about the various animals he saw. Around the corner from the hotel was a crippled vendor with a monkey and once a month he'd visit the zoo. The zoo's attractions were a single Bengal tiger and two mangy elephants. The tiger he called Charlie and the two elephants Ike and Mike. In his frequent trips to the countryside he'd see water buffalo and pigs, and once he'd taken a photograph of a marine major with an eighteen-foot anaconda wrapped around his neck. Dietz hated snakes but his children didn't. He invented wild and improbable stories about the animals, giving them names and personalities and droll adventures. From time to time he'd give the girls a glimpse into his own life, opening the door a crack and then shutting it again. He thought the letters and his motives for writing them were straightforward, but his former wife did not. On one of Dietz's visits home she told him that the letters were interesting, but not much use to the children. "You're really writing those letters to me," she said.

Dietz was very serious about the letters; in three years in the war zone he missed a week just once. He wrote the letters early in the morning, before he began the day's work. When he expected to be out of touch for any length of time he'd leave several letters with the concierge of the hotel, with instructions to mail one every three days. It was important to him to be part of the lives of his children, and he considered the letters as valuable and necessary substitutes for personal visits. The letters were as long as they needed to be, and were posted with exotic stamps.

However, he was careful never to disclose too much. Because he lived in a war zone he felt entitled to keep his personal life to himself. He did not want to alarm or upset the children, nor did he want to leave the impression that he was enjoying himself. He thought if he phrased the letters with care, the girls would understand his obligations to himself and to his work. Dietz never had the slightest feeling of heroism, still less of advancing any national interest. He was a newspaper correspondent and believed in journalism. He believed in his value as an expert witness whose testimony might one day prove valuable. The work was demanding and not to everyone's taste, but Dietz found it congenial. Because the war zone was dangerous he felt he had the right to make his own rules, and that meant the right to withhold certain information from his children and the others.

There were several love affairs, and many friends both male and female. During the worst part of the war scarcely a week went by without someone he knew, or knew of, being wounded or killed. There was one terrible week when five correspondents were killed and a number of others wounded, but Dietz did not mention this to the children except in an oblique way. In a letter home he told a long and complicated animal story and assigned the names of the dead to various enchanting animals. Dietz felt in that way he commemorated his colleagues.

He worked eighteen-hour days and considered himself at the top of his craft. Everyone he knew had difficult personal problems that obliged them to sail close to the wind, as his friend Puller expressed it. Puller described the war zone as a neurotics' retreat no less than the Elizabeth Arden beauty farm or the Esalen Institute. While recognizing the truth of what Puller said, Dietz did not apply it to his own life. The various personal problems, serious as they might appear to outsiders, were not allowed to interfere with the job he was paid to do.

Therefore, the letters home were not factual but invented. Dietz did not completely understand this until years later, when he chanced upon the correspondence and reread it. Dietz kept carbons of everything he wrote.

. . .

Odd — there was not a line in any of the letters about the good times
he'd had. It was awkward to talk of good times because people put
you down as a war lover, a man who drew pleasure from the suffering
of others. And from *this* war, no less. Borrowing a concept from
older writers who had covered earlier wars, Dietz told himself that a
sense of carelessness and adventure was necessary in order to remain
sane. In order not to become permanently depressed. He explained
this idea one night to an experienced woman who had witnessed a
number of European wars and she laughed in his face, not unkindly.
The other wars were sane, she said. This war was insane.

"And?"

"Draw your own conclusions."

Still, in his letters home, there was not a word about casual things
— pleasant walks through the damp scented air in the deserted parks
early in the morning. Nothing about late night swims in the pool at
the old country club, or afternoons at the run-down racetrack. Nothing about the long evenings playing bridge, or the occasional sprees
at restaurants in the Chinese quarter. There was nothing at all about
the constant noisy laughter as the correspondents drifted down the
boulevard to a café where there were drinks and hot roasted peanuts
in shallow dishes. There were no descriptions or explanations of the
many wonderful friendships he'd made.

While there was nothing at all in the letters about the good times,
there was nothing about the bad times either.

Having decided to cut himself off from America, Dietz felt it was
important and necessary to take an aggressively neutral stance in his
attitude toward the war. He felt that the one could be justified only
in terms of the other — for he had *fled* the United States; no question
about that. This belief was reflected both in the letters and in the
articles he wrote. His heaviest gun was irony. Dietz acquired an uncommon ability to turn sentences in such a way as to leave his readers
empty and puzzled and, when he was writing at the top of his form,
depressed. The facts he selected implied foreboding, and his descriptions suggested darkness and disease. This was done subtly. He
wheeled his irony into position at the end of every story, and gave his
readers a salvo. Standing outside events, even-handed Dietz believed
he was uniquely equipped to describe an enterprise that was plainly
misconceived: deformed, doomed. He never wrote of anything as
crude and obvious as wounded children or wrecked churches. Instead, he devoted a series of articles to the remarkable military hospitals and their talented surgeons, who saved lives and left men
vegetables or worse. He became something of a social historian, de-

scribing the furious whims and customs of those involved in the war.
Dietz developed a theory that there was a still center in the middle of
the war, a safe location without vibrations of any kind, and if he
could occupy that center he could present the war from a disinter-
ested position. A moral fortress. It would be the more precise and
persuasive for being factually impartial, because it was evident to him
that the public was skeptical of anything that hinted at the lurid or
the grotesque. Dietz worked at trimming adjectives from his prose,
and was careful to spell everything out with near-mathematical pre-
cision.

He wanted to describe the war with the delicacy and restraint of
Henry James setting forth the details of a love affair.

His life enlarged and grew in harmony with the war. He was rooted,
comfortable, and at ease, feeling himself outside the war and inside it
at the same time. Dietz refused to learn the history of the country or
its language or the origins of the struggle, in the belief that the war
was necessarily a sentient experience. He brought emotion to his
portraiture, but the emotions were solidly based on fact.

He was scrupulous. Aircraft, artillery, small arms, battalions, bat-
tlefields — all of them were precisely identified by name, number,
or location. Dietz's room at the hotel was covered with American
military maps, and he'd obtained weapons manuals from a friendly
colonel at American military headquarters. Readers understood immediately where they were and what was happening, who was doing
the fighting, and with what weaponry, and the name and age of the
dead and wounded. These facts, so precise and unassailable, gave
Dietz's journalism the stamp of authenticity and therefore of authority. Dietz believed that facts described the truth in the same way that
shapes and colors describe a landscape, and in that way journalism
resembled art.

One April afternoon he was almost killed.

They'd encouraged him to accompany a long-range patrol. They
did not conceal its danger: this was a reconnaissance patrol that
would establish beyond any doubt the existence of sanctuaries in the
supposedly neutral country to the west. They were frank to say that
public knowledge of these sanctuaries would be . . . helpful. Dietz
was free to write what he pleased, and of course it was entirely
possible that there were no sanctuaries. But they trusted Dietz to
write what he saw.

Dietz was eager, listening to them explain the mission. This was not a patrol that would engage the enemy. It was purely reconnaissance for the purpose of intelligence gathering. But they did not lie to him about the danger. There was at least an even chance that the patrol would be discovered in some way, and that would mean serious trouble. They would be deep in enemy territory. However, the commander would be the best reconnaissance man in the zone and his team would be hand-picked. It would be an all-volunteer force. A helicopter squadron would monitor their progress and be prepared for immediate action. The mission had the highest priority and Dietz was free to go along without restraint. It was appealing, the story was appealing on a number of levels; Dietz put danger out of his mind.

On the second day the patrol was ambushed and nearly annihilated. The commander and his number two were killed, and Dietz and half a dozen others were wounded. They owed their lives to the quick reaction time of the helicopter force, though for an hour they were obliged to defend themselves without aid of any kind. Of course they found no sanctuaries or anything else of value, and in that sense the mission was a failure.

Dietz was five days in a field hospital, half delirious and very weak from loss of blood. They watched him around the clock. As soon as they were able, the authorities moved him to a small private clinic in the capital. Having urged him to undertake the mission, they now felt responsible. They'd make certain he had the best medical attention available in the zone.

In ten days the danger was past, though the effects lingered. Dietz was euphoric.

His friend Puller, looking at him lying in bed, remarked, "You look like hell."

"Feel fine," Dietz said.

"White as a sheet," Puller said.

"Lost all my blood," Dietz said.

"You need a drink. Can you have a drink?"

Dietz laughed and extended his hand, and Puller poured him a gin and tonic.

"Actually you look OK."

The nurse was working on his arm, cutting the steel sutures that bound his wounds. "It's a load off my mind," Dietz said.

"How's that?"

"This can only happen to you once. The odds. I've used up my ticket."

Puller looked at the nurse and asked her in French how Dietz was. The nurse said, Fine. Recovery was rapid.

How long would Dietz remain in the hospital?

Perhaps a week, the nurse said. But he would have to remain quiet when he got out. He sustained shock and was more disoriented than he realized. If Monsieur Dietz were wise, he'd take a long holiday.

Puller observed that his friend seemed in very good spirits.

The nurse nodded. Indeed. A model patient, always cheerful.

Puller turned back to Dietz. "I talked with your office on the telephone today." He smiled. "They wanted to know when to expect the story."

"I'm writing it in my head," Dietz said.

"Well, they said not to worry. They're giving you a month's leave, you can have it whenever you want it. They'd like you to return to the States for a couple of weeks. But you can do what you want."

Dietz winced as the nurse washed and dried the large wound on his forearm. "Ask her how long I'll be in here."

"You really don't know any French at all?"

"Only the basics," Dietz said.

Puller smiled; Dietz made no concessions. He was the same wherever he was: the Middle East, Latin America. He didn't know Arabic or Spanish either. He was like a camera; his settings operated in any environment. "She says you'll be out in a week but you'll have to take it easy."

Dietz pointed to a pile of mail on the bureau. There was a foot-high stack of letters and telegrams. "Did you pick up any mail today?"

"None for you," Puller said.

Dietz looked puzzled. "Nothing at all?"

"You're a greedy bastard. Christ, you've heard from everybody but the secretary of defense."

"I love to read expressions of sympathy," Dietz said.

"When are you going to write the story?"

"Well, I told you. I am writing it. In my head."

"I mean for the newspaper."

"I have to write it for the kids first."

"Oh, sure," Puller said.

"I have to get the characters straight. These stories are damn complicated, and the kids count on them."

"Right."

"Got to get the plot worked out."

"Do you want your portable?"

"No, I'm writing it in my head, memorizing it. I'll memorize it and write it up in longhand. But it's taking a hell of a long time, I'm only up to the first night." He smiled benignly. "Bivouac."

Puller put two ice cubes and a finger of gin in Dietz's drink, watching the nurse frown and turn away. He told Dietz that he had to leave but would look in at dinnertime, perhaps bring a few friends. He moved to go, then looked back at the bed. "What did you mean a moment ago, that you've used up your ticket? What does that mean?"

"I'm invulnerable. This can only happen to you once. The odds are all in my favor. I've done everything now, I'm clean. They've got nothing on me."

"I'd like to know the name of that odds maker. That bastard is practicing without a license."

Dietz laughed. "It's true!"

"And who hasn't got anything on you?"

"They don't. None of them do." Dietz said, "I've paid my dues." That was a private joke and they both laughed. "I'm in fat city."

"Jesus Christ," Puller muttered. "I suppose you are, as long as you're here."

Dietz drained his glass and grinned. "When you come back tonight, bring me some stationery. The kids are probably worried, they haven't heard from me in two weeks. Probably don't know where the hell I am."

Puller nodded. Sure. Then: "Well, they know you got hit."

"No reason for them to."

"But —"

"Listen. It's a long story, so bring plenty of stationery."

"Honest to God, you look in damn good shape," Puller said.

"Feel fine," said Dietz.

In the end Dietz wrote a story for the children and the newspaper, and they were entirely different stories. The story for the children was witty, crammed with incident, and populated with strange animal characters in a mythical setting. He set one character against the others, though all of them were friends. The story began darkly but ended sweetly, it was very exciting and covered twelve sheets of paper. In the act of writing it, Dietz discarded most of the myths and composed a lovable story about animals. The article for the newspaper was deft and straightforward. He wrote the article in one draft from memory and did not consult his notebook at all. Reading it over, he was alarmed to find he'd neglected his facts, save the central incident and one or two names. To his surprise and confusion it was a cruel but cheerful story, and somehow uplifting despite its savage details. He kept himself out of it and most readers did not understand until the final sentences that it was an eyewitness account. But the editors liked it and put it on page one with a box and a picture of Dietz. The picture caption read: "Dietz at War."

He cabled the story, then did a strange thing. He wrote the editor of the newspaper and told him to inform his ex-wife when the article would be published. The editor was to tell the ex-wife to keep the newspaper out of the house that day. Under no circumstances were the children to see the article Dietz had written about himself.

Dietz went from success to success. He matured with the war, developing a singular style of journalism in order to arrive at the still center of the violence. In the years following the murderous afternoon in April he devoted himself entirely to journalism and to his letters home. He removed himself from the life of the capital and ventured ever farther afield for his stories. He'd spend two weeks among the mountain people, then a week investigating the political structure of an obscure coastal province. His dispatches contained detailed descriptions of the flora and fauna of the country, its landscapes and population. There were many places where the war was not present and he was careful to visit those as well. Often Dietz's stories contained no more than two or three facts — the dateline, the subject, the subject's age. No more, often less.

But his sense of irony, his understanding of awful paradox, was exquisite. He saw the war in delicate balance and reported it as he would report the life and atmosphere of an asylum, or zoo. He adopted various points of view in his reportage, convinced that each moment possessed its own life; he often impersonated a traveler from abroad. Energetic and restless in his inquiries, he occasionally published fictitious information. These were the devices he used to move the emotions of his readers. As the dead piled on dead his images became blacker and more melancholy, though he fought for balance. He'd bring himself back into equilibrium by writing a long letter to his children. Every month he spent at least a fortnight with troops on the line, though he always refused to carry a weapon.

During one of the periodic cease-fires (they came as interregnums, pauses between seizures), Dietz's old friend Puller returned from the United States. Puller'd done a year's time in the zone and departed without hesitation. That was two years ago, and now Puller was back for a visit. They spent a long and sour night drinking in Dietz's hotel room.

♦

Puller demanded, "Why are you still here? No one cares anymore. What are you doing here?"

"I live here. It's my home."

"It's a forgotten front, I'll tell you that."

"Not by me."

"No one gives a damn anymore."

"Well, I do."

"Odds in your favor, is that it?"

"Well, I'm here. In one piece. Healthy. Sound."

"You ought to quit it," Puller said. "There's a limit —"

"It's a rich vein," Dietz said. "Hardly touched."

"A vein of pure crap."

"The rest of you, it's all right. You can watch it from the United States. The point is, you can't *know* this place until you've lived here. You have to *live* here, in it."

Puller looked at him. "It's a place like any other. One more place to get stale in."

"You think I'm stale?"

"The stuff you're writing, a lot of it doesn't make any sense."

"Are you reading it?"

"Well, no. I don't read it much anymore."

Dietz smiled. His expression was one of satisfaction. "Well, it's strange. Perhaps true." He smiled warmly, and poured fresh drinks for them both. "You know, because of the cease-fire there's been no dead this week. No killed or wounded. No casualty lists." He shrugged, amused, amazed. The casualty lists had been part of his life for so long that he could not imagine their absence. They and the war were what he lived with. He had not come to terms with parting from either of them, the dead or the war. America seemed to him remote, at an infinite remove; the back of beyond. "None," he said.

"You think you're *part* of this war. You think you can't leave it. You think that if you go away, the war will disappear."

"No man is indispensable." Dietz grinned.

"Paying your dues. You're *paid up!*" Puller glanced around the familiar room; it hadn't changed in two years. The transistor radio, the bottles on the sideboard, the photograph over the typewriter — Dietz in fatigues, fording a nameless river in the jungle. Puller had taken the picture, catching Dietz's winning smile as the water washed over his chest. Dietz had hung the picture — why? Perhaps it reminded him of hardship. Whenever he looked up from the typewriter he saw himself in fatigues, fording some nameless river, smiling.

"Yes, I am," Dietz agreed.

"Then why —"

Dietz roared, "My God, Puller — how can that compare to *this?*"

Puller left shortly after midnight (they were both drunk, and less friendly than at the beginning), and Dietz prepared another drink and set about securing himself for the night. A hotel room was a world away, a haven in its safety and invisibility; its neutrality. No man's land. Drink in hand, he set the latch and the chain and the bolt, and tucked the desk chair under the doorknob. He checked the tape that crisscrossed the windows that looked out onto the main square of the capital; on advice of army friends, he'd taped the windows to prevent flying glass in the event of an explosion. He locked the windows and carefully removed the pictures from the walls and stacked them under the bed, where they'd be safe. The bottles of gin and whiskey were placed in the closet, next to the carbine and the filled canteens. There was a full clip of ammunition taped to the stock of the carbine; he inspected that to verify that it was clean, and that the breech was oiled and the barrel spotless. His steel pot and knapsack were in their places, on the shelf in the clothes closet. He drew the blinds and covered his typewriter and put the table lamp on the floor next to his desk.

Dietz took a long pull on his drink and looked around the room, satisfied. He undressed slowly, taking small sips every few seconds. He listened for any disturbance in the street but heard nothing. The sentry was still in the square — how did they expect one man to fend off an attack if it came? The sentry was leaning against a lamppost like some dapper soak in a Peter Arno cartoon; it was useless, he was probably asleep. He was either asleep or working for the other side. The most dangerous time was between midnight and three A.M.; he'd learned that much from the military authorities. It was during the early morning hours that the enemy struck without warning, moving anonymously from the shadows, planting satchel charges and mines. A month earlier there'd been a scare in the hotel and half a dozen downtown restaurants were now off-limits to American personnel. His drink empty, Dietz flicked on an overhead light and the two lamps next to his bed. The desk lamp on the floor was already burning, as were the lights in the bathroom. He stripped and lay naked on the sheets, listening to the hum of the air conditioner. Then he reached for his pen and the box of stationery.

· · ·

Dietz never wearied of writing to his children. Over the years the letters grew prolix, four and five letters a week, some of them five and six hundred words long. Dear Girls, Much Love from Dad. It didn't bother him that his children didn't reply for months at a time, and it did not occur to him at all that one of them was too young to write anything. His former wife, suddenly sympathetic, kept him informed of their progress. He had not been to America in more than three years; his vacations were limited to long weekends at a secure seaside resort. He felt it would be a tragedy to be out of the country the day it "blew," so he kept himself in constant readiness. He invented wonderful stories about the animals in the zoo, and his letters home were entirely concerned with the Bengal tiger, the two elephants, the zebra, the monkey, the antelope, the water buffalo, the snake, and the civet cat. These animals were assigned personalities that corresponded to the men who managed the war.

Dietz stayed on in the zone, assembling ever more powerful ironies with which to ravage the consciences of his readers. After five years the management of the newspaper insisted that he come home for good. When he refused, the publisher of the paper sent him a brief note informing him that he would either come home or consider himself fired. Dietz scanned the note and decided there were loopholes; they would not dare to fire him. He'd plead for time, and if necessary take leave and file on a free-lance basis. He knew that in the last analysis they would not fire him; they never fired anybody.

Dietz's critics insisted that he was out of touch with the realities of the war. It was no longer a war but a depredation. The realities had changed but Dietz had not. He was rarely seen at the various important news briefings, preferring instead to investigate the mood of the provinces. In the provinces he found life and therefore hope, and from time to time a strange sweetness infused his copy. He had long since given up his love affairs and was an infrequent visitor to the downtown cafés. It was true that his ironic turn of mind no longer puzzled or depressed his readers, as it was true his children found his letters home tedious. However, his readers still thought him authoritative and his children assured him they loved him. He was a majestic figure inside his moral fortress, healthy, astute, and entirely free of bias. In that way the war never lost its savor, and Dietz was free of facts forever.

# ABOUT BOSTON

◆

BETH WAS TALKING and I was listening. She said, "This was years ago. I was having a little tryst. On a Thursday, in New York, in the afternoon. He telephoned: 'Is it this Thursday or next?' I told him it was never, if he couldn't remember the *week*. Well." She laughed. "It makes your point about letters. Never would've happened if we'd written letters, because you write something and you remember it. Don't you?"

"Usually," I said.

"There isn't a record of anything anymore, it's just telephone calls and bad memory."

"I've got a filing cabinet full of letters," I said, "and most of them are from ten years ago and more. People wrote a lot in the sixties, maybe they wanted a record of what they thought. There was a lot to think about, and it seemed a natural thing to do, write a letter to a friend, what with everything that was going on."

"I wonder if they're afraid," she said.

"No written record? No," I said. "They don't have the time. They won't make the time and there aren't so many surprises now, thanks to the sixties. We're surprised-out. They don't write and they don't read either."

"That one read," she said, referring to the man in the tryst. "He read all the time — history, biography. Sports books, linebackers' memoirs, the strategy of the full-court press." She lowered her voice. "And politics."

"Well," I said. I knew who it was now.

251

"But he didn't know the week." She lit a cigarette, staring at the match a moment before depositing it, just so, in the ashtray. "You always wrote letters."

I smiled. "A few close friends."

She smiled back. "Where do you think we should begin?"

"Not at the beginning."

"No, you know that as well as I do."

I said, "Probably better."

"Not better," she said.

"I don't know if I'm the man —"

"No," she said firmly. She stared at me across the room, then turned to look out the window. It was dusk, and the dying sun caught the middle windows of the Hancock tower, turning them a brilliant, wavy orange. In profile, with her sharp features and her short black hair, she looked like a schoolgirl. She said, "You're the man, all right. I want you to do it. I'd feel a lot more comfortable, we've known each other so long. Even now, after all this time, we don't have to finish sentences. It'd be hard for me, talking about it to a stranger."

"Sometimes that's easiest," I said.

"Not for me it isn't."

"All right," I said at last. "But if at any time it gets awkward for you —" I was half hoping she'd reconsider. But she waved her hand in a gesture of dismissal, subject closed. She was sitting on the couch in the corner of my office, and now she rose to stand at the window and watch the last of the sun reflected on the windows of the Hancock. A Mondrian among Turners, she called it, its blue mirrors a new physics in the Back Bay. And who cared if in the beginning its windows popped out like so many ill-fitting contact lenses. The Hancock governed everything around it, Boston's past reflected in Boston's future. And it was miraculous that in the cascade of falling glass the casualties were so few.

I watched her: at that angle and in the last of the light her features softened and she was no longer a schoolgirl. I checked my watch, then rang my assistant and said she could lock up; we were through for the day. I fetched a yellow legal pad and a pen and sat in the leather chair, facing Beth. She was at the window, fussing with the cord of the venetian blind. She turned suddenly, with a movement so abrupt that I dropped my pad; the blind dropped with a crash. There had always been something violent and unpredictable in her behavior. But now she only smiled winningly, nodded at the sideboard, and asked for a drink before we got down to business.

. . .

I have practiced law in the Back Bay for almost twenty-five years. After Yale I came to Boston with the naïve idea of entering politics. The city had a rowdy quality I liked; it reminded me of Chicago, a city of neighborhoods, which wasn't ready for reform. But since I am a lapsed Catholic, neither Irish nor Italian, neither Yankee nor Democrat nor rich, I quickly understood that for me there were no politics in Boston. Chicago is astronomically remote from New England, and it was of no interest to anyone that I had been around politicians most of my life and knew the code. My grandfather had been, briefly, a congressman from the suburbs of Cook County, and I knew how to pull strings. But in Boston my antecedents precluded everything but good-government committees and the United Way.

Beth and I were engaged then, and Boston seemed less daunting than New York, perhaps because she knew it so intimately; it was her town as Chicago was mine. I rented an apartment in the North End and for the first few months we were happy enough, I with my new job and she with her volunteer work at the Mass. General. We broke off the engagement after six months — the usual reasons — and I looked up to find myself behind the lines in enemy territory. I had misjudged Boston's formality and its network of tribal loyalties and had joined Hamlin and White, one of the old State Street firms. I assumed that H,W — as it had been known for a hundred years — was politically connected. An easy error to make, for the firm was counsel to Boston's largest bank and handled the wills and trusts of a number of prominent Brahmin Republicans, and old Hamlin had once been lieutenant governor of Massachusetts. In Chicago that would have spelled political, but in Boston it only spelled probate. There were thirty men in the firm, large for Boston in those days. The six senior men were Hamlin and Hamlin Junior and White III, and Chelm, Warner, and Diuguid. Among the associates were three or four recognizable Mayflower names. The six senior men were all physically large, well over six feet tall and in conspicuous good health, by which I mean ruddy complexions and a propensity to roughhouse. They all had full heads of hair, even old Hamlin, who was then eighty. Their talk was full of the jargon of sailing and golf, and in their company I felt the worst sort of provincial rube.

Of course I was an experiment — a balding, unathletic Yale man from Chicago, of middling height, of no particular provenance, and book-smart. I was no one's cousin and no one's ex-roommate. But I was engaged to a Boston girl and I had been first in my class at Yale and the interview with Hamlin Junior had gone well. All of them in the firm spoke in that hard, open-mouthed bray peculiar to Massachusetts males of the upper classes. The exception was Hamlin Junior, who mumbled. When it was clear, after two years, that their experiment had failed — or had not, at any event, succeeded brilliantly — it was Hamlin Junior who informed me. He called me into his dark brown office late one afternoon, poured me a sherry, and rambled for half an hour before he got to the point, which was that I was an excellent lawyer mumble mumble damn able litigator mumble mumble but the firm has its own personality, New England salt sort of thing ha-ha mumble sometimes strange to an outsider but it's the way we've always done things mumble question of style and suitability, sometimes tedious but can't be helped wish you the best you're a damn able trial man, and of course you've a place here so long's you want though in fairness I wanted mumble make it known that you wouldn't be in the first foursome as it were mumble mumble. Just one question, I've always wondered: 'S really true that you wanted to go into politics here?

It was my first professional failure, and in my anger and frustration I put it down to simple snobbery. I did not fit into their clubs, and I hated the North Shore and was not adept at games. I was never seen "around" during the winter or on the Cape or the Islands or in Maine in the summer. I spend my vacations in Europe, and most weekends I went to New York, exactly as I did when I was at law school in New Haven. New York remains the center of my social life. Also, I was a bachelor. Since the breakup of my engagement, I had become an aggressive bachelor. Beth was bitter and I suspected her of spreading unflattering stories. Of course this was not true, but in my humiliation I believed that it was and that as a consequence the six senior men had me down as homosexual. In addition, I was a hard drinker in a firm of hard drinkers, though unlike them I never had whiskey on my breath in the morning and I never called in sick with Monday grippe. I could never join in the hilarious retelling of locker room misadventures. They drank and joked. I drank and didn't joke.

When I left H,W, I opened an office with another disgruntled provincial — he was from Buffalo, even farther down the scale of things than Chicago — half expecting to fail but determined not to and wondering what on earth I would do and where I would go, now that I'd been drummed out of my chosen city: blackballed. Young litigators are not as a rule peripatetic: you begin in a certain city and remain there; you are a member of the bar, you know the system, you build friendships and a clientele and a reputation. Looking back on it, Deshais and I took a terrible risk. But we worked hard and prospered, and now there are twenty lawyers in our firm, which we have perversely designed to resemble a squad of infantry in a World War II propaganda movie: Irish, Italians, Jews, three blacks in the past ten years, one Brahmin, Deshais, and me. Of course we are always quarreling; ours is not a friendly, clubby firm. In 1974, we bought a private house, a handsome brownstone, in the Back Bay, only two blocks from my apartment on Commonwealth Avenue. This is so convenient, such an agreeable way to live — it is my standard explanation to my New York friends who ask why I remain here — that we decided not to expand the firm because it would require a larger building, and all of us love the brownstone, even the younger associates who must commute from Wayland or Milton. Sometimes I think it is the brownstone and the brownstone alone that holds the firm together.

I suppose it is obvious that I have no affection for this spoiled city and its noisy inhabitants. It is an indolent city. It is racist to the bone and in obvious political decline and like any declining city is by turns peevish and arrogant. It is a city without civility or civic spirit, or Jews. The Jews, with their prodigious energies, have tucked themselves away in Brookline, as the old aristocrats, with their memories and trust funds, are on the lam on the North Shore. Remaining are the resentful Irish and the furious blacks. Meanwhile, the tenured theory class issues its pronouncements from the safety of Cambridge, confident that no authority will take serious notice. So the city of Boston closes in on itself, conceited, petulant, idle, and broke.

I observe this from a particular vantage point. To my surprise, I have become a divorce lawyer. The first cases I tried after joining forces with Deshais were complicated divorce actions. They were women referred to me by Hamlin Junior, cases considered — I think he used the word "fraught" — too mumble "fraught" for H,W. In Chicago we used the word "messy," though all this was a long time ago; now they are tidy and without fault. However, then as now there was pulling and hauling over the money. Hamlin Junior admired my trial work and believed me discreet and respectable enough to represent in the first instance his cousin and in the second a dear friend of his wife's. He said that he hoped the matter of the cousin would be handled quietly, meaning without a lengthy trial and without publicity, but that if the case went to trial he wanted her represented by a lawyer ahem who was long off the tee. You know what it is you must do? he asked. I nodded. At that time divorces were purchased; you bought a judge for the afternoon. Happily, the cousin was disposed of in conference, quietly and very expensively for her husband. The success of that case caused Hamlin Junior to send me the second woman, whose disposition was not quite so quiet. Fraught it certainly was, and even more expensive.

I was suddenly inside the bedroom, hearing stories the obverse of those I had heard after hours at H,W. The view from the bedroom was different from the view from the locker room. It was as if a light bulb joke had been turned around and told from the point of view of the bulb. Hundred-watt Mazda shocks WASP couple! I discovered that I had a way with women in trouble. That is precisely because I do not pretend to understand them, as a number of my colleagues insist that they "understand women." But I do listen. I listen very carefully, and then I ask questions and listen again. Then they ask me questions and I am still listening hard, and when I offer my answers they are brief and as precise as I can make them. And I never, never overpromise. No woman has ever rebuked me with "But you *said*, and now you've broken your word."

The cousin and the wife's friend were satisfied and told Hamlin Junior, who said nothing to his colleagues. He seemed to regard me as the new chic restaurant in town, undiscovered and therefore underpriced; it would become popular soon enough, but meanwhile the food would continue excellent and the service attentive and the bill modest. For years he referred clients and friends to me, and I always accepted them even when they were routine cases and I had to trim my fees. And when Hamlin Junior died, I went to his funeral, and was not at all startled to see so many familiar female faces crowding the pews.

My divorce business was the beginning, and there was a collateral benefit — no, bonanza. I learned how money flows in Boston, and where; which were the rivers and which were the tributaries and which were the underground streams. Over the years, I have examined hundreds of trusts and discovered a multiformity of hidden assets, liquid and solid, floating and stationary, lettered and numbered, aboveground and below. The trusts are of breathtaking ingenuity, the product of the flintiest minds in Massachusetts, and of course facilitated over the years by a willing legislature. And what has fascinated me from the beginning is this: the trust that was originally devised to avoid taxes or to punish a recalcitrant child or to siphon income or to "protect" an unworldly widow or to reach beyond the grave to control the direction of a business or a fortune or a marriage can fall apart when faced with the circumstances of the present, an aggrieved client, and a determined attorney.

This is not the sort of legal practice I planned, but it is what I have. Much of what I have discovered in divorce proceedings I have replicated in my trust work, adding a twist here and there to avoid unraveling by someone like me, sometime in the future. Wills and trusts are now a substantial part of my business, since I have access to the flintiest minds in Massachusetts. Turn, and turn about. However, it is a risible anomaly of the upper classes of Boston that the estates have grown smaller and the trusts absurdly complex — Alcatraz to hold juvenile delinquents.

So one way and another I am in the business of guaranteeing the future. A trust, like a marriage, is a way of getting a purchase on the future. That is what I tell my clients, especially the women; women have a faith in the future that men, as a rule, do not. I am careful to tell my clients that although that is the objective, it almost never works; or it does not work in the way they intend it to work. It is all too difficult, reading the past, without trying to read the future as well. It is my view that men, at least, understand this, having, as a rule, a sense of irony and proportion. At any event, this is my seat at the Boston opera. It is lucrative and fascinating work. There was no compelling reason, therefore, not to listen to the complaint of Beth Earle Doran Greer, my former fiancée.

She said quietly, "It's finished."

I said nothing.

She described their last year together, the two vacations and the month at Edgartown, happy for the most part. They had one child, a boy, now at boarding school. It had been a durable marriage, fifteen years; the first one had lasted less than a year, and she had assumed that, despite various troubles, this one would endure. Then last Wednesday he said he was leaving her and his lawyer would be in touch.

"Has he?"

"No," she said.

"Who is he?"

She named a State Street lawyer whom I knew by reputation. He was an excellent lawyer. I was silent again, waiting for her to continue.

"Frank didn't say anything more than that."

"Do you know where he is?"

"I think he's at the farm." I waited again, letting the expression on my face do the work. There were two questions. Is he alone? Do you want him back? She said again, "It's finished." Then, the answer to the other question: "There is no one else." I looked at her, my face in neutral. She said, "Hard as that may be to understand."

Not believe, *understand;* a pointed distinction. I nodded, taking her at her word. It was hard, her husband was a great bon vivant.

"That's what he says, and I believe him. His sister called me to say that there isn't anybody else, but I didn't need her to tell me. Believe me, I know the signs. There isn't a sign I don't know and can't see a mile away, and he doesn't show any of them. Five years ago — that was something else. But she's married and not around anymore, and that's over and done with. And besides, if there was someone else he'd tell me. It'd be like him."

I nodded again and made a show of writing on my pad.

"And there isn't anyone else with me either."

"Well," I said, and smiled.

"Is it a first?"

I laughed quietly. "Not a first," I said. "Maybe a second."

She laughed, and lit a cigarette. "You were afraid it would be another cliché, she would be twenty and just out of Radcliffe. Meanwhile, I would've taken up with the garage mechanic or the gamekeeper. Or Frank's best friend; they tell me that's chic now." She looked at me sideways and clucked. "You know me better than that. Clichés aren't my style."

I said, "I never knew you at all."

"Yes, you did," she said quickly. I said nothing. "You always listened; in those days you were a very good listener. And you're a good listener now."

"The secret of my success," I said. But I knew my smile was getting thinner.

"The mouthpiece who listens," she said. "That's what Nora told me when she was singing your praises. Really, she did go on. Do they fall in love with you, like you're supposed to do with a psychiatrist?"

Nora was a client I'd represented in an action several years before, a referral from Hamlin Junior. She was a great friend of Beth's but a difficult woman and an impossible client. I said, "No."

"It was a pretty good marriage," she said after a moment's pause. "You'd think, fifteen years . . ." I leaned forward, listening. Presently, in order to focus the conversation, I would ask the first important question: What is it that you want me to do now? For the moment, though, I wanted to hear more. I have never regarded myself as a marriage counselor, but it is always wise to know the emotional state of your client. So far, Beth seemed admirably rational and composed, almost cold-blooded. I wondered if she had ever consulted a psychiatrist, then decided she probably hadn't. There was something impersonal about her locution "like you're supposed to." She said abruptly, "How did you get into this work? It's so unlike you. Remember the stories you told me about your grandfather and his friend? The relationship they had, and how that was the kind of lawyer you wanted to be?"

I remembered all right, but I was surprised that she did. My grandfather and I were very close, and when I was a youngster we lunched together every Saturday. My father drove me to the old man's office, in an unincorporated area of Cook County, near Blue Island. I'd take the elevator to the fourth floor, the building dark and silent on Saturday morning. My grandfather was always courteous and formal, treating me as he would treat an important adult. On Saturday mornings my grandfather met with Tom. Tom was his lawyer. I was too young to know exactly what they were talking about, though as I look back on it, their conversation was in a private language. There was a "matter" that needed "handling," or "a man" — perhaps "sound," perhaps "a screwball" — who had to be "turned." Often there was a sum of money involved — three, four, fi' thousand dollars. These questions would be discussed sparely, long pauses between sentences. Then, as a signal that the conversation was near its end, my grandfather would say, "Now this is what I want to do," and his voice would fall. Tom would lean close to the old man, listening hard; I never saw him make a note. Then: "Now you figure out how I can do it." And Tom would nod, thinking, his face disappearing into the collar of his enormous camel-hair coat. He never removed the coat, and he sat with his gray fedora in both hands, between his knees, turning it like the steering wheel of a car. When he finished thinking, he would rise and approach me and gravely shake hands. Then he would offer me a piece of licorice from the strand he kept in his coat, the candy furry with camel hair. He pressed it on me until I accepted. I can remember him saying good-bye to my grandfather and, halting at the door, smiling slightly and winking. Tom would exit whistling, and more often than not my grandfather would make a telephone call, perhaps two, speaking inaudibly into the receiver. Finally, rumbling in his basso profundo, he would make the ritual call to the Chicago Athletic Club to reserve his usual table for two, "myself and my young associate."

In those days children were not allowed in the men's bar, so we ate in the main dining room, a huge chamber with high ceilings and a spectacular view of the lakefront. We sat at a table by the window, and on a clear day we could see Gary and Michigan City to the southeast. Long-hulled ore boats were smudges on the horizon. Once, during the war, we saw a pocket aircraft carrier, a training vessel for navy pilots stationed at Great Lakes. The old man would wave his hand in the direction of the lake and speak of the Midwest as an ancient must have spoken of the Fertile Crescent: the center of the world, a homogeneous, God-fearing, hardworking *region*, its interior position protecting it from its numerous enemies. With a sweep of his hand he signified the noble lake and the curtain of smoke that hung over Gary's furnaces, thundering even on Saturdays. Industry, he'd say, *heavy* industry working at one hundred percent of capacity. Chicagoland, foundry to the world. His business was politics, he said; and his politics was business. "We can't let them take it away from us, all this . . ."

When the old man died, Tom was his principal pallbearer. It was a large funeral; the governor was present with his suite, along with a score or more of lesser politicians. Tom was dry-eyed, but I knew he was grieving. At the end of it he came over to me and shook my hand, solemnly as always, and said, "Your grandfather was one of the finest men who ever lived, a great friend, a great Republican, a great American, and a great client." I thought that an extraordinary inventory and was about to say so when he gripped my arm and exclaimed, "You ever need help of any kind, you come to me. That man and I . . ." He pointed at my grandfather's casket, still aboveground under its green canopy, then tucked his chin into the camel hair. "We've been through the mill, fought every day of our lives. I don't know what will happen without him." He waved dispiritedly at the gravestones around us, stones as far as the eye could see, and lowered his voice so that I had to bend close to hear. "The world won't be the same without him," Tom said. "The Midwest's going to hell."

Tom died a few years later, without my having had a chance to take him up on his offer. But from my earliest days in that fourth-floor office I knew I would be a lawyer. I wanted to be Tom to someone great, and prevent the world from going to hell. Tom was a man who listened carefully to a complex problem, sifting and weighing possibilities. Then, settled and secure in his own mind, he figured a way to get from here to there. It was only an idiosyncrasy of our legal system that the route was never a straight line.

"I mean," she said brightly, leaning forward on the couch, "listening to a bunch of hysterical women with their busted marriages, that wasn't what I expected at all."

"They are not always hysterical," I said, "and some of them are men."

"And you never married," she said.

That was not true, but I let it pass.

"No," she said, rapping her knuckles on the coffee table. "You *were* married. I heard that, a long time ago. I heard that you were married, a whirlwind romance in Europe, but then it broke up right away."

"That's right," I said.

"She was French."

"English," I said.

"And there were no children."

"No," I said. We were silent while I walked to the sideboard, made a drink for myself, and refilled hers.

"Do you remember how we used to talk, that place on Hanover Street we used to go to, all that pasta and grappa? I practiced my Italian on them. Always the last ones out the door, running down Hanover Street to that awful place you had on — where was it?"

"North Street," I said.

"North Street. We'd get to dinner and then we'd go to your place and you'd take me back to Newton in your red Chevrolet. Three, four o'clock in the morning. I don't know how you got any work done, the hours we kept."

I nodded, remembering.

"And of course when I heard you'd been sacked at H,W, I didn't know what to think, except that it was for the best." She paused. "Which I could've told you if you'd asked." I handed her the highball and sat down, resuming my lawyerly posture, legs crossed, the pad in my lap. "Do you ever think about your grandfather? Or what would've happened if you'd gone back to Chicago instead of following me here? Whether you'd've gone into politics, like him?"

"I didn't follow you," I said. "We came together. It was where we intended to live, together."

"Whatever." She took a long swallow of her drink. "Chicago's such a different place from Boston, all that prairie. Boston's close and settled and old, so charming." I listened, tapping the pencil on my legal pad. It was dark now. At night the city seemed less close and settled. The cars in the street outside were bumper to bumper, honking. There was a snarl at the intersection, one car double-parked and

•

another stalled. A car door slammed and there were angry shouts. She looked at me, smiling. "I don't want anything particular from him."

I made a note on my pad.

"I have plenty of money; so does he. Isn't that the modern way? No punitive damages?" She hesitated. "So there won't be any great opportunity to delve into the assets. And Frank's trust. Or mine."

I ignored that. "Of course there's little Frank."

She looked at me with the hint of a malicious grin. "How did you know his name?"

"Because I follow your every movement," I said, with as much sarcasm as I could muster. "For Christ's sake, Beth. I don't know how I know his name. People like Frank Greer always name their children after themselves."

"Don't get belligerent," she said. "A more devoted father —" she began and then broke off.

"Yes," I said.

"— he's devoted to little Frank." She hesitated, staring out the window for a long moment. She was holding her glass with both hands, in her lap. She said, "What was the name of that man, your grandfather's lawyer?"

"Tom," I said.

"God, yes," she said, laughing lightly. "Tom, one of those sturdy Midwestern names."

"I think," I said evenly, "I think Tom is a fairly common name. I think it is common even in Boston."

She laughed again, hugely amused. "God, yes, it's common."

I glared at her, not at all surprised that she remembered which buttons worked and which didn't. Beth had an elephant's memory for any man's soft spots. Why Tom was one of mine was not easily explained; Beth would have one explanation, I another. But of course she remembered. My background was always a source of tension between us, no doubt because my own attitude was ambiguous. She found my grandfather and Tom . . . quaint. They were colorful provincials, far from her Boston milieu, and she condescended to them exactly as certain English condescend to Australians.

"It's a riot," she said.

"So," I said quietly, glancing at my watch. "What is it that you want me to do now?"

"A quick, clean divorce," she said. "Joint custody for little Frank, though it's understood he lives with me. Nothing changes hands, we leave with what we brought, status quo ante. I take my pictures, he takes his shotguns. Except, naturally, the house in Beverly. It's mine anyway, though for convenience it's in both our names. He understands that."

"What about the farm?"

"We split that, fifty-fifty."

"Uh-huh," I said.

"Is it always this easy?"

"We don't know how easy it'll be," I said carefully. "Until I talk to his lawyer. Maybe it won't be easy at all. It depends on what he thinks his grievances are."

"He hasn't got any."

"Well," I said.

"So it'll be easy," she said, beginning to cry.

We had agreed to go to dinner after meeting in my office. I proposed the Ritz; she countered with a French restaurant I had never heard of. She insisted, Boylston Street nouvelle cuisine, and I acceded, not without complaint. I told her about a client, a newspaperman who came to me every six years for his divorce. The newspaperman said that the nouvelle cuisine reminded him of the *nouveau journalisme* — a colorful plate, agreeably subtle, wonderfully presented with inspired combinations, and underdone. The portions were small, every dish had a separate sauce, and you were hungry when you finished. A triumph of style over substance.

She listened patiently, distracted.

I was trying to make her laugh. "But I can get a New York strip here, which they'll call an entrecôte, and there isn't a lot you can do to ruin a steak. Though they will try."

"You haven't changed," she said bleakly.

"Yes, I have," I said. "In the old days I would've been as excited about this place as you are. I'd know the names of the specialties of the house and of the chef. In the old days I was as al dente as the veggies. But not anymore." I glanced sourly around the room. The colors were pastel, various tints of yellow, even to a limp jonquil in the center of each table, all of it illuminated by candles thin as pencils and a dozen wee chandeliers overhead. It was very feminine and not crowded; expensive restaurants rarely were in Boston now; the money was running out.

"I'm sorry about the tears," she said.

I said, "Don't be."

"I knew I was going to bawl when I made that remark about Tom and you reacted."

"Yes," I said. I'd known it too.

"It made me sad. It reminded me of when we were breaking up and all the arguments we had."

I smiled gamely. "I was al dente then, and I broke easily." I knew what she was leading up to, and I didn't want it. When the waiter arrived I ordered whiskey for us both, waiting for the little superior sneer and feeling vaguely disappointed when he smiled pleasantly and flounced off. I started to tell her a story but she cut me off, as I knew she would.

"It reminded me of that ghastly dinner and how awful everything was afterward."

I muttered something noncommittal, but the expression on her face told me she wanted more, so I said it was over and forgotten, part of the buried past, et cetera. Like hell. We had argued about the restaurant that night, as we had tonight, except I won and we went to the Union Oyster House. My parents were in town, my father ostensibly on business; in fact they were in Boston to meet Beth. The dinner did not go well from the beginning; the restaurant was crowded and the service indifferent. My parents didn't seem to care, but Beth was irritated — "The Union Oyster Tourist Trap" — and that in turn put me on edge, or perhaps it was the other way around. Halfway through dinner, I suspect in an effort to salvage things, my father shyly handed Beth a wrapped package. It was a bracelet he had selected himself; even my mother didn't know about it. It was so unlike him, and such a sweet gesture, tears jumped to my eyes. Even before she opened it, I knew it would not be right. Beth had a particular taste in jewelry and as a consequence rarely wore any. I hoped she could disguise her feelings, but as it happened she giggled. And did not put the bracelet on, but hurried it into her purse after leaning over the table and kissing my father. He did not fail to notice the bracelet rushed out of sight. Probably he didn't miss the giggle, either. In the manner of families, after a suitable silent interval my father and I commenced to quarrel. On the surface it was a quarrel about businessmen and professional men, but actually it had to do with the merits of the East and the merits of the Midwest and my father's knowledge that I had rejected the values of his region. The Midwest asserted its claims early, and if you had a restless nature you left. It forced you to leave; there were no halfway measures in the heartland, at that time a province as surely as Franche-Comté or Castile, an interior region pressed by the culture of the coasts, defensive, suspicious, and claustrophobic. When I left I tried to explain to him that a New Yorker's restlessness or ambition could take him to Washington as a Bostonian's could take him to New York, the one city representing power and the other money. No Midwesterner, making the momentous decision to leave home, would go from Chicago to Cleveland or from Minneapolis to Kansas City. These. places are around the corner from one another. The Midwest is the same wherever you go, the towns larger or smaller but the culture identical. Leaving the Midwest, one perforce rejects the Midwest and its values; its sense of inferiority — so I felt then — prevented any return. In some way it had failed. What sound reason could there be for leaving God's country, the very soul of the nation, to live and work on the cluttered margins? It had failed you and you had failed it, whoring after glitter. My father's chivalry did not allow him to blame "that girl" publicly, but I knew that privately he did. Too much — too much Boston, too much money, too determined, too self-possessed. He hated to think that his son — flesh of my flesh, blood of my blood! — could be led out of Chicagoland by a woman. The image I imagine it brought to his mind was of an ox dumbly plodding down a road, supervised by a young woman lightly flicking its withers with a stick. That ghastly dinner!

"The thing is." She smiled wanly, back in the present now: that is, her own life, and what she had made of it. "It's so — *tiresome.* I know the marriage is over, it's probably been finished for years. But starting over again. I don't want to start over again. I haven't the energy." She sighed. "He's said for years that he's got to find himself. He's forty-eight years old and he's lost and now he wants to be found. And I'm sure he will be."

"Usually it's the other way around," I said. "These days, it's the women who want to find themselves. Or get lost, one or the other."

"Frank has a feminine side." I nodded, thinking of Frank Greer as a pastel. Frank in lime green and white, cool and pretty as a gin and tonic. "But the point isn't Frank," Beth said. "It's me. I don't want to start over again. I started over again once and that didn't work and then I started over again and it was fun for a while and then it was a routine, like everything else. I like the routine. And I was younger then."

I did not quite follow that, so I said, "I know."

"Liar," she said. "How could you? You've never been married."

"Beth," I said.

♦

She looked at me irritably. "That doesn't count. You've got to be married for at least five years before it's a marriage. And there have to be children, or at least a child. Otherwise it's just shacking up and you can get out of it as easily and painlessly as you got into it, which from the sound of yours was pretty easy and painless."

I looked away while the waiter set down our drinks and, with a flourish, the menus.

"How long ago was it?"

"Almost twenty years ago," I said.

"Where is she now?"

I shrugged. I had no idea. When she left me she went back to London. I heard she had a job there; then, a few years ago, I heard she was living in France, married, with children. Then I heard she was no longer in France but somewhere else on the Continent, unmarried now.

"That's what I mean," she said. "You don't even know where she *is.*"

"Well," I said. "She knows where I am."

"What was her name?"

"Rachel," I said.

Beth thought a moment. "Was she Jewish?"

"Yes," I said.

Beth made a little sound, but did not comment. The amused look on her face said that my father must have found Rachel even more unsuitable than Beth. As it happened, she was right, but it had nothing to do with Rachel's Jewishness. She was a foreigner with pronounced political opinions. "And you like living alone," Beth said.

"At first I hated it," I said. "But I like it now and I can't imagine living any other way. It's what I do, live alone. You get married, I don't. Everyone I know gets married and almost everyone I know gets divorced."

"Well, you see it from the outside."

"It's close enough," I said.

"Yes, but it's not *real*." She glanced left into Boylston Street. It was snowing, and only a few pedestrians were about, bending into the wind. She shivered when she looked at the stiff-legged pedestrians, their movements so spiritless and numb against the concrete of the sidewalk, the sight bleaker still by contrast with the pale monochrome and the fragrance of the restaurant. Outside was a dark, malicious, European winter, Prague perhaps, or Moscow. "We might've made it," she said tentatively, still looking out the window.

I said nothing. She was dead wrong about that.

She sat with her chin in her hand, staring into the blowing snow. "But we were so different, and you were so bad."

The waiter was hovering and I turned to ask him the specialties of the day. They were a tiny bird en croûte, a fish soufflé, and a vegetable ensemble. Beth was silent, inspecting the menu; she had slipped on a pair of half-glasses for this chore. I ordered a dozen oysters and an entrecôte, medium well. I knew that if I ordered it medium well I had a fair chance of getting it medium rare. Then I ordered a baked potato and a Caesar salad and another drink. The waiter caught something in my tone and courteously suggested that medium well was excessive. I said all right, if he would promise a true medium rare. Beth ordered a fish I never heard of and called for the wine list. The waiter seemed much happier dealing with Beth than with me. They conferred over the wine list for a few moments, and then he left.

She said, "You're always so defensive."

"I don't like these places, I told you that." I heard the Boston whine in my voice and retreated a step. "The waiter's OK."

"You never did like them," she said. "But at least *before* . . ." She shook her head, exasperated.

"Before, what?" I asked.

"At least you were a provincial, there was an excuse."

I pulled at my drink, irritated. But when I saw her smiling slyly I had to laugh. Nothing had changed, though we had not seen each other in fifteen years and had not spoken in twenty. The occasion fifteen years ago was a wedding reception. I saw her standing in a corner talking to Frank Greer. She was recently divorced from Doran. I was about to approach to say hello; then I saw the expression on her face and withdrew. She and Greer were in another world, oblivious of the uproar around them, and I recognized the expression: it was the one I thought was reserved for me. Now, looking at her across the restaurant table, it was as if we had never been apart, as if our attitudes were frozen in aspic. We were still like a divided legislature, forever arguing over the economy, social policy, the defense budget, and the cuisine in the Senate dining room. The same arguments, conducted in the same terms; the same old struggle for control of our future. Her prejudice, my pride.

"You have to tell me one thing." She turned to inspect the bottle the waiter presented, raising her head so she could see through the half-glasses. She touched the label of the wine with her fingernails and said yes, it was fine, excellent really, and then, turning, her head still raised, she assured me that I would find it drinkable, since it came from a splendid little château vineyard near the Wisconsin Dells. The waiter looked at her dubiously and asked whether he should open it now and put it on ice, and she said yes, of course, she wanted it so cold she'd need her mittens to pour it. I was laughing and thinking how attractive she was, a woman whose humor improved with age, if she would just let up a little on the other. Also, I was waiting for the "one thing" I would have to tell her.

I said, "You're a damn funny woman."

"I have good material," she said.

"Not always," I replied.

"The one thing," she said, "that I can't figure out. Never could figure out. Why did you stay here? This isn't your kind of town at all, never was. It's so circumspect, and sure of itself. I'm surprised you didn't go back to Chicago after you were canned by H,W."

"I like collapsing civilizations," I said. "I'm a connoisseur of collapse and systems breakdown and bankruptcy — moral, ethical, and financial. So Boston is perfect." I thought of the town where I grew up, so secure and prosperous then, so down-at-heel now, the foundry old, exhausted, incidental, and off the subject. We lived in Chicago's muscular shadow and were thankful for it, before the world went to hell. "And I wasn't about to be run out of town by people like that," I added truculently.

"So it was spite," she said.

"Not spite," I said equably. "Inertia."

"And you're still spending weekends in New York?"

I nodded. Not as often now as in the past, though.

"Weird life you lead," she said.

I said, "What's so weird about it?"

"Weekdays here, weekends in New York. And you still have your flat near the brownstone, the same one?"

I looked at her with feigned surprise. "How did you know about my flat?"

"For God's sake," she said. "Nora's a friend of mine."

It was never easy to score a point on Beth Earle. I said, "I've had it for almost twenty years. And I'll have it for twenty more. It's my Panama Canal. I bought it, I paid for it, it's mine, and I intend to keep it."

She shook her head, smiling ruefully. She said that she had lived in half a dozen houses over the years and remembered each one down

to the smallest detail: the color of the tile in the bathroom and the
shape of the clothes closet in the bedroom. She and Doran had lived
in Provincetown for a year, and then had moved to Gloucester. That
was when Doran was trying to paint. Then, after Doran, she lived
alone in Marblehead. When she was married to Frank Greer they
went to New York, then returned to Boston; he owned an apartment
on Beacon Hill. They lived alone there for two years, and then moved
to Beverly — her idea; she was tired of the city. She counted these
places on her fingers. "Six," she said. "And all this time, you've been
in the same place in the Back Bay." She was leaning across the table,
and now she looked up. The waiter placed a small salad in front of
her and the oysters in front of me. The oysters were Cotuits. She
signaled for the wine and said that "Monsieur" would taste. She told
the waiter I was a distinguished gourmet, much sought after as a
taster, and that my wine cellar in Michigan City was the envy of the
region. She gave the impression that the restaurant was lucky to have
me as a patron. The waiter shot me a sharp look and poured the wine
into my glass. I pronounced it fine. Actually, I said it was "swell,"
and then, gargling heartily, "dandy." I gave Beth one of the oysters
and insisted that she eat it the way it was meant to be eaten, naked
out of the shell, without catsup or horseradish. She sucked it up, and
then leaned across the table once again. "Don't you miss them, the
arguments? The struggle, always rubbing off someone else? The
fights, the friction — ?"
I laughed loudly. "Miss them to death," I said.

We finished the bottle of white and ordered a bottle of red; she said
she preferred red with fish. I suspected that that was a concession to
my entrecôte, which at any event was rare and bloody. She continued
to press, gently at first, then with vehemence. She was trying to work
out her life and thought that somehow I was a clue to it. At last she
demanded that I describe my days in Boston. She wanted to know
how I lived, the details, "the quotidian." I was reluctant to do this,
having lived privately for so many years. Also, there was very little to
describe. I had fallen into the bachelor habit of total predictability.
Except to travel to the airport and the courts, I seldom left the Back
Bay. My terrain was bordered by the Public Garden and the Ritz,
Storrow Drive, Newbury Street, the brownstone where I worked, and
Commonwealth Avenue where I lived. I walked to work, lunched at
the Ritz, took a stroll in the Garden, returned to the brownstone, and
at seven or so went home. People I knew tended to live in the Back

Bay or on the Hill, so if I went out in the evening I walked. Each year it became easier not to leave the apartment; I needed an exceptional reason to do so. I liked my work and worked hard at it.

She listened avidly, but did not comment. The waiter came to clear the table and offer dessert. We declined, ordering coffee and cognac.

"What kind of car do you have?" she asked suddenly.

I said I didn't own one.

"What kind of car does she own?"

I looked at her: Who?

"Your secretary," she said. "I hear you have a relationship with your secretary."

"She's been my assistant for a very long time," I said.

"Her car," Beth said.

I said, "A Mercedes."

"Well," she said.

"Well, what?"

"Well, nothing," she said. "Except so do I."

"Two cheers for the Krauts," I said.

"Is she a nice woman?"

I laughed. "Yes," I said. "Very. And very able."

"She approves of the arrangement."

"Beth," I said.

Beth said, "I wonder what she gets out of it."

"She won't ever have to get divorced," I said. "That's one thing she gets out of it."

"Was she the woman in the outer office?"

"Probably," I said.

Beth was silent a moment, toying with her coffee cup. There was only one other couple left in the restaurant, and they were preparing to leave. "You were always secretive," she said.

"You were not exactly an open book."

She ignored that. "It's not an attractive trait, being secretive. It leaves you wide open."

For what? I wondered. I looked at her closely, uncertain whether it was she talking or the wine. We were both tight, but her voice had an edge that had not been there before. I poured more coffee, wondering whether I should ask the question that had been in my mind for the past hour. I knew I would not like the answer, whatever it was, but I was curious. Being with her again, I began to remember things I had not thought of in years; it was as if the two decades were no greater distance than the width of the table, and I had only to lean

across the space and take her hand to be twenty-five again. The
evening had already been very unsettling and strange; no reason, I
thought, not to make it stranger still.

I said quietly, "How was I so bad?"

"You never let go," she said. "You just hung on for dear life."

"Right," I said. I had no idea what she was talking about.

"Our plans," she began.

"Depended on me letting go?"

She shrugged. "You tried to fit in and you never did."

"In Boston," I said.

She moved her head, yes and no; apparently the point was a subtle
one. "I didn't want to come back here and you insisted. I was depending on you to take me away, or at least make an independent life.
You never understood that I had always been on the outs with my
family."

I stifled an urge to object. I had never wanted to come to Boston.
It was where she lived. It was her town, not mine. Glorious Boston,
cradle of the Revolution. I had no intrinsic interest in Boston; I only
wanted to leave the Midwest. Boston was as good a city as any, and
she lived there —

"You were such a damn good *listener*." She bit the word off, as if
it were an obscenity. "Better than you are now, and you're pretty
good now. Not so good at talking, though. You listened so well a
woman forgot that you never talked yourself, never let on what it
was *that was on your mind*. Not one of your strong points, talking."

"Beth," I said evenly. She waited, but I said nothing more; there
was nothing more to say anyhow, and I knew the silence would
irritate her.

"And it was obvious it would never work; we never got grounded
here. And it was obvious you never would, you could never let go of
your damn prairie *complexe d'infériorité*. And as a result you were"
— she sought the correct word — "*louche*."

"I am not André Malraux," I said. "What the hell does that
mean?"

"It means secretive," she said. "And something more. Furtive."

"Thanks," I said.

"It's a mystery to me why I'm still here. Not so great a mystery as
you, but mystery enough. You had to lead the way, though, and you
didn't. And I knew H,W was a mistake."

"It was your uncle who suggested it," I said.

"After you asked him," she said.

"At your urging," I said.

"When it looked like you wouldn't land anything and I was tired of the griping."

"You were the one who was nervous," I said.

"I didn't care where we lived," she said. "That was the point you never got." Her voice rose, and I saw the waiter turn and say something to the maître d'. The other couple had left and we were alone in the restaurant. Outside, a police car sped by, its lights blazing, but without sirens. The officer in the passenger seat was white-haired and fat, and he was smoking a cigar. It had stopped snowing but the wind was fierce, blowing debris and rattling windows. The police car had disappeared. I motioned to the waiter for the check. But Beth was far from finished.

"So I married Doran."

"And I didn't marry anybody."

"You married Rachel."

"According to you, Rachel doesn't count."

"Neither did Doran."

The waiter brought the check and I automatically reached for my wallet. She said loudly, "No," and I looked at her, momentarily confused. I had forgotten it was her treat. I had become so absorbed in the past; always when we had been together, I had paid, and it seemed cheap of me to let her pay now. But that was what she wanted and I had agreed to it. She had the check in her hand and was inspecting it for errors. Then, satisfied, she pushed it aside along with a credit card. She exhaled softly and turned to look out the window.

She said quietly, talking to the window, "Do you think it will be easy?"

"I don't know," I said.

"Please," she said. She said it hesitantly, as if the word were unfamiliar. "Just tell me what you think. I won't hold you to it if you're wrong."

"His lawyer," I began.

"Please," she said again, more forcefully.

"You're asking me for assurances that I can't give. I don't know."

"Just a guess," she said. "In your line of work you must make guesses all the time. Make one now, between us. Between friends."

"Well, then," I said. "No."

"The first one was easy."

"Maybe this will be too," I said.

"But you don't think so."

"No," I said. I knew Frank Greer.

She said, "You're a peach." She put on her glasses.

I did not reply to that.

"I mean it," she said.

Apparently she did, for she looked at me and smiled warmly. "I have disrupted your life."

I shook my head no.

"Yes, I have. That's what I do sometimes, disrupt the lives of men."

There was so much to say to that, and so little to be gained. I lit a cigarette, listening.

With a quick movement she pushed the half-glasses over her forehead and into her hair, all business. "Get in touch with him tomorrow. Can you do that?"

"Sure," I said.

"And let me know what he says, right away."

"Yes," I said.

"I don't think it's going to be so tough."

"I hope you're right," I said.

"But I've always been an optimist where men are concerned."

I smiled and touched her hand. I looked at her closely, remembering her as a young woman; I knew her now and I knew her then, but there was nothing in between. That was undiscovered territory. I saw the difficulties ahead. They were big as mountains, Annapurna-size difficulties, a long slog at high altitudes, defending Beth. I took my hand away and said, "You can bail out any time you want if this gets difficult or awkward. I know it isn't easy. I can put you in touch with any one of a dozen —" She stared at me for a long moment. In the candlelight her face seemed to flush. Suddenly I knew she was murderously angry.

"I think you're right," she said.

"Look," I began.

"Reluctant lawyers are worse than useless." She took off her glasses and put them in her purse. When she snapped the purse shut it sounded like a pistol shot.

"I'll call you tomorrow," I said. I knew that I had handled it badly, but there was no retreat now.

She stood up and the waiter swung into position, helping her with her chair and bowing prettily from the waist.

Outside on Boylston Street the wind was still blowing, and the street was empty except for two cabs at the curb. We stood a moment on the sidewalk, not speaking. She stood with her head turned away, and I thought for a moment she was crying. But when she turned her head I saw the set of her jaw. She was too angry to cry. She began to walk up the street, and I followed. The wind off the Atlantic was vicious. I thought of it as originating in Scotland or Scandinavia, but of course that was wrong. Didn't the wind blow from west to east? This one probably originated in the upper Midwest or Canada. It had a prairie feel to it. We both walked unsteadily with our heads tucked into our coat collars. I thought of Tom and his camel-hair coat. At Arlington Street she stopped and fumbled for her keys, and then resumed the march. A beggar was at our heels, asking for money. I turned, apprehensive, but he was a sweet-faced drunk. I gave him a dollar and he ambled off. Her car was parked across the street from the Ritz, a green Mercedes convertible with her initials in gold on the door. The car gleamed in the harsh white light of the streetlamps. She stooped to unlock the door, and when she opened it the smell of leather, warm and inviting, spilled into the frigid street. I held the door for her, but she did not get in. She stood looking at me, her face expressionless. She started to say something, but changed her mind. She threw her purse into the back seat and the next thing I knew I was reeling backward, then slipping on an icy patch and falling. Her fist had come out of nowhere and caught me under the right eye. Sprawled on the sidewalk, speechless, I watched her get into the car and drive away. The smell of leather remained in my vicinity.

The doorman at the Ritz had seen all of it, and now he hurried across Arlington Street. He helped me up, muttering and fussing, but despite his best intentions he could not help smiling. He kept his face half turned away so I would not see. Of course he knew me; I was a regular in the bar and the café.

Damn woman, I said. She could go ten with Marvin Hagler.

He thought it all right then to laugh.

Not like the old days, I said.

Packed quite a punch, did she, sir? Ha-ha.

I leaned against the iron fence and collected my wits.

Anything broken? he asked.

I didn't think so. I moved my legs and arms, touched my eye. It was tender but there was no blood. I knew I would have a shiner and wondered how I would explain that at the office.

Let's get you into the bar, he said. A brandy —

No. I shook my head painfully and reached for my wallet. The doorman waited, his face slightly averted as before. I found a five, then thought better of it and gave him a twenty. He didn't have to be told that twenty dollars bought silence. He tucked the money away in his vest and tipped his hat, frowning solicitously.

You wait here one minute, he said. I'll fetch a cab.

No need, I replied. Prefer to walk. I live nearby.

I know, he said, looking at me doubtfully. Then, noticing he had customers under the hotel canopy, he hurried back across the street. I watched him go, assuring the people with a casual wave of his hand that the disturbance was a private matter, minor and entirely under control.

I moved away too, conscious of being watched and realizing that I was very tight. I was breathing hard and could smell my cognac breath. I felt my eye beginning to puff and I knew that I would have bruises on my backside. I decided to take a long way home and walked through the iron gate into the Garden. There was no one about, but the place was filthy, papers blowing everywhere and ashcans stuffed to overflowing. The flurries had left a residue of gray snow. I passed a potato-faced George Washington on horseback on my way along the path to the statue facing Marlborough Street. This was my favorite. Atop the column a physician cradled an unconscious patient, "to commemorate the discovery that the inhaling of ether causes insensibility to pain. First proved to the world at the Mass. General Hospital." It was a pretty little Victorian sculpture. On the plinth someone had scrawled UP THE I.R.A. in red paint.

I exited at the Beacon Street side. A cab paused, but I waved him on. I labored painfully down Beacon to Clarendon and over to Commonwealth, my shoes scuffing little shards of blue glass, hard and bright as diamonds; this was window glass from the automobiles vandalized nightly. While I waited at the light a large American sedan pulled up next to me, its fender grazing my leg, two men and a woman staring menacingly out the side windows. I took a step backward, and the sedan sped through the red light, trailing rock music and laughter. Tires squealed as the car accelerated, wheeling right on Newbury.

My flat was only a few blocks away. I walked down the deserted mall, my eyes up and watchful. Leafless trees leaned over the walkway, their twisted branches grotesque against the night sky. I walked carefully, for there was ice and dog shit everywhere. The old-fashioned streetlights, truly handsome in daytime, were useless now. It was all so familiar; I had walked down this mall every day for twenty years. Twenty years ago, when there was no danger after dark,

♦

Rachel and I took long strolls on summer evenings trying to reach an understanding, and failing. I remembered her musical voice and her accent; when she was distressed she spoke rapidly, but always with perfect diction. I looked up, searching for my living room window. I was light-headed now and stumbling, but I knew I was close. The Hancock was to my left, as big as a mountain and as sheer, looming like some futuristic religious icon over the low, crabbed sprawl of the Back Bay. I leaned against a tree, out of breath. There was only a little way now; I could see the light in the window. My right eye was almost closed, and my vision blurred. The wind bit into my face, sending huge tears running down my cheeks. I hunched my shoulders against the wind and struggled on, through the empty streets of the city I hated so.

1983

◆

# MAINTENANCE

◆

ONE OF THE THINGS I liked about living in the Northeast Kingdom was the weather report on the evening news, Channel 8. For many years I lived in a coastal metropolis, and the contrast between the adolescent good cheer of the meteorologists of the city and the dour inland pessimism of Burns was marked, and even now makes me nostalgic for my years in the woods. Burns was preoccupied by comparative statistics, record highs and lows, degree-day units, volume of snow or rain, and, always, the menacing low-pressure zones to the west and north. He had a special affinity for the winter, recognizing the immense effect it had on all our lives, and he reported it as a foreign correspondent would report a losing war. His was truly a weather report, not a forecast; he was less interested in what might happen tomorrow than in what had happened yesterday and today and, as a matter of fact, he was a terrible forecaster. No one depended on him for predictions and indeed more than once when he was upset he would neglect to furnish them. In his forecasts he was about as reliable as the average racing handicapper. Burns was a fussy little man with narrow eyes and a reedy voice, but he could rise to eloquence on those occasions when a record seemed imminent.

This pause is the fourteenth consecutive day of pause below-zero weather silence smile. And if we can *maintain*. If we can hang *on* for another three days we'll pause match the record set in nineteen and eleven. Wind-chill factor today silence, minus twenty. *Five* degrees colder than yesterday, thanks to the great Arctic air mass over pause the Hud-son Bay.

With the pauses and the silences, the Gothic solemnity of his face, and the suggestion of anarchy as he reported the inexorable facts, I thought of him as a character from a play by Harold Pinter. After a year or so listening to him I came to know that Burns was no ordinary television hack, bucking for promotion to the network. He was obsessed by the weather in Vermont, being a connoisseur of bad news.

Burns had a drinking problem. I used to see him at the bar in Lyndonville. Things were going badly for me, too. Often in the evenings, after the news was ended and the dinner eaten and the children in bed, I would leave my wife and go to a place in Newport and sit and drink and read the newspaper. Then when that bar became overrun with young people I went to a place in St. Johnsbury. St. J. was an hour's drive from my house, however, and therefore inconvenient and dangerous late at night after an evening's drinking. So I sought another anchorage and in time found the bar in Lyndonville.

At first I did not recognize him; Burns in no way carried the authority of a television "personality." In fact, he was quite anonymous. I was at the bar in Lyndonville two or three nights a week and he was always there, so I assumed that his was a seven-nights-a-week habit. Burns did not give the appearance of a drinker, being fine-featured, almost dainty, and neatly dressed in a dark suit and sweater. He looked like someone's clerk. His costume on television every night was a dark suit and red sweater with a polka-dot tie. Apparently he drove to Lyndonville directly from the studio. He always sat quietly on a stool at the far end of the bar drinking boilermakers, a small pile of bills and change in front of him. When he finished one drink he'd push a dollar bill forward and Stuart, the bartender, would fetch him another. Often Burns would essay a small joke, such as "It's getting wet out tonight."

Do you think it will ever stop snowing? Stuart would ask.

Always has, Burns would say, and cackle softly. He had a lifetime supply of droll Vermont jokes.

The bar in Lyndonville was not popular, so most evenings there would be just the two of us customers, seated at opposite ends of the long bar, with Stuart standing strategically in between; we were like the points on a triangle.

The only time Burns showed any interest was when the eleven o'clock news came on Channel 8. He listened to the weather report

attentively, frowning when it became evident that the forecast had
changed from his own six o'clock version. The eleven o'clock meteorologist was a young woman with no flair for the report but an
unerring eye for accurate prediction.

More than once, in point of fact, she would confuse or misstate the
day's weather. She was so anxious to move from the present to the
future.

Oh dear, Burns would mutter.

Stuart would look at him sideways, silent.

She got the Celsius wrong, Burns would say.

Stuart would nod.

Nice enough girl, Burns would say, but she doesn't really get it.
She gets it but she doesn't *get* it, do you see what I'm saying? It's so
necessary to be accurate with the Celsius, we've a number of regular
viewers across the border. You know Vermont. Close to God and
Canada.

She's nice to look at, Stuart said. She's got a pleasing smile.

She's a knockout, Burns said, shaking his head. She's just a peach.
He turned to look down the bar, politely including me in the conversation. This was rare; conversation was almost never general; mostly
we were silent drinkers, me with my newspaper and Burns with his
droll jokes. Burns cleared his throat and continued: At eleven o'clock
it doesn't matter so much because you know up here in the north
country at eleven o'clock P.M. we're either drunk or in bed asleep. At
six, that's when it counts. At six the events of the day are still fresh
and our people want confirmation. They want the numbers and the
comparisons, this day to the day before; how this season compares
to last. How bad has it been *really;* that's what they want to know.
So the forecast is a mug's game, it's so risky and gives such a false
sense of security. Do you see what I'm saying? We have to describe
exactly the flow of the thing now because tomorrow's always another
day, and different. And you can't do anything about it. Maintenance,
that's the essence of the north country. "Use it up, wear it out, make
it do, or do without." Tomorrow depends on today and yesterday,
that's obvious, isn't it? We're tough, here in the north country; we go
the last inch, we don't waste. And that's why the forecast isn't the
only thing. It isn't even the main thing, if the north country's your
place of residence. And that's what she doesn't get. I'll have another.

Stuart made the drink and said it didn't matter anyway, because
he, Burns, was in charge of the six o'clock report. And as he'd pointed
out, they're usually awake and not drunk at six.

Burns nodded morosely and didn't say anything. There was a long silence.

I'd like to buy a drink, I said.

Stuart prepared one for me and another for Burns and drew himself a draught beer.

I said, You're right about the comparisons. You've got to know where you've been and where you are today before you can plan tomorrow. Because tomorrow never comes and predictions are empty, it's always a question of acting on what you know. That's why the six o'clock report is so salient, because you describe where we've been.

Thank you, Burns said.

We were silent for a moment. I moved over two stools, tightening the triangle as Stuart moved to a point midway between us. The atmosphere was easy now, like a men's club. We were all in agreement, three middle-aged drinking men, each a resident of the Northeast Kingdom, each with a specialty. Burns threw down his shot and chased it with a beer. I did likewise. In the easy silence I watched the last of the news on the television set. This was the sports report, mostly schoolboy stuff from the local high schools. Really, it was just an announcer reading the news wire. There was no film, or animation of any kind.

Well, Stuart said when the news ended. He switched off the set.

They're thinking about a change, Burns said. That's the thing that's got me wiped out. They're going to try her in my slot when I go on vacation. That's the gist. It could be pretty awful.

Burns explained that he always took his vacation in July and August, when the weather was benign, except of course for the violent summer thunderstorms. The other ten months he worked seven days a week. He called summertime the months of truce. It was obvious that his main and most important work occurred during the ponderous and unpredictable winter months, and on the shank of the seasons. March and April, for example, could be tragic and required an experienced eye, a veteran meteorologist with a memory and the authority to make his estimates stick. There were three records set last March alone. The situation obviously required a senior man.

So, Burns said dispiritedly, there's that to worry about, along with everything else.

I said, That's a hell of a thing.

They're beginning the buildup next month, Burns said. Ads were already in preparation, a film strip of the young woman standing in front of a weather map. These contained the obnoxious slogan "Whether it's rain or shine, she'll brighten your tomorrow."

I said, It cheapens everything.

He looked at me and asked if I was married.

I said I was.

Then you know all about it, he said.

That's right, I said. I've been through the mill.

Stuart said, It's about time to close up, boys.

One for the road, Burns said.

One, I said.

Stuart said, This last one's on the house.

Burns said, There's nothing to be done about it.

I shook my head sympathetically. I knew what Burns meant. Things were falling apart. I tried to think of a consoling thought. I said, They don't get it and they'll never get it.

And there's been some complaint, he said.

Always is, I said vehemently. Always. You can count on it. Man tries to do a job, there's always a complaint waiting for him when he gets home. Especially when he gets home.

I'll get the light outside, Stuart said. He placed fresh boilermakers in front of Burns and me.

Burns said, I was married once. All she ever did was watch television, the soaps. She hated it up here and moved to Bradenton, Florida, taking the kids, the car, and the bank account. But she left me the dog.

I said, It's hard on some people, they don't understand the drill. You expect one thing, you get another thing. We're so remote here, and they don't get it. You don't advance. There's no such thing as an advance. You *maintain*. Isn't that right?

Right as rain, Burns said.

Stuart was looking at his watch, and calculating. He said, Jeezum. You boys've got to get out of here. I should've closed an hour ago, we're going back on the standard time tonight.

So there were always complaints, I said, when you don't want them and can least afford them.

They've been writing letters to the station, Burns said. Vicious stuff, about my forecasts. What they don't understand is that the forecasts're not the point, but these new people over at the ski areas don't see it that way. They don't care about today and yesterday, it's only tomorrow and whether there's snow or rain so they can spend twenty-two dollars a day falling into snowbanks. The turkeys. So I'm supposed to forecast bluebird days for turkeys.

I laughed. From New Jersey and Massachusetts, I said.

They'll get the snow soon enough, when the Big Freeze comes. The goddamned turkeys.

You guys've got to clear out, Stuart said.

No, I said. You've forgotten. This season it's the other way around. We've got an extra hour, and we're still well within the law, by my watch. And in that event, why don't we have another little drink for the road?

Stuart's right, Burns said.

I put my glass down.

"Spring forward, fall back," Burns said.

There were many such nights at the bar in Lyndonville. Things were going no better at home for me, so my two or three nights a week turned into four or five. Vermont is not the rustic paradise it's cracked up to be, and we all felt the pressure. I got to know Burns very well. I was not surprised when he told me he had been a businessman before moving to Vermont, intending to farm. But that didn't work out and then his wife left him. Burns took instruction at UVM to become a meteorologist and then found work at Channel 8, at first on the weekends and then full time when the regular man had a heart attack and died on the air. That was twenty years ago.

I became even more attentive to the six o'clock news, knowing Burns so well. He always presented the same face to the world, and in that I admired him. Same dark suit, red sweater, polka-dot tie, dour expression; but in his own way he was a passionate man. When he stood with his pointer in front of the map of Vermont — it was not a regional map but a state map, with the surrounding districts unnamed except for Hudson Strait and Hudson Bay — he was as authoritative as your family doctor. He did love bad news.

The drinking got worse. One night Burns fell off the bar stool and I took him home with me, bundling him into the back seat of my car after Stuart revived him with smelling salts. This was in March during a sudden thaw. The false spring had made us all giddy, and when I got home that night I forgot that he was in the back seat. I was a little the worse for wear myself.

When I told the story later, it broke people up. It was so ludicrous, they laughed until they cried. I said that the next morning I was awakened brutally by my wife's fists pounding me on the back. She was cursing and yelling and I didn't know what it was about until I turned over and pushed her away. I related that she fell over something and lay there prone, still yelling. "The Christ," I said she said, "the Christ's the Channel 8 weatherman's doing in the back seat of the Subaru, shitfaced?" Of course that was mostly invented; it made such a funny story. The truth is, I don't remember our first words. I remembered struggling out of bed, realizing that I had forgotten about Burns. "Is he all right?" I asked her.

"I've had it," she said, "up to here." She made a leveling motion with her trembling hand, right at the Adam's apple.

"Hold your horses," I said. "The bastard's been out there all night."

She commenced to yell and curse but I wasn't listening at all. I couldn't get it straight. I didn't remember driving home, and didn't recollect Burns in the back seat. Apparently I forgot all about him, listening to tapes on the way home. I thought to myself, Thank God for the false spring. In deep winter he would've frozen to death. The thought frightened me. That sort of thing happened all the time in the north country. I was in bed fully dressed and my wife was in the doorway of our bedroom with her parka on, the car keys in her hand. She said she had thrown Burns out of the car.

"You just wait," she said. Then she was gone, for good, as it turned out.

When I got downstairs, Burns was at the kitchen table nursing a beer. He looked fine, though there was a hurt expression on his face. He had taken off his suit coat and hung it on the back of the chair. I stoked the Defiant and lit a cigarette while I made myself a cup of coffee. I apologized for my wife's behavior. Burns declined my offer of bacon and eggs, and in any event the refrigerator was empty; and she had thoughtlessly left the dirty dinner dishes in the sink. I had one cup of coffee and then another. When I was steady again I cracked two beers, one for him and one for me. The house was so quiet.

He said, "You're in Dutch with your wife."

I shrugged and made a wisecrack. I was trying to recapture the hilarity of the night before.

"I'm sorry as hell about it," Burns said. "I think it's my fault."

I laughed gamely and said I was always in Dutch with my wife. She always came around, on reflection. My wife, I said, laughing. "Whether it's rain or shine, she'll brighten your tomorrow."

Burns frowned and said nothing.

We went into the living room and sat on the couch to watch the weather approach. My house was situated near the top of a mountain and commanded a wide view to the west. Really, it was one of the most spectacular views in that part of the state and a source of consolation to my wife and me when we first moved north. We had trouble adjusting to the country, and whenever anything went wrong, and much did, we would say to each other, "At least we've got this wonderful view." We boasted about the view in the way that some people boast about their health. Excellent health, never been sick a day in their lives, never a night in a hospital, no insomnia, no dread. We were both late risers, so we seldom saw the dawn — which in any case was a show that could be seen only from the windows with the eastern exposure, and they looked into the deep forest. The house was backed into a mountainside. We specialized in dusks, through the glass sliders we called the Viewmaster. We arranged drinks to go with dusk, which made for long evenings in the winter. In the beginning we thought we were fortunate that there were no houses nearby, and therefore no lights; there was no manmade thing to spoil the view. It was like being at the far end of the world during the previous century, which was fine in the beginning. Then when things began to go badly it was hard on everyone. The children became uncommunicative. In the winter and spring there was gray day after gray day, the weather enlivened only by snowstorms and the occasional daylong thaw, which didn't fool anyone. The snowstorms were never a surprise, because we could see them approaching from the west. There were never any surprises on that mountain, after the first year or two; then each year was measured by the year before, the base year being the year we arrived. We called that Year One and when anyone asked us how long we'd been in the north country we'd laugh and say, Since Year One.

Burns was sitting quietly, not saying anything, sipping his beer.

I said that we depended on him. My wife and I did. We watched him every night. I said he was our official historian, and we never missed an installment. I pointed at the television set in the corner. I had bought a special antenna in order to receive the clearest possible picture. I noticed that Burns had finished his beer and rose to get two more from the refrigerator. They were the last two.

Then she fell off the train, I said.

He took a long swallow and walked over to the sliders and stood looking into the gray. There was no breeze and no movement anywhere. The clouds hung over us, stationary.

I explained that the third year we were in the north country someone gave my wife a stash of dope and she became fond of it, finding
sundown even more spectacular when she was stoned. She gave up
liquor entirely and relied on dope for her pleasure at dusk. She
thought she saw friendly faces in the shadows, and then the faces
became ideas; she counted seven different shades of blue in the mountains when the sun went down.

Burns nodded, still looking out the window. It was not an unusual
story for the north country. Even middle-aged people smoked dope
regularly and had a fine time. My wife deliberated while she watched
the dusk come. She wanted to know what the future held.

They all do, Burns said.

That's the trouble, I said.

He looked at me suddenly, a hard expression on his face. She
wasn't into the serious stuff? he asked.

Oh, no, I said, laughing. Not my wife. It was just pot, locally
grown. I told him I couldn't stand the stuff. It made me sick, and of
course I worried about the children. I depended on spirits. But I didn't
like her when she was stoned, and she didn't like me when I was
drunk. She would have these visions of the future, and I couldn't see
where they fit into anything. She couldn't be realistic when she was
stoned. We had wonderful times drinking together in front of the
Viewmaster, and dope pulled us apart.

Well, he said.

I was in the kitchen checking out the supply. There was a half a
fifth of gin and most of a half gallon of Johnnie Walker Red. There
were two jugs of Zinfandel. Back in the cabinet was an inch of Mount
Gay. There was a quart of Popov and various mixers, tonic water,
soda, and tomato juice. I checked the ice, no problems there. We
would be all right for a couple of days. I mixed two highballs and
gave one to Burns and we stood together at the Viewmaster. The gray
was thickening and beginning to move. Burns described the process.
The barometer would be falling now. I opened the sliders and we
stepped onto the deck. A breeze came up and it was abruptly cold.
He pointed at the horizon, where the mountains rose in tiers; seven
different shades of gray. He described to me the low-pressure system
that dominated the north country. Yesterday it was west of Hudson
Bay; no doubt it was moving now. There might be a storm or there
might not be; it was too early to tell. I listened closely, not looking at
him, hearing only his familiar reedy baritone. I looked away into the
distance, still listening, wondering how I could put his intelligence

report to good use. March was a bad hat any way you cut it. We had had such a good time the first year, everything fresh and unexpected; we told each other that we had gone back to the fundamentals, and that was certainly true. My hand was cold around the highball and I took a sip. A sharp breeze swept across the deck and I knew that the thaw was ended. I put my arm around Burns's shoulder. What a good guy, I thought. He was so keen and dependable. He'd been through the mill, too, and had come out the other side. And he remained a passionate inhabitant of the north country, pouring his heart and soul into the weather, weighing and measuring for the rest of us, who wanted only to know how bad it really was.

1982

◆

# A GUIDE TO THE

# GEOGRAPHY OF

# VERMONT

◆

THIS IS NOT an exemplary story, though some of the angles should be familiar. There are no exemplary stories of my "generation," which I narrowly define as the one that had only the dimmest memory of the spring and early summer of 1945, the explosions of Little Boy and Fat Man, and the end of the war in Europe and Asia. No recollection of the beginning of the war, only its end; and now it is only the memory of a memory, news of one holocaust half the world away. My older brother, born in 1935, has had a different experience altogether, and my younger brother, born in 1948, is dead. Thirteen years separated them; it could have been fifty.

But this is not the story of me or my brothers. This is Hank Beers's story, and in telling it I am conscious of disjunction. I think of my own life as a timorous negotiation with a roulette wheel. Beers's as anything but. Nothing has encouraged me to believe in direct cause and effect, anything reliable. It may be, as Hank maintained, that life is a row of falling dominoes, but my experience is that the dominoes are arranged haphazardly and like the headstones in a New England graveyard some are erect and others aslant; they are secure or unstable depending on age and the soil in which they are entrenched.

I have always been fascinated by the careers chosen by my friends — this one became a lawyer, that one an insurance executive, another one a screenwriter, and now it seems impossible for them to have been anything else, yet they chose carelessly. These three men I knew in college and have kept up with ever since. Tommy has written my

will and George has insured my life and each Sunday I faithfully turn
to the entertainment section of the paper for news of Carl's latest
movie or television serial. They are not alike in temperament, but I
believe with a different throw of the dice in 1964 it could be George
writing films and Tommy writing insurance and Carl writing wills.
They agree.

"Hank Beers," Carl says, believing he has clinched the point. Hank
Beers, the exception that proved the rule. Hank Beers, who never
wanted to be anything but an architect, who even as a student was
regarded as a professional. It only serves to emphasize the difference
between us to point out that none of us has commissioned a Beers
house, nor would ever consider doing so.

We four came to know Hank at New Haven. He was a friend of
Carl's sister Charlotte and was finishing up at the architecture school.
He was two years older than we were and it is unlikely we would
ever have come to know him except for the connection with Char.
Hank was not our kind; he was the first zealot I ever knew, a true
believer whose sect was architecture. I remember him well in those
days, large, muscular, and long-haired, always carrying a T square
and slide rule, his conversation dense with the vocabulary of construction and design, and always with the look of the magician about
him, as if one day he'd turn and gesture with the T square and the
divinity school would vanish and the Bauhaus rise in its place. He
was tolerant of, if puzzled by, Tommy, George, Carl, and me, who
had no idea what we would "do," only that it should be agreeable
and somehow significant. However, the prospect of a Goldwater administration was moving us rapidly to a decision, any decision so
long as it precluded military service. In 1964 that was a definite possibility — "a definite poss," in the phrase of the time — so Tommy
eventually went to law school, George got married, Carl had a long
talk with his family doctor, and I joined the Peace Corps.

Hank Beers did nothing. Listening to the four of us scheme, his
eyes would glaze and turn inward and he would mutter, "Negative
energy," nod at Char, and in a moment they would be gone, off to
his apartment to talk about buildings. She was a second-year student
at the architecture school and believed Hank the genius who would
lead American architects out of Le Corbusier's concrete wilderness.
*Hank Beers,* she said, emphasizing the name as if it were one that we
had *better remember,* possessed a sublime mind and transcendent
spirit and would in time become a master, the Wright or Gropius of
his generation.

We listened politely. Charlotte was openly condescending to the four of us, so immature, so unfocused and doubtful about what we wanted to make of ourselves. (George was to enter the family insurance business, and Carl's doctor had found an obscure allergy that required rustication on the West Coast.) The last three months of our senior year we were stoned most nights and it was a noisy *Schadenfreude* with which we greeted the news that Beers had been drafted and was due to report to the infantry one month after graduation. He had done nothing to prevent it, in fact had ignored the government's notices until receiving one by registered letter that threatened prosecution.

Stupid, Carl told his sister. Fatally flawed, your Hank. A man with no sense of the future, and no grasp of the way the world worked.

You understand nothing, she said.

I understand enough to know he's going to that pointless war, Carl said. And he could've avoided it.

She said, When it's done, it's done. *Hank Beers* doesn't care about it. It doesn't matter to him at all. It's a matter of no importance.

Carl said, No importance maybe. Consequence surely.

You still don't get it, she said.

I listened to all this, enchanted. Hank Beers may have lacked simple common sense but he did not lack attraction for women. This woman was fighting mad and it was obvious as she argued with her brother that an attack on *Hank Beers* was an attack on her.

"Adolescents," she said finally. "Spoiled brats, all of you. *He* doesn't care about it. It doesn't matter to him at all. *It is not worth his attention.*"

This was true. The last three months of the school year he was engaged in the design of a three-family communal house. Nothing else was important to him. The truth was, he didn't have the initiative to do what nearly every other Yale graduate did, which was find ways and means to avoid the army. There was nothing patriotic about it; he simply couldn't be bothered spending the energy required to avoid the draft. As Charlotte said, it was not worth his attention. Later, obliged to think about it, he reasoned that three years in a law school or four in a medical school or in the Peace Corps would be three years or four away from architecture, so what was the point? It never occurred to him to falsify his medical history, and the idea of marrying someone and becoming a father as a way of placing himself beyond the reach of the authorities was ludicrous. He did not intend to become a breadwinning family man at twenty-three; he intended to *build*. He might as well be in the army, and it was typical of him that once committed he began to consider military architecture. Surely they required architects as they required riflemen. Possibly some of these architects had gone to Yale or to MIT and, who knew, given the chance he could design a concrete bunker in the manner of Le Corbusier, a none too subtle parody. Bunkers were the same the world over, the design had not changed since Wellington, and could be a fascinating structural problem. Perhaps each bunker could be self-contained, circular, wings feeding off a central War Room and prefabricated so it could be moved easily from place to place as the front shifted; a circular building could be easily disguised from the air . . .

His enthusiasm was infectious and after graduation he and his friends went ardently to work designing the Corbu Bunker, amid wild laughter. Beers always carried jokes to an extreme. He approached the dean of the architecture school and asked him to write a letter to the secretary of the army. The dean liked Beers (everyone did) and thought him a highly original student. He wrote a serious letter and a reply came by return mail, a two-sentence reply from the secretary himself. The first sentence read, "Thank you for your letter." The army was satisfied with the architects it already had. It did not need architects. It needed riflemen.

He had been lucky all his life, indulged by fond parents, enjoying robust good health, and knowing exactly what he wanted to do from a very early age. In later years he came to believe that the luckiest he had ever been was in 1964. He had the good luck to be drafted in that year and do his time in the zone before the war became criminally dangerous. He had the further good luck to be assigned to G-2 (Intelligence), owing to a high IQ and a fluent knowledge of French, learned solely to understand and therefore dispute Le Corbusier. Stationed at Pleiku, he never fired a shot in anger and was remote from the violence of the war.

All this was in retrospect.

He did not consider it lucky then but knew later that he was *very* lucky to be twenty-three and out of graduate school in 1964 and not in 1968, because in 1968 he would have fled to Canada or Sweden rather than fight in the war. In 1964 he would have been hard put to locate the war zone in an atlas; it was just another noisy episode on the eleven o'clock news, random news — casualties in Turkey, fatalities in Bolivia — that filled the room, unheard, while he bent over the drawing board late at night. Scotch-taped to the wall in front of him was an anonymous mountain panorama, Vermont in deep winter, an aerial shot of a pristine slope and rectangular fields where it leveled off into a narrow solitary valley. From time to time Beers would glance at the picture as a sculptor would at a model. He was visualizing the location of the three-family communal house; it would be *there* halfway up the slope, a southern exposure and protected from the northwest wind. The television set was always on but never watched or heard, so the war was far away.

In 1968 and later a number of his younger friends went to Canada or Sweden rather than fight in Indochina. Most of them had the support and blessing of their families, but the act took something out of them. Ten years later they were still in search of themselves and nostalgic — wanting to feel again the romance and vitality of resistance. Of course there were others who were simply down and out, then and now. In a way they reminded Beers of the veterans of the same period, embittered and angry at the indifference of the government and the short memory of the population. Both groups, those who went and those who didn't, were in thrall to the past. The war was the single most important event in their lives, and perhaps always would be. And there was no question, none at all, that if Beers had been called up in 1968 or later — with the issue of the war always present, a specific problem that required a specific solution — he would have gone to a neutral country, too. The war would have made its claim on his conscience and his ambition and he would have refused to go.

So he was lucky in five ways. He had gone to the war, had not killed anybody, had not been killed himself, had assimilated the experience — and had an extraordinary moment of revelation.

This happened one afternoon in November 1965, near the end of his tour in the zone. He was flown to a mountain village to interrogate a defector. The helicopter touched down in a clearing outside the village, then flew away, leaving Sp/4 Beers standing alone under a hot sun in a rice field, so excited he was trembling. Before him, framed on three sides by jungle, was a settlement of a dozen houses, deserted and immaculate, the houses vivid in their primitive austerity. They were raised on short stilts, dark wood against the green of the forest, sloping roofs thatched with bamboo. The structures seemed to him in some mystical harmony with the curving chaos of the forest and the high hills rising beyond, all of it as spare and radical as

Euclidean geometry. The rising heat made the field shimmer in the bright sun and he saw the settlement as a mirage. He closed his eyes and then opened them, imagining the dark hills drenched in snow, with open fields here and there for perspective. The straight lines of the houses defined sanctuary or refuge as the forest defined hazard. The houses were built into the forest, not taming it but complementing it; the houses had their claim and the forest had its, neither impeaching the other. He thought immediately of the maestro, Frank Lloyd Wright — how astonished Wright would be! Beers wanted to devise a mountain style as Wright had devised his prairie style, the buildings enhancing the land as the land enhanced the buildings. He had dreamed of working in rugged Vermont, feral terrain, and now saw his ecstatic dream declare itself. Always he had known that his conceptions were ingenious in detail but inchoate in the sum, a series of brilliant images that tailed away into confusion. He had waited for his vision, knowing it was there to spring up some lucky day, not something you could hasten or force but something simply allowed to occur. Patience, optimism, and confidence were always rewarded. Dominoes never fell of their own accord.

An American officer was waving at him from the village. He heard shouts. Still, he could not move. The sight delighted him. Then, rising from his reverie, he shouldered his rifle and began to move slowly toward the houses. He looked at them now with a practical eye. How deep were the footings? What was the precise angle of the slope of the roof? The ratios, floor to ceiling? *How had these people managed so exquisite a balance between the architecture and the geography?* It was breathtaking, this chaste and formal balance.

A hundred feet from the settlement he paused, suddenly unnerved and terribly afraid. He had never been afraid before, he was a rear-echelon intelligence man. It was very quiet in the field; he heard his own breathing and the whirr of insects. Even now, *right this minute*, he thought, the Viet Cong could be surrounding the village, sappers in the forest just beyond the silhouette of the buildings. It was their terrain, and they would fight for it as he would fight for his; and they would prevail. The American officer disappeared into the house and Beers knew for a certainty what he must do. His mind was as uncluttered as the vision before him. He knew that if he remained he'd be killed, enemy fire, friendly fire, a random accident, or disease. He could not allow that to happen and knew then that the time had come to seize the future. Seize it or lose it. He took a last excited look at the village, burning it into his memory.

Then, with a quick positive movement, he pressed the trigger of the M-16 and shot himself in the foot.

From this distance, fifteen years later, it is tempting to read too much into Beers's decision to wound himself, "a stateside wound." But it was symmetrical. In the beginning the war wasn't important enough to notice and in the end it was too important to ignore. He spent a month at Walter Reed and the remainder of his tour at the Pentagon. The army released him unconditionally after a month, an honorable discharge — he was a staff man and demonstrably incompetent with weapons, so it was not surprising that when he tripped he thumbed the safety and accidentally discharged the weapon. Of course there was nothing suspicious in his record, nothing to indicate he was in any way a malcontent or subversive or cowardly. He walked out of the Pentagon one day in February, took a cab to the nearest automobile dealer, bought a second-hand Jeep on the spot, and headed north.

Beers had money, not a great deal but enough to purchase three hundred acres on the slope of any mountain in the Northeast Kingdom. In 1966 land was cheap. He spent a month cruising the frozen roads north of St. Johnsbury and in time came to know the country towns as well as he knew the suburbs of his hometown, St. Louis. There was Barton, East Burke, Johnson, Newport, and half a dozen others, interchangeable until you spent time in them and learned their characteristics. Beers divided the territory into grids and drove methodically, knowing exactly what he wanted. It was February and each day seemed colder than the last, but when he saw likely terrain he would stop the car, haul on his snowshoes, and strike out cross-country.

He wanted an enclosed valley that was already populated, a place where the land was worked but not yet exhausted. He did not want lush country with gentlemen farmers — lush country, indeed! — of the species found in the southern part of the state, stocky gray-haired men who inspected their cattle in jodhpurs and J. Press jackets out at the elbows, accompanied by accountants from Morgan's bank. The Northeast Kingdom was something else altogether, impoverished but not yet exhausted, redneck country: dirty white clapboard farmhouses with television aerials that resembled radar apparatus, ancient barns and tractors, mutts, tomcats, snowmobiles and abandoned sedans rusting in the front yard, the windows broken and the interiors filled with snow. Close to God and Canada. Weathered men, husky women, and sly children. Beers believed he could inspire the region, his own sense of possibility encouraging the inhabitants. New blood! And if he failed, it was as it was; but not for lack of effort.

The plan was this. To buy three hundred acres at one end of the valley, the northern end to take advantage of the southern light; in Vermont, all valleys ran north and south. Each house would be backed into the mountain, protection against the northwest weather. This was timber country, so he would find a parcel with a logging road and subdivide along the road. His partners would buy into the venture in two-acre lots. The remainder would be common land and wild forever. There would be orchards and a meadow to support sheep and vegetable gardens, panoramic views and cross-country ski trails and a market town nearby.

Lab conditions.

In the end Beers found exactly what he wanted and bought it after a week of fierce haggling, the owner suspicious because he could not imagine the use to which the land would be put. Irritated by Beers's beard, he believed him a draft dodger with Communistic tendencies until Beers casually mentioned that he was a veteran. He did not display his damaged foot with its livid scar but was prepared to do so in order to secure the land; he'd cooked up a story to go with the scar. After the documents were signed, the older man told him about the original inhabitant of the mountain, a recluse and migrant from Portland, Maine. His shack still stood near the top of the mountain, more than a hundred years old now. Beers was interested and pressed for details, but there were no details. The recluse disappeared in the early 1920s, '21 or '22, he couldn't rightly recall; simply disappeared, no trace ever found. Disappeared into the forest as a fallen tree does, returning to the earth, dust to dust.

What was his name? Beers asked.

The older man didn't know or couldn't remember. In the region he was known as the *old* bastard. But the shack still stood. When he offered to draw Beers a map to its location, Beers demurred. He wanted that pleasure for himself.

I'll find it, he said.

There were five friends, all former classmates, and he wanted them to join him. These friends were working in cities and bored in the usual ways. They were restless and avid for adventure, a life more dangerous than "inking" for senior partners and designing dentists' offices in Larchmont or Winnetka. Carl's sister Charlotte was the first to reply, writing Beers that Vermont would be her Canada, a refuge from conscription into the American way of life. She was not a flamboyant woman, so she did not say that they would build the New Jerusalem, but that is what she meant. As for Beers, he could scarcely wait to replicate the serene village and the forest surrounding it. All one, the structures, the forest, and the community of architects, each complementing the others in unexpected ways, isolated from the random violence and cheap success of commercial America. In 1966 Hank Beers was twenty-five years old and saw himself as an explorer, the Magellan of a great movement that would change the visage of the nation.

That June his five friends joined him and by Thanksgiving they'd built their first house, in which they lived communally. It was a cooperative project, though the design was pure Beers. A failure by the standards of Yale or MIT, the house bore scant resemblance to any house in the mountains of Pleiku Province or anywhere else in Indochina. Only Beers saw the connection, the structure converging into the terrain and somehow an extension of it. It seemed to be an exercise in angles, most of them oblique; there were no curves anywhere. It was like living inside a trapezoid that leaked. It was very exciting to look at and daring to live in, though Charlotte complained that the atmosphere was often hostile. A trapezoid schizophrenic, she called it. Living under radical angles was in no way cozy and always disconcerting, except when one was smoking grass. The trouble was, one never forgot for a moment where one *was;* she thought in that way it resembled living at Versailles or a state prison — though she agreed, too, that it was extraordinary and somehow suited to the land, the steep slope of the mountain and the enormous thick-bellied spruce, the spruce in snow looking like benign hoop-skirted women. Perhaps it was disconcerting, inconvenient, and hostile and in those ways a failure, but she knew, and the others knew, that they were on to something original. There was no dwelling like it anywhere in America. And as for being a "failure" — that depended entirely on the definition of failure, and by Beers's definition it was not a failure at all but a conspicuous success. Beers's design set the example for all the houses to follow: a precipitous perpendicular, fitted snugly into the womanly spruce.

Other friends arrived that winter and the following spring and summer. Beers's mountain became a way station on the underground. Many of the visitors stayed on, camping out, and before the end of 1967 there were twenty people in more or less permanent residence, a few of whom bought land, though most wanted only to stay a while and observe the construction. (Much later Beers would see this as an early version of the California light bulb joke. How many architects does it take to build a house in Vermont? Twenty. Six to build the house and fourteen to share the experience.) It was a time of great entertainment and consanguinity; the six original settlers had three ideas a day and energy to burn and now there was an audience. Beers had never been happier, and if he had been in the least political the experience of the first year would have turned him to Marxism. *Class distinctions have disappeared, and all production has been concentrated in the whole nation.* That was true; even the visitors contributed in their own way. They were like foreign correspondents come to view the future working. *Political power, properly so called, is merely the organizing power of one class for oppressing another.*

There were no politics on Beers's mountain, nor oppressors.

To which my older brother, with the generosity of spirit that has characterized all his works and days, replies, "Believe that and you'll believe anything."

◆

I t existed as a haven, "form follows function," and in those days was certainly not unique. There were similar settlements all over northern New England and if many of them now seem romantic relics of the fly-by-night 1960s, flotsam casually tossed on the beach from the storms of assassination and war and just as casually returned when the weather eased, it only serves to emphasize the durability and good character of those that did survive. Let no one believe it was easy. The seasons in Vermont are more oppressive than any ruling class. Keeping the egos in harness, maintaining idealism and allowing a certain self-indulgence and failure for failure's sake without it all degenerating into a woodsy, free-spirited Gulag Archipelago, was hard work requiring subtlety and persistence. By the early 1970s there were seven houses, Beers's the centerpiece. Scarcely a week passed without a delegation of architects from one city or another arriving to inspect the famous mountain, the houses that were now part of it, and the Gropius of the movement, Beers. While almost no one "approved," everyone was fascinated. Original. Utterly original, they said, without knowing exactly how to approach the designs. Unfortunately, there was nothing useful to be learned from them; or so it seemed to conventional minds. The houses were unlivable in the

strictest sense, impractical, uncomfortable, and clumsily constructed. ◆
(The amateur builders had not begun to solve the structural problems
presented by the professionals' advanced designs.)

Interesting, a Boston architect wrote in a critique published in *Ar-
chitectural Review*, in the way a thumb screw is interesting.

It was fashionable to believe that Beers had painted himself into a
corner. The houses were coelecanths, cul-de-sacs off the main stem of
Western architecture. They would survive, as the coelecanth survives,
but nothing would come of them. They were situated beautifully into
the mountain and thrilling to look at; but they were not of the real
world, and not for any theoretical reason. ("He has tried to construct
a countercultural Shangri-la and failed dismally," the Boston architect had written, seeking political significance in what he had seen
and disliked so.) It was simply that the angles were too numerous
and aggressive and therefore unsettling — "hostile," as Charlotte said
again and again. It was as if Beers was indifferent to how people
actually *lived*. To that accusation he replied that he wished to change
the way people lived. The hostility was in the mind's eye only, a
learned response to God knows what. The memory of barbed wire.
The mystery of the Pyramids. Beers did not find his house hostile; he
had learned to live in it. And of course he knew its provenance. He
never spoke of his vision in the zone. Only Charlotte knew of it and
she was sworn to silence. He conceded that the connection was mystical, but most spiritual occasions were. At any event Beers's prediction that the hostility was temporary turned out to be true; the longer
one lived in a Beers house, the less threatening it seemed. Beers argued
that it would take a lifetime to adapt completely.

Like a spy behind the lines, she joked.

No, he said. Like a fish in water. "We are the water, the structures
are the fish."

But in the narrow world of modern architecture Beers's buildings
were seen not as a beginning but as an end. The mountain came to
be known as Dead End and in the mid-1970s the delegations ceased
to arrive from New York, Montreal, and Boston. It was old hat by
then.

I arrived at about that time. In fact it was 1975, and after eleven
years in the Peace Corps I was tired and stale. I had joined up in the
summer of 1964 to avoid the inevitable war and with some vague
idea of carrying on John F. Kennedy's legacy, de rich man's burden
in de southern latitudes, "waging peace." I went to Morocco, which
was interesting, then returned to headquarters. In early 1969 my

younger brother, Timmy, was killed in Indochina. I stayed on in the
Peace Corps *faute de mieux;* one more turn of the wheel. I knew my
work had nothing to do with John F. Kennedy's legacy or any legacy.
The Peace Corps was by then a mature Washington bureaucracy, no
different from the Agriculture Department or the FCC. By 1975 the
city seemed terminally ill, a chronic invalid wasted by assassination,
war, and scandal, and the building in which I worked increasingly
came to resemble a mausoleum.

I cannot fairly present myself as a casualty of the 1960s. My brothers are the casualties, Timmy because he is dead and Lew because he
turned a blind eye to the decade, sailing through it like a Bourbon
king, nothing learned, nothing forgotten — but I was a witness, and
that gives me a claim on Hank Beers and the other inhabitants of the
mountain, and the spirit that animated them. We had risen through
the years together and everything that rises must converge.

I resigned on May 1. I knew of the mountain from Carl, who was
in constant touch with his sister. I had no reason to remain in Washington, so I decided to visit Beers and Charlotte and see what they
had made of their lives. I had money enough for a year or two and
had an idea that I would write a memoir of life in the Peace Corps.
But that was secondary to my interest in Beers and Charlotte, who
seemed to represent so many of the hopes we had had for ourselves
in the early sixties. I began by saying that there are no typical stories
of my generation, and surely that is true; Hank was in no way typical. Still, we shared a few goals. We were distrustful of leaders and
institutions and like the radicals of the thirties we opposed people who pushed other people around. Above all else we believed in
personal happiness; each person had to choose, and the more au-
dacious the choice the greater the likelihood that it would prove
"correct."

So I drove to the Northeast Kingdom, where Charlotte had arranged for me to live in the topmost loft of Hermann Goering's
house. All the men had nicknames. Hermann Goering was a Californian of German birth. There was Fido, Slugger, Dirty, Banjo, A-
Frame, and Bad-Debt. The women did not have nicknames. In the
beginning Beers was cordial but remote. I commenced my memoir
right away, believing it necessary to appear occupied at serious work.
Beers's mountain was like a nation, with its own laws and history,
language, economy, and cuisine. Its cultural pull was as strong in its
way as Morocco's and I did not want to succumb. I resisted as I had
in Morocco years before, all too easily seeing myself as some charac-

ter out of a Paul Bowles story, gone to seed in an unfamiliar climate, drenched in kif and damp memories. Beers's mountain seemed to combine the most dramatic features of a religious retreat and a men's locker room.

It was a month before I had my first serious conversation with Charlotte.

"How do you like it?" she asked. We were at a party at Banjo's house, though perhaps "party" gives it a formality that is misleading. The volleyball game ended at seven and then everyone went swimming. Slugger and June Bell drove into town for hamburger and beer. We ate by the side of the river and then everyone adjourned to Banjo's. There was a shifting population on the mountain, arrivals and departures every week, many of them women. There was a women's house down the road from Hermann Goering's and the women would check in there first, and remain or not as they chose. Sexual arrangements were loose without being chaotic. There had been two marriages but the couples had left after a few months, preferring to live closer to town. The place had a relentlessly masculine atmosphere which most of the women found attractive; Charlotte was an exception.

I said it was all new but fascinating. The mountain suited my mood in ways I didn't entirely fathom. I felt the need to say something agreeable, so I shook my head and said I couldn't understand the complaints about the construction. Hermann Goering's house was watertight and evenly heated, altogether as well built as any house I had seen anywhere.

She nodded vigorously. "That was a bum rap from the beginning." They had always known those problems were merely structural and would be solved in time. "They were *not easy* to solve," she said, looking directly at me. "But we knew they would be and of course the nitwits that complained about that in their tight-assed little articles in the *AR* haven't acknowledged it." She looked away and I saw her eyes fasten on Beers, surrounded at the other end of the room; he was telling a story and the others were laughing. "You're here at an interesting time." I said nothing. Charlotte had always been very direct, assuming you knew as much as she did. She never bothered with background information.

"That one," she said, pointing at Beers. "He understands it. Not so sure if he understands the implications."

"The bum rap," I said.

"No," she said. "The fact that the problem's been solved. That's what's important. It was solved two years ago. Essentially it was a problem" — she moved her hands together in the manner of a pilot demonstrating an aerial maneuver — "of receiving surfaces." She went on to explain the breakthrough, Beers's inspiration, A-Frame's carpentry. She made it sound preposterously simple, as obvious as the design of a light bulb.

"I see," I said, following the bureaucratic principle of never confessing ignorance about anything.

"It hung us up for years and consumed a lot of energy. Even though we knew the solution" — she smiled grimly at me, her Washington connection — "was at hand."

"Now it's solved."

"Has been for two years," she said, still smiling at me. When I didn't reply, she abruptly shifted direction. "This is a wonderful community. It's been my turf for nine years. It must seem weird to you as one of your government buildings would seem weird to me. Of course you and Carl . . ." She let her voice trail off. "You know last year we had our first birth on the mountain. I," she said, grinning broadly, "was an assistant midwife. Banjo's girlfriend, who's split now, though we're hoping she'll come back this winter. Wonderful person. Banjo's promised to fix the roof and" — she looked around the room, in motion now, a dozen people talking and laughing — "the other things." She said, "I'd guess before the year is out we'll have another wedding, probably in the meadow behind Hank's. That's where we have them, it's a gorgeous setting. Births, marriages. Then I suppose we'll have our first death, we almost had one three years ago when A-Frame fell off the roof. But we've been here nine years and, oh, the people who said we wouldn't make it through the first winter. And we almost didn't."

Someone replaced the recording on the stereo and suddenly guitar music filled the room, loud and insistent.

I asked, "What about you?"

"That depends partly on him."

"Hank," I said.

"As I mentioned, though you didn't get it, the structural problems have been solved."

"Okay," I said. I had it now.

"This place lives on the horizon, always has, meaning something that's always in sight but never *achieved,* you know? That's the point of it. From my window I look down the valley, and in the morning, early, when the sun's rising, I'll believe anything, anything in the world . . ." She paused, listening. "Hear the music? You've never heard of this group, I won't even bother telling you the name. Banjo has a connection in L.A. and she sent him the record, which hasn't even been released, and we've been playing it for a week. You'll hear about it in a year or so, maybe later because it's *news*, this music. This music brings the news and you'll hear about it and then you can say," she said, laughing, "that you heard it here first."

I said, "New music."

"The cutting edge," she said. "You bet."

"So it depends on Hank."

"Mostly," she said.

"Is it true what they said? Carl told me."

"That he's in a cul-de-sac? Dead End Beers?" I nodded. "No," she said stiffly. "It is not true. God damn Carl."

I held up my hand. The music roared around us. "He was just reporting," I said. "It wasn't his opinion —"

"What Carl doesn't know about architecture would fill an encyclopedia."

"Wait a minute," I said.

"*Hank Beers*," she said, and for the first time the tone was reminiscent of our days at New Haven. She hesitated, groping for words. "Understand one thing. Hank Beers decided to go up against Corbu. That's what he announced. He didn't know how he was going to do it, I mean the technique, he only knew that he'd make it his life's work. Corbu, the friggin' robot. Anyway. I never knew a man with more ambition and more confidence in his ambition, even though in the beginning he didn't know how he'd subvert. That's what it was, subversion, because he was dealing with a *regime*. Then he had an — experience." She pressed her palms together, hard. "After the experience he knew what he was going to do and came up here and bought this place. *There wasn't anything here nine years ago.* Just this mountain with nothing on it except for the old bastard's shack near the top. No houses, no fields, and no community. Look around. Everything you see. He's done this —"

She went on in that way, but I was thinking of something else. Perhaps we all have buried within us the characteristics of the things we hate, but it seemed to me that Hank Beers's architecture was as fully dehumanized as Le Corbusier's, though it was clumsy, comparing the plain materials and dramatic landscape of the Vermont community with Villa Savoie at Poissy. Corbu was parched and austere

♦

on the outside, Beers on the inside. His houses were as unbeautiful to dwell in as Le Corbusier's were unbeautiful to look at.

"— so that isn't the point," she said, "and to say he's at a dead end is wrong and and and . . ." She stuttered, searching for the word.

"Charlotte," I began.

"— mischievous," she said.

I laughed. That was not the word I expected.

"Kiss my ass," she said.

"Stop the bombing."

"Eat it."

I said, "Still —"

"No," she said firmly.

"— what about you?

She looked away and mumbled something I did not catch. The music was very loud now.

"I'm thirty-four," she said.

I knew what she meant by the tone of her voice, and I was surprised. In this environment I did not connect her with traditional values: a family, a husband, children, or any desire for them. I had a moment of satisfaction; things were not as unmoored as I thought. Attractive women, even attractive women living unbuttoned lives in Vermont, still wanted the usual things. But of course that was not what she meant at all.

She said, "I did something on a lark, something without thinking much about it. I entered a competition."

I suppressed a smile. She said it as another woman might confess to one of the seven deadlies.

"What happened?"

"I won," she said miserably.

"That's what happens on a lark," I said lightly. She looked at me and began to rise, slowly uncurling her middle finger. She was furious. I touched her arm and apologized. "I didn't mean that the way it sounded," I said, though the truth was I meant it humorously, nothing more.

She slowly resumed her seat.

"It isn't the worst thing," I said gently. "Entering a competition and winning."

"This isn't the Nobel Prize."

I sighed. The phrase then was not "laid-back." Laid-back came later, anyway to Vermont; the next year, I think. But on the mountain there was an almost frantic willingness to discount any secular achievement. I said nothing, waiting for her to continue.

"It's important to have the right enemies."

I nodded. "Absolutely."

"My enemies, *Hank's* enemies, were judging this competition. Mine, Hank's, Banjo's, A-Frame's. All of ours. I didn't know that until after I'd entered. I didn't know who the judges would be, I didn't pay any attention to that. It was last winter, obviously we weren't building anything here, by Jesus there was a hundred and ten inches of snow on the ground and you couldn't get down the road for a week, so I just sat at the drawing board, waiting for a break in the weather. And I designed this *house*." She looked away and I saw a smile beginning to form at the edges of her mouth. "Someone sent Hank these forms, thinking that he would enter, and the forms were just lying around. Well, it wasn't just someone. It was Hank's *mother*, who won't be satisfied until he designs Taliesin North. I sent the thing off when the weather broke and I could get to the post office, and didn't think about it again until I got the letter. I won."

"You won," I said.

"Five thousand dollars," she said.

"Congratulations."

"I didn't tell anybody, which was a mistake, because Hank, like, found out about it. I don't know how." She caught the expression on my face because she shook her head. "He didn't care about *that*," she said.

"Of course not."

"He was *not* jealous." She smiled. "Except maybe a little."

I smiled back, ready to support any move by Charlotte to begin the demystification of Hank Beers. Oracles were tiresome. So I said exactly the wrong thing. "I'm glad to know he's as insecure as the rest of us."

"He's not," she said, "but I take your point." She looked at me evenly, irritated again, and I was on the edge of proposing to her that I would try to forget her adolescence if she would try to forget mine. It seemed to me that we were mired in the 1960s, forever the upperclassman and the graduate student, Carl's friend and Carl's sister. But that was eleven years ago, and I believed we had both come a long way since New Haven; and Carl had nothing to do with it any longer.

"Will you listen a minute?" I said.

"You really ought to make an effort to understand what's happening here. You made an effort to understand Morocco. Why is this so threatening to you?"

"It isn't," I said. It seemed impossible to me then to explain my life to her. The government, less yielding even than Vermont. Timmy.

♦

My brother's relentless cynicism and love of disorder. I did not have a large reservoir of faith.

She was silent a moment, then began to talk matter-of-factly. When Hank learned the identity of the judges, he was merciless. They were all enemies, with the exception of one judge who was too craven to declare himself on the side of any one school. "It was like winning a humanitarian award from the Joint Chiefs of Staff."

"Hank said that?"

"Yes."

"How generous of him."

"It was true."

"I think it's for you to say, not for him to say."

She considered that, then looked away. "It was a competition for a row of houses in Newark. An urban renewal project. Federal money, the government has to approve. The government seal of approval." She smiled at me. "Does that make me an accomplice? Accepting the seal of approval of the government? Do I get indicted along with Hunt and Liddy?"

"Hank —" I began.

"Is still merciless," she said.

"You can give back the five thousand dollars."

"It isn't the money," she said patiently. "That isn't the point. They've offered me a job." She spoke softly, and I could hardly hear her over the music. "One of the judges has this firm in New York and he's offered me a job, pretty good job. Latitude." Then: "I have to let them know next week."

"And?"

"And it's a problem." She was staring somberly into the middle distance, her cool gray eyes thoughtful and troubled. The party swirled around us, a separate thing. "And I'm waiting for Hank Beers to decide where we go from here on the mountain. I've been with him for nine years and I'm not going to leave now, without knowing the direction he's headed. This mountain isn't just any project, I've spent most of my adult life here and I'm not leaving until I see" — she hesitated and I had the feeling that this was the first time she'd spoken the words out loud, giving voice to the thoughts that possessed her — "how he's going to *continue,* and if it's going to be here or some-place else. He won't talk about it. I don't know," she said, facing me, returning now from the middle distance. "I just don't know if this mountain is large enough to contain . . . it's so private, you know, it's just us. We're a family and this is our homestead. We don't know the country. If you think of the country, our nation, as a body, this is the healthiest organ in it, but it's a very small organ and the body is huge and diseased and all the diseases are contagious. I don't know if he's prepared to *continue* —" She turned away again, openly desolate.

I moved toward her, wanting to console in any way I could. I did not know how to reach her in this state of Excellent Health. My time had been spent in the diseased nation. But it seemed to me that we were kin. We both wanted to do great things, the greatest things we were capable of, and that meant seizing new ground — for me it was moving to the mountain and for her it was moving off it. I was sure of that. Restless, we would always be restless, and *Hank Beers* would be forever at once mentor and deadly enemy. Just then a loud crash threw the room into turmoil. I began to speak, determined to ignore the commotion. One of the men had fallen and smashed a lamp. There was laughter and someone turned up the volume on the stereo. I was moved by her pride and her confusion; and I believed that she had come ever so much farther than I had. Suddenly Hank was between us, laughing and flapping his arms like a great bear. Sweat poured down his red face and he was shirtless and shoeless. Charades! he cried. It was time for charades! He seized Charlotte and moved away to the center of the room, calling for quiet. Three teams of four each. He and Charlotte and June Bell and Hermann Goering would make up one team. Five minutes' thought, then action! The room fell silent while he spoke, then erupted again. The joint came around to me and I took a drag, watching the sport. I saw Charlotte's oval face darken and then lift to look at Hank. He swept her up in a bear hug and began to spin in slow time and suddenly she was all smiles. Bad-Debt was arm-wrestling with Slugger while Dirty took bets. An anonymous girl was asleep on the ottoman. I observed the melee through a thick blue haze, thinking how natural it all was, the irregular walls and high sharp ceilings, this eccentric geometry so appealing and harmonious, enhancing the pandemonium. Inside the restless motion it seemed to me there were fragments of twenty shouted conversations, a modern opera to the music of a slide guitar. Then they were playing charades, Charlotte perched on Hank's shoulder like a circus performer. There were shouted answers and laughter in return. I passed the joint and strolled blissfully into the kitchen to fetch a beer. The noise was deafening and incoherent, esoteric slang words and phrases that had meaning only to the inhabitants of Beers's mountain. I cracked the beer and stood with my skull pressed against the cool refrigerator door. Above me the ceiling soared twenty feet. The kitchen was pyramidal and I was standing at the epicenter, my head swimming, staring at the converging planes. In this moment of confusion I felt the blood drain from my head. I saw dark plywood walls, shadows dancing on the ceiling; the nails were bright as footlights. I imagined all the clamor gathered above me, sounds collected as a dealer collects a deck of cards, shuffles once, twice, then deals with razzle-dazzle —

The noise swelled, gathering motion, rising to a terrible crescendo, a mighty physical thing. The foundations trembled, as if assaulted by a force of nature.

My last clear thought was that they had it wrong at MIT. Beers had proven them wrong, for whatever it was worth. *Function follows form.*

Nothing happened quickly on the mountain. Hours of furious work would be followed by hours of equally furious play, and sometimes it was difficult to distinguish between the two. I never learned how they arrived at decisions; decisions somehow materialized after the hours of work and days of play. The human voice travels at 740 miles an hour and listening to them in the evenings was to gain a fresh perspective on the science of ballistics. Beers presided but he did not rule.

It was months before Charlotte was able to talk seriously with him. Of course the job in New York was no longer open, and I suppose a cynic would conclude that this was calculated by Beers. But Charlotte didn't think so. It was simply true that time, or the concept of time, was different on the mountain. One day was much like another, and chronology was measured in terms of construction schedules; foundations were dug in the spring. One ate when hungry; one skied any time. It amused her; part of the charm of the mountain was the short attention span of the residents.

A kindergarten, she said, except when they were drawing. It was not unusual for them to work forty-eight hours at a stretch on a particular design, and at those times they reminded her of monks patiently tinting illuminated manuscripts. They were less attentive when it became necessary to translate the design into a structure, a physical thing with dimensions: height, depth, width, and weight.

The party at Banjo's was in mid-July. Charlotte spoke with Beers once in September, then again in November. She and Hank shared meals and occasionally bed and in important ways were as close as or closer than many married couples, and she knew it was senseless to try to force him; he would talk about the future when he was moved to, and not before.

The November conversation was the decisive one. She told me much later that it was obvious Hank had devoted considerable thought to the future, and the ways and means by which he intended to "continue." Charlotte made me understand that she was in no way giving him an ultimatum, nor did she believe she had any right to demand that he disclose his plans. It was his choice, she said. But it was also true that she was thirty-four and restless. She did not have the power to change the mountain, nor would she exercise the power if she had it. Her point was this: she was changing, and she wanted to know if the mountain would change also. But she suspected that the laboratory days were gone forever.

The others had decided to go into town to a movie. When Hank declined to go with them, she knew they would talk at last. They sat in front of the Jötul, watching the season's first snowfall, and talked from seven in the evening until six in the morning. They began by reminiscing about the old days at New Haven. She found this charming and surprising; Hank Beers never reminisced about the pre-Vermont days. Charlotte was startled at his memory, almost total recall of conversations from twelve years before, of designs begun and abandoned, the names of professors, buildings, books, telephone numbers, what they had said on this occasion or that, and the dreams they'd shared —

"Corbu," she said, grinning.

He waved his hand in dismissal, but not before raising his eyebrows. They had not talked about Le Corbusier in years.

"The opposition," she said.

"Not any longer." He looked at her, the force of his personality like a magnetic field. She leaned into him, drawn. "I don't think about him anymore. Corbu! He's as irrelevant as the Sears Tower."

She said, "Negative energy."

He hesitated; it was a phrase they used often in the old days. It was his phrase really, and it surely struck some chord deep in his memory. He said slowly, "That, too."

"Bear." It was an old nickname she seldom used anymore. "Bear, who replaces Corbu? Someone has to. We're not meant for vacuums, either of us. We like to push and shove and there's got to be something *to* push and shove. And this" — she gestured around them, the stove, the glass sliders, the unfinished walls and all that lay beyond — "do you work on this forever?"

"Can't keep her down on the farm," he said archly.

"That's damn unfair," she said quickly.

"What is it exactly that you want here?"

"Not what I want," she said. "I don't know exactly what I want. I want to know how you're going to continue. Then I can discover whether I want to continue with you. I don't know what it is you've got in mind anymore. Always before I sensed a goal, though we never talked about it. Not cool to talk about goals, though I knew it was there and you did, too. I don't know where your ambition is now. I mean *what* it is."

"I don't have to justify myself."

"Not asking for that," she said. "If you never do another thing you'll've done more than any architect I know. No apologies, you need never make any. You can remain here for the rest of your life, it's enough. It would be enough for anyone, or almost anyone. This place, the community. You're the" — she smiled encouragingly — "founding father. And it's special, what we have here. But you're a large man, Bear. I'm surprised that you still find this stage — large enough."

He looked at her, expressionless, and moved to the stereo to replace the record. He leafed through the albums on the floor, then turned the machine off and stood in the silence looking out the sliders into the darkness; snowflakes bounced off the glass. He was silent a very long time and when he finally spoke he did not turn toward her but remained staring out the glass. "Nothing here when I came. Logging road, the old bastard's shack at the top of the mountain; took me three days to find it. Some iron spouts in the sugarbush, only signs of habitation. That shack, those spouts. That tough old bastard, think of the work it took, and the yield — only a few gallons of maple syrup. But apparently it was enough. Hard to believe but you have to believe it. As we both know, it doesn't take much to live in Vermont. Money." He paused and she was certain he was trying to visualize his predecessor, the mountaineer, his red face and huge hands, breath pluming in the cold. He said, "I bought it, the old bastard's legacy, and made something of it. We did. You, me, A-Frame, Banjo, Bad-Debt, the others. Of the original six, four have stuck. The two who left weren't suited from the beginning, we agreed about that, weren't prepared to work in a community. Weren't suited after the first year and like, what the hell, this place isn't a *Stalag*. And Corbu doesn't come into it anymore." He sighed, turning finally to face her. He wore a bright red shirt and heavy tweed trousers with wide white

suspenders; she smiled at the trousers, two inches too short and the
patching in the crotch coming undone. He'd worn the trousers for
years, ever since she could remember. Leon Bean's best.

"So we've stuck and I suppose it's true that in terms of" — he
hesitated — "novelty. Artistic orgasm. The mountain isn't what it
was, or how we want to remember it. What are we doing, 'consoli-
dating our position'? I don't know about that because it doesn't
matter a goddamned bit to me. Some nitwit sociologist from Yale
was up here a few months ago, it was while you were visiting your
folks, and told me we were a 'mature society.' Maybe that's so.
Anything in this country lasts for nine years, maybe that makes it
mature. But I don't care about sociologists from Yale. I don't give a
damn about the outsiders who don't understand or care what we're
doing here. What am I supposed to do? Come twelve times when that
banker from Saint J. tells me what a Boy Jesum Grahnd thing it is,
I've cleaned up my act and'm paying off the mortgage, punctual with
the monthlies, and how would I like some tax-free municipals now
that the corporation has some loose change? That's all materialism
and I don't like it now any more than I did then. This is what I have,
right here, and I remember —"

"Hank," she began.

"— that village near Pleiku. That's what I've had in the back of my
mind all these years and I've come closer to it. The idea of an idea.
Than I ever thought I would. I *don't care* what they're doing in
Newark or anyplace else. Go ahead," he said.

"Nobody comes here anymore."

He shook his head, staring at her. "I don't care about that either.
And I'm surprised that you do."

She said, "I'm trying to be honest."

"If it matters to you so much, you can count on it. They'll be
back."

"I liked it when they came, so sure of themselves. They didn't know
*what* to make of it, or us either. God, I loved watching them watch
you and the buildings, muttering to each other. You could see their
eyes widen and they'd all take out cigarettes at the same time, smiling
a little because they knew they were going to have a dandy story to
tell at the country club or the next AIA convention. Then Banjo
would appear with a beer in his hand and that woman, my God she
must have weighed three hundred pounds, twice as big as he was.
They'd watch all this, eyes getting bigger. Except there would always
be one or two of them, the young ones, who were looking at the

buildings, really *seeing* them, instead of looking at her, and you knew
they were coming away with something. You knew that for an afternoon you'd invaded their minds and life was no longer a series of
twelve-by-sixteen rectangles and stylish ovals. They'd seen something
new, and while they wouldn't have the balls to do anything about it,
at least you'd touched them for an afternoon —" Her words came in
a rush, tumbling from her, and now she laughed. "I've got a little of
the preacher in me."

"There are no pulpits here," he said sourly.

"Used to be," she said. "And what's wrong with it? What's wrong
with sharing it. Giving a little. It used to be, like, *fun* when those
idiots from Boston —"

"That was before we were mature," he said, grinning suddenly.

"Pisses you off a little, doesn't it?"

He didn't reply. "As for the size," he said after a moment, "there
is no larger place than this mountain. This is the world. The world is
wherever you happen to be and there are no limits to it, and this is
where I happen to be. And as for continuing." He reached behind the
chair and brought out a rolled blueprint, spreading it on the floor,
securing the four corners with empty beer bottles. She looked at it,
puzzled for a moment. "Look at this. I'm going to replace *this* and
*this*, eliminate them entirely, then tear down this wall. The stairwell
will go *here* . . ."

She nodded, listening to him. It was a revision of the interior of his
house. He was softening some angles and hardening others. As he
explained it she was reminded of a writer revising a manuscript. The
structure remained the same, though a sentence was turned here and
there; one sentence in, another out. The writer himself would be the
only one who noticed.

When he was finished she said nothing. Dawn was commencing
over the mountain and far away she heard the sputter of a chain saw.
In the city you heard horns; here you heard chain saws. The dawn
was gorgeous, yellow over the brilliant white of the mountain. A foot
of snow, the first of the season; it brought tears to her eyes just
looking at it; her eyes filling, she watched the shadows shorten.

"But before I begin this," he said, "there's the small matter of
wood. We're cutting this week and next. I want twenty-five cords
before Christmas, not like last year —"

Maintenance, she thought. That was what it was in Vermont. One
maintained in order not to break down. She understood suddenly
that it was a pessimist's state — perseverance, patience, fatalism. The
region was littered with false beginnings, buildings abandoned or

burned, mills empty, fields lying fallow, the deer dying for lack of forage.

"— when we were caught short, you'll remember."

"Yes," she said. She stopped crying.

They sat watching the dawn, more brilliant each second. The corners of the house caught the light and held it. It was a house that worked best in the early morning and superbly in November, the month of its completion eleven years ago. It was designed for November's infrequent golden sun.

"Never again," he said.

"Happens every year. We run short."

"Remember, the first year? You couldn't get the hang of the chain saw." He touched her wrist with his rough fingers, turning it. "I thought you'd torn the vein, it scared hell out of me. Dear Char."

She shuddered, remembering the look of her wrist, the ragged skin and ivory bone, blood everywhere.

"Lucky," he said. "You were lucky that day. This has always been a lucky place for you." Lucky? She'd almost severed her arm. "And lucky for me too," he said. "I've been lucky all my life."

"It's true," she said.

He leaned away from her to turn on the radio, the local station. They listened to it for the news and the weather, the weather always a presence and more important than the news. It was a radio station that had just three announcers. They had terrible voices and were unprofessional in other ways, but familiar and close as neighbors.

He said, "You're one of the originals. What's wrong with our life here? With what we've done? *What more could you possibly want?*"

She could not reply to that. What was it? She didn't know for sure, understanding only the restlessness inside her. She did not desire security, never had. She guessed it was the horizon. In the beginning the geography extended the boundary, *her* boundary, and now it no longer did; she felt pinched. She knew she needed to live with the horizon in sight and here it was closed off by mountains.

She rose. "I've got to think about it."

He said, "Negative energy." They listened for a moment to the radio: clear skies today and tomorrow and for the rest of the week, a high pressure zone centered in Canada . . .

He said, "I don't want you to leave."

They had been together for so long. "What's this?" She smiled, reaching toward him, snapping his suspenders. "A proposal of marriage?" Her dearest friend, he was closer to her than anybody.

He threw up his hands in mock horror. "Anything but that!"

Sunlight flooded the room. He looked as alert as a prizefighter before the bell. *Hank Beers,* forever refreshed. Looking up at him, his massiveness so close, she thought of him suddenly as a mountain, one of the Granite Hills; his steepest slopes would remain forever uninhabited.

He stook looking down at her, grinning. He said, "You're looking for another Corbu."

She shook her head, unconvinced; then she reconsidered. "Maybe."

"That's the difference between us, Char."

Oh? She smiled back at him. He was nobody's fool.

"You," he said. "I think you're the opposition now."

"I may be at that," Charlotte said.

◆

$A$t Christmas, Charlotte left. There was no note taken of the event; one day she was there, the next day she wasn't. Of course her absence was felt; she was the most practical of the original settlers, and for some time to come the mood on the mountain was quarrelsome and dissonant. Beers was unapproachable during this period, throwing himself into a design for a house to be situated on the shore in Connecticut; he worked on it for months before resigning the commission and returning his fee to the client.

Charlotte did not sell her house but gave it to the corporation, for use as a guest house "or whatever." That was sentiment on her part and the house was seldom used. Unoccupied, it deteriorated and five years later it had disappeared altogether. I heard that it burned to the ground one summer night in 1979; the only visible remains after the fire were the concrete footings and a year later they too had vanished, overgrown with brush.

I departed six months after Charlotte. I attempted a correspondence with Hermann Goering and with Beers but neither man cared much for the written word, so the correspondence languished. In the late spring of 1980 my brother insisted I come to Middlebury for his son's graduation. After the ceremonies I began to reminisce about the mountain and in the course of talking about it I felt an irresistible desire to return. I talked Lew into driving to the Northeast Kingdom the next morning, lying about the time it would take us, and insisting he owed it to me to see the place where I'd spent a year of my life. A happy year, too, in retrospect.

I don't know what I expected. A condominium development, perhaps, or a sports center complete with racquetball courts and putting
greens and a swimming pool occupied by debutantes in bikinis. But
there was none of that; in fact there was very little change in five
years. I noticed one new house, less extreme than the experimental
models of the early years. Hank Beers's house had not changed at all.
There was junk in the driveway and a rusting iron sculpture lying
broken in the front yard. The Jeep was still there, though it hadn't
run in years. Beers himself was nowhere to be seen.

Across the road a young woman worked the vegetable garden,
topless. She waved cheerfully at my brother, who was staring. She
must have been amused at his city clothes, the cord jacket and gray
flannel trousers and penny loafers. I did not recognize her but walked
across the road to inquire about Beers. She watched me while smil-
ingly pulling on a T-shirt.

I asked her where Hank was.

"Gone up to town," she said. The Vermont accent was unmistak-
able. She didn't know when he'd be back, maybe an hour, maybe
two. "You a friend of Hank's?" she asked, her eyes narrowing.

"I used to live here," I said.

She looked at me. My brother and I were identically dressed. She
laughed, shaking her head, and went back to digging. Then: "You
*did?*"

"It was five years ago," I said.

"I thought you was from Boston or someplace."

I said no. Then I asked her where the others were. When she looked
puzzled, I named them all, Banjo, Slugger, Fido, Hermann Goering.
She shook her head.

"Those names don't mean anything to me."

"Bad-Debt, Dirty, A-Frame."

She brightened "Bad-Debt lives over there. A-Frame's gone to
Mexico."

"And Hank Beers?"

She smiled and cocked her head. "He lives with me," she said. "I
come from around here. That's where Hank is now, with my folks
up to town. My daddy needed some help with the back hoe." I
nodded. "Hank's helping him out. They're good friends," she said
proudly.

"And Bad-Debt?"

"Bad-Debt got *married* last week," she said. "My daddy married
them in the church. Hank was best man. I was bridesmaid."

♦

The preacher's daughter. She was so cheerful and composed it was impossible not to smile along with her, as if her information signaled an end to unhappiness everywhere.

"What's your name?"

I told her, and asked her please to remember me to Hank. I still wondered where the others had gone and turned to put the question to her. Surely Hank saw them from time to time. But she was bent over the hoe, our conversation apparently at an end. Perhaps then she remembered Hank's compulsive hospitality, for she looked up and asked if we, my brother and I, would like a glass of cold cider or a beer. I glanced at my brother, who shook his head.

I thanked her and then, backing away, asked her where the others lived now. She shrugged, a smile wide on her face. She didn't know; they had all left before she came. Hank talked about them sometimes. Sometimes they telephoned late at night and the men all laughed together. They were just — gone.

The geography of Vermont is different from New Hampshire. The mountains of Vermont are less majestic, and the valleys narrower and more self-contained. In the Northeast Kingdom the mountains are known as the Granite Hills and are gentle in contour, giving no hint of the hardness and density beneath. Of course Vermont is land-locked; it is an inland state in all respects. There is more forest now than at the turn of the century, owing to the unprofitability of lumbering the high country. Walking away, I thought about that.

I left my brother standing in the driveway of Beers's house and walked up the road, locating Charlotte's site. I knew about the fire and had difficulty locating her land. The forest had changed in five years, being both higher and thicker. I saw Slugger's house and, on the other side of the road, Fido's. Both appeared to be deserted; they were certainly neglected. Farther up the road were A-Frame's and Banjo's houses, sturdy as monuments. I was surprised; the houses were not as conspicuous as they had been; the wood sidings had weathered, darkening, and they had grown into the maturing forest. The forest had welcomed Beers's houses at last.

The atmosphere was wonderfully peaceful. Somewhere off in the woods I heard the banging of a hammer. But the sounds were desultory in the soft warmth of the June afternoon. I imagined the carpenter was thinking of a swim or a nap.

I hurried back down the road to Beers's house, confused by the change in five years' time. My brother was leaning against the car, smoking a cigarette and watching the girl in the T-shirt. I was un-nerved and began to describe for him the way it had been, the clamor, stereos blasting from every house, volleyball games, barn raisings, men always shouting at each other. But my description was unsatis-factory, and sentimental because it bore no relation to the surround-ings now.

"Well," my brother said at last. "Satisfied?"

I took a last look around. I wanted to burn the place into my memory so that I could describe it in a letter to Charlotte. Still, I was reluctant to leave with so many mysteries still in place. I nodded at the girl. "She's very pretty."

Lew grunted. "She's very *young*, Brother John."

We got into the car and I backed carefully out of the driveway. I waved again at the girl but she was concentrating on her garden and didn't notice. I drove slowly down the hill, unaccountably elated. My brother was talking but I wasn't listening. I thought of Beers remain-ing and Charlotte leaving and what that meant for them both. I had heard Char was happy, working productively in a prairie city. These surroundings gave no hint of Hank Beers's state of mind. Things were settled, though. Perhaps inside his house had changed and I cursed myself for not asking the girl if I could look around. Perhaps he had made all the changes he'd promised Charlotte and promised himself, the result a sublime interior. Heavenly biases. An interior free of hostility.

My brother was still talking and I sneaked a look into the rearview mirror, a final glance at Hank Beers's Shangri-la. I saw it reversed through the trees, the twin triangular peaks soaring above the thick-waisted spruce. His was the only house visible. I remembered the first time I'd seen it, how I'd laughed out loud. A triumph of obliquity, I'd thought then. Delinquency. Megalomania. It did not seem so now.

Then we were off the hill and onto the highway. I was driving very slowly. A mile from town a damaged pickup truck accelerated around a curve and was by me before I could react. It was Beers, unmistak-able in his bright red shirt and white suspenders. I heard the horn and watched him bring the truck to a skidding stop. I reversed and pres-ently we faced each other across the median stripe.

"Nego!" he shouted. My brother looked at me queerly. I had not told him my nickname. Beers had assigned all the nicknames, and mine was the diminutive of "negative."

"Had to come up for a look," I said. "Place's changed," I added.

"What did you expect?"

I smiled. "Extinction?"

"No," he said. "Transformation. Nothing ever dies. It's just trans-formed." He made a little motion with his fingers, like a diner asking for the check.

"Looks good," I said. I suddenly imagined him bent over his draw-ing board alone, turning frequently to stare out the window at the slope of the mountain, hearing crickets but seeing the land drenched in snow. Winter and summer would always exist simultaneously in his mind. I asked him what he'd done to the interior of his house.

"Come on back, I'll show it to you."

"Got to move along," I said hastily, indicating my brother. He had not said a word, leaning forward and listening to us talk. "An ap-pointment in Middlebury."

Beers laughed, revving his engine. "Old Nego."

"Why not?" Lew asked, looking at me.

"No," I said, my tone harsher than I'd intended.

"I'm John's brother," Lew said.

"I guessed," Hank said.

"We're late," I said. I reached across the stripe to shake hands with Hank Beers. I did not want to go back with him. I had my own conception of the mountain and did not want it tampered with. The nature of the transformation did not matter as much as the fact. I suppose there was some fear in that, too; either that he had failed completely or succeeded wonderfully; either of the above. I preferred to believe the latter, because if the last two decades had taught me nothing else they had taught me the necessity of mystery to faith. I said, "Good to see you, Hank."

He put the truck in gear. "Ever hear from Char?"

"Christmas card," I said. "Nice card, it's a drawing of your house in winter, a wreath on the door —"

He nodded, pulling away. "I know. Poor Char." I put my car in gear and we separated at a crawl, both of us leaning out the window looking at the other. Then with a wave he was gone, gathering speed as the road rose in the direction of the mountain.

Lew was silent a moment, then began to chatter. It was some family matter, a personal complication. I nodded at the words but did not truly listen. I was trying to apply the austere lessons of Hank Beers to my own life, and not succeeding. We had started the sixties together and had lived through the seventies, he maintaining in his way, I in mine. Of course I had returned to the government. This was a fresh decade and for the life of me I could not decide which of us had a purchase on the future. I was suddenly sympathetic to him and wanted to believe that as he succeeded, so did we all. But that was nonsense. He managed to endure in an extreme climate, and what could that imply for the rest of us?

My brother touched my arm. What do you make of him? Lew asked. "Give me the word, old Nego. What is he? Hermit? Guru? *Agent provocateur?* Prophet? Coward?"

God damn Lew. But this is not his story, is it? Or Timmy's. Or mine.

I said I imagined Hank Beers today and for all the days to come at work alone on his mountain, blending into it and continuing to grow and thicken. His houses would remain, some deserted, others not. He has not forsaken and is not forsaken. He is thirty-nine and his dream still surrounds him. I explained to my brother that it was a metamorphosis, this conversion of Hank Beers into a feature of the geography of Vermont.

1980

◆

# THE NORTH SHORE,

# 1958

◆

Swan and I discovered the Art Institute of Chicago in the summer of 1955, the year of our great rebellion, three or four years
after I learned to drive. The Art Institute was a secret between us; if
anyone asked where we were going, we told them the club to play
golf. We would drive into Chicago on weekday afternoons, taking
the slow way, Sheridan Road through Highland Park and Wilmette
and Evanston, making the turn at the Edgewater Beach Hotel, then
flying down the Outer Drive past the high-rise apartments and yacht
basins to Grant Park and the fine gray building on Michigan Avenue.
    Swan and I drove to Chicago in my Chevrolet convertible, the top
down, the radio turned loud to the afternoon opera. In Winnetka,
Swan always turned up the radio another notch, hoping to attract the
attention and disapproval of the matrons in their station wagons; the
matrons reminded her of her mother. The pretty North Shore towns
were uniformly quiet and monotonous and it was a tranquil drive,
majestic oaks and elms arching overhead, the car tires swishing on
the narrow road, dipping, curving, and dipping again. From time to
time we would see the lake, flat and placid as a prairie, lukewarm
under the milky summer sun. Swan and I were never closer than when
driving up Sheridan Road to the Art Institute, sharing an excitement
our parents must have felt going to their first speakeasy. The Art
Institute — its somber rooms, its chaste alienation from Chicago's
grab, its Renaissance sensuality — was an underworld as exotic as
Capone's.
    That summer we wanted to meet Jews. We had never met one,

except in books. I had read "A Perfect Day for Bananafish" in *The New Yorker* and had identified with the desperate hero. I did not know what, if anything, was specifically Jewish about Seymour Glass's predicament in Miami, but I knew he wasn't a Presbyterian. After reading "In Dreams Begin Responsibilities," Swan wanted to meet Delmore Schwartz. I said I didn't think Delmore Schwartz was Jewish. Oh, yes, she said; yes, he was, definitely. She had read an article about him in the library at school and there was no question about it, Schwartz was a Jew, though probably not a practicing Jew. He didn't wear a skullcap or anything. But he was a prophet, with a prophet's premonition. Swan had laughed wickedly, inventing a meeting with Delmore Schwartz; it would be in New York, a chic literary bar in Greenwich Village.

"*That* would show them," she said. What if she met Delmore Schwartz and fell in love with him, and he with her, a *coup de foudre?* They would be seen all over New York, and their affair would find its way into Winchell's column; it would be a great scandal. He was a passionate man, she knew that much — though what he could possibly see in a drab little debutante from the North Shore, she couldn't possibly guess. He wouldn't look at her twice, and it was too bad because if she became his mistress she could bring him home and introduce him to her parents. They would have cocktails and Delmore could read "In Dreams Begin Responsibilities" to her father, and what a riot it would be! Her father hated Jews almost as much as he hated her mother.

"Come off it," I said.

She said, "It's true."

"You're not drab," I said.

"Yes I am," she replied. She was not fishing; she believed it. Her mother thought she was drab; not a great beauty, not an easy conversationalist, a difficult girl, willful. Swan ruffled her hair and sighed. Her ears were too big and her bosom too small, and she hated polite conversation; she was a charmless dinner partner. But she had a dream, meeting Delmore Schwartz and bringing him home; if only he lived in Chicago, then there would be the possibility of a meeting by chance at the Art Institute.

In any event, we never met anyone at the Art Institute. We never met a soul we knew, nor any Jews. It was always just Swan and me alone on summer afternoons, escaping Lake Forest.

The first time we visited the Art Institute we stayed with the Impressionists until closing time. Someone had told Swan that the

French collection was the class of the field, and we looked at it with longing and envy; this was a world far from the one we knew. We remained a long time before Degas' *The Morning Bath*. It was not until the following week that we came upon the room containing the work of Edward Hopper. He was unfamiliar to us, being an American Artist; of course we favored the Europeans. Hopper's oils were a revelation, and not only for their reductive technique. Dazzled, we saw the desolate soul of the Midwest: empty streets, dark light, and turbulence under the still skin of things. Also, it seemed to me that Hopper identified the dead hand of the past: his people were rooted, in place forever, imprisoned by memory. And memory was an unrequited love. Hopper confirmed all that we thought and felt about Illinois and its bourgeois Republican values, its conformity and repression and suspicion and yahoo chauvinism, America First. In 1955 we had such loathing for the heartland and wanted so to break out, to resign in protest, spitting in La Salle Street's eye. I have never felt such certitude about anything since.

Swan said, "Oh, look. *Look*." We entered the room and began to move slowly in front of the pictures (there were not many), avid to observe each detail. Hopper's light was so hard and bright that it hurt your eyes to look at it.

She said, "He takes you so far in that you can almost see the other side."

I said, "I know what you mean." Behind Hopper's motionless housewives, Degas' dancers. The one seemed to suggest the other.

She said, "On the other side of that, just beyond the light and shadows and the silence." She stepped closer to *Nighthawks*, peering at it, her eyes squinted, shining. She bent to take off her Capezios, and now they swung free from the fingers of one hand. She moved soundlessly, on tiptoe. I had a vision of her entering the diner barefoot and disappearing through the yellow door behind the coffee urns, the heads of the patrons and the counterman turning, surprised, *Lady, where do you think you're going?* But she was already gone, the door slowly swinging to. Swan drew back and said softly, "On the other side of that is something *great*."

"I don't know," I said. I was looking at it again.

"Oh, yes," she said. "I know it."

I said, "What is it, then?"

"My own life," she said proudly.

"Your morning bath," I said. I was making a joke.

"Nothing but," she said. She pointed at the picture. "I'm going to have to go through this to get to that. I'm going to walk right by all those people, all that loneliness —"

"You and Delmore Schwartz." Hand in hand, I thought. Another joke.

"I'm serious," she said.

"And that's what you want?"

"Yes," she said. "Yes, I do. That's what I want." She paused. "And it frightens me."

The atmosphere of the painting fascinated me. I did not see it, or what it represented, as something to be overcome. It was not threatening. It seemed to me that a world was contained there, a solitary planet, with nothing at all beyond it. It was an isolated world I knew well; I knew its interior. I had never been in a diner at night, but I knew the life there; I knew the town, its cabs and red brick storefronts and its silent inhabitants, its bleak churches. I said; "I love it, it's real just the way it is."

She turned to look at me. "And that's what *you* want?"

"Not what I want," I said. "What *is.*"

"And what you want, also."

"That's not the point," I said stubbornly. "I recognize it. I see what Hopper sees. If I could paint, that's the way I would paint. That's not some ideal dream" — I was thinking of *The Morning Bath,* but did not say so — "that's *real.* That's life, right there. And that's the point."

She nodded sadly, apparently unconvinced; or perhaps she was disappointed.

"That's the world that you have to live in," I said, saying more than I meant, certainly more than I understood. In some way I knew I was defending my own life — what I had made of it to this date, and what I would make of it henceforth. "You have to live in that before you can live in anything else. Do you see what I mean?"

"Yes," she said after a moment. "And I don't agree with you." There was a strained silence. She dipped her head and I saw she was crying. She made no sound. She stood staring at the floor, lightly tapping the heels of her pumps, heel to heel; that was the only sound in the great room. "Yes, it's real. Good, it's real. It's so real it hurts. But that's not all there is. And it's not enough."

She spoke with such emotion that I reached out to touch her arm. But she eluded me, smiling grimly, already sliding away to the next Hopper, slipping her feet into her pumps. Subject closed.

It was years before I learned that Edward Hopper was from the

East, born in a suburb of New York City. I thought he was a Midwesterner through and through, and had gone to paint in Cape Cod
and Maine as Hemingway and Fitzgerald had gone to France: to live
the life of a Midwestern exile, believing that his natural material — a
street, a farmhouse, an El, an automat, a woman alone in a room —
was seen from afar, perhaps only seen from afar. As everyone knows,
Midwesterners are great travelers. Swan and I spent many afternoons
in the Hopper room at the Art Institute. We would view the Italians,
and French, the Germans, Picasso, and Hopper, in that order. Then,
driving slowly back up Sheridan Road to Lake Forest, we would
argue endlessly over the import of *Nighthawks* and the others. She
was troubled, I consoled.

That time is so scattered now, a universe of dead stars, cold and
untouchable. I am almost fifty, and its design seems beyond the reach
of my eyesight. But its pull is still strong, and thinking of it now is
like meeting a childhood enemy years later and finding him charming,
not at all the bully of memory. My past is like a picture gallery, with
specimens from the various schools. Imagine oils displayed on the
bone-white walls of a conservative museum. Up close they have a
familiar logic, but as you move back from them the logic fades and
finally dissolves altogether and you are left wondering what it was
that had been so vivid. And of course the reverse is also true.

This much I know for certain: my great rebellion lasted just that
one year; one summer, really. I returned to college in September, and
in January of 1956 I fell in love with a girl from the East, a Vassar
girl, and although the romance ended, my friendship with her and
her family did not. Rebellion suddenly seemed adolescent, a waste of
time, and beside the point. My girl was Jewish and came from a
family of lawyers — witty, rowdy, disputatious, rich — and I determined that I would be a lawyer, too. It seemed a fine way to mix
public and private lives, and somewhere in the back of my mind was
the idea of a political career. I wanted to be like them, or as I conceived them to be: cosmopolitan, free from regional prejudice, living
in the present, and looking to the future without entangling alliances.
That is, no longer possessed by the facts of the past. No question,
mine was the eye of a Midwestern provincial; I tended to see things
in primary colors, and my grasp of irony and paradox was incomplete. At any event, Sophie's family seemed somehow to transcend
region, capable of picking up and moving on at a moment's notice;
and they studied the past, not with any particular nostalgia or affec-

tion, but with the singlemindedness of mathematicians working on an equation whose answer was eternally elusive. "The trouble with loving the past," Sophie said, "is that it doesn't love you back."

I thought those the wisest words I had ever heard from a woman, and they sealed my decision. That I would leave the North Shore was by 1958 a closed question; of course I would. I realized I could walk through an open door.

However, with Swan it was different. And this is Swan's story, not mine. It is a story of the time, Ike's and Adlai's America. In those days it was difficult for girls like Swan to find their feet, and leave their families to make lives of their own. The way out was marriage, and too often that meant only a regional trade — the North Shore of Boston or of Long Island for the North Shore of Chicago. That would never be Swan's way; she was far too intelligent. Her expectations ran so high, and her passions so deep; and she was mature beyond her years. She fastened on things that were just out of reach, in the shadows beyond the light; that was where her fate lay. The Midwest in those days was a landlocked region, the coasts were out of sight over the horizon. For a young woman of Impressionist temperament, it was not a journey made solo. So she waited for a kindred spirit, someone as high-reaching and hungry as she was, someone with whom she could share what she called the ethical life. She maintained her crush on Delmore Schwartz, though she found she liked the poems less than the stories, "Dreams" especially. She told me once that she thought he must lead an ideal life, the reward for being a great writer, universally admired, even loved. "He must be a happy man," she said. But that was a rare lapse of insight.

Swan was patient, always watchful, confident that even on the North Shore there were surprises — unusual men, gallant men, men cut from a different cloth, adventurous men, Impressionist men who in a few inspired strokes could create a world.

Art Reisinger had been a marine in Korea, and badly wounded in the murderous retreat from the Thirty-eighth Parallel. He had been a volunteer, joining up in his sophomore year at Yale; and he did not go to O.C.S. with his friends, but enlisted as a private. He came home with a false hand, which he concealed in a black leather glove. The first time Swan met him, he shook hands with his left hand, palm down. She did not notice the false hand, she said later, because he was wearing a tuxedo and it was dark. She did not know his military history and was not prepared for a false hand inside a black glove.

Never had a war been forgotten so quickly and thoroughly as the war in Korea.

She thought he kept his right hand in his jacket pocket as a Continental mannerism; he was obviously a worldly man. She was charmed by the left-handed shake before she knew the practical reason behind it. "Right away I knew he was different from the rest of you," she said much later.

I introduced them at a party at the country club. Swan and I were standing at the bar watching people dance. It was a warm evening with a full moon, the steely water of the lake shining in the distance. The clubhouse was perched on a bluff overlooking the lake. There was a hardwood dance floor under a green and white tent, the band at one end of the tent and the bar at the other. It was a lively season that summer, parties every weekend. The crop of debutantes was especially vivacious and carefree, and in that respect Swan was remarkable. She was shy and serious-minded. Her mother urged her to be more outgoing, to at least try to be popular, and her friends thought her "deep."

Swan murmured, "Who is that?"

Reisinger was leaning against a tent pole, his feet crossed at the ankles forming a figure 4. His jacket was buttoned. I did not recognize him immediately, he had been gone so long. After he was separated from the service he remained on the West Coast to finish his education; then he dropped out of sight. He slipped out of our suburban orbit, and no one heard anything reliable, only garbled and incomplete reports from his sister. There were reports that he was drifting, reluctant to return home, working as a lumberjack, then as a roughneck in the oil fields, finally that he had settled somewhere in Northern California. There was a rumor that he had gotten into a scrape serious enough to require the intervention of the family lawyer, but no one knew any details. He was five years older than I, and taller and thicker than I remembered. His hair was long, and that was not the fashion then. He was drinking a gin and tonic and after each swallow he would put the glass on a table at his elbow. The floor was a swirl of color and sound, everyone unbuttoned and in motion. Lester Lanin himself was leading the ensemble. Reisinger was alone and standing quite still, his shoulder against the tent pole.

"That's Art Reisinger," I said.

"Linda's brother?" Swan said. "So *that's* Linda's brother."

"He's been away," I said.

She said, "I know. Linda said he might be home this summer. They haven't seen him in years —" Just then he turned toward us, an inquisitive look on his face. We were obviously talking about him, and he had caught us off-guard. Flustered, I made a sign of recognition and Swan and I walked over to him. I introduced them and it was then that he put out his left hand, palm down. Swan took it, giving a little delighted laugh and saying how nice it was to meet him, she had heard so much. I remembered immediately about the false hand and that made me even more ill at ease. I thought he might misinterpret Swan's enthusiasm, which to me sounded forced.

I asked him how long he had been in town and he said not long. He was living with his family while he waited for people to vacate an apartment on the Near North Side.

"Well," I said. "You'll find the place hasn't changed much." I gestured at the dancers, Lanin, the lake, the bartenders.

He said, "Yes, it has."

Swan said, "You've been on the West Coast." She said it as she might have said Samarkand or Copenhagen.

He nodded, turning to watch the floor. He had picked up his drink and stood clinking the glass against his teeth. His manner was so abrupt that I looked around for a means of escape. I thought suddenly that I was too old for these parties. I was twenty-three and had been going to them for five — no, six — years. Compared to most of those on the dance floor, I was an older man. Of course I wanted to marry and settle down, but that would have to wait a year; too bad Swan was only eighteen. I turned to Swan, intending to suggest that we dance, but Reisinger was talking and she was intent, listening to him. He said, "How do you know that?"

"Your sister. Linda and I are friends."

He leaned down so that his ear was close to Swan's mouth. The music was very loud and it was hard to hear conversation. He used an expression that was unfamiliar to me then, but that I have since recognized as military argot: "Say again?"

"Linda," she said. "Your sister."

He nodded sourly, turning to look at the dance floor. "And what else did Linda tell you?"

"Linda's very mysterious about you. My brother Arthur, the mystery man from the West Coast. Is there a great deal to tell?" She cocked her head, smiling brightly. I thought she looked tight, though she rarely drank. "Why did you decide to come back here, after all that time out there? Your seven years, so far away. The West Coast, gosh. And what are you going to do, now that you're back?"

♦

He said, "It remains to be seen."

"Brokerage, I suppose," she said. She pronounced it *brrroke-erage.* "Or banking or real estate, solid La Salle Street stuff. Or selling foreign cars. Or maybe you'll be an ad man, that's a productive thing, very popular. It's what a lot of your crowd is doing now, advertising. J. Walter Fathead. Batton, Barton, Durstine and Halfwit."

I looked on, amused. The advertising industry was everyone's whipping boy that year, but I hadn't known that Swan knew or cared. And she was never aggressive, except when defending Delmore Schwartz. Now she was baiting Reisinger; she seemed to be challenging him to something, and his condescending manner was not encouraging. He looked like a man who wanted to back life into a corner, and not with Thoreau's intention of reducing it to its simplest terms. Swan rocked forward on the balls of her feet, her head tilted provocatively. She was waiting for him to reply.

"No," he said.

"Maybe law," she said, with a nod in my direction.

"Not law, either," he said.

"Pulla-tics," she said. "Is that your game?"

He smiled a little.

"Do you like to dance? Do they dance on the West Coast?"

He said nothing to that.

"Why don't you ask me to dance?"

Reisinger looked at her a long moment, then shrugged and very deliberately put his glass on the table. He put his hands out to her, palms up, as if he were handing her a plate. Here, his manner said, what are you going to do with this? Swan looked at his black glove, and then at him. Lanin was playing a waltz. She took both his hands in hers and they stood a moment, looking at each other. Then they moved off to the center of the noisy floor, turning slowly, then faster and faster. Reisinger was a fine dancer. His false hand rested inert on the soft shelf of crinoline at the small of her back. After a moment she deftly switched hands and they twirled in the center of the floor. Now she was leading, her white hand over his black glove. Her head was thrown back and she was looking at him solemnly as they turned to the music. At once she looked years older, not a suburban debutante, but a woman of character. I watched them, fascinated and envious — and with foreboding, too, because they seemed to be out of this world. Swan was leading him in triple time. Young people on the floor made way for them. The floor was abounce with music and color and shouted conversation, the disheveled stag line in constant

motion; but Swan and Reisinger retained a kind of detached stillness
and authority. Lanin always conducted waltz music as if it had been
invented by Irving Berlin, but they were dancing the real thing,
Strauss or Brahms, gallant and serious in the crowd of college-age
debs and their escorts.

"What are you doing here all alone? Where's Swan?"

I reluctantly turned to say hello to Swan's mother. We chatted a
moment and when she saw her daughter in Reisinger's arms she
shuddered and gave a sharp, nasty laugh. She asked me who he was
and when I told her she nodded firmly: Oh, yes, *him*, the crippled
marine who couldn't make a go of it. She knew he was back; Eileen
Reisinger had said something the other day. Her prodigal son, returned at last. And it was inevitable, him finding Swan, though it was
more likely that Swan had found him. "What I've never understood
about Swan," she said, talking into my ear, smothering the music, "is
these boys she finds who all look exactly, but *exactly*, like her father
at that age. *God*, it's too strange."

There was a certain physical resemblance. Both men were tall, dark,
and reserved, and looked at the world with vehemence. Lee Emerson
was a bad-tempered and somewhat controversial criminal lawyer; he
and his wife had never gotten on, hence her spiteful comment. She
had a sharp tongue and was disagreeable in other ways, so of the two
I preferred him, a tough attorney of the old school, fiercely proud of
his law practice. His interests in life were his golf game, Swan, and
his practice. He was not particular about his clients, many of whom
turned up in the local papers in the glare of flashbulbs, fedoras held
over their faces, manacled to federal agents. My father believed that
he had a grudge against the world, and the controversial law practice
was his way of getting even.

No question, he and Reisinger shared a muscular, sardonic presence. They had weight, and with the weight the bookmaker's air of
knowing the odds. The night that Swan and Reisinger waltzed at the
country club remains in my memory, a scene quite out of character
for our Midwestern suburb, where everyone tried to fit in — the architecture was borrowed from Europe, but the manners were not.
And there was something ineluctably European about them that
night, a denseness and fatalism, as if theirs were a love affair just past
its prime. They looked as if they had shared a dark history together.

Swan and Reisinger dropped out of sight for a while, then reap-
peared. Three weeks later they eloped, or "eloped" because it was an

elopement only by the standards of the North Shore in 1958. Swan's
mother always referred to it as "Swan's elopement." Her parents and
her brother and Reisinger's parents and his sister were present at the
ceremony, and there was a reception later at the Emersons'. There
were only a few people at the reception and the new Mr. and Mrs.
Reisinger stayed for just an hour. It was obvious that even the hour
was a trial, a concession to the parents, both sides. I had one hurried
conversation with Swan before their departure.

She kissed me warmly and I said, truthfully, that she looked lovely.
She had a new haircut. I said, "All the best."

"We did it, didn't we?"

I said, "You sure did."

"No, no," she said. "I mean *we*. *We* did it." I mumbled something
affirmative. She looked at me slyly, smiling. "*We got me out of here.*
This ghastly place, the way people have to lead their lives. Remember
the arguments we had? We were so over our heads, you and I. But
that's all finished now. Arthur —" She looked around the room, and
when she found Reisinger, she blew him a kiss. "Arthur and I are
moving to the Near North Side and I'm going to a real school, the
University of Chicago." She said this defiantly and I grinned; the
Midway then was thought to be under the influence of Communists
and their dupes. I wondered what Reisinger intended to do, brrroke-
erage, banking, real estate, advertising, and law being out. Perhaps it
would be pulla-tics after all. She said, "He's so different, you can't
know how serious he is, what he's seen and done and been through,
and what he's made of it. Did you know he was in the Korean War?
He volunteered, and then he went to school in California to try to
figure it out, the reason for the war. He knows what it is to be
intimate, and who your enemies are. And how you have to protect
yourself." She was breathless, talking so fast that the words tumbled
over themselves. "And you introduced us and that makes you a special friend. I fell in love right away, but I suppose you guessed that. It
was love at first sight, him too. Arthur's an individualist. I took him
to the Art Institute. But we didn't go our way, we started with the
Hoppers and ended with the French. And he agrees with me, and that
made me so happy. It used to bother me so, the way you felt, because
we were such good friends. You were the only friend I had. All this."
Her voice deepened and fell as she gestured out the window at the
lawn and the swimming pool shaded by oak trees. A few guests,
Reisinger's parents among them, stood under trees, drinks in their
hands, the men in white ducks and blazers and the women in loose
dresses and floppy hats. "All this means nothing to him," Swan con-

tinued, "*rien du tout.* They're not there when you need them." She glanced at her father, standing alone near the front door. "They thought they made everything so safe." She laughed again and I realized how young she was. Two months before she had been a debutante, coming out.

I said, "What happens after the University of Chicago?"

"Ah," she said. "Who knows?"

I said, "I'll bet you have a million children."

She said, "I doubt it. Maybe one or two." She looked sideways at the guests on the lawn. Sunlight fell through the trees, dappling the grass. "We are going to have a great life together," she said. "We are *like that.*" She pressed two fingers together and whispered, "Arthur's hard to know but I hope you'll try." I smiled, she was so hopeful and spirited; I was convinced she was pregnant.

Later, I stood in the Emerson driveway with Swan's father and watched them depart in Reisinger's old Austin-Healey. He still had his California license plates. I had managed a handshake with him, but that was all. He accepted my congratulations but did not seem eager to talk. He kept looking over his shoulder, searching for Swan. Everyone applauded as they sped out of the driveway, the car tires scattering gravel. But there was no rice and Swan did not throw her garter. Her mother was not present for the farewell.

"Where are they going?" I asked Swan's father.

"Door County," he said morosely.

"It's very pretty this time of year." He looked at me. In fact, as we both knew, Door County was hot, flyblown, and crowded. I raised my glass. "Good luck to them."

"Yes," he said.

I had known Lee Emerson all my life, and liked him despite his bad temper and disreputable law practice, and his grudge. He and my father were golfing friends, and once a few years before, when I was going through a bad patch with my parents, he had allowed me to come and stay for a week, "a change of venue." That was the year before the year of my great rebellion, and the beginning of my friendship with Swan. Making conversation, I said, "Where did you and Mrs. Emerson honeymoon?"

"We went to Europe," he said. "It was 1939 and they were getting ready to blow everything up. The world just went to hell. That goddamned Roosevelt."

I did not want to talk politics with him. I said, "Well, it was a nice ceremony."

"Nice?" He looked at me, his eyes watery and vague. He said, "She looked beautiful, as always. She is a beautiful girl, isn't she? She looks the way all girls should look at eighteen. She has always been precocious. She has a subtle mind. She has a mind like mine and was going to Vassar to get it educated. An untrained mind is worse than useless. Now she's going to the goddamned University of Chicago, the Great Books and all that crap. It's a crime. Of course now, to me, she is a hostile witness. She has married a man who is beneath her in every way. Who doesn't have it *here*." He pointed to his stomach. "He is a son of a bitch. Her *husband*." He bit off the word. "Is an oddball."

"Lee," I said. It was the first time I had ever called him by his first name. I was appalled at what he had said, and did not know how to reply. I had affection for Swan, too.

"Weren't you supposed to be engaged?"

"Engaged to be engaged," I said.

"What happened?"

"It broke up but we're still friends. She's a wonderful girl," I said loyally, adding, "You'd like them, a family of lawyers."

"Sophie something," he said. "From the East."

I said, "Yes." Then: "New York."

He said, "Your father told me." He started to say something more, then changed his mind. He looked away, then back at me, nodding sharply. "You're smart. Or lucky. You're too young. So's she. My daughter's even younger than you are. Except she's not smart. Or lucky. She needed some help and no one gave it to her."

I did not understand this remark. I said, "It'll be fine."

"No, it won't." His voice was loud and people near us turned to hear the conversation, Swan's father's courtroom baritone. He stood looking at the place in the driveway where the Austin-Healey had been, but when he spoke it was to me only. "I wish to Christ you'd stood up to be counted when it counted. I wish to Christ you'd done that, it might've helped. But you didn't. I suppose you had reasons. Did you have a reason?" He didn't wait for an answer and probably he knew there wouldn't be one; no lawyer asks a question without knowing the answer to it. "Now she's ruined her life," he said.

The summer of 1958 was my last on the North Shore. I was entering my final year at law school and after graduation I would go to work, I hoped in the East. On the Labor Day weekend four of us decided to give an end-of-the-summer party, a kind of valedictory to the Charleston and the waltz. We had in mind a pleasant, boozy, light-hearted evening. No dance bands, no debs, no sophomores, no crashers, no marrieds.

Terry Harris's parents were away for the weekend, so we assembled at his house, my old red Webcor stacked with Chicago music, Muggsy Spanier, Georg Brunis, Wild Bill Davison, Art Hodes. Around eight o'clock a sudden rain forced us inside. The party seemed to grow throughout the evening, and in fact a few debs did show up, along with a few marrieds. The marrieds gave the party an air of seriousness and maturity.

Five of us were playing poker in the den when George Field came up behind me and whispered, "There's some trouble." I looked at him and folded my hand. He took me off into a corner and said there was trouble in the kitchen. Reisinger was acting crazy.

"I didn't know he was here," I said. "Where's Swan?"

"In the hall," he said. "She's pretty damn upset. He's threatening people."

"Well, is he drunk?"

George looked at me and shrugged. With Reisinger, it was impossible to tell. But he didn't think so.

I found Swan sitting on a chair in the vestibule, alone. She had her raincoat on and looked frightened. She stared at me a moment and said, "You."

"Me," I said.

"It's nice to see you," she said.

"You, too."

"It's been a while."

"Well," I said. "Since your wedding. You're an old married woman now."

She said, "I guess I am."

"And you've cut your hair."

"No more drab little Swan. Too bad I can't do anything about my ears." She unbuttoned her raincoat and leaned forward, looking at me. Her hair was parted on the side and swept back, the fashion then. "I hoped you'd be here, and now you are."

"George," I began.

"Never mind George," she said.

I knelt beside her and asked what the trouble was, but she only shook her head. We could both see into the kitchen from the vestibule. George and Bill Darcy were crouched by the door, posed as if they were waiting for a serve at tennis. Reisinger was out of sight. There was no conversation at all.

Swan moved closer and said in a flat voice, "We only came at the last minute. I wanted to, the last party of the summer. We only just got back from Fish Creek. What a nice trip we had."

"You look great," I said.

"Do I?" She turned away, glancing in the direction of the kitchen. "I don't feel so great."

"We'll fix it up," I said.

She nodded, arching her eyebrows, but did not reply for a moment. She said, "Now's the time you can be a special friend to us, if you want to. It isn't a question of fixing anything up." She looked at me again and I nodded. "He ordered me to leave when it began. But if you can get him out of there, get him close to me. Do you understand that?" She put her hand on my arm, squeezing, and I noticed her wedding ring, a plain gold band. She brought her face close to mine, her eyes shining, squinted. "I'm the only person he trusts."

I said, "What happened?"

"Someone said something stupid." Then: "His hand hurts all the time, even though it's not supposed to. It hurts him and he takes stuff for the pain." She paused and said, "Sometimes he doesn't know what he's saying, and when he gets with *them* —" She gestured at George and Bill, their backs to us.

I said, "Swan."

She smiled and said, "We had such a nice honeymoon. We rented a house and went sailing. He taught me how to fish, fly cast. We didn't see a soul."

"I've been meaning to call you."

"We've been looking for a place in Chicago."

I nodded. It was still quiet in the kitchen.

"The South Side, near the university." And in answer to my unspoken question, she said, "Arthur doesn't know what he's going to do yet, but he's got lines out everywhere. I've been encouraging him to write a book."

I started at that. Then I rose to my feet, putting my hand on her shoulder. I did not see Art Reisinger as a writer of books, and I wondered what sort of books she was encouraging him to write. "OK," I said. "But —"

She said slowly, "They were arguing. Someone tried to bait him, and that's the wrong thing to do. That's a big mistake with Arthur. I'm the only one he trusts around here, and for good reason." Her voice was low and controlled, with a timbre I did not recognize. She said, "We're so close it's as if we're the same person. I love him so, and when we're together, only us —" I listened, flattered that she would confide in me. I felt brotherly toward her, but uneasy listening to her confessions. "I need him and he needs me." She sighed, her shoulders sagging, looking again into the kitchen.

"What were they arguing about?"

"It doesn't matter," she said brusquely. "They're such shits, they don't *know anything* about *anything* beyond this town." She smiled, an odd, private smile. "And they don't know anything at all about Arthur, but they're going to find out."

I left her and went to the kitchen door and looked in. There was a breakfast table in the center of the kitchen, and behind the table Reisinger and Terry Harris. Reisinger had a knife at Terry's throat. Terry looked like a child next to Reisinger, who stood behind him, one long arm around his chest and the knife drawn up under his chin. He looked as if he were demonstrating some commando tactic. Terry was a full head shorter than Reisinger, but that was not what made the contest so unequal. They were a boy and a man, and no matter that only a few years separated them. There was the fact of Reisinger's war, his mysterious past on the West Coast, and the false hand inside the black glove. He did not seem to notice me, and I thought his eyes looked unfocused. The muscles in his forearm bulged. His arm was covered with thick, black hair, and there was a tattoo on the biceps: SEMPER FI.

I felt a motion at my elbow and turned to see one of the debs. She was very pretty and quite tight and did not seem to understand the situation, because she giggled. She must have thought we were playing The Game. Seeing her, Terry tried to struggle free, but Reisinger, grinning, held him fast, tickling his puffy chin with the blade of the knife. The knife was military issue, its pistol grip and pommel familiar from photographs and movies; none of us had ever seen the real thing.

I tried to move the deb out of the doorway — this had nothing to do with her — but she wouldn't go. There were now six of us in the kitchen. The others looked naturally to me; I was Swan's friend, I would have some authority. I looked at them. There was no question of us "taking" Reisinger, not one of us was a brawler. When we were hot, we had another drink and cooled off. Fighting was not our style because it was not adult, as we understood "adult." It was true that once or twice a summer someone would throw a punch, but it always seemed they were married men defending their wives' or friends' honor. They were quick fights, broken up almost as soon as they began, invariably late at night in sporting circumstances; the last scrap was in the sand trap off the ninth tee. But this was different, and our experience was not equal to it. We did not know where to begin.

George had said there had been an argument. Terry had said something that Reisinger misinterpreted, though it was obvious that Reisinger wanted to fight, obvious from the moment he walked into the house, Swan on his arm. Misjudging the situation, Terry had asked him about the war. Reisinger took offense. Terry apologized, but it didn't seem to matter.

I said, "Art."

He said something I didn't understand but which sounded to me like garbled military language.

I said again, "Art."

He said, "Roger that," and lowered the knife a little.

I said, "Swan's outside. She wants to go home."

He said, "Get her in here."

I said, "She's in the car."

"Get her in here!"

I was afraid for her. I said, "She won't come."

He cursed once and looked at me sideways with the purest malevolence. I took a step backward, confused. I didn't know what he wanted. Whatever it was, I didn't have it. I thought that probably Swan did, or anyway knew what it was.

George said, "Put the knife down, Art. For God's sake, we're all friends here. And Terry's apologized. Who the hell cares?"

Reisinger said, "I care." Terry made a sudden movement and Reisinger pressed him again, hard, digging his false hand into Terry's chest. Terry looked at the black glove and closed his eyes. Reisinger moved as if in a trance, his face flushed, skin drawn tight over the bones, eyes wide and accusing. I wondered what the memory was, for surely he was now back in his memory. I supposed it was Korea and what had happened there, the retreat from the Thirty-eighth Parallel and the phantom pain in his false hand. But I knew nothing about the war and could not imagine living with a false hand.

I said, "What's it all about, Art?"

He said, "You'll get what's coming to you."

The deb, who had been watching all this, said in a strained voice, "I'm going to call the police."

Bill Darcy said, "No," and grabbed her arm. I knew his concern: it was unthinkable that the authorities, the town, be brought into this. Everyone's reputation was at stake, and it was all so weird. Poor Swan. Of course the police would be discreet; there was no question of any arrest or investigation or formal report or newspaper story. That was not the way things were done in our town. The point was, *they* would know and that would mean gossip and comment. And eventually the story would get out and ruin everything; we would be seen to be incapable of managing our own affairs. Bill said something to the deb and she nodded, apparently agreeing that this was not a public matter. It was an incident in the Harris kitchen, too many cocktails and someone spoke out of turn.

Reisinger sighed and muttered something. Then I heard Spanier's cornet, muted, *waa-waa*, so blue. It was one of the sides with Frank Teschmacher and Dave Tough. George looked at me and winked, wiggling his shoulders. This was the party we had planned, an end-of-the-summer celebration with Spanier's music, happy blues. It had nothing to do with Korea or Swan or Reisinger's pain or me getting what was coming to me.

"Come on, Art," I said. "It was a long time ago. Listen to Muggsy. Have a drink."

Reisinger said, "You dirty little Jew."

I said, "What?"

In the stunned silence he glanced around him, as if searching for something; or perhaps he had forgotten where he was. He brought his arm up so that the false hand was resting under Terry's ear, black on white, inert.

I said, "What the hell are you talking about?"

"Politics. I'm talking about a conspiracy."

I said, "Wait a minute."

"You and your Jew friends."

I looked at George Field, casually lighting a cigarette; we had known each other all our lives, and had had many escapades together. But George did not look at me. The Harris kitchen suddenly seemed very small, claustrophobic as a cell, and the atmosphere filled with — it wasn't menace, more a kind of morbid curiosity mixed with fear. George said mildly, "Come on, Art." No one moved.

"Your Jew war."

"That's not nice," the deb said.

George laughed, a sharp little snicker.

"Well, it *isn't*," the deb said.

Reisinger seemed not to hear. He spoke directly to me, though his eyes were every which way; I did not know if it was me he saw or someone else. He said, "You don't care about anything, you Jews. You entitled people. So long as you get yours, you don't care how many of us you kill. And the question I've always asked is: What's the motive? *Why?*"

"Stop it," the deb said.

"What are you talking about?" I said again. But I knew what he was talking about, and I didn't think it had anything to do with Jews.

"Jews," Reisinger said. "Jews." The word spoken out loud seemed to give him particular pleasure, for he grinned widely. "Jews and politics. Money and Jews."

Bill Darcy said, "I don't get it."

"No?" Reisinger said. "Well, you'd better."

I said, "Let's have it, then."

He said, "You're asking for it."

Listening hard, I said nothing. Reisinger was deep into the regional subconscious, a forbidden country, unexplored; his vulgar tongue cast it in a shocking light. The Jewish threat was never very far below the surface in our town, yet the word itself was always spoken sotto voce, a side-of-the-mouth word of opprobrium, a whispered word not suitable at the dinner table or in the drawing room. It was not a nice word. By their language shall ye know them, and this was the Anglo-Saxon vernacular of the polite Midwest: accurate, blunt, but with much left unsaid, much concealed, much implied. The word "Jew" was an inch wide and a mile deep, a slender iceberg of a word, brutal as a dagger. Its open acknowledgment was in the locker room jokes of the period, men talking to like-minded men, the punch line in a dialect joke, and a blast of laughter. But this was not the locker room and there was no camaraderie, and Reisinger did not seem that kind of man. In the silence, George Field leaned forward, expectant.

George said, "Tell us about the war, Art." He lifted his chin and smiled halfway.

Reisinger said, "You stabbed us in the back, and then you let us fade away. A common Jew trick, chaos."

George laughed. "No argument so far."

Reisinger did not seem to hear him. He said, "Killers."

I started to say something, then didn't. I recognized the tone, a Midwestern defensiveness, so familiar. I heard my own voice, the near whine of an aggrieved subordinate, or a child who believes that a promise has been made and broken. This was the dark side of prairie fatalism, what Midwesterners liked to believe was their unique steadiness, simplicity, and resistance to anything modish — their stubborn belief that there was no human conspiracy, only an inscrutable and farseeing God. But this belief was often strained, and from time to time there were heroes. And if in this world there was a hero, there had to be a villain; and if the hero was also a victim, well then.

Things got off the track. I imagined Sophie listening to all this, and
wondered at her reaction. I could hear her precise, angry voice, slicing
at supercilious George Field, then turning on Reisinger. And when
she looked at him, whom would she see? Dr. Goebbels? Ezra Pound?
George Babbitt? Or a shell-shocked soldier with his foot in his
mouth?

Reisinger said loudly, "*Where were you?*" He turned then toward
the wall, and I saw the framed photograph and knew right away
what the argument was about, and how it had begun. Next to the
refrigerator was the famous picture of Douglas MacArthur, the taut
profile with the corncob pipe under the battered officer's hat with the
scrambled eggs on the bill. The photograph was signed and dated.
Terry's father had been one of the founders of a committee to draft
MacArthur for the 1952 presidential nomination, believing Eisenhower too liberal and Taft unelectable. Taft lacked the common
touch. Terry's father thought that the nation's corruption could be
traced to the refusal of the Republicans to turn to MacArthur, general, proconsul, and patriot, thereby leaving the destiny of the Republic in the hands of the Eastern bankers, the national press, the unions,
the Democrats, and the Jews, a junta directed by the quisling Thomas
E. Dewey. Terry was very much his father's son, without the certain
faith and hatred of the true believer. So they had been talking about
the war, he and Reisinger, and Terry had said something about the
great general, the tactician, the architect of victory, ruined by a Democrat haberdasher, and Reisinger had taken it badly. Probably it was
not what Terry had said, but that he had said anything. Dugout Doug
or General Jesus: Terry Harris was not entitled to speak of Reisinger's
war, none of us was. It would have been like speculating openly about
his intimate life with Swan. Reisinger had been there, a volunteer
marine, a witness, in the line, a casualty of General MacArthur's
command. The rest of us were outsiders, and would always be outsiders. And of course Reisinger's view of the war would be perverse:
he would enlist our sympathy, but discourage our understanding.

"You bastards." Reisinger sighed, a kind of exasperated sigh of
contempt, and placed the blade of the knife flat on Terry's neck.

"Please," the deb said. She was trembling and I thought she was
going to cry.

Reisinger looked at her curiously.

George murmured, "Not the time or the place, *definitely* not the
time or the place."

"You ought to try it sometime, you and your Jew friends."

"Try what, Art?" I took a step forward.

Bill Darcy said to me, "Easy now."

George said slyly, "Tell us about the war, Art. Tell us what you did in the war."

Bill said, "Shut up."

"Cowards. You. Him. You're cowards now." He pointed at George, who still wore his half smile. "You people really wanted it, didn't you? Just couldn't wait for it. Wanted it so badly you could taste it, except not so badly that you'd go to it. You people, so safe, so out of it, so protected, you stabbed us in the back, and left us there." He said, "I came in at the end of everything."

His next sentences were incoherent, something about a fifth column and a conspiracy against the volunteers. He mentioned Hiss, Acheson, the Rosenbergs, Truman, and Cohn. He was talking faster and faster, the names running together helter-skelter. Then he began to lose speed and finally stopped, silent. He rubbed his chin with his false hand, and suddenly I understood that he was back in the here and now, out of the shadows. He was in the near distance. I tried to look behind the surface, to penetrate the skin and discover the life there, but I could see nothing. I thought that we were all strangers, to ourselves and to each other. When he began to speak again it was with the gentlest tone, as if he were explaining the position to a curious child. "It was so cold and nothing like our prairie cold, our Windy City; the cold that exists outside a warm house. It was northern cold, colder than hell. It was wind all the way from Siberia. Every one of us had frostbite, even old Gunny, and when they started up again it didn't get warm and I thought it would. Everyone said it would. It always had. It was just as cold as before except they were coming down on us and just shooting everything to hell. You knew they were going to attack when they blew their bugles. That's the way it was. The lieutenant ran away. We were unprotected, and it was a massacre. I got separated from my unit. That's how I got this, look at it." He moved his arm up and down like a semaphore. "Our weapons misfired. Our food was gone. And the water froze in our canteens." He paused and seemed to concentrate on the music, Spanier's old-fashioned Chicago horn, hot and blue. I held my breath. Reisinger listened to Spanier with the offended expression of a man listening to a joke that irritated him and that he didn't get. Then something in him seemed to ignite, and he looked at each of us in turn, a look I had never seen before on anyone's face. He looked as if he were breaking apart; there were tears in his eyes. I felt that somehow I owed him an apology, or anyway a word of consolation. But he turned suddenly, pulling Terry around until their faces were almost touching. I thought for a moment that they would kiss. Then Reisinger pushed him away, hard. Terry crashed into the kitchen table, and then to the floor.

We all stood a moment, uncertain whether it was over or just beginning. Reisinger still had the knife. We stood frozen, watching him and listening to the rain tap-tap on the roof, and Spanier in the distance. The deb moved behind me and I knew without looking that Swan was in the doorway. I heard her breathing, and smelled her distinctive scent. I turned to her but she did not seem to notice. She stood with her hands in the pockets of her raincoat, staring into the middle distance; her gaze and Reisinger's seemed to meet at an indefinite point between them, and hold. Her face told me nothing, but I deliberately moved to give her room. I had thought, unreasonably, that it was her show. He was her husband, and it was up to her to get him out of Terry Harris's kitchen. But as I looked at her I knew that it wasn't her "show" at all, and that she and Reisinger were using calculus while the rest of us were in simple arithmetic.

"Well," Reisinger said. "You're back. Get bored in the car?"

She shook her head and replied, almost inaudibly, "I wasn't in the car. You know better than that." She looked at me. "Why did you say that I was in the car when I wasn't?"

There was no simple answer I could give to that.

To the middle distance, she said, "I was inside, waiting for you. So we could go home."

Reisinger opened the refrigerator and took out a bottle of beer. He searched for an opener, and finally knocked the cap off on the counter's edge with the heel of his false hand. It made an odd sound and we all looked at him as he drank. No one spoke.

Terry shook his head as if to clear it, but of course his purpose was the reverse. He wanted to cloud the episode. We must all forget what had happened. It was an embarrassment, inexplicable, an aberration. We had all wandered away and forgotten ourselves, and there had been a kind of breakdown of civilization. Something dreadful had gotten loose but now it was back where it belonged. Terry said at last, "Let's shake hands, forget it."

I turned away; how like Terry. He observed the conventions and probably somewhere in the back of his mind was the old rule that a gentleman never insulted someone unintentionally. I had watched Terry as Reisinger spoke, Terry's eyes wide with disbelief; Reisinger might as well have been reciting the plot of a movie, or been lecturing about Stalingrad, Freud, or the Red Queen. *The water froze in our canteens. The lieutenant ran away.* And the statement that had begun it all: *You dirty little Jew.* And what had he meant when he said, *I came in at the end of everything?* Whatever Reisinger's experience, it had no connection with our pretty suburb with its curving streets and turn-of-the-century railroad station, and Republican values. It seemed likely in those days that our bellicose fathers had given us a world that would last forever, a structure as secure and tidy as a city-state of the Middle Ages — a prosperous suburban stronghold where everything was built to look like something else, a Cotswold cottage, a château of the Loire, a teahouse in Kyoto, a *Platz* in Lübeck, with restrictive convenants more formidable than any battlement or moat. But where was the bedrock, the natural thing? The human result had seemed to me a weird composite of Bertie Wooster, the Budden-brooks, and Natty Bumppo — and my attitude toward it could only be ironical, a popgun on that field of fire. What was serious? Atoms for Peace? Adlai Stevenson? All abstract and far from home. And then there was Reisinger and his teeming memory of the retreat from the Thirty-eighth Parallel, his dead hand, his knife at Terry's throat, and his extraordinary tirade, and the acquiescence with which we listened to it. Now, in the thick Hopper silence, we waited.

Reisinger had not moved. He ignored Terry's hand, and the truth is, I doubt if he noticed; eventually, Terry withdrew it. Swan walked slowly from the doorway to her husband's side, her eyes still focused on the middle distance. I wondered what she saw there — Degas, *Nighthawks*, Delmore Schwartz, or the first time she had seen Reisinger, so composed and debonair in black tie. Probably none of the above; no doubt she was not in her memory at all, but in the present moment. She moved in an odd hesitant shuffle. They stood there together stiffly, as if posing for a formal portrait. She looked us over one by one. Reisinger's face was blank, drained of all heat or passion. He looked like an animal caught in the glare of headlights.

Suddenly he kissed Swan, a lingering kiss, a lover's kiss. She closed her eyes and did not move; she did not look at him, nor react at all except to put her fingers to her mouth when he finished. Then she put her hand on his arm, leaning close to him, but whether the gesture was meant to steady her or steady her husband, there was no way of telling. She took his hand, then said something inaudible, lifting her face to whisper into his ear. Reisinger nodded. He finished his beer and put the knife in his belt, pirate-fashion. Then he swaggered out

of the kitchen. Swan watched him, every step. We heard the front
door slam. Swan seemed so alone and defeated, and there was nothing we could say. To comfort her now would be an intrusion, a
confirmation that her great adventure, her "great life," was over
almost as soon as it began.

The silence was so close as to be unendurable. I said, "Are you all
right?" She nodded. "Can I take you home?"

She looked at me. "Arthur's in the car."

I said, "You shouldn't drive with him."

She smiled fractionally, and glanced at Terry.

I said quickly, "He's been drinking."

Terry said, "That's the trouble."

She said, "No, it isn't."

I said, "He's had a lot to drink."

She said, "So have you."

I said, "Yes, but."

"What do you think?" she said. "What are you imagining? Do you
think he'll mistake me for Ethel Rosenberg? Do you think he'll stick
me with his knife?"

I shook my head.

"He won't," she said.

"Of course not," I said.

"He would never hurt me."

"No," I said.

"*Never*," she said fiercely.

I opened the refrigerator and fetched a beer. I did not want to
argue with her about Reisinger, or about anything; and I did not
want her to think me an enemy. And what was there to be said,
beyond what had been said? I wondered what it was that brought
them together and inspired such loyalty. I couldn't believe it was
marriage alone, or three weeks together at Fish Creek, hot, flyblown,
and crowded. They had known each other only for a summer, and
had married in such haste, as if time would run out, as if they both
had just this one chance. Swan had committed herself, though; she
had bet all her chips. I thought of Reisinger's past, a darkness and
disorder greater than anything Swan could imagine or prepare for.
What the Jews had to do with it I had no idea; perhaps convenience,
a historical mission. Perhaps Reisinger, on reconnaissance in his
memory, had recalled a conversation in the locker room, or on the
street, or in someone's back yard, or around the dinner table. Anywhere, really. Jews screwing people, Jews in control, Jews always

wanting in, Jews sticking together, Jews united in opposition, Communist Jews. And I wondered if everyone felt the heat when Reisinger was at the height of his tirade; there was lust in the air, perhaps of the sort that rises when a man finds a fancy sexual game that excites him, and of which he is ashamed.

Terry said, "Well, the party's over."

Swan said, "What did you say to my husband?"

Terry shrugged and mumbled something about MacArthur, the marines, and the war, "the police action." It was innocent enough, he said, the sort of casual remark people made all the time. "Hell's bells," he said, "it was just politics."

"I'll tell him that," she said.

"And Art took offense and he shouldn't have."

She said, "I'll tell him that, too."

I thought for a moment that she would offer some explanation, but of course she didn't. Why would she? The explanation, whatever it was, was private between them. They were side by side — *like that*, as she said — and that was why her eyes were fixed on the middle distance and why, when he kissed her, she remained silent, undemonstrative. Swan heaved a great sigh and turned to Terry and smiled. The smile was off-key, but it could be interpreted as an apology, or anyway an expression of regret. Terry was happy enough to accept that, and they embraced awkwardly. Actually, it was Swan who embraced him, her arm around his waist, a maternal gesture.

"Take care, Terry."

"You, too, Swan."

Suddenly there were loud voices and jostling as others, married men, pushed into the kitchen. I wondered what had taken them so long, the cavalry. One of the married men looked at Terry with an I'm-in-charge-here expression, and demanded an explanation. They heard there was trouble, someone acting crazy. What was it about? He looked belligerently from one face to another, avoiding Swan. Terry said there was no trouble, just a misunderstanding, everything's fine, party's over.

Swan examined the married man up and down, as if measuring him for a suit of clothes. She said, "Who are you?"

Her tone was so cold, he moved back a step and did not reply.

"It was my husband," she said.

He nodded. No harm done then.

"No," she said. "Not to you, anyway."

"Just a second here," he said.

"Yes?" She leaned toward him, balancing on the balls of her feet. For a moment I thought she was going to hit him, and he thought so, too, and moved back another step; but she only grinned, a cat's grin, inscrutable and without mirth.

I said, "Art was telling us how the Jews started the Korean War."

"What are you talking about —" he began.

"Jews," I said. "The Rosenbergs, Hiss, Acheson, Truman, Greenglass."

"Watch your language," he said.

"Or what?" said Swan.

"Just so you know what it was about," I said. "What the trouble was here."

He was a tall, slender, married man, a stockbroker, good on the golf course; I had seen him around for years. He had been confused, but now he had his issue: manners. He looked sternly at me, pointing his finger as a schoolmaster might. He said, "Cool off. We don't use that kind of language around here, in this town, mixed company."

Swan looked at me, and I thought I saw a flicker of a smile; it was the distracted smile of a woman looking into a distant mirror. I flickered back. Then we heard the toot of a car horn and Swan left the kitchen. I was waiting for a sign, any sign at all that we were not natural enemies. But she did not look at me. She seemed collected, her hands in her raincoat pockets, pushing past the newcomers. She paused when the deb reached out to her; the deb squeezed Swan's hand and they stood a moment together, silent. Swan looked much older, though in fact they were the same age exactly; they had gone to the same school, but had never been particular friends.

After the front door slammed there was more bluster in the kitchen but I paid no attention to it. I looked out the window; a spotlight illuminated the lawn, brilliant and glittering in the rain. Shade trees threw thick black shadows. A car's headlights moved on the periphery, Reisinger's Austin-Healey. I thought of them together in that small space, staring into the rain on the edge of our bright green watery world. I imagined her hand over his, white on black. And I imagined her troubled voice, low and hushed in the darkness, soothing, consoling. Then they were out of sight around the corner, and I was left with the bluster and Spanier's muted horn. People were laughing now. I heard the clink of ice cubes, and someone mimicking Reisinger's thick speech. Things were familiar again, safe and fearless; we were home. George Field started to tell the joke about the dog and the Jew sitting at the bar. I continued to look out the window, at the darkness beyond the light. The Reisingers would be home soon. I tapped on the windowpane, a farewell to Swan. There was a little embarrassed silence behind me, and then someone snickered.

◆

We corresponded for a while, Swan and I, then drifted apart. The 1960s were not a good time for staying in touch. I had heard that she and Reisinger had moved west after Swan got her degree at the University of Chicago, honors in twentieth-century American poetry. I had also heard, but somehow did not believe, that Reisinger enrolled at the university, too, earning a master's degree and then a Ph.D. in history. I did not think of him as a scholar, and I could not imagine him on the Midway. Of course by then I was out of law school, and very much involved with my own life in Boston; I was courting the girl I later married and divorced.

As my father used to say, "There are only a hundred people in the world and they all know each other." I was brought up to date only the other day by Swan's daughter, whom I met quite by chance at a reception in Cambridge. Susan Reisinger was happy to talk about her mother. She related that Swan had a substantial career working for the governor of Colorado and was thinking about elective office, perhaps Congress, except that she didn't want to spend half the year in dreary Washington. She loved the West, her adopted home, especially Colorado, highest state in the union. She loved the people, rugged individualists, always laughing and carrying on. She had taken up skiing and of course Reisinger was a great fisherman, so they often spent weekends in the high country, fly casting for trout. Swan had become ubiquitous on television, talking about the various threats to the Colorado environment. That was her specialty, the environment, though she was also a hero to feminists, and a great favorite of the men, too. "You wouldn't have any trouble recognizing her," Susan said; "she hasn't changed a bit. She looks like a teenager. It's the healthy Western life. And doing what you were meant to do. And not giving up."

Reisinger died two years ago. He had taught history at the university, a respected and popular instructor; he was a full professor when he died. He was dedicated to the discipline of history, it being both his profession and his avocation. He loved to teach, though he held the unorthodox view that Santayana was a windbag: history repeated itself whether it was remembered or not. Still, he believed it his mission to elucidate the more obvious calamities. In the evenings, Susan said, he would often retire to the basement alone and remain there long after everyone had gone to bed. The basement was filled with war memorabilia, and a sand table to replicate the notable battles of the Korean War: the defense of the Pusan perimeter, the offensive of 25 September 1950, the Inchon landing, the advance to Manchuria, and the retreat from Manchuria. He recreated the battles according to data furnished in the *West Point Atlas of American Wars* and a Chinese text someone gave him. "He was trying to find a way to make the chaos visible," she said; "it's harder than it might seem." He even wrote a book about his own experiences, and had it published privately, his contribution to the short shelf of literature of the war in Korea.

Susan said, "He only taught one course in the Korean War, because there wasn't much interest in it. They were interested in him, because he had such a good reputation as a teacher; and of course they knew that he had a personal connection with it. As a matter of fact, there was quite a lot about the war that was still unresolved, according to my father. Motives, and so forth and so on."

She said they led a comfortable life, near Boulder. They lived on the grounds of a country club, in a rambling house on a hill adjoining the fifteenth tee, with a gorgeous view of the mountains.

"It sounds like the ideal suburban life," I said.

Susan laughed, raising her eyebrows; at that moment she looked remarkably like her mother, though she had her father's composed bearing. We were at the Faculty Club at Harvard, an awards ceremony; the recipient of the award was a friend, so she had come down from New York. He was also a friend of mine, and when he introduced us the names registered right away. "You grew up with my mother," she said. "My mother often speaks of you."

I said, "We were great friends. But we lost touch."

"Well, she remembers."

I said, "So do I. I had heard that she was living in the West."

"And she knew you were in the East." There was a little silence and then she said, "You'd probably be interested to know that my mother owns a Hopper etching. It cost her a bundle."

"I believe it," I said. "Which one is it?"

"It's one of the reclining nudes," Susan said. "Very simply done." She paused two beats. "Degas is way beyond her budget."

I smiled, then laughed. What a pleasure it must be to have a subtle daughter! I envied Swan. It was obvious they were very close, and that would be a pleasure too. I remembered Swan's mother, and wondered how they were able to break the pattern. Then I thought of the woman in *The Morning Bath*. A few years ago it came to the Museum of Fine Arts in Boston and when I saw it I was immediately reminded of Swan, something about the awkward angle of the model's leg; nothing about it had changed. The unexpected sight of *The Morning Bath* inspired such a rush of memory that I went immediately to look at the Hoppers, of which the MFA has a fine collection. Of course *Nighthawks* was still in Chicago. But I stayed an hour, moving slowly in front of the pictures — I thought *Ryder's House* was particularly provocative — remembering the old days, especially the year of our great rebellion. I wanted to ask Susan about her father, the circumstances of his death, and whether or not he and Swan had had a successful marriage. I said instead, "What do you do in New York?"

She said, "Medical school." Then: "Psychiatry. I'm going to be a psychiatrist. My two closest friends also had parents who were ill, it's a fairly common motivation; we three are planning to open an office together when we finish school and our residencies." She looked at me and smiled, waiting. "Would you like me to tell you the rest of it? I'd be happy to."

I said, "Please."

She said that her father had been in and out of hospitals with a variety of ailments, many of them obscure. He had one breakdown and then another and a third. They were frightening breakdowns, always predictable, like a barometer signaling a violent change in the weather. He went to a private hospital in Boulder, never remaining more than a month; her mother usually stayed with him, nights. When he came out he was fine, his old self, until the next episode. He was always on medication of some kind, and the ghost pain in his hand never left him. However, his death had nothing to do with that or with the breakdowns. He died of a heart attack on the golf course; he had been walking alone early in the morning, as he often did, and they didn't find him right away. We always thought, If they had —

The odd part about it was that he was in great shape, very fit from his active life in the West.

Susan said that her parents were the most devoted couple she knew. Everyone said that. She felt sometimes that they didn't need anyone but themselves, they lived in a sweet private world, so close — they had a private language, unintelligible to outsiders — and when she was younger she hated it; she felt excluded. But as she got older she

understood how rare it was, and how beautiful, her parents' love
affair. And he was not an easy man, though men are not usually easy;
women, either. And when he died so suddenly, her mother was unspeakably low and broken up. She went to Mexico, where she had
never been, and then on impulse to Europe. And then she came home
for good, and picked up her career where she had left it.

Swan believed he had saved her life, and not only that, he had
sacrificed his life for hers, like someone in a war who throws himself
on a live hand grenade.

Susan said to me, "I don't believe it, but she believes it. I thought
he had more reason to think that than she did, what with his illness
and so forth and so on. She was always there for him, always. But he
was there for her, too. And perhaps what she needed was not quite
so visible. But what do you think? You knew them when."

I said, "They were very special."

"Yes," she said, "they were."

I hesitated a moment, watching her; Swan's memories would be
very different from mine, and what she made of them would be
different also. I said, "You know, we had a year of rebellion, your
mother and me."

"She told me," Susan said. "She told me all about it. And she
always wondered what became of you. She knew you were a lawyer
in Boston. She heard you specialized in divorce law. Is that right?"

"Yes," I said.

"She thought that was funny. She said she couldn't believe it. Anyway. You were saying . . ."

I said, "What's so funny about divorce law?"

Susan said, "I don't know. Are you married?"

"Briefly," I said. "Once, a long time ago."

"My mother thought it was funny. She said she didn't know
whether you'd be good at it or not. She thought probably you
would." Susan smiled brightly. "She said probably you'd never overpromise."

"I never do," I said. She did not reply, waiting for me to answer
the other question. Had her father thrown himself on a live hand
grenade? In my experience, people did not sacrifice themselves. I was
going to say something about Marx in the British Museum and Swan
and me in the Hopper room at the Art Institute, alert for Delmore
Schwartz, but I didn't. It sounded frivolous and cynical and Susan
Reisinger was anything but. I said, "With me, the great rebellion
lasted only a year, and after that it didn't seem so important. The

world was so large and our part of it so small. The Midwest is just a region like any other. It isn't an earth spirit or Mother Russia, that's what I decided when I went away to law school." Susan looked at me queerly. I went on, "But not to your mother. It was a prison she had to fight her way out of. Not retreat from. Not sneak away from. Not merely leave it or be paroled from it, time off for good behavior. No. She had to *struggle* with it. She had to defeat it. She had to defeat its hold on her. Her parents' hold on her. And your father —" I paused. What was there to say about Reisinger? "And your father was the man she wanted to fight beside; she used to say they were together *like that.* Maybe she thought he had experience. Maybe she knew that with what he'd gone through, he'd never give up. Or allow her to."

Susan nodded thoughtfully.

"And he didn't," I said.

She said, "I guess not."

"And what a great thing that they stuck together."

Susan looked at me sharply. "You wouldn't even have wondered about that if you really knew them, or saw them together."

"I didn't mean it that way," I said. "It was that in the sixties everything broke up." But she was also correct. I looked away. The room was dark, dark paneling, men and women in dark winter clothing; a Harvard occasion, the talk low, intense, and obscure. Outside a light snow was falling. Twenty-five years ago I would never have imagined myself at a reception at the Harvard Faculty Club, an insider knowing most of those present, at ease in the surroundings. In the corner next to the sherry table three men in dark suits stood in a tight triangle, murmuring as if exchanging state secrets. One of them was an old friend, an economist; I had represented him in his divorce. He had wanted me to conceal his government consultancy fees on the novel ground that if revealed they would compromise national security. He had a particular expertise in the Chinese railway system. A memorable exchange with the judge and with opposing counsel . . . I wondered if it were true, what I had heard about life in the West; I had never been to Colorado. I had been to Los Angeles and San Francisco, and once to Phoenix, but that was not the West as Susan Reisinger was describing it.

"Well," she said. "It's been nice talking. What a surprise, seeing you here."

I said, "It surprises me, too."

"I'll tell my mother I saw you."

"Tell her I send my best. Maybe I'll find myself in Boulder some-
day." I had one last question that had edged its way into my mind.
"Tell me one last thing. Where does she hang the Hopper?"
"The living room," Susan said, smiling broadly.
I asked her why she was smiling.
"She bought it, it cost her a bundle, and the truth is that she doesn't
like it much. But she keeps it around anyhow."
"I think I can guess why," I said.
" '*To remind*,' she says," Susan said. "Do you know what else she
says about you?"
"No, but you'd better tell me."
Suddenly she began to laugh, leaning toward me. People looked at
us, curious; her laughter was gay in the dark formality of the room. I
knew that she would say something extraordinary. "My mother said
this. She said, 'We are so different. He is the only man I know who
could look at the work of Edward Hopper and find consolation.' "

My law practice brings me back to Illinois now and then, and I am
always overwhelmed by memory, from the moment the plane floats
down over the lake, the towers of Chicago bunched together, a raised
hand of metal and glass, and the neighborhoods spreading from it in
orderly straight lines. On a clear day you can see north to Wisconsin,
and south past the suburban lawns to the prairie itself, flat, fertile,
and unwelcoming. I conduct my business on Michigan Avenue, then
check into the Drake. I rent a car and drive north on the Outer Drive
to Sheridan Road, the old way, the way Swan and I went back then,
before the Edens Expressway was constructed. I frequently miss my
turn out of the city; so many landmarks are gone, replaced by buildings of no distinction. Once I leave the city, nothing seems changed;
I am twenty, driving in a Chevrolet convertible. It is the region as I
knew it, frozen in the 1950s, William G. Stratton in the governor's
mansion, Adlai Stevenson in Libertyville, Colonel McCormick in Tribune Tower, Art Hodes at the Blue Note. Evanston is still dry; North-
western still seems the model of an unpretentious rah-rah Midwestern
campus. I ignore the protestors surrounding the Baha'i Temple in
Wilmette, and drive slowly up the North Shore beside the flat gray
lake.
    My father is retired, and he and my mother live in Florida; the
house I grew up in has long since been sold. Most of my old crowd
has moved away, though Terry Harris is still around, managing the
family real estate business. His parents are dead and he lives in their

house, off Green Bay Road. After dinner, his wife goes out; to her discussion group, she says. He married the girl in the doorway, the deb who thought we were playing The Game, the one who held out her hand to Swan. Terry and I have a nightcap and he tells me that things are very different now, and that the old rules no longer apply.

He is willing to describe the changes. "You know how it used to be around here, everyone knew each other, and things were reliable, day to day. It was like —" he searches for the word, and finds: "Europe. But we didn't keep it, and that's our fault; no one to blame but ourselves. Things moved so fast. Still, compared to most places . . ." The proles are everywhere now, he says, and the police are vicious. You should see the traffic on Saturday mornings. And the taxes! The clubhouse by the lake burned down last year, and there are no plans to replace it; of course there are other clubs, but still. And the debutantes, *gad* the common accents they have now. You know, we used to have a distinctive accent around here, it meant something. Now they all sound like Mayor Daley, when they're not stoned on white powder or chemicals.

"Or reefers," I say.

"Oh, they've been around forever," he replies.

Naturally the *Tribune* no longer has a society page, so it is difficult to know who is coming out in Society. As if anyone cared. There are so many new people, people you never heard of from places you never heard of. And out beyond the old mill, they're building condominiums, can you believe it? For the new people to move into, as if this were Fort Lauderdale. They wanted Harris and Partners to go into it with them, provide some of the financing and this and that, and I told them no, absolutely not; this is my *home.*

"It must be great, living in Boston," he says. "Where do you live? Manchester? Beverly?"

"The Back Bay," I say.

"That's what I mean," he says. "A place where things mean what they used to mean. The *Back Bay,* that's great."

We have another nightcap.

A little later I remind him of the night in the kitchen with Reisinger. We are sitting in that same kitchen, and he turns to look at the framed photograph of the old warrior, a portrait as familiar as Stuart's historic Washington or Brady's ravaged Lincoln. He frowns and shakes his head, and then he laughs. "Weren't we crazy back then? Gosh, don't you wish we had those days back? What a lot of fun we had —"

Then something stirs in his memory, and a shadow crosses his face. After a moment, Terry says, "Art Reisinger wasn't quite all there, was he? I guess it was the war. Not a bad chap, though, all things considered . . ." He brightens, letting the sentence hang. "And that Swan, what ever happened to her? Wasn't she a piece of work? She just loved him to death." And then he changes the subject.

And I brutally change it back. Remember Reisinger's tirade? *You dirty little Jew!* Jew! Jew! Jew! And the knife at the throat, and Reisinger's judgment: *You cowards.*

Terry shrugs, and seems to nod in agreement; that is, he remembers. But when he speaks, he says this: "Well, as you know, you couldn't say that now. The Jews are all over the place."

He looks away, and the atmosphere chills; the chill is palpable. This is obviously an embarrassment still. I am sorry that I brought it up at all. Terry would not think me a gentleman. I look at my watch: time to go back to the city. I do not tell him that Reisinger is dead, and Swan a Democrat. Instead, I try to make him laugh by saying there was a Woody Allen routine there somewhere, Reisinger's Jew cold and Jew wind, Chinese Jews sweeping down from Manchuria, slant-eyed Hasidim in side curls and yarmulkes, slaughtering leathernecks left and right, all of it supervised by the Rosenbergs and Dean Acheson.

He laughs dutifully, then turns to me with a puzzled expression. He gives another short, helpless laugh. "Who's Woody Allen?" he asks.

Our local chroniclers insisted that the summer of 1958 was the last of the brilliant seasons, really a superb season — though Swan Emerson's elopement was a surprise and a scandal. It set an unfortunate precedent, everyone agrees; and she was such an attractive girl, though not outgoing. The next year the debs seemed plainer and their parents not so conspicuously rich, and there was a general insolence and disregard for the conventions. And the year after that was the summer of 1960, and everyone sensed the change.

1985

◆

# THE COSTA BRAVA,

# 1959

◆

T ED had been terribly sick in Saulieu, a combination of too much wine and a poisonous fish soup, and no one to blame but himself. He had chosen the night in Saulieu to be difficult about money, explaining to Bettina that a room and dinner for two plus wine at the glorious Côte d'Or was an extravagance they could not afford. It was only their third day in France, and he was not yet comfortable in francs. Gasoline was expensive, and it was necessary to keep a reserve for contingencies. The travel agent had said that Spain would be cheap, but she had also said that it would be warm in Europe; and when they had landed at Orly it was cold, forty degrees, and raining. And the room at the Continental had been very expensive, though he had wisely prepaid in Chicago.

They had driven hesitantly into the parking lot at the Côte d'Or, their little rented Renault conspicuous between two black Citröen sedans. The Côte d'Or had the appearance of an elegant country house. A bushy cat lay dozing on the doormat, and the trees in the courtyard were changing in a blaze of red and gold. Bettina read the specialties from the Guide Michelin: terrine royale, timbale de quenelles de brochet eminence, poularde de Bresse belle-aurore. Two stars, twenty-three rooms. She rolled down the window and smiled slowly, arching her eyebrows. They could smell the kitchen.

He asked if she minded, and she said she didn't.

"It's so damn expensive," he said.

She said, "I'm so tired."

Ted said, "We'll take a nap before dinner."

They booked into the shabby hotel down the street, and Ted took a stroll around town while she slept. In the Basilique St.-Andoche he sat a moment in meditation, and then in prayer — her good health, his good health, their future together. Then he lit a taper and stood watching it burn; the air was chilly and damp inside the church. Later, they had an apéritif in a café and returned to the hotel to dine at a table by the front window. From the window they could see the Côte d'Or through the trees, a little privet hedge in front and a rosy glow within. It had begun to rain, and the hotel dining room was drafty and cold. Ted ordered the fish soup and roast chicken and knew right away that he had made a terrible mistake. Bettina ordered a plain omelet, and they ate in silence, looking out the window through the rain at the alluring Côte d'Or. He knew he had been very stupid; it was one of the best restaurants in France. To kill the taste of the soup, he drank two bottles of wine. Bettina, exhausted, went to bed immediately after dinner. Ted walked across the street alone to have a cognac at the tiny bar off the dining room of the Côte d'Or. There were two large parties still at table, and much laughter; they were talking back and forth. Ted's French was not good enough to eavesdrop seriously, but they seemed to be talking about American politics, John F. Kennedy, and the primary campaign, still months away. He heard "Weees-consin" and "Wes Virginia" and then a blast of laughter. He wondered who they were, to have such detailed knowledge of American elections. The room was very warm. Ted picked up a copy of *Le Monde*, but the text was impossible to read. Inside, however, was a piece on the Kennedy *stratégie*. It depressed him, not speaking French or reading it. It would be better in Spain, where he knew the language and admired the culture. His stomach was already sour, and he had three cognacs before returning to the hotel to be sick.

The weather improved as they drove south. They had a cheerful, lovely drive on secondary roads to Perpignan. They lunched on bread and cheese, choosing pretty places off the road to eat. And Bettina's strength returned. Her color improved, and she lost the preoccupied look she had had for three weeks, ever since the miscarriage. Five months pregnant, and it had seemed to Ted that she could get no larger. When she began to cramp early one evening, neither of them knew what it was, or what it meant; she was alarmed, but passed it off as an upset stomach. At midnight he had rushed her to the hospital, and in two hours knew that she had lost the babies, a boy and a girl. She had been pregnant with twins, and that was such a surprise because there were no twins on either side of the family. Of course there was no chance of saving either one, they were so tiny and undeveloped. The doctor said that Bettina was perfectly healthy, it was just something that had happened; she would have other children. Ted listened to all this in a stunned state. He did not know the mechanics of it, and when the doctor explained, he listened carefully but did not know the right questions to ask. There were certain obvious questions, but he did not want to seem a fool. Bettina had been wonderfully brave that evening, and later in the car rushing to the hospital, displaying a dignity and serenity that he had not known she possessed. It was the first crisis for either of them, and she had been great. To Ted, the doctor said that the twins were a shock to her system. She was a perfectly normal, healthy girl, but this was her first pregnancy and twins after all, what a surprise; it was simply too much. All this in the corridor outside Bettina's room, the two of them whispering together as if it were a conspiracy. The doctor had taken him out of earshot, but the door was open and Ted could see Bettina in her bed, and he knew she was watching them even though she was supposed to be asleep. Dr. McNab put his hand on Ted's shoulder and spoke confidentially, man to man. Ted gathered that this was information best kept to himself, the "shock to her system." He was flattered that the doctor would confide in him; the night before, the nurses had been brusque. He had sat in the waiting room for two hours with no word from anyone, and no idea what was happening except that it was precarious. The truth was, he had not had time to become accustomed to the idea of being a father; and now he wouldn't be one, at least not this year. But he accepted without question the doctor's explanation (such as it was) and cheerful prognosis. Of course they would have other children.

Bettina was not communicative, lying in her bed, the stack of books unread, staring out the window or at the ceiling. She cried only once, the next morning, when he arrived in her room with a dozen roses. No, she said, there was no pain; there had been, the night before. Now she was — uncomfortable. She wondered if, really, she was not the slightest bit relieved. She looked at him and frowned. Wrong word. Not *relieved*, exactly. But they had been married only a year and hardly knew each other, and children were a responsibility. Wasn't that what her mischievous friend Evie had said? Didn't everyone say that children would change their life together, and not absolutely for the better: diapers, three A.M. feedings, colic, tantrums, unreliable baby sitters? She had quoted an Englishman to him: *The pram in the hallway is the enemy of art.* Ted was not amused. So she had reassured him, of course, that that was no argument for not having children; children were adorable and everyone wanted a family, but still. As the doctor said, they were both young. And they were happy on the practical surface of things: their house, their friends, Ted's job. And Ted was preoccupied, too; as it happened, he was working with the senior partner on his first big case. The senior partner was a legend on La Salle Street, and he seemed to look on Ted as a protégé. Ted described the case in detail to her as she lay in the narrow hospital bed; and as if to confirm his estimate of his excellent prospects with Estabrook, Mozart they were interrupted by the nurse bearing an aspidistra with a get well card signed by the man himself in his muscular scrawl, E. L. Mozart.

Bettina was home in four days. She went immediately to her desk in the bedroom to look at the poem she had been writing. She had been very excited about it, but now the poem seemed — frivolous. About one inch deep, she said to Ted that night at dinner. And derivative, and the odd part was that it was derivative of a poet she did not admire: e. e. cummings, with his erratic syntax and masculine sensibility. She had not seen that when she was working on the poem, nor had it seemed to her one inch deep. As she spoke, she knew that her life was changed in some unfathomable way. It was not simply the miscarriage, it was something more; the miscarriage had released hidden emotions. How strange a word it was, "miscarriage," as in miscarriage of justice. And the form that Ted had been given to sign did not use the word at all; the word on the form was "abortion."

That night he got the idea of a vacation.

*Europe,* he blurted. It was entirely spur of the moment, and she doubted it would ever happen. What about Mozart and the big case? The trip would have to wait until the case was settled — as, miraculously, it was, the following week, a fine out-of-court settlement for the client. This was an omen, and Ted was elated. He had never been to Europe or even out of America. Bettina had been two years before, the summer of her senior year in college. Ted was courting her then and wrote her every day from Chicago, where he was in his final year at law school. She had given him an itinerary, carefully typed by her father's secretary. Ted had sent her three or four long letters to every city on the itinerary, places he knew only from an atlas: London, Amsterdam, Paris, Lausanne, Venice, Florence, Rome. The letters were his way of holding her. Ted was terrified that she would meet

♦

someone sexy in Europe and would have a love affair that would change her forever. And then she would be lost to him. Later, he learned that the letters were the cause of much hilarity, some of it forced. Bettina was traveling with her roommates, the three of them determined to have an adventure before settling down and marrying someone. The letters were somehow inhibiting, and irritating in their wordy insistence and blunt postmark, CHICAGO.

All those damn letters, Evie St. John said later. *God, Ted. It was like being followed by your family, watched. Just once we wanted to arrive at the hotel and find nothing at the desk. It was as if you were on the trip with us, and it was supposed to be girls-only. Or maybe Peggy and I were jealous. The only letters we got were from our mothers, asking us about the weather and reminding us to wash our underwear. But really, it was a bit much, don't you think?* Bettina couldn't get away from you, even when we found those boys in Florence, *especially* when we found those boys in Florence. The cutest one was after Bettina. But there were four letters of yours at the hotel in Florence and it just made her sick with — it wasn't guilt.

What was it? he had asked.

I don't know, Evie replied. Disloyalty, perhaps.

Well, he said. What happened in Florence?

Laughing: I'll never tell.

They arrived at last on the Costa Brava. Spain was everything he imagined. They chose a pretty whitewashed town with a small bull-ring, a lovely fourteenth-century church, and two plain hotels. The hotel they chose was near the church, perched on a cliff overlooking the sea. The room was primitive, but they would use it only for sleeping. It was late afternoon, and they changed immediately and went to the beach. Bettina smiled happily; it was a great relief being out of the car.

The path to the beach wound through a stand of sweet-smelling pines. They spread their towels on the rough sand, side by side. Bettina was carrying a thick poetry miscellany. She murmured, "Isn't this nice," and at once lay down and went to sleep. She didn't say another word. Her forehead was beaded with sweat. She was lying on her side, her thighs up against her stomach, her cheek dead against her small fists. Her brown hair fell lifeless and tangled in a fan over her forearm. She looked defenseless, fast asleep. Ted looked down at her, his shadow falling across her stomach. He thought she needed a new bathing suit, something Bardot might favor, black or red, snug against the skin. The one she had on was heavy and loose, made in America. In her Lake Forest bathing suit she looked complacent and matronly, though she was obviously worn out from the drive, all day long in their small car on narrow roads, dodging diesel trucks and ox carts and every fifty kilometers a three-man patrol, the Guardia Civil, Franco's men, sinister in their black tricorns and green capes and carbines, though they looked scarcely older than boys, nodding impassively when Bettina waved. She thought they looked more droll than sinister; as Americans, she and Ted had nothing to fear from the Guardia Civil. He stepped back and looked at Bettina again. From her rolled-up position on the towel, she might have been at home in bed on the North Shore instead of on a sunny Mediterranean beach. Her skin was very white in the fading sun.

Ted turned and walked to the water's edge. There were no waves. The water seemed to slide up the sand, pause, and die. He looked left and right. The beach was wide, crescent-shaped and cozy. There were two other couples nearby, middle-aged people reading under beach umbrellas. Down the beach a girl stood staring out to sea. Presently a man joined her and they stood together. They were very tan, and Ted was conscious of his own white skin and frayed madras trunks. The girl wore a white bikini, and the man had a black towel around his waist. The girl stood with her legs apart, her arm around the man's dark shoulders; they were both wearing sunglasses. Ted looked back at Bettina. She was faced in his direction, but she had not moved. He turned back to the water, thinking how different it was from the shore at Lake Michigan — the fragrance of the beach, pine mixed with sea and sand, and the swollen bulk of two great rocks a hundred feet offshore. This coast was complicated and diverse, a place to begin or continue a love affair *sin vergüenza*. It was nothing at all like mediocre Lake Michigan; it was as different from Lake Michigan as he was from his American self. He walked into the water, chilly around his ankles. The woman in the bikini and the man in the towel were walking up the beach in the direction of the hotel, holding hands.

Ted began to swim in a slow crawl, feeling the water under his fingernails. He wished Bettina were with him at his side. The water slid around his thighs, slippery, a sexual sensation. He imagined them swimming together nude, unfettered in the Mediterranean. He swam steadily, kicking slowly, hot and knotted inside, his throat dusty and the sun warm on his back. Bettina would never swim nude but now and again he could coax her out of her bra and she would swim

around and around in circles; this was always late at night in the
deserted pool of the country club, after a party, illicit summer adventures before they were married. He slowed a little, lost in the sentimental memory of them together. The sensation mounted, a thick
giddiness, incomplete. Ahead were the great rocks rising from the
water ten feet apart. From his perspective they looked like skyscrapers, and beyond them nothing but the serene blue-gray Mediterranean and the milky sky overhead. He wanted to climb the nearest
rock to the summit and sit in the last of the afternoon sun. But above
the waterline the rock was smooth, no handholds anywhere. The
stone was warm to his touch and smooth as skin. When he tried to
climb, his hands kept slipping, and at last he gave up and floated, the
curve of the brown rocks always on the edges of his vision. Then on
impulse he took a deep breath and dove, kicking and corkscrewing
through the murky water. He could not see the bottom. Almost immediately the water chilled, offering resistance. He did not fight it,
saving strength and breath. He struggled deeper, hanging in the heavy
water, darkness all around him, the bottom out of sight. Something
nudged his arm, and he felt a moment of panic. Lost, he had the
sensation of rising in an elevator. The elevator was crowded with old
men, their faces grim. Mozart was in front of him, lecturing in his flat
prairie accent. There was a ringing in his ears, and he tried to push
forward to get out through the heavy doors, away from the old men.
He was dazzled by a profusion of winking red lights, a multitude of
floors, all forbidden. Mozart would not yield, and the elevator came
slowly to a halt, the atmosphere morbid and unspeakably oppressive.
He recognized the faces of those around him, friends, colleagues,
clients. Then his hand struck stone and the hallucination vanished.
He had arched his back like a high-diver in midair, hanging upside
down, watching afternoon light play on the flat surface of the water.
Losing breath, he thought of the girl in the white bikini, so trim and
self-possessed, and provocative as she stared out to sea. He wondered
if she had had many lovers. Certainly a few, more than he had had;
and more than Bettina, though they would all be about the same age.
It was hard to know exactly how old she was, she could be eighteen
or twenty-five; but a hard-muscled and knowing eighteen or twenty-
five, having grown up in Europe. If the three of them met, what would
they have to say to each other? He could describe for her the ins and
outs of an Illinois land trust and the genius of E. L. Mozart. Bettina
could talk to her about pregnancy or e. e. cummings. Well, there
would be no common experience. And Bettina was so shy and he so

green. She looked like a girl who would know her own mind, where she had been and where she was going. The cavalier with her looked as if he knew his own mind, too. She moved beautifully, like a dancer or athlete. He thought of embracing her in the darkness and silence of the deep water.

When he broke the surface, gasping, he heard his name and turned to see Bettina on the beach, calling. The people under the umbrellas had put their books down and were rising, curious. Bettina saw him and dropped her hands, in an abrupt gesture of irritation and relief. She stood quietly a moment, shaking her head, then walked slowly back to the towel. The bells of the church began to toll, the dull sounds reaching him clearly across the water. He smiled, never having heard churchbells on a beach. He shook his head to clear his ears of water. The bells stopped, and there was no echo; the girl and her escort had disappeared down the beach. Ted remained a moment, treading water, looking closely at the rocks and knowing there was a way up somehow. There was always a way up. Perhaps on the far side; he could look on it as the north face of the Eiger, an incentive for tomorrow's swim. He pushed off and began a slow crawl back to the shore, where Bettina was already gathering their things.

They went directly to their room and made love, quickly and wordlessly; a model of efficiency, she thought but did not say. Ted had been ardent and a little rough, and now they lay together in the semidarkness, smoking and listening to two workmen gossip outside their window. Ted lay staring at the ceiling, blowing smoke rings. She was looking into an oval mirror atop their dresser beyond the foot of the bed. She was nearsighted and could not see her features clearly, but she knew how drained she looked, her sallow complexion, dead eyes, and oily hair, the pits. She hadn't washed her hair in a week, since they left Chicago. She touched it with her fingertips, then worked it into a single braid and brought it over her shoulder and smelled it — sweat, fish, and seaweed, ugh. It had to be washed, but she had no energy for that or for anything; no energy, or taste for food, drink, or sex. She had loved listening to the bells, though. The truth was, she looked the way she felt. Her looks were a mirror of her state of mind as surely as the mirror on her dresser reflected her looks, and there was no disguise she could wear. What should she do, put on a party hat? Pop a Miltown? No chance of that; she distrusted tranquilizers and had not filled the prescription the doctor gave her. She disliked suburban life as it was — how much more would she dislike it tranquilized? She felt as if half of her was empty. She was a fraction, half empty. She thought that something had been stolen from her, some valuable part of herself, and it was more than a fetus; but she did not know what it was or who had taken it. She felt so alone. She inhabited a country of which she was the only citizen; one citizen, speaking to herself in a personal tongue. Sometimes in her poetry she could hear a multitude of voices, a vivifying rialto in the dead suburban city. On the beach she had felt abandoned; and when she looked across the water and did not see him, she didn't know what to do; he had been there a moment before, looking at that girl. So she had gone to the water's edge and called, in a joky way; then she was filled with a sudden dread and called again, yelled really, just as he broke the surface, spraying water every which way, his arm straight up — and looked at her so shamefacedly, as if he had been caught red-handed. Then the bells began to toll and she listened, startled at first; they were so mournful and exact, churchbells from the Middle Ages, tolling an unrecognizable dirge. The church would have been built around the time of the beginning of the Inquisition, and she imagined the altar and the simulacrum behind it, an emaciated, bloody, mortified Christ, wearing a crown of thorns sharp and deadly as razor blades, the thorns resembling birds' talons. And for a long moment, within hearing of the bells, everything stopped, a kind of ecstatic suspension of all sound and motion. She turned away, fighting a desire to cry; she wanted tears, evidence of life.

She felt a movement next to her, Ted extinguishing his cigarette, sighing, and closing his eyes. Smoke from the Spanish tobacco hung in layers in the air, its odor pungent and unfamiliar. She stubbed out her own Chesterfield. He murmured, "Forty winks before dinner, Bee." She absently put her hand on his chest, his skin slick with sweat though the room was no longer warm — watching herself do this in the mirror, her hand rising slowly from her stomach, making its arc, and then falling, and he covering her hand with his own. He had nice hands, dry and light, uncalloused. She felt his heart flutter, and the tension still inside him; she wondered if he could feel her tension as she felt his. Probably not, she was so emotionally dense sometimes, and he was not that kind of man.

It was almost dark now. The workmen had gone and she could hear gentler voices, hotel guests moving along the path to the terrace.

She said, "Teddy?"

He made a sound and squeezed her hand.

"Nothing," she said.

He said, "No, what?" in a muddy voice.

She said, "Go back to sleep, Teddy." He stirred and did not reply. It was quiet outside. She said quietly, "It's silly." She looked at the ceiling, there was a ghost of a shadow from the light outside. "Are you still sexy?"

He laughed softly. "A little."

She said, "Me, too."

He rolled over on his side, facing her.

She smiled at him, wrinkling her nose in a way that he liked; this was a sign of absolution. "Did you know that?"

He grunted ambiguously and kissed her stomach. Then he reached over her shoulder and took one of the Chesterfields from the pack on the bedside table, lit it, and offered it to her. She shook her head, watching all this dimly in the mirror; she had to crane her neck to see over him when he reached for the cigarette. Then the flare of the match in the glass.

She turned to look at him squarely. "I'll bet you didn't."

He said, "Did too."

She shook her head. "Unh-unh."

"I know all about you, Bettina."

Dense, she thought; an underbrush. Her poetry was dense, too, but she liked it that way.

He began to make jokes about the various ways he knew all about her, "Bettina through the ages." He always knew what she was thinking, as she was an open book; she wore her heart on her sleeve, more or less. Then he began to talk about himself, his disappointment with his white skin and college-boy bathing suit, as obvious as a fingerprint or a sore thumb. He said he wanted to lose his nationality, and she should lose hers, too. They would become inconspicuous in Europe, part of the continent's mass. Perhaps he would become an international lawyer with offices in Lisbon and Madrid, master of half a dozen languages, a cosmopolitan. They would have a little villa on the Costa Brava within sight of the sea, a weekend place. He knew they would love the Costa Brava. He described swimming alone to the rocks, thinking of her, then diving, the water cold and heavy below the surface, and the hallucination that had transported him to La Salle Street, an elevator crowded with old men, red lights everywhere and no exit, a morbid oppression. The stone was slippery and warm to the touch, unfamiliar, the rocks sheer as Alps, no inhibitions on the Costa Brava — though what that had to do with it, with *her*, he couldn't say. At any event, he didn't.

She said, "Thinking about me? And then a real hallucination?"
He said, "Yes."
She said, "Nuts. You were watching that femme fatale in the bikini.
The one with the flat stomach."
"No," he said. "It was you. You're my favorite."
She lay quietly, holding her breath; she had a moment of déjà vu,
come and gone in an instant. She tried to recapture it, but the memory
feathered away. Distracted, she said, "I'll never have a flat stomach,
ever again." She prodded her soft belly. It was as if there were an
empty place in her stomach, an empty room, a VACANCY. There was
no spring or bounce to her; her muscles were loose. Almost a month,
and she had not returned to normal; depressed, always tired, petulant, negative, frequently near tears. But what was normal? She was
an anomaly. She had a young mother's flabby body, but she was not
a young mother. "And I need a new bathing suit." She looked at the
coral-colored Jantzen lying crumpled in the corner; ardent Teddy, he
couldn't wait. He couldn't get it off fast enough. What a surprising
boy he was in Europe, so curious about things, a young *husband*. At
home he was reserved, wanting so to fit in. They both looked at the
bathing suit. There were bones in the bra and she didn't need bones.
She didn't need bones any more than the femme fatale did, except
now she might, now that she looked like a young mother. Was her
body changed forever? She looked at him in the darkness and then
turned away, blinking back tears. She wanted him to touch her and
say that he loved her body, would love it always, that it was a beautiful young body even in the coral-colored Jantzen, Marshall Field
chic. His cigarette flared and he blew a smoke ring. She sighed; there
would be no tears after all. And he would not tell her that she had a
beautiful young body, even if he believed it. Tomorrow she would
buy a new bathing suit, a bathing suit à la mode. No bikinis, though.
Bikinis were unforgiving. She said, "He was much too old for her."
    "Who was?" Teddy rose and stepped to the window, peeking out
through the blind.
    "That man she was with. That señorito in the black towel."
    "So," he said. "You were watching him."
    "Why not?" she said. "Jesus, he was a handsome man."

She took her time bathing and dressing, selecting a white skirt and a
blue silk shirt and the pearls Teddy had given her at their wedding.
She washed her hair, and took care making up her eyes. It was nine
before they presented themselves on the terrace. Lanterns here and

there threw a soft light. Each table had a single candle and a tiny vase of flowers and a jar of wine. The tables were set for two or four; they were round tables with heavy ladder-back chairs. One of the waiters looked up, smiling, and indicated they could sit anywhere. It was an informal seating. The terrace was not crowded, and conversation was subdued in the balmy night. The handsome señorito and his girl were at a table on the edge of the terrace, overlooking the sea. They were holding hands and talking earnestly. Bettina led the way to an empty table nearby, also on the edge.

The moon was full and brilliant. The sea spread out before them, steely in the moonlight, seeming to go on forever. The drop to the sea was sheer, and although it was a hundred feet or more Ted felt he could lean over the iron railing and touch the water. The rocks were off to their left, dark masses in the water. From the terrace the rocks did not look as large as skyscrapers. A way out to sea there was a single light, a freighter bound for Barcelona. Ted looked at Bettina, but she was lost in some private thought, absently twisting her pearls around her index finger, her eyes in shadows. She did it whenever she was nervous or distracted, and he wondered what she was thinking about now, so withdrawn; probably the handsome couple at the table nearby. She had seated herself so that she could look at them, and perhaps guess their provenance. She loved inventing exotic histories for strangers.

The waiter arrived and took their order. Conversation on the terrace rose and fell in a low murmur. There was laughter and a patter of French behind him. Bettina looked up, raising her chin to look over his shoulder, her fingers working at the pearls. Ted sat uncomfortably a moment, then poured wine into both their glasses. Bettina touched hers with her fingernails, *click,* and smiled thanks. She was still looking past him, concentrating as if committing something to memory.

"Isn't it pretty?"

She said, "Another world."

"Did you imagine it like this? I didn't."

She said, "I didn't know what to expect."

He said, "You're twisting your pearls."

"You gave them to me." She took a sip of wine. "I have a right to twist them if I want to." She said after a moment, "I wish I had brought my poem with me, the one I was working on. It was the one that began as one thing and then when I got out of the hospital it was another thing, the one I told you about after, that night. There's one part of it that I can't remember. Isn't it a riot? I wrote it and now I can't remember it."

"Begin another," Ted said. "That's the great thing about writing poetry, all you need is a pencil and a piece of paper." And a memory, he thought but did not say.

"No, there's this one part. I have to know what it is because I want to revise it. I want to revise it here. It means a lot to me, and I know I'll remember if I try."

"Is it the beginning or the end?"

"The middle," she said.

"Good," he said and laughed.

She looked at him, confused.

"I figured the poem was about me. Or us. Us together."

"No," she said. "It wasn't."

"What was it about, Bee?"

She looked away, across the water, her chin in her hands. The breeze, freshening, moved her hair, and she tilted her chin and shook her head lightly, evidently enjoying the sensation. "Me, the baby, that's what the poem was about." She smiled without irony or guile. "What happens when things are pregnant." She took a sip of wine, holding the glass by its stem in front of her eyes. She said, "I'll never be able to think of them separately, as distinct and different person-alities, a brother and a sister. It'll always be just 'the baby.' "

"You were extremely brave," he said.

She gestured impatiently. "No," she said. "That isn't it."

"Still," he began, then didn't finish the sentence. Why was she so reluctant to take the credit that was hers? If you couldn't take the credit you deserved, you couldn't take the blame either and you ended up with nothing, always in debt to someone else. But he did not want to argue, so he said, "I didn't know what was going on."

"Like the other night in Saulieu."

"What night was that? You mean when I got so sick?"

"Teddy," she said. "Sometimes, you know, you could just *ask.*"

"All right then," he said. "I'm asking."

She looked at him innocently, the beginnings of a smile. "I thought a lawyer never asked a question without knowing the answer to it." When he reacted, she said, "Please, don't be angry. This is so pretty, and I'm happy to be here. I feel like a human being for the first time in ages, and I feel that it's *possible,* right here. This country is so old, and it's gone through so much." She glanced over his shoulder and smiled; he heard a flurry of laughter. "You know, we're not so dumb. We don't know everything. Probably we don't know as much as

those two, but we can learn. I feel." She leaned toward him across
the table, sliding her hand forward like a gambler wagering a stack
of chips. "I feel we don't try for the best there is. We're surrounded
by nonentities, like you in your elevator, all those organization men.
What did you call it? You called it morbid, that atmosphere."

He nodded, touched by her sincerity. But what they didn't know
would fill an encyclopedia. And he didn't like her reference to organization men, and he didn't know what she meant about the night in
Saulieu; then he got it. "It was just a restaurant, Bee. I didn't have
the money straight and didn't know how expensive things were. And
how lousy that hotel would be. I thought it was important to keep a
reserve for emergencies."

She nodded, Sure.

"See?"

She looked at him across the table, wondering if she could make
clear what it was that she felt. She wanted him to listen — and here,
this terrace, this table, the Mediterranean, this was the place. She had
been stupid to mention Saulieu, off the subject. She took another sip
of wine. "But there are times when you shouldn't leave me. The night
in Saulieu was one of the times, and the night in the hospital another.
You and McNab in the corridor, talking about *me*. You wouldn't
look at me while you were talking to him, and I didn't know what it
was that was so secret. If it was secret, it couldn't be anything good,
isn't that right? So I thought something was being kept from me, and
I felt excluded, you two men in the corridor and me in bed."

He said, "I didn't know. I thought you were asleep. It's what
McNab wanted. I didn't know what he was talking about, and I was
too dumb to ask the right questions." He looked around him, embarrassed; their voices were sharp in the subdued ambience of the terrace.

"It's that you have to stand up for what's yours, Teddy." She filled
his wineglass and her own. She looked at both glasses, full, and
smiled. She watched him closely, wondering if he had really listened,
and if he understood. Probably he had; he looked bothered. In the
candlelight she thought him good-looking, a good-looking American;
he only needed a few years. The Costa Brava became him. And her,
too. Spain gave her courage. She gave a bright laugh. "I was brave,
was I?"

"Yes."

"Tell me how brave?"

He said, "Brave as can be." Her eyes were sparkling, brilliant in
the soft light.

"Oh," she said suddenly, lowering her voice. "Oh, Teddy. Turn around."

He did as she directed. The handsome señorito and the girl were embracing. She had her bare arms around his neck. Her head was thrown back as she leaned into him, on tiptoe. Against the light and motion of the moon and the sea, it was an exalted moment. Bettina whispered, "I know who they are." She commenced a dreamy narrative, a vivid sketch of him, a romantic poet and playwright like García Lorca, close to the Spanish people. There was definitely something literary and slightly dangerous about him. As for her, she was a political, a young Pasionaria, a woman of character and resolve. They had been in love for ages, exiled together, now returned to Catalonia incognito . . .

Bettina took his hand and held it. She described the poem she had been working on, reciting a few of the lines, the ones she could remember. She was going to write another poem, and McNab would be a character in it. She was going to write it tomorrow on the beach while he climbed to the summit of the largest rock. What better place to write? The Costa Brava was a tonic. In time she would be as healthy and resolute as the girl in the bikini, and he would be as lean and dangerous as the man in the towel.

Ted opened his mouth to make a comment, then thought better of it. He looked out to sea and it occurred to him suddenly that they were sitting literally on the edge of Europe, the precipice at their feet a boundary as clear and present as the Urals or the Atlantic. He had never considered the Mediterranean a European sea, and Spain herself was always on the margins of modern history. A puff of wind caused the candles to flicker and dance. Ted imagined the air originating in North Africa, bringing the scent and languor of the Sahara or the casbah. There were two lights now on the horizon. What a distance it was, from their stronghold in the heart of America to the rim of Europe! Was it true that everything was possible in Europe? Ted thought of the Spanish war and the twenty years of peace, the *veinte años de paz,* that had followed. Franco's hard-faced *paz.* He had read all the books but could not imagine what it had been like in Catalonia. He had thought he knew but now, actually in the country, face to face with the people and the terrain, he had no idea at all.

# A WOMAN OF

# CHARACTER

◆

In TELLING HER STORY, which she was happy to do from time to time, Sally did not varnish the truth. She spoke of her life with impetuous candor, fully describing both her achievements and her mistakes. She did not neglect her personal life either, though reporters did not seem especially interested in it. Questions about her son, Charlie, usually came at the end of the interview, and were asked out of a sense of politeness. Yes, she had come to Washington in the first year of the Kennedy administration. Yes, she had one son, age twelve. No, she was not married nor did she believe in marriage. "I was married for a year but it didn't work out."

She was friendly with the political correspondent of one of the Chicago papers, having grown up in Chicago, where her father, now dead, had been a well-known trial lawyer. Sally Sutton was vaguely "known" in the region the newspaper called Chicagoland. She'd watched with amusement and fascination her passage through the news columns of the paper as she fed the political correspondent bits and pieces of information. In ten years, she'd advanced from "source" to "knowledgeable source" to "well-informed source" to "highly placed official." She imagined that one day there would be a magic moment in Chicago journalism when she would be a proper noun: knowledgeable, well-informed, highly placed Sally Sutton.

Sally did not lack detachment or a sense of irony, but she was fiercely proud of what she'd done and the person she'd become.

She was one who'd succeeded on sheer animal energy, though for years her various bosses regarded her as one more star-struck political dilettante. Her personal style was deceptive and tended to conceal her ability. The first to take notice of her was a congressman who observed that she was "that rarity" among women, a born administrator. She'd laughed and thanked him and said, Yes, lacking natural rhythm she'd turned to administration instead. The congressman was mystified: How could she work so hard at the office and raise a young boy as well? Her reply was uncharacteristically oblique. "I couldn't do any of it without Charlie," she said.

Eventually she was hired by the national committee after years on Capitol Hill. The job paid thirty thousand dollars a year, plus perks, and if they ever elected a President, she'd be in line for an important political appointment. She was eager for it, believing herself extremely disorganized on the outside but tidy within. She knew her good qualities: at the office she was singleminded and a shrewd judge of people and generally high-spirited, though she often slid into depressions. The depressions: she believed they were a function of the times, like pollution and war. She'd been lucky enough to discover a practical though cynical psychiatrist who listened patiently for a month, then told her to go home. Forget it. Relax. Of course she was depressed sometimes; depression was a fundamental condition of the human organism no less than of national economies. He told her to think of them as temporary recessions, downturns, cyclical, inevitable. She'd hesitated; it sounded too easy, though the explanation appealed to her sense of humor. She'd asked him, Do you think I need a husband — someone permanent? The psychiatrist laughed and said, Sure. Perhaps. Then you could deal with his depressions as well as your own, and of course he could deal with yours and possibly that would be a comfort. Doubtless it would. Then you could both come and see me on alternate days and I'd get $150 a week from you and from him, too. Then I could afford to see a psychiatrist, or perhaps spend the winter in Jamaica. He'd laughed again; depression was a perfectly normal neurotic condition. She'd asked him seriously about the boy, what effect did her depressions have on him? And what about the way she lived? The psychiatrist shrugged; he didn't know about the boy. The boy sounded all right to him. What did she want? Vat is it you vimmen vant? he roared in a mock-Viennese accent. Where did she think she was living, Plato's Republic?

He said, "I'm sure there are dozens of unresolved conflicts, and you've got a pretty good case of the guilties about the kid. But I don't believe the conflicts are serious or in any way out of the ordinary, and you know in your heart you're an attentive mother and that the guilties, therefore, are not warranted. You know that. Hell, Sally, you're not some silly housewife with only her orgasms or her bridge games to worry about. You've lived, you've been around —"

"I appreciate the thought," she said dryly.

"I suppose you want me to be supportive. OK, I'll be supportive. You're clever, you're healthy, you've got looks. Your sex life satisfies you, and God knows it's varied. You love to laugh. You're good at what you do and you're well paid for it. I've got women who would give their left tit —"

She laughed. "You're a con man!"

"The Ponzi of the profession," he said.

"And a cynic."

"Baby, that's how I survive."

"And you've been trying to get me into bed from the first day I walked into this office."

"Sally, you're a peach."

So that night they had dinner together and he seduced her, or perhaps it was the other way around, and that was the end of her formal therapy.

She had an episodic love affair with the psychiatrist, who appealed to her because he cared nothing about politics. He heard enough about politics in his office; he did not care to hear about them in bed. It was a relationship that suited her because both of them maintained absolutely separate identities: no professional competition, no sexual minuets. It was tricky because when the depressions came upon her she wanted to talk about them with him, and that bothered her because she felt she should be paying for the privilege. It was like sleeping with a lawyer and asking him for tax advice. Sally prided herself on her understanding of mutual interests, her deft estimates of how much should be given and how much taken in any transaction. It was one reason for her success in politics; she learned very early that temporary advantage nearly always led to long-term loss. Except of course with enemies; that was different. With enemies, you used every trick you knew. But with friends the best agreement was an equal agreement, one in which all parties left the table satisfied that they'd gotten what they wanted, or most of what they wanted; in any case, what they had to have. To an outsider it might sound bloodless, but it was important and pertinent to Sally. She'd worked too hard establishing her independence to throw it away lightly.

They were reading in bed when she turned to him. It was serious and she respected his judgment, and she made it plain that in talking to him she was asking a favor from a friend. But she wanted his professional opinion.

She said, "Sam, I have to talk to you about something. I got a call from Charles at the office this morning. He was calling from Chicago with what he said was a 'dynamite idea.' He wants Charlie to come and live with him full time. I'd have exactly the same visiting rights that Charles does now. Those are unlimited, no problems there. Charles and Charlie would live in Winnetka. He says it's very important for a son to know his father."

Sam lit a cigarette and looked at her. "And what was your first reaction?"

"Hostile," she said. "Very hostile. Maybe it's selfish, but that boy is part of my life and I'm part of his. Sending him to Winnetka would be like sending him to . . . Cairo. A completely different culture, for God's sake. Charles probably belongs to a country club. Look, I've raised him and I provide for him . . ." She shuddered. "A country club. Where they probably don't even allow Jews. Or Irish. I don't know anybody who isn't Jewish or Irish, and Charlie doesn't either. He's comfortable here, and the fact of the matter is that I'm a damn good mother."

He smiled. "You are a good mother."

"Very funny," Sally said sharply.

"I don't understand the objection, though. Is it political? Are you saying that Charles's ADA rating isn't high enough to suit you? He's the boy's *father*, not his congressman."

Sally laughed. "OK, touché."

"Is he a son of a bitch?"

"No, not a son of a bitch. As I've explained, he's one of those let's-lower-our-voices-and-be-reasonable people. One of those types. It's weird, we never got along. Never did, never would."

"Why never?"

"Second law of thermodynamics," she said. "While it is perfectly obvious that heat always passes from a warm body to a cold one, it is not so obvious that the reverse is never true. You think it's obvious but it isn't. It isn't obvious at all."

"I thought you were a politician, not a physicist."

"Works in politics, too." She sighed. "The trouble is, maybe Charles has a point."

He did not reply for a moment. Then he spoke to her very quietly. "Sally, you are talking about something *else*."

She shrugged sadly and lit a cigarette. "I don't want him to go away," she said. "I do not expect you to understand this entirely, but for ten years that boy has been part of everything I've done. When he was a baby I had to borrow from my mother to have a person live in while I was working. And I had to organize my life in order to spend as much time with him as I could without getting angry or resentful about it. I'm proud of what I've done. If we can get Numbnuts elected President, I'm going to have a very, very good job. I mean top of the line, probably in the White House. I've done that all alone, by myself, no help from anybody. At the same time I've raised Charlie. And brought home the bread. Now that I've done all that and Charlie is just reaching the age where he can fend for himself, when our life here really makes sense, that goddamned father who never did anything when it counted wants him —"

"What's so hard to understand about that?"

"Well, some people don't."

"But you've got to understand your true motives."

"I know," she said miserably.

"You're worried about the way you live, you think you're disorderly. You wonder about the effect on him and you begin to lose your nerve." He kissed her and smiled reassuringly. "You're a libertine on the outside but on the inside you're square as hell." She laughed; it was true. She adored men and men adored her and God knows her life did not run on schedule. But did that matter? Charlie was growing up without illusions, except the best illusion of all: he knew that she loved life, loved what she did, offered no apologies, and took responsibility for her actions.

"I can't let him grow up the way Charles grew up. *I can't do that.*"

"What does he do? I've forgotten."

"What do you mean? Job? Well, as I told you, he screwed around for ten years. When we were first married he joined a third-rate law firm. He was there about a year and then dropped out but went back later. When one of the partners left to join a chemical company, Charles left with him. That was, oh, five years ago. All of a sudden he's vice president of the chemical company and lives in Winnetka. Big deal."

"You mean he's successful."

"Not as successful as me," she said.

The note was short and formal. Charles was coming to Washington on business. Could he have dinner with her? The Mayflower, eight o'clock? The Mayflower, she thought; that was typical. The dining

room of the Mayflower, first choice for big butter-and-egg men. She
wrote him back that dinner would be all right, but why didn't they
meet at Le Steak instead. Better food, warmer atmosphere. She'd meet
him at the small bar in the front of the restaurant; they could rendez-
vous there at eight-thirty, after work. She'd have her secretary make
the reservations.

She knew what she was doing and disliked herself for doing it.

Sally arrived at nine to a chorus of greetings from the *patron* and
a table of journalists near the door. It took her a few moments
to extract herself from the journalists. She found Charles at the end
of the bar, pretending not to notice her arrival. She reflected that
only by wearing earplugs could he have ignored the cries of welcome.

She said, "I'm sorry I'm late. A meeting. Tied up."

He said, "I only just got here."

It was apparently true. The bill in front of him showed a single
drink and that was resting at his elbow, untouched. She looked to see
if the ice had melted, but it had not. Round one to Charles, except as
she looked at him she knew he was not aware of any of it. He'd
grown heavier, almost ponderous, and his hair was thinning at the
top. He'd always looked younger than he was, he'd always looked
the youngest man in the room; now he looked older. He was dressed
in a muted glen plaid suit and a striped tie, a uniform from the 1950s.
Her attitude suddenly softened; at least he didn't dye his hair or wear
double knits. He'd always been hesitant and a bit vague, and now his
manner was weightier than she remembered. She hadn't seen him in
two years.

She'd arranged for a table in the rear of the restaurant. All the
tables were close together, but by ten o'clock the place would begin
to thin out and they would have privacy enough to talk. She'd arranged it that way; she wanted to get a sense of him before they got
into the question of Charlie. So they talked casually. Charles was
never a very precise man; he spoke to her as if reading from a poorly
prepared lawyer's brief, using as much psychology as he was capable
of using.

"You've done very well, Sally," he said in his careful voice. "I see
your name in the paper occasionally. I came across your name in the
paper the other day, some political thing . . ."

"What connection?"

"Well, you know I don't follow politics anymore. Don't have the
time or the interest. Is there an important race in California?"

"Oh, that. Yes, there are two actually, one for the Senate and the other for the governorship . . ."

"They quoted you about some polls that had been taken."

"Damn them," she said. "It was supposed to be a background interview, no names. Well, I haven't heard anything about it, so no one saw the piece. No one sees the Chicago papers here."

He smiled. "A backgrounder, was it? Secretive Sally, the woman of mystery."

She looked at him, wondering if he meant to cut her. Probably not; he was too obtuse for that. "A tomb of secrets, that's me."

"Well," he said awkwardly. "It must be quite a lot of fun, and profitable too, I suppose. I think you've done damn well. Really damn well . . . this success . . ." She smiled, though she did not care for open praise. She preferred the style of politicians, which was to make a joke when they wanted to pass a compliment.

"What about you?" she asked. "This new job."

"It's rather funny, as a matter of fact. My company that everyone thought was going to be a bust isn't a bust after all. It's quite a success and I'm in on the ground floor." He grinned disarmingly. "A new experience for me. For the first time in my life I've got some money and that's one of the reasons I want to talk about Charlie. You've done a wonderful job with Charlie. I can't imagine anyone doing any better. But at this time in his life he needs a . . . father."

"Why now, particularly, rather than ten years ago? Or five? What, you think he's going to turn into a woman or something?" When he looked at her sourly, she turned away. "Sorry, but this whole thing makes me nervous."

"All I'm proposing is that we reverse the situation."

She laughed. "Oh, is that all?"

"Well, the truth is that I've got a responsibility and I want to meet it. And the other thing is this. All the shrinks say that children have got to know their parents, the good and the bad. Charlie doesn't know me. He sees me on vacations, he doesn't see me leading a normal life. Forget for the moment whether my life is a life you approve of. I assume that you don't. But it's different from yours, that's the main point. Half of that kid is *me*. If he doesn't come to know who I am or what I'm about, he'll never come to understand himself . . ."

"And what are you about, Charles?"

He took her hand, and then released it. "I'm about to order another bottle of wine."

♦

"Well, you look very prosperous."

"I'm making up for the lean years."

The remark stung her. She remembered him coming home from the office the year they were in Washington. They had very few friends and spent evenings plotting their rise in Camelot. Empty dreams: they never came close, and she knew that it would never happen; he would never fit into the town. He had no instinct for it. He was bright enough and personable enough but he had no instinct, and would not persevere. Everyone then was placing bets, and he was not a gambler. Bright, someone had said, but not attached to anything. She said, "You look older."

"I know it, and I don't mind. I suppose it's partly the new job, the responsibility."

"And now you want to be responsible for Charlie."

"That's it. I believe he needs a full-time father."

She thought of her cynical psychiatrist. What would he have said? They never talked about Charlie in those terms. She remembered him saying that if the boy seemed happy, all was well. Don't worry. Never fret. Go home. Relax. She felt herself being edged into a corner and she didn't like it. "Why this concern, all of a sudden?"

He looked at her. "People change, Sally. People really do change. And the truth is, I couldn't afford him before. I couldn't afford a housekeeper during the days. And I didn't want him, that's the truth too. I could invent other reasons but those are the main ones. Those sleazy apartments I lived in. Half of what I made went to you."

"Some months, not others," she said.

"Do you think," he said evenly, "do you think we can bury that particular part of the past and concentrate on the present? We can't remake or repair what's gone before. And who would want to? They were bad years." He smiled. "Can't we begin now, ground zero so to speak?" He turned to search for the waiter, his hand half raised. When he caught the waiter's eye he pointed at the empty wine bottle and motioned for another. It seemed to her out of character and she wondered why. Then she remembered. In the old days he would have asked her if they needed another bottle, and if so, which one. Then he would have gone ahead and done what he was going to do anyway.

"It would mean quite a change in my life," she said.

"Mine, too."

"Understand this. For the first time in a long time my life is ordered the way I want it. Charlie is part of it, part and parcel. Perhaps in some ways Charlie is responsible for it —"

"In what way?" He stared at her; she thought he was about to press an advantage.

"Well, it's not important." She saw him watching her, a slight smile on his face; the smile irritated her, it was almost a smirk. A salesman's smile; she supposed he used it in his business. "Charlie has never been better. Top marks in school. He's something of an athlete. He . . ." She could not understand why she was on the defensive.

He said, "Maybe we ought to ask *him*."

She quickly shook her head. "No, I would never put a child in that position. A child of that age. Are you seriously proposing that I ask him to choose between his mo——, between you and me? No. Not on your life. There's no way I'm going to do that. Absolutely not. From your point of view that's a ridiculous suggestion; you know very well who he'd choose."

"All right, perhaps that's not such a smart idea."

"No. It is not."

"But just on the general principle. Think about *his* life for a moment. Not mine. Not yours. His life."

"I am," she said.

"For one thing, I can't believe that Charlie's a bed of roses twenty-four hours a day. At times he's got to be a pain in the ass."

"Of course," she said.

"All right, you like to have fun. God knows you always liked to have fun. If Charlie were living with me, it would give you freedom you've never had before."

She looked away. How possibly could she have more freedom than she had now? Charlie was not a burden to her; he was part of her life. He was part of the freedom that she had. He was part of its definition. Without Charlie her life would be less free because it would be less tidy. She meant her inner life, which was the only life that counted. He did not inhibit her, except perhaps occasionally. But it was nothing serious. Freedom did not mean license. That was anarchy. She was not an anarchist, she did not want to lead her life as one.

"Will you let me talk to Charlie about it?"

"No!"

"We can talk to him together, the three of us. We can work it out. I promise I'll put on no undue pressure. We can work it out as a family."

♦

"But we're not a family," she said harshly. "We've never been a family."

"Well, we can try. We can try this once." He leaned across the table; their hands were almost touching. She tried to remember what there had been about him that had so attracted her, and recalled at once that it was his sincerity. His apparent solidity. His imperturbability and earnestness. Reliable Charles. Serious. Sober. Responsible. Fair. Or seemed to be fair; his language was always moderate. Charles saw both sides of every question and never forced an issue. His mother had probably warned him that it was bad manners to force anything. But he was forcing this issue: perhaps it meant that he was at last settled and secure. "Sally, I want some time with my *son*. I want something continuous."

She felt herself compelled by his logic. His reasonableness against her desire.

He looked at her across the wineglass. "My spies tell me you're quite the hot property. Politically."

She laughed. "That's me."

"Weren't you working for some congressman before this job?"

She shook her head. Charles never followed politics. Elections to him were like the box scores of baseball games to her, so many meaningless statistics. The congressman had been the subject of a cover story in *Time* and nightly reports on the television networks. She said, "He was defeated. By the astronaut, remember?" She watched the slow dawn of recognition, or feigned recognition; it was ludicrous, like a comedian's double take in a silent movie. She said patiently, "I'm working now for the national committee."

"Yes," he said. "I know that. But doing what?"

"This and that," she said. It was pointless to discuss it in any detail.

"Well, is it a secret?" He laughed. "Like the formula for New Blue Cheer?"

Why was she on the defensive? *Why?* "As a matter of fact, it is," she lied.

"You're on the road quite a lot."

She said, "One or two trips a month." Then she added, "About as often as you are."

He poured the last of the wine into his glass. Hers was still full. "Yes," he said.

"I will think about Charlie. I'll write you next week. It's a big step. I'll let you know."

Charles looked at her for a long moment. At last he said, "At least we've never been enemies."

She drove him to his hotel and then returned to her own house in Georgetown. She wanted to be where she could think straight. When she dropped him off at the Mayflower, he'd muttered something vague about his "rights" and how nasty it would be for everyone concerned if they had to go to lawyers "to settle it." She did not respond. When he was out of the car, she simply drove away.

She wandered into the kitchen and poured herself a glass of milk, then thought better of it and made a weak highball. She turned toward the stairs, but thought better of that, too; she needed to think straight by herself. She moved into the library and stood staring out the window. A single fact: she had never thought of the boy as his. For the first five years of Charlie's life, Charles was never there. At that time he was in the process of "finding himself." (So much for her estimate of his character, sober, responsible, reliable Charles.) Now he'd fetched up on the shores of Winnetka and that was typical. He'd grown up in a suburb and now he was back there, free to pursue his conception of the well-modulated life. She thought that in the most complete sense the boy was *not* his. He was Sam's as much as he was Charles's. And had been Peter's before he had been Sam's. She smiled to herself; that was *definitely* the wrong train of thought. Before Sam, Peter. Before Peter, Alex. Before Alex . . . all the way back to the Englishman, Ian. The man with the funny accent who told ghost stories. When she came home at night and when she woke up in the morning, Charlie was always there. Others came and went, but Charlie was always there, constant, faithful. And no, she was not mistaking her twelve-year-old son for a husband or lover. He was exactly what he was, Charlie, a twelve-year-old boy *whom she provided for.* Who was part of her life. He was as happy as any of the other children she knew, the progeny of cheerful, durable marriages (to the extent there were any in Washington; most of the married people she knew seemed to go through life with clenched teeth). To take Charlie out of her environment, in which he was perfectly secure and at ease, and thrust him into Winnetka . . .

She sat in the big leather chair in the library, staring at her books and half listening to the stereo. She'd put on a recording of the MJQ and turned it low. Drawn back against her will into her own childhood, she saw her father sitting where she was sitting, in a leather chair in a library. Her big, careless father, who seemed to gulp life like a swimmer perpetually surfacing from under water. He was the source of her energy and her pride and her ambition. He was the source, but not the sustenance. She wished she could ask his advice; he was always very good about advice. She would not be bound to follow it, but at least she would have it. She concentrated, recalling various typical pronouncements of her father's. She sought gravity, but in her memory there were only wisecracks.

Well, perhaps that was narrow and snobbish of her. Winnetka wasn't the end of the world. A number of people lived there and seemed to thrive. But she didn't think they'd have any connection, Charles and the boy. She'd taken him to meetings, encouraged him to read the newspapers and the news magazines, and four years before, they'd attended the convention at Miami Beach. They'd talk politics at the breakfast table: who was up and who was down in the Senate; where Big Labor was going in November; whether the young Southern governor had a chance; the idiocies of the opposition. Charles knew nothing of this world and cared less. It was impossible; for Charlie, Winnetka would be a death sentence.

She hugged her knees and looked around the room. There was a photograph on the mantel of her and Charlie on a sloop on the Chesapeake Bay with friends. The wind was blowing her hair, and Sam had caught them in a look-alike moment. She stared at the picture and thought of herself and the boy standing together against the world, so loose, their lives fused, each a part of the other. In the background, the congressman grinned for the camera: it was an unaffected smile of paternity for them both. Her eyes welled up and she saw her life in Kodachrome: her son had his arm lightly around her waist, they were clowning together. His head was high (as tall as she was, now), her hand rested on his shoulder. They were unconfined, separate centers of gravity, but they were connected, too. They depended, each on the other — not for support alone but for love. That boy was hers, no one else's.

No, she thought. She would not do it. She knew how to fight and she would fight like hell. He could get himself another son to love. And he was quite wrong in what he'd said. They were enemies, always had been. She knew it, and so did he.

She turned back to the photograph, crying freely now. God, she loved it. She loved her life and what it meant. In this life you took what you wanted. She turned toward the stairs, momentarily confused. You took what you wanted, when you wanted it badly enough. That was what you had to do. "*I mean to survive,*" she said aloud.

Sally hurried up the stairs, stumbling once, then moved down the long hallway to his bedroom door. She hesitated, her hand on the knob. She stood motionless for a long moment, then turned away. No, she did not need an accomplice. She released the knob and stood listening for a sound, any sound apart from the beating of her own heart.

1975

◆

# SHE'S NOT DEAD,

# BELLE

◆

THIS WAS THE YEAR the summer would not end in Europe. Even
the terrorists went about their work in short-sleeved shirts and
sandals, hurtling from target to target in air-conditioned BMWs. It
was the Chernobyl summer also, and a Polish émigré she knew linked
the hazy sunny days and humid nights to the Soviet rads in the atmosphere, a deliberate provocation whose consequences would not
be known for decades — centuries even! Summer went on and on,
until one day in late October it ended. A drenching rain, rain all day
long, and suddenly a northern European chill in the air. Well, that's
it until May, the Parisians said; it could have been worse, and it was
good while it lasted. Sunbathers went back to their apartments, and
the hard-faced gendarmerie continued to patrol the streets, bulky in
combat boots and blue flak jackets, grateful for the chill.

The resident Americans liked the return to normal temperatures,
meaning a more familiar ambience, something predictable. It had
been a dangerous summer, so unsettling, and then to have continued
for so long, hot as the devil. Except in early November it got warm
again and then, not suddenly this time but gradually, cold, and then
it was as cold and gray as any French or North American winter. The
streets seemed to empty overnight, café tables and chairs disappearing
from the sidewalks. The tourists went home and the terrorists went
to ground in the cold weather.

She wanted to take the Polish émigré to see Flaubert's house, but the
émigré declined: Flaubert's hand was as reactionary as Stalin's. So

she went alone to Rouen. The house was closed because it was Sunday, but she stood outside a few moments to gaze at the door, which hung at a rightward tilt. It was a scarred door with a sturdy lock and oiled hinges, and looking at it she had to agree that it had a Stalinist aspect. The door gave no hint to what lay behind; that something *was* behind it, there could be no doubt.

She ate a large meal, looked at the churches, and returned on the six P.M. train to Paris. On the platform, ten minutes before the train was to depart, an old man had a heart attack and died. Railroad officials clustered around him, no one knowing what to do; there was no question of mouth-to-mouth resuscitation. He was dead before he hit the ground. Watching this from the bar car, she did not move; other passengers clustered around the windows, but she thought that an invasion of privacy; impolite, though that was hardly the word under the circumstances. The body was left on the platform uncovered, and the railroad officials gathered in the bar car, drinking from a half bottle of cognac. They were very upset, talking in low tones and covering their eyes with their hands.

Later that night, in Paris, she was having a drink with an old friend. She told him the story, beginning with Flaubert's door and adding all the details: the old man's wife in shock, comforted by the officials, one of whom embraced her like a father. The teenage girl in front of her was horrified at the sight, smoked Marlboro after Marlboro, and finally began to cry. She had stepped across the aisle and had spoken to the girl, offering a few words of consolation in her halting French; but the girl only bit her lips between puffs on the cigarettes. That poor girl, she said, and added, unneccessarily, that the train left on time as European trains generally did. Her friend listened, making no comment. And as she added detail after detail he became bored, stifling a yawn, steepling his fingers and peering at them closely, his eyes narrowed, eager to resume the previous line of conversation. He had been talking about South Africa and the cupidity of the West, and she finally figured out that the sudden death of an old Frenchman did not have the moral significance of a comrade in Soweto. It was a natural death, after all, not death by truncheon, bomb, or torture, death instead by Bordeaux. From the look of him, the Frenchman was no stranger to the pleasures of the table.

She said, You don't mean cupidity. Cupidity means lust.

That is *exactly* what I mean, he said.

. . .

◆ In the great caves of the Dordogne a few weeks later with the same friend she bought a postcard depicting the Cro-Magnon man, knuckles dangling near his ankles, a skull shaped like a football helmet. She wrote to a colleague: *This is the earliest known sculpture of a university president. Note the fine features, the look of compassion. Observe the hand outstretched for money. Notice the worry lines, the weak knees, the high mind, and the absence of balls. Love, Belle.*

That ridiculous name.

That night at dinner he returned to South Africa, and then to Central America and Indochina. They had been in Indochina together two decades before, he working for a magazine, she with a grant from the university. Someone had unearthed new documents showing American mendacity extreme even by the standards of the period. Hard to imagine, she said. Well, no, he replied. That's the *point*, Belle. It isn't hard to imagine at all. Quite a lot of people imagined it at the time. You, for example, if you'll remember. And it's going to get worse, this is only the tip of the iceberg.

You mean, there's nine-tenths to go?

You know what I mean, he said.

But she didn't know, really. She said, There're probably lies on the walls at Lascaux. That perfectly thrown spear into the heart of the mammoth, the one we saw this afternoon, probably missed because the poor baby who threw it was too scared to get close enough or aim properly. What we were looking at there, Ice Age disinformation. The artist, some broken-down hack of an illustrator turned press secretary. Drew what his boss told him to draw. The people were discouraged. Boss wanted a victory over the mammoth, so the hack gave him one.

Very funny, he said. I think you've had enough sabbatical. Time for you to get back to work —

It's only a half sabbatical, she said.

— in the real world.

She thought about that a moment, the real world of chalk on a blackboard, blue books, office hours, and her monograph. But she knew that wasn't what he had in mind. She said, Gabe, Gabe, who cares about what they said or didn't say in Indochina twenty years ago?

I care, he said. And you should care, too, you of all people. They've falsified the record. They've trashed history, the liars . . .

While he talked her eyes wandered to the corner of the restaurant where two old men were playing chess. They sat motionless over the board, elbows on their knees, while the waiter leaned on the bar, reading a racing paper. They seemed to be enacting some ancient ritual, looking as if they belonged not to this century but to the one before, or the one before that. He said, What are you thinking about now? You're a million miles away. He turned, frowning, to look at the two old men.

No, she said. I'm right here.

Do you play chess, Belle?

No, she said. But I like watching them.

The inertia, he said.

The concentration, she said.

They're carved in stone, those two.

She said, No they're not.

Whatever, he said.

She said, I was thinking about the dead man on the platform, the other day at Rouen; at Rouen weeks ago, it just seems like the other day. She remembered the old man's heavy face and the stubble on his chin, and his eyes, half closed. Or half open; at any event, sightless. She remembered his worn-out shoes and the shapeless black suit, and the woman, so suddenly a widow, beginning to tremble uncontrollably. It could happen to anyone. It could have happened to her; her ex-husband drank like a fish; still did.

Well, he said.

So public, she said.

Public? He looked at her, beginning to smile.

An old man should die alone, not on a train platform, his wife at his side. They were probably going home for dinner. Except maybe they were getting on the train, not leaving it. Going to visit their children. And his heart stopped.

Belle, he said. No one should die alone.

She wasn't listening to him. She was thinking about the old man, and about Andy, her ex-husband. She said, Strangers all around. Strangers looking out the window of the bar car, watching him die. Not so good for the strangers, either. That teenage girl will never forget it.

They were silent a moment, watching the chess players. White raised his hand as if to move a piece, then shook his head and resumed staring at the board. Belle sighed and signaled the waiter for the check.

I know, she said. This is definitely not cheerful.

It's morbid, he said. Not your style at all.

.   .   .

They were on the train returning to Paris; he was leaving for Boston the next day. She was reading, absorbed in the newspaper, and he was watching her. Suddenly he leaned forward and began to talk in a hoarse whisper. He reminded her how long they had known each other, and how much they'd been through together, how fond he was of her, and, he knew, vice versa. We're buddies, he said; you and I, we're the representative *carte*. He said fiercely, *What are you doing here?* Then he began to lecture her on her self-absorption, her stubbornness and morbidity, her self-indulgence. Not the Belle Browne-with-an-*e* he had known for twenty years; the Belle Browne he knew was engaged with work and life, with real things, with seeing issues clearly and insisting that the record be straight. The Belle he knew would never ask what difference it made. Would never have said, *Who cares?*

What's wrong with you? he asked.

Go to hell, Gabe, she said quietly.

He hesitated, then disclosed that he was leaving the magazine to work for a senatorial candidate. Off the record, he said; the idiot editor doesn't know yet. I've known Jim on and off for years, he said, still whispering, as if fearful they would be overheard by the other Americans in the car. And he'll win, too, unlike most of the candidates we've supported over the years. He's a good man, he said. And there's not only me who's involved, but a couple of others from the old days, people who dropped out and decided to drop back in again because it was Jim. He mentioned three names from the old days.

And Joanna, he said.

My God, she said. I thought she was dead.

She is not *dead*, Belle.

I heard she had an accident. She remembered it very clearly, Joanna Cooper killed in an automobile accident somewhere on the West Coast; or Nantucket, one of those two.

She is alive and very well, Gabe said.

I thought she was dead. Could have sworn it.

Gabe said, There's a role in the campaign, Belle. I mean for you. His foreign policy section is weak. The people he has are very, very bright; oh, God, they're bright. But they're young, too, and sometimes abrasive. You know, overconfident, the way we were. He could use someone like you, who's been around the block a few times, who knows the graveyard. A Ph.D. will take you only so far, right?

She nodded, smiling.

It might take you a minute to learn to work with the young people, though.

More than a minute, she said.

He looked at her, exasperated.

She said, You have to get used to them.

And you'd like Jim, he said. He's not blow-dried, he's genuine, and he knows what he's doing, knows what has to be done. And he'd like you, too, but not the morbid you. Not the stubborn and self-absorbed and exhausted you. So do yourself a favor and come home and get involved. We'd have a great time.

She was watching cows motionless in a field. They were lying down and that meant rain, though the sky was cloudless. In the distance was a village, its ochre roofs bunched like the knuckles of a fist, church spire aloft, glittering in the sun, a venue for ordinary life. They said that in France all ambitious people went to Paris; the provinces were dying.

So what about it? he asked.

I like it here, she said.

But what does it lead to?

Thanks but no thanks, she said.

You'd rather waste away here.

She said, It's a sabbatical, not a convalescence. And I have two months to go; but maybe I'll stay. Maybe I'll stay and get a house in the country.

You're bored to death, he said. He sat back in his seat, looking at her. Then he leaned forward again, tapping her knee for emphasis, enumerating the ways in which she was bored. The evidence of boredom: exhaustion, stubbornness, and self-absorption.

She said, Maybe I'll find a boy. Nice curly-haired boy, history student. I can tutor him on the Ice Age.

Ha-ha, he said.

There are a lot of boys in Paris and in the provinces, too.

How about a man, Belle? I think you're old enough now for a man.

OK, she said. Either one.

You could make a difference, you know. The Republican he's running against is such a twit, though he has money; not enough money, however. Jim has real money, in hand and absolutely committed. It's a great opportunity, if he wins, and he will win, take it from me. Who knows what might happen.

What might happen, Gabe?

Never mind, he said. One election at a time.

She heard something in his voice, and smiled.

It's a possibility, he said defensively.

Got your office picked out, Gabe?

No, he said. She knew he was lying.

OK, she said. I'm not bored, by the way.

You act bored. You look bored to death, though I like the way you've done your hair. And this place — he gestured out the window, at the bright placid fields, narrow roads empty of cars — is an antique shop. Who cares? And as you very well know, it wouldn't do you any harm.

She looked at him and smiled. He meant, A fresh and convincing credential in the dossier, helpful when applying to the government or to the foundations for a grant. She wondered if the CIA would be interested in a military appreciation of the Ice Age, roles and missions, strategy and tactics, weapons, breastworks, fully footnoted, all the scholarly apparatus. They funded everything else, why not that?

I liked the caves, she said.

He nodded sourly, turning away.

They were moving slowly through a construction zone. Four men were straining at a railroad tie, levering it with crowbars, and making no progress. In the warm sun they were shirtless and their backs were slick with sweat. Two of the men, boys really, had red bandannas around their necks. She thought they looked chic, blue-collar boys from the pages of *Vogue* or *Elle*. She continued to watch them as the train slid by, thinking that working on the railroad had not changed much since the nineteenth century. A broad back and a crowbar laid the rails from coast to coast in America. One of the boys looked up, saw her, and waved. She waved back, nodding sympathetically. Andy had a term for railroad men, Andy with his inexhaustible supply of Americanisms. He called them gandy dancers. The train began to pick up speed and in a moment they were quit of the construction zone, the train making a wide arc. She craned her head to look back. The men were straining again at the tie, stubborn as ever.

She said, It's a very old part of the world, where we were.

Yes, he said.

They don't know anything about it, really, how people organized their lives, who was in charge, the economic arrangements, the rituals. They have bits and pieces of this and that, nothing firm, no written record to go on, of course; nothing to indicate what mattered to them desperately, and what didn't matter at all.

What mattered to them was staying alive, Belle.

There's always that, she said.

It's the only issue of any importance.

Do you really think so?

Yes, he said.

She said, Rouffignac. That's where I'll go when the balloon goes up. Remember Rouffignac, with the tram, the drawings on the walls? The damp and the echoes, the cavern was eight kilometers long . . . When he rolled his eyes she told him the story of the Polish émigré who attributed the warm summer to the rads from Chernobyl. Nuclear summer, she said. Summer all year long, thanks to the Soviet Union.

*It's not funny,* Gabe said furiously.

She had three weeks remaining on the Eurail pass and decided to go to Zermatt. She had kept meticulous records of her trips, what the cost would have been if she hadn't bought the pass. Zermatt, eight hundred kilometers distant, would be a completely free journey. And in the off-season, only weeks before the skiers arrived, it would be quiet and orderly. She had never been to Switzerland.

She was walking out the door with her bags when the telephone rang, Gabe calling from Boston. He wanted to give her one last chance to join the crusade. He mentioned a dollar figure and the new polls, better than before. No, she said. Thanks but no thanks.

Then on impulse she said, Have you heard anything from Andy?

No, he said. Not a thing lately. Why?

Just wondering, she said.

Last I heard he was in Kentucky.

That's what I thought, she said. American idioms. He's taping oral histories in the hill country.

There must be a hell of a lot of them, Gabe said.

People or idioms? she said, laughing.

*Jesus,* he said grimly. Kentucky.

What's wrong with Kentucky?

Everything's wrong with Kentucky, he said.

When she rang off she was behind schedule, and had to forgo the Métro for a cab. It was a matter of principle never to take a cab in daylight. She made the train with a few minutes to spare and settled herself in a window seat. Her suitcase was heavy, owing to her hiking boots and parka. She began to read the *Herald Tribune* but nothing interested her except the crossword. So she did the crossword as the train hurtled toward Geneva. She finished the crossword in thirty minutes and sat back to enjoy the scenery, flashing by like a film on fast forward beyond her own reflection in the glass. She was dressed in her new outfit, fawn-colored corduroys and a black cardigan sweater with an ascot, no jewelry. She had had her hair cut, and thought she looked rather smart. Across the aisle a curly-haired boy smiled at her but she did not smile back; instead, she blushed. She was not in the mood for conversation, especially a conversation that might lead to something. She did not want to lead, neither would she be led. She was due at Zermatt in midafternoon, time enough for a short hike. Then she would have dinner quietly and read her Gogol biography in bed; and she would be asleep before midnight and on the trail before nine the next morning. There were trails that would take you more than halfway up the Matterhorn. She could stuff a sandwich and a flask of wine in her parka and take lunch on the mountain, alone in the chilly clear air, under the thumb of the Matterhorn. She looked at her reflection in the glass and wondered if she had the guts to tell the dean good-bye, she wasn't coming back this term or any term. That would be unfair to her colleagues, but everything that you did that you really wanted to do was unfair to someone. There were farmhouses in the Dordogne for sale for a song; one of them had its own hill and sheep in a field nearby, three hectares, and only a short walk to the river itself; Rouffignac was a thirty-minute drive. She could live in the old-fashioned way, far from Boston and Boston's suburbs, far from Cambridge and the Cape. Suddenly she saw America as old and Europe as new; worn-out, exhausted America, in some respects a Third World country. In some respects older than God, as Andy liked to say. Far from the lecture hall and office hours and meetings, she would have the opportunity to live in her own way, whatever way that was. That would be what she would find out.

The train pulled into Bellegarde. The platform was crowded with travelers and she felt a moment of apprehension, observing an elderly couple carrying parcels, moving slowly. The woman had her hand on the man's arm, and they looked angry with each other. They looked as if they hadn't said a kind word to each other in years, but that did not stop her from saying a short prayer; if anything happened to either of them, right there before her eyes, it would be a terrible omen. But it was all right. They passed from view, safe.

The train began to move, rapidly picking up speed. She cocked an eyebrow at herself in the glass; the scenery was rushing by her eyebrows, the mountains rising. From somewhere nearby she smelled the pungent odor of pipe tobacco, a mixture that reminded her of roast chestnuts. She tapped the glass, slick and cool on her fingernails. The curly-haired boy leaned across the aisle and asked if she had a match, his mouth smiling around the words; he had a cigarette in his fingers. No, she said, she did not smoke. Well, then, did she mind if he — No, she said, she liked the smell. And turned abruptly back to her window, looking again at the countryside tumbling by, herself imposed on it — or the reverse, depending on the angle of vision. All these sensations at once, it reminded her of the time she was pregnant, and all her senses seemed redoubled, stretched to the limit. She was a Geiger counter of sight, sound, smell, touch, and taste. She popped a mint into her mouth. It was years ago, that pregnancy, and she had miscarried. And felt so ill and alone for months after. She thought of herself as an hourglass turned upside down. Everything flowed out of her. But she remembered the intensity of things when she was pregnant, remembered them as vividly as the letdown later. She did not believe it while it was happening. Such a thing had never happened in her family, to her knowledge. In the hospital she refused to believe what she knew was true. She remembered the pregnancy and its aftermath equally. Just then the train entered a tunnel and she smelled cigarette smoke along with the pipe, and soft laughter. When the train shot out of the tunnel the sunlight was brilliant, so sharp it hurt her eyes. She heard laughter again and looked around, but the curly-haired boy was no longer there. She began to smile, looking into the window; she saw herself smile, and felt herself fill almost to bursting. On this train she felt now exactly as she felt then, before the aftermath.

1989